MW00620996

Cover Design: Christine.vanbree@gmail.com
Interior Design: TracyCopesCreative.com

Title Info:
978-1-61088-664-2 HC
978-1-61088-665-9 PB
978-1-61088-666-6 Ebook
978-1-61088-667-3 PDF-Ebook
978-1-61088-668-0 Audiobook

Published by Bancroft Press
"Books that Enlighten"
(818) 275-3061
4527 Glenwood Avenue
La Crescenta, CA 91214
www.bancroftpress.com

Printed in the United States of America

THE PLAYBOO

A NOVEL

GARY E. PARKER

bancroft
press

BANCROFT PRESS

As a former athlete in Greenwood, South Carolina
(years ago), I played for some amazing coaches
and want to dedicate this story to their memory
and to the thousands of other men and women
who serve as mentors, leaders, and coaches
for young people across America.

Coach Roper, Coach Yonce, Coach Riddle, and Coach Babb
were men of character, discipline and sportsmanship and
I'm grateful for what they meant to me and others like me.

Approximately 1,088,000 high school students play the game of football each week. Of these, about 2,400 are female.

Occasionally, one of these young women loves the game so much she carves out a career in the male-dominated arena. The story you're about to read isn't true.

But some day, it may be.

CHAPTER ONE

Her stomach flipping like pancakes in a diner, Chelsea Deal crouches on the sidelines of a packed, brightly lit stadium and rolls a football in her slender, well-manicured fingers. Glancing quickly at the scoreboard through cobalt blue eyes, she struggles to stay calm. It's just high school football, she reminds herself as she stands. Though you wear the purple jacket of a Rabon Knights' coach and your team wobbles within seconds of its first loss in two years, this is nothing compared to. . .

She pushes away the memory of another night on a football field and chews off what remains of her lipstick as she edges closer to Dub Klein, the Knights' head coach standing beside her. A mid-fifties gentleman with skin the color of charcoal, Dub wears a gray suit, purple tie, and snappy dress hat.

"Zebra, fifty-four, Y Go!" shouts Dub, his hands busy signaling to his offense. "Go! Go! Go!"

Completely focused again, Chelsea keys on Ty Rogers, the Knights' quarterback, as he rushes the purple-clad offense to the line of scrimmage. The clock continues to tick as Ty, a six-feet tall, seventeen-year-old African American with a thick chest and strong legs, barks the signals. The Dragons' defense, dressed in red, shifts left as the center snaps the ball to Ty. He drops back to pass but the defense sticks to his receivers like lint on Velcro and no one breaks open. Ty scrambles toward the Knights' sideline but, not fast enough to outrun the defense, he's caught by a tackler, who yanks him to the ground. The Dragons celebrate, jumping up and down, chest-bumping.

Chelsea and Dub run ten yards onto the field and yell simultaneously at the referee, "Time Out! Time Out!" The referee waves his arms and the clock stops. Chelsea glances at the scoreboard again as Dub frantically waves the team over to him. KNIGHTS: 27. DRAGONS: 31. Eight seconds left.

The players and coaches hustle toward Dub, their breath puffing gray plumes in the cold. Chelsea scans the stadium as everyone gathers. The smoky aroma of Southern barbecue drifts through the air. The roar of the crowd, bundled up to protect against the cold October night, echoes off the nearby Smoky Mountains. An elderly woman in a seat close to the sideline bows her head, her hands positioned in prayer.

The players surround Dub, and he pulls Ty close as the crowd noise drops. Still holding the football, Chelsea bends to listen. Dub speaks softly but firmly, his accent southern but with distinctly clear diction. "I love you, Ty," Dub says. "But I've told you a thousand times. Never try to run. You're too slow."

Ty pants heavily. "I thought I saw a lane, Coach."

"I'm talking a turtle in wet cement slow," replies Dub. "You're the starter because you're smart. If I want a fast quarterback, I'll put Palmer in."

Dub and Chelsea glance at Palmer Norman, a lanky blonde standing on the fringe of the huddle. A younger kid, he's taken his helmet off and his head is down.

Ty shakes his head. "Palmer won't know the plays, Coach."

"I'm just making a point, Ty," says Dub.

"What's the play?" Ty asks.

Dub resets his hat and turns to Chelsea. "Call the play, Coach," he says to her.

Chelsea looks at him like he's ordered her to jump from a plane without a parachute. "You've never let me call a play in a game," she says.

"It's the ninth game, Coach," counters Dub. "You're my Offensive Coordinator. Time you earned your paycheck."

Her mind a jumble, Chelsea quickly hands Dub the football, jerks a play sheet from her back pocket, and stares hard at it.

"Forget the analytics, Chelsea," says Dub, leaning closer. "Just do something they won't expect."

"Call it, Coach," Ty encourages her. "I'll make it work."

Pushing down her nerves, Chelsea brushes her blonde hair from her eyes and studies the play sheet again.

"Make a decision and live with it!" Dub says.

Chelsea runs a finger over a play on her sheet but she's uncertain whether to call it. She's imagined a moment like this for a long time, but her mind feels stuck, the gears glued in place.

"Chelsea!" whispers Dub. "Time's up!"

Chelsea swallows, steps to Ty, and whispers in his ear. A referee blows his whistle for play to resume.

"I like it." Ty grins at Chelsea.

"Make me look good," she says, hoping he's more confident in the play than she is.

Ty snaps his chinstrap and leads the offense back to the middle of the field as Chelsea returns to the sideline with Dub on one side and Buck Jones, a lean, ramrod straight, mid-forties coach dressed fully in purple, on the other.

"You let her call the play?" Buck asks Dub, talking across Chelsea as if she's not there, his voice thick with disapproval.

"Not now, Buck," Dub says sternly.

"Just surprised is all."

Dub grunts and Buck peels away as the teams on the field approach the line of scrimmage.

"Ignore him," Dub tells Chelsea as they face the field again.

"Copy that," says Chelsea.

Dub chuckles and hands the football back to her as Ty lines up in a shotgun formation and Swoops, a lean wide receiver with dredlocks dangling below his helmet, positions himself near the left sideline. The field announcer booms: "LAST PLAY OF THE GAME! SWORDS OUT, KNIGHTS!" Thousands of fans hold up plastic silver swords and wave them in the air.

"What play did you call?" Dub asks Chelsea, his eyes lasered on the offense.

Chelsea stares straight ahead. "I'm too scared to tell you."

"That's not comforting."

The center snaps the ball to Ty and he sprints left like he's going to run. His offensive line bangs against defenders rushing at him. From the left sideline, Swoops sprints toward Ty.

Spotting Swoops, coaches on the Dragons' sideline start screaming, "REVERSE! REVERSE!"

A defender smacks into Ty's left knee but he pitches the ball to Swoops just before he hits the ground.

"Swoops!" Chelsea shouts as he grabs the pitch out of the air and jets toward her on the right sideline. She's caught the Dragons off guard and she knows it! Swoops dodges one defender, stiff arms another, and turns the corner right in front of Chelsea.

"Swoops!" Chelsea raises her football into the air as Swoops sprints away from her, his long legs eating up the grass. Defenders chase him but they're too late and Swoops outruns them into the endzone for the winning touchdown.

As the Knights' crowd erupts in celebration, Chelsea spikes the football and rushes the field with Dub and her players. Wristbands, sweaty towels, hats, and even a couple of purple shoes fly into the air.

"I never would've called that play!" Dub shouts at Chelsea over the noise of the celebration.

Chelsea laughs and shouts back. "Expect the unexpected, Coach!"

Dub doffs his hat and bends at the waist, formally bowing to her. She laughs again and they slap palms in a high-five as the team continues to rejoice.

Close to an hour later, the stadium is mostly empty, but the players' parents, girlfriends, and scores of buddies still hang outside the Knights' locker room, waiting for the players to shower and change. Gradually, the combatants emerge. A couple of coaches drift out among the players, their faces beaming as they wave to the fans, pile into their cars, and drive through the exit gate.

A couple minutes later, Ty limps out of the locker room beside Sean Johnson, the second-string quarterback, a skinny guy with curly red hair and arms that reach the tops of his knees. A handful of fans quickly surround them, offering congratulations and slaps on the back. Ty and Sean fist-bump some fans, high-five others.

Slowly making his way past the group, Ty spots his mom and dad, Vanessa and Russell, waiting by his dad's glistening black Aston Martin. Both former athletes, his dad sports a Super Bowl ring, and his mom wears a pair of diamond earrings big enough to choke a snake.

"Later, Dude," Ty says to Sean.

"Tomorrow," says Sean.

Ty limps to Russell and Vanessa as Sean hurries away. Vanessa hugs Ty.

"Close game," says Russell.

"We had it all the way," chuckles Ty.

"You're limping," says Vanessa, "Your knee bothering you again?"

"It's not too bad," says Ty.

"We're not debating it anymore," says Russell. "You're seeing a doctor on Monday."

"I don't need a doctor," argues Ty, climbing into the back of the Aston Martin. "Monday, Ty," insists Vanessa. "No more argument."

His face lit with a toothy smile, Coach Dub exits the locker room a few seconds later and the remaining fans start clapping and patting him on the back.

"Thanks," he says over and over as he works his way through the crowd. "Appreciate your support. The players deserve the credit."

After several minutes, he finishes the last handshake and reaches his designated parking spot. where his wife Patrice, a handsome, busty woman with bright eyes and a welcoming face, greets him with a hug.

"Shall we go out or head home?" Dub asks hopefully, reaching for her hand.

Patrice steps back, her hand in his. "You know the drill, Coach," she says. "Victory party with the Booster Club before we go home. You need to see and be seen after a game."

"I'll make it worth your while if we drive straight home," Dub offers with a cheeky grin.

"You're a devil in a fancy suit," laughs Patrice. "But, in the interest of your job security, I'll resist your temptations."

Dub shakes his head as he opens the passenger door of his silver SUV and ushers Patrice in. "All right," he laments. "But I remember a day when you would've jumped at an offer like that."

He closes her door, circles to the driver's side, and joins Patrice in the car. "I let Chelsea call that last play," he says proudly as he fastens his seatbelt.

"Look at you," grins Patrice. "Trusting a woman with the game on the line."

Dub chuckles and starts the car. "I'm a credit to my gender."

An empty, boiled peanuts bag blows across the parking lot as Palmer Norman, dressed in scuffed black boots, a faded denim jacket, and blue jeans, walks unnoticed by the remaining crowd to an old but clean motorcycle parked behind the locker room. Strapping on a battered brown backpack, he quickly straddles the bike and kicks the pedal. The bike doesn't start.

A couple of tall, heavy-set teenage brothers, Don and Strick, amble up and stop as Palmer kicks the starter again. Both guys wear baggy jeans low on their hips, high-top sneakers, and a Knights' football jersey and hat. Dark hair pokes out from Don's cap and reddish curls escape from Strick's. Cigarettes dangle from their mouths.

Strick laughs as Palmer tries to start his motorcycle a third time. "What's up, Hillbilly?" he asks.

Palmer glances at Strick. "That ain't my name," he says, his accent Southern, country, and unpolished.

"You like Rube better?" mocks Strick. "Hick? Cracker? I got a million choices for you."

Ignoring Strick, Palmer hops off the motorcycle and examines the engine, his fingers busy as he checks it over.

Don steps closer. "I personally like Yokel best. That good by you?"

Palmer looks up. "You no better than me," he mumbles.

"Your bike is roadkill," offers Strick.

"We headed to toke up," says Don, as if offering a truce. "Want to join?"

Palmer climbs onto his bike again and kicks the starter, but it still won't start. "I got work in the morning," he says to Don. "Give me a ride home?"

Strick grunts. "We look like Uber to you? Call somebody."

"I got nobody to call." Palmer hops off and reexamines the engine.

A posse of girls walk up and Bridget, a leggy, green-eyed blonde dressed in a chic leather jacket and stylish black slacks and boots, steps to the motorcycle, slowly straddling the front wheel and gripping the handlebars. "You're new at school the year, aren't you?" she coos as she leans towards Palmer.

Palmer's eyes widen as he glances at Bridget. Though she's in his math class, he's shocked that she's noticed him. "I moved in right before school started," he answers quickly. "Live with my uncle."

"What about your parents?" asks Bridget, leaning in so close he can smell her perfume.

Palmer eyes Bridget, wondering what her game is. Girls like her don't talk to guys like him.

"You making some new friends?" she asks.

Palmer feels all eyes on him—the girls with Bridget, plus Don and Strick. He stares at Bridget, her elegance pouring off like heat from a July sidewalk. He stands slowly and eases Bridget's soft, manicured hands off the handlebars.

Don steps towards Bridget. "Leave him be, Princess," he says. "Yokel is way below your social register."

Bridget smiles at Palmer as he lets her hands go. "You get your bike fixed, you let me know," she says. "We'll take us a ride." She tosses her hair and leads the girls off, Don and Strick trailing behind.

Relieved to be alone again, Palmer quickly tries his bike one last time. It still won't start. Drops of rain suddenly patter down and Palmer hurriedly dismounts, pushes the bike behind the locker room, and jogs past the exit gate and onto a dark road.

Her phone to her ear, Chelsea hops into her black pickup, flips on the windshield wipers, and exits the parking lot. The wipers thump rhythmically, working hard against the splashing rain as she turns left onto the road. A coach's whistle hangs on the rear-view mirror and a notebook titled "Player Profiles" rests beside her in the leather seat. Still smiling from the game, she chats on the phone, her voice excited.

"You won't believe what happened tonight, Bo!" she chortles as she adjusts the heat.

"I can't believe you're still coaching football," grunts Bo.

"Dub let me call the last play!" she says, happily ignoring his dig. "And it worked! We won!"

"It's just, you know, you're a lawyer, Chelsea."

"Was a lawyer," she corrects him.

Silence falls for a second, then Bo changes the subject. "I finally got your diploma fixed," he says, a little sheepishly.

Chelsea chuckles. "Well, you are the one who broke it."

"I already apologized, multiple times."

"I appreciate that." She stops at a red light. "You still driving up Sunday?"

"You promise you won't wear khakis?"

"You make spaghetti for me and I'll wear a dress. Plus some earrings I just made."

"I actually get to see your legs?"

"From stem to stern."

"My world-famous spaghetti it is."

"It's world famous now?" she teases him.

"Well, it should be."

"I can't wait." The light changes and Chelsea drives off, her face still aglow from calling the game's winning play.

A circular driveway and manicured lawn frame a large contemporary home. Giant square windows, a flat roof at three distinct levels, lots of steel, and a brick façade. A four-car garage sits on the left side and a giant swimming pool and recreational area, including a basketball court, a putting green, and a volleyball court, stretch out beyond the right.

Inside the house, Ty limps into his second-floor bedroom, drops his gym bag by a king-sized bed, and flops down. Trophies and awards—academic and athletic—fill every nook of the room. Two computer screens sit on a desk, and pictures of Ty and his parents decorate the walls. The three of them at the Eifel Tower, the Lincoln Memorial, in Yankee Stadium. The biggest picture—Ty shaking President Obama's hand——hangs over the desk, and framed posters of Desmond Tutu and Martin Luther King, Jr., border it.

Ty pulls his phone from a pocket as Vanessa enters and plops down beside him.

"Let me see your knee," she demands.

"It's nothing, Mom," he grunts, still eyeing his phone. "A little pain, that's all."

"We need to make sure there's no structural problem," she says firmly. "You have a lot of football ahead of you."

"Drop it, Mom," he says, irritated at her insistence. "I have just one more year after this one."

"Stop saying that," Vanessa orders.

"I'm just facing facts," he insists as he looks up at her. "I'm not Dad. Won't be an All-American, or an NFL All-Pro. And I'm okay with that."

She reaches for his hand and he lets her hold it. "Don't sell yourself short, Son," she says.

"I know what I am, Mom," he says gently. "An average high school quarterback, smarter than most but slower too, and a slightly below-average passer. I do fine with the skills I have, but I play primarily because it's what you and Dad want for me."

"You like it too," Vanessa pouts.

"But I'm not obsessed with it."

They stare at each other, neither backing down.

"I'm as stubborn as you are," Ty says, determined to hold his ground.

"Show me your knee," she insists.

Ty drops her hand and pulls up his pants' leg.

"It's the size of a grapefruit!" moans Vanessa as she sees the knee.

"I'll ice it down," says Ty.

Vanessa carefully examines the swollen knee, probing and pressing like the nurse she once was. Ty winces a couple of times as she works, and she shakes her head as she finishes. "I'm cancelling your throwing session with Coach Paul tomorrow," she says.

"Don't do that," Ty says. "I'll wear the brace you bought me."

"You think that will help?"

"It has before."

She leans back. "Okay. But you're definitely seeing the doctor on Monday."

Secretly relieved that he'll finally see a doctor, Ty nods and pulls his pants' leg back over his knee. Though giving into his mom irks him, he also knows that something inside his knee is wrong, perhaps greatly so.

The rain splatters down in sheets, flooding Chelsea's windshield in spite of her busy wipers. Squinting though the deluge, she spots somebody running on the roadside. Swerving to the left, she glances over and recognizes Palmer's vague outline. Slowing the truck, she hits a button and lowers the passenger window. "Hey, Palmer!" she yells. Palmer turns to her but keeps running.

"Hop in!" Chelsea yells. "I'll give you a ride!"

Still running, Palmer waves her off. Rain splashes into the truck from the open window.

"Come on!" Chelsea orders. "You're soaking wet! Get in!"

Palmer stops and she brakes and pushes the passenger door open.

"You sure?" Palmer calls over the rain. "You know, these days. A woman coach, a..." he hesitates to say it.

"A male player?" Chelsea finishes the sentence for him. "Don't worry about that! It's a monsoon out there! Climb in!"

Palmer hops in and brushes water off his face as Chelsea hits the button to roll the window up.

"Thanks," Palmer says, catching his breath.

"No problem."

Palmer leans toward the heat vent as Chelsea drives off. "Your place?" she says. "How far from here?"

"Couple miles up this road," says Palmer. "Take a left. Four miles past that."

The windshield wipers thump as Palmer shivers and the heater blows. They ride in silence for a minute and Chelsea glances at Palmer, then back to the road. "Something happen with your ride home?" she finally asks.

Palmer stares out the window for a few seconds. "My motorcycle broke down," he finally says.

"A bad night for that to happen."

Palmer lays his hands on the vent and falls silent again as Chelsea turns left.

"You like it here?" she asks, trying to make conversation.

Palmer shrugs. "It's okay."

"You live with your uncle if I recall."

He nods but doesn't speak.

"What does your uncle do?" she asks.

"He plays music."

"You play too?"

He blows on his hands. "You ask a lot of questions," he says.

Chelsea hesitates, not sure whether to press ahead. But she knows almost nothing about Palmer and, because he hardly ever speaks when he's with the team, this is probably her only chance to find out anything but the bare facts about him. "I'm your coach," she explains. "But the truth is you're a blank page to me. And you don't know me either. So..."

She waits for him to respond but he's staring out the window like he's watching a parade march by.

"I'm not trying to intrude," she says, still hoping he'll loosen up. "But you, and all my players, are important to me."

Palmer turns and eyes her as if trying to x-ray her insides. "Me and Dirk," he finally answers. "We play music together when he's home."

She smiles. "Thanks," she says. "For telling me that."

He stares out the window again.

"Can I ask another question?" she asks gently.

"I don't reckon I can stop you, can I?"

She laughs. "What kind of music do you and Dirk play?"

"All kinds. But mostly country."

"My law firm played country music in the lobby on Tuesdays and Thursdays," she says, glad to find a connection, even if slight, with him.

"You were a lawyer before this?" He faces her and finally asks a question of his own.

"Six years in litigation."

"You make more money as a lawyer?"

"Stacks more."

He laughs a little. "You must like coaching."

Chelsea chuckles too. "Most days."

Palmer shivers again and Chelsea turns the heat to its maximum. "You have a lot of potential, Palmer," she says.

"You ever play football?" he asks.

"High school, then small college. I was a kicker."

"I reckon there ain't a lot of woman coaches."

"True dat." She slows the truck as they approach a run-down farmhouse with a small porch with two steps on the front. "This the place?" she asks.

Palmer nods and she stops and puts the truck in park. An old tractor rusts in a weedy yard to the side of the house. One light burns in a window. A beat-up shed sags out toward the back.

Palmer pulls a wet dollar from a pocket and offers it to her. "For gas," he explains.

"It's okay," says Chelsea, refusing the money.

"Well," he says, pocketing the dollar and reaching for the door. "Thanks for the ride."

"Don't forget, Palmer," Chelsea says. "You could be really good."

Shrugging, he hops out and rushes to the run-down house as Chelsea, feeling sad for reasons she can't explain, pulls away into the rain.

CHAPTER TWO

A Saturday morning sun brightens a double-bay window. Inside, in a large family room, Coach Dub, standing barefooted and wearing red flannel pajamas, holds a paintbrush by an artist's easel. Paintings of flowers and fruits hang in various spots on the walls. Patrice, fully dressed in a tan sweater and brown slacks and shoes, enters with two cups of coffee on a tray. She hands one cup to Dub and eases down to a chair beside him.

Dub takes a sip of coffee with one hand and points to the easel with his brush. A candy-red apple stares back at him from the canvas. "My teacher is making me paint fruit, Patrice," he complains.

"Most people like fruit," Patrice replies, sipping coffee as she studies the painting.

"But I'm a football coach! She should take that into consideration!"

Patrice smiles. "I think a fruit-painting man is kind of sexy."

"Well, I am a sensitive guy." He grins at her.

Patrice sips some more coffee and clears her throat.

"Thirty minutes to lose the jammies, Van Gogh," she says. "I'm ready for brunch." She stands, pats him on the back, then hurries out.

Dub makes one more stroke on the apple, lays down the brush, and studies his work with a raised eyebrow. "That's one fine piece of fruit if I say so myself."

Dressed in baggy navy pants and a matching shirt with "Rabon Motel" stitched over the front pocket, Palmer walks into a dirty motel bedroom and glances around. An overflowing trash can fills one corner, empty beer bottles another. Filthy towels lay over a lamp on a dresser and at the foot of a messy, slept-in bed. Several plastic cups, teeming with cigarette ash complete the disarray.

Stepping into the hallway, Palmer pulls a clean-up cart into the room and starts to work, jerking the filthy sheets off the bed, hauling them to the cart, grabbing fresh ones, and beginning to make the bed. A pretty but tough-looking teenage girl, with a tattoo on the inside of her left wrist and dressed exactly like Palmer, saunters in as he slips the clean sheet over the mattress.

"Hey, Molly," he says as his stomach churns, as it does every time she enters a room with him.

Molly pushes brunette hair from her face and studies him through deep brown eyes. "You again?" she asks as if irritated by his presence. Her accent is Southern and a bit rough around the edges.

"I been here every weekend for the past two months," Palmer says as he drapes a clean bedspread over the sheet.

Molly grunts and dumps the ash-filled cups into the trash bag on the cart. "What a buncha idiots," she complains. "It's a non-smoking room."

Palmer pulls clean pillowcases off the cart and weighs his response. Though he wants Molly to like him, she pushes his buttons in ways that frustrate him to no end. "You smoke," he finally says, unwilling to give her the final word.

"I smoke outside, Idiot. In the fresh air."

"That don't matter to your lungs."

Molly stops and stares at him. "How I treat my lungs is none of your business."

Palmer speaks again before he can stop himself. "It's disgusting, is all."

"I expect you an expert on disgusting."

Angry that he took the bait she always seems to throw at him, Palmer stuffs a pillow into a cover. "You know zero about me," he grumbles.

Molly stops dead still and stares at him as if she's a queen about to pounce on a rebellious servant. "What are you?" she asks. "Fifteen? Sixteen, tops?"

Her phone dings and she glances at it. A text. "It's the front desk," she says. "Some idiot puked in 112."

Relieved to have escaped her wrath, Palmer quickly finishes with the bed. "I'll clean 112," he offers. "Since I'm the expert on disgusting."

Molly laughs for a moment, grabs a hotel pen and notepad from the cart, scribbles a number on the pad, and hands it to him. "Reach out if you want," she says.

"You not even nice," he says with a pout, though pleased that she's given him her phone number.

Molly hops onto the bed and starts swirling, her arms out like a ballerina in a play. "I know you been watching me," she laughs as she spins. "You want some a this. You know it, I know it, all God's children know it."

Palmer tries to ignore her, but his thrumming heart won't let him, so he watches her, a doll twirling around and around as he stands still, in a trance. Gradually, she slows and finally stops.

"Don't hold your breath on me calling," he says softly as he pockets the number.

"We both know you're bluffing," says Molly. "Just do it, Idiot."

Unable to speak, Palmer turns away and hustles out, his stomach doing flips as he touches his pocket where her number rests.

A metal rack filled with footballs stands alongside Ty on the Knights' football field. He's wearing his Knights' helmet, football shorts, and jersey. Reaching to the rack, he pulls out a ball, drops back, and throws at a stationary target forty yards away. Almost immediately, he grabs another ball and spins it toward the target. Over and over. Ball after ball.

Coach John Paul, a short, stocky man in his fifties with a Knights' hat on backwards, a purple lollipop in his mouth, and a towel dangling from a pocket, runs down the balls Ty throws and drops them into a gray bag, then hustles back and refills the rack.

After throwing thirty passes in a row, Ty stops to adjust his knee brace as Paul reloads the rack.

"What's with the brace?" Paul asks.

"Got hit last night," says Ty. "The last play." He grabs a football from the rack and drops back, His throw misses the target by a couple of feet.

"Load up on your back foot," Paul coaches. "And whip the ball all the way through."

Ty nods, drops back, and throws again, this time hitting the center of the target.

Paul whoops his approval and waves his towel in the air. "That's it! Perfect! Take a break."

Ty pulls off his helmet and jogs over to Vanessa and Russell, who are watching from the sidelines.

"You're throwing clean today," Russell says, patting Ty on the back as Paul joins them.

Vanessa hands Ty a water bottle. "Should you move back to the fifty-yard line?" she asks. "Make some throws from there?"

"I'm good from forty to forty-five," replies Ty. "Not so much at fifty."

Vanessa turns to Paul. "He needs accuracy from fifty yards, doesn't he? To play college ball?"

Paul sucks his lollipop, raising an eyebrow at Ty. They've both heard the question before. "Fifty is a minimum," agrees Paul.

"What can he do to add that next ten yards?" Vanessa asks.

"Sometimes it's just the tools you're born with," suggests Ty, frustrated that his mama is re-plowing the same ground for the thousandth time. "You either can or you can't."

Vanessa ignores Ty and presses Paul. "Your job is to turn his can't into a can," she says.

"Maybe you'll grow another inch or two," says Paul, addressing Ty. "Extra height means extra leverage and that could mean extra distance on your throws."

"Whatever he needs, Coach," interrupts Russell. "Nutrition. Speed training. Strength coaching."

Ty winks at Paul to make sure he's in on the joke. "I hear good things about growth hormones," he offers.

Vanessa cuts her eyes at him. "Don't be silly."

"I'll check with Coach Dub again," Paul says, backing away from Vanessa's anger. "See if he's heard of any new training techniques we can try."

"We just want Ty to maximize his chances," says Vanessa.

Paul nods. "We're all on board with that."

"Don't discount the hormones," Ty teases again.

Vanessa waves a finger at him, and Ty slips his helmet back on and hustles back to the field.

"Fifty more throws!" he yells. "Maybe I'll find that magical ten yards on the last one."

A banjo in hand, Palmer lounges on a worn-out green sofa in his uncle's living room and picks softly as the late-afternoon sun drops outside. A wood fire burns in a fireplace across from him, the crackling somehow comforting in the quiet of the house. A couple of wood chairs frame the fireplace, and a rectangular coffee table fronts the sofa. Nothing decorates the dingy beige walls. One lamp burns on the mantle over the fireplace and a TV hangs on the wall over that.

Palmer begins to sing as he plucks the banjo, his voice gritty but clear and pure. A tinge of sadness paints the notes of his music, and that sadness adds color to his singing, a touch of darkness born by suffering somewhere along the way.

Wind whips outside and something clacks across the roof. Palmer thinks of Molly's number in his pocket. He considers calling her but isn't sure what to say if he does. She's older than him and he's a new kid in town with barely a dollar in his pocket. Plus, with his motorcycle broken down, he's got no way to go see her even if he asked and she said "yes."

He stares into the fire. Suddenly, the front door opens and a rugged, mid-thirties guy with long dark hair and a groomed beard walks in.

"Hey, Dirk," says Palmer, rising and placing the banjo on a stand as Dirk lays a travel bag and guitar case on the floor. "It's been a minute."

"What's up, Dude?" asks Dirk, stepping to him with open arms.

"This and that," says Palmer, accepting the bro hug. "You grow another inch since I been gone?" asks Dirk as they back away from each other.

"They measured me for the football program. I'm six feet, four inches."

"Wow," says Dirk, walking to the fireplace and warming his hands. "You getting to be a big one."

"I didn't hear you drive up," says Palmer.

"My truck is part ninja."

"It's prime for a proper burial is what it is."

"I'm thinking about buying a new one," Dirk says, throwing another log on the fire. "Get me some leather seats this time."

"How long you home for?" Palmer asks, hoping one thing but expecting another.

"Not long. The band's playing in Nashville again real soon."

Palmer pushes aside his disappointment. "Ya'll are killing it these days," he offers.

"We're not big time," Dirk says humbly. "But we're earning our share of gigs."

The fire blazes higher. "There's a couple slices of left-over pizza in the kitchen," he says.

17

"Any mold on it?" teases Dirk.

"Not that I noticed."

"Then I'm all in."

They laugh as they head toward the kitchen. "By the way," says Palmer, "this town sucks."

Dirk shrugs. "Nobody's holding a gun to your head to stay."

Dressed in black sweatpants and a Georgia Bulldogs jacket, Ty limps slowly down the winding second-floor staircase to the family room. A picture of Russell in a Falcons' uniform hangs on one side of a stone fireplace, and one of Vanessa accepting a Volunteer of the Year Award from Rabon's mayor adorns the other. Clear windows cover the opposite wall, offering a view of a yellow moon staring down on the mountains in the distance.

Russell enters the room from one side, Vanessa from the other. Russell grabs car keys off the mantle as Vanessa pulls a coat from an entry closet. "Come on, Ty," she encourages as he gingerly reaches the landing halfway down the stairs. "We're starving."

"Sorry I'm so slow," he apologizes. "But my knee has swollen some more." He takes another step, stops, grimaces in pain. Tries to walk again but his knee suddenly buckles, and he sags down on the steps.

Moving like the wide receiver he once was, Russell dashes up the stairs, pushes up the leg of Ty's sweatpants, and examines his knee. "It's twice its normal size!" Russell says as he turns to Vanessa.

"Forget dinner!" she demands. "We're driving to the emergency room right now."

"I'll call Dr Ramirez," says Russell.

"You think he's available this late?" asks Ty, acknowledging at last that he needs to see a doctor. "On a Saturday?"

"If he's in town, he'll make himself available." Russell says, helping Ty stand.

"I'll bring the car to the front door," says Vanessa, already moving toward the garage.

Russell tosses her the keys, and she rushes out as Ty leans on his dad's shoulder and hobbles the rest of the way down the stairs.

Palmer and Dirk sit at a small blue dining table in a cramped kitchen, their chairs pushed back as Palmer finishes off the last piece of pizza and Dirk sips a beer. The kitchen is clean, the sink empty of dishes, the floor swept, the counters wiped.

"You certainly keep it spic and span around here," Dirk says approvingly as he surveys the room.

"I got mad skills with a vacuum cleaner," says Palmer. "Learned it working at a high-class motel."

"The job going okay?"

"It pays nine bucks an hour," Palmer says with fake enthusiasm. "And they let me use a brush when I clean the toilets. I'm living large."

Dirk laughs. "You're turning sarcastic in your old age." He picks up a piece of pizza crust, nibbles it a few moments, turns serious. "I wish I could do better by you."

Palmer stands and throws the empty pizza box in the trash can. "You doing more for me than anybody else, Uncle. And I'm obliged to you for it."

"School going all right?"

Palmer grunts as he leans against the counter. "School is the light of my life. That what you want me to say?"

"Just asking the question, Dude. Answer however you want."

"School blows, Uncle."

"But you're keeping straight with it?"

Palmer stares at the floor, not wanting to confess the truth but seeing no way out of it. "I missed a few days here and there. Worked some extra shifts at the motel, you know. I need the money more than the classes."

Dirk finishes the pizza crust. "School's more important than work, Palmer. You understand that, don't you?"

"I suck at school," Palmer counters, his shoulders slumped in frustration.

"No excuses, Dude. School is the top priority."

Palmer angrily grabs a rag from the sink, wipes off the table, and throws

Dirk's empty beer can into the trash. "I'm glad you home," he says. "But I don't need no lectures about the virtues of school."

Ty perches quietly on a doctor's examination table, Vanessa and Russell sitting across from him in hard-backed chairs. A mid-fifties man, Dr. Raoul Ramirez, dressed in a red golf shirt and gray slacks, enters and shakes hands with Vanessa and Russell.

"Thanks for seeing us on the weekend," says Vanessa.

"No problem," says Ramirez, stepping to Ty. "If my favorite Knight needs me, I am there. Unless my wife says otherwise."

Vanessa and Russell laugh while Ty stays quiet.

"Let's look at this knee," says Ramirez.

Ty rolls up his sweatpants as Ramirez slips on a pair of medical gloves and gently raises the knee. "Any pain just lifting it?" asks Ramirez.

Ty shakes his head. "Nope."

"Did it get hit recently?"

"Last night, the last play of the game."

"Did it hurt any before that?" Ramirez rolls the knee to the left, then to the right.

"Off and on. Three weeks ago, the game against Thurman, I took a shot from behind. The knee swelled some that night but felt fine after a couple days."

Ramirez stretches out the knee, pressing it from the back. Ty winces and Ramirez presses it again. Ty grunts in pain and Ramirez relaxes the stretch. "A scale of one to ten," says Ramirez, "how bad does this hurt?" He presses hard on the front of the knee.

Ty groans and sweat pops out on his face. "Eight, maybe 9," he says through gritted teeth.

Ramirez stops pushing and lowers the leg. "We will need X rays. An MRI. Blood tests and a bone scan."

Ty glances at Vanessa and Russell. "What you think it is, Doctor?" he asks, looking him straight in the eyes.

Ramirez shrugs. "Let's run the tests before we do any speculating."

"How soon will we know something?" asks Vanessa.

"It's Saturday," says Ramirez, peeling off his gloves and tossing them in a trash can. "But I'll get things moving. Do what tests we can tonight, the rest tomorrow morning. We should have a preliminary diagnosis soon after that."

"You think it's serious?" asks Russell.

"Patience, Russell," says Ramirez. "And prayers."

Ramirez turns to Ty. "I hope you don't have big plans for tonight."

Ty shrugs and Ramirez continues: "I need to check you into the hospital to move the tests along as quickly as possible."

"I'm all yours, Doctor," says Ty, tamping down his worries. "Counting on you to patch me up before the playoffs start."

Ramirez pats him on the back. "We'll do all we can to make that happen."

CHAPTER THREE

F all colors glint off the last of the autumn leaves as Chelsea and Bo jog along the edge of a quiet, winding country road on a Sunday morning. Wearing black running shorts and shoes plus a bright red pullover jacket, Chelsea presses up a gradual slope, her stride smooth, her breath slow and steady. About fifteen strides behind her, Bo—a mid-thirties, preppie type with wavy brown hair tucked under a baseball cap—breathes like a scuba diver with an empty oxygen tank.

Reaching an overlook, Chelsea stops at the edge, sucks in a breath, closes her eyes, and revels in the sun on her shoulders. Bo stumbles up behind her a few seconds later and bends over, his hands on his knees, gasping for air. "You're killing me, Chelsea," he pants.

"You're the one who wanted to see my legs," she teases as she opens her eyes.

"In that dress you promised," he huffs. "A frisky pair of heels. Not gym shorts and Nikes." He stands up straight and manages to catch his breath.

"I want you to see a house," she says, ignoring his complaints. "Another mile up the road. It sits on the ridge. Looks down on Rabon. I might buy it."

"You want to buy a house in this god-forsaken backwater town?" he asks with exasperation.

"It's a fixer upper," Chelsea counters. "With great bones. On ten acres."

Bo sets his jaw. "Look, Chelsea," he starts, his tone frustrated. "I've waited, patiently I think, for you to work this football thing out of your system. But—"

Chelsea's phone suddenly dings, and Bo pauses as she pulls it from her jacket, checks the number, and declines the call. "Go on," she says. "Finish your thought."

Bo starts to speak but the phone dings again and he stops as Chelsea shuts it off. "Really," she says, focusing on Bo. "What's on your mind?"

"No, it's okay," he says, impatiently. "Show me this house. We'll talk tonight at dinner."

Chelsea smiles and pecks him on the cheek. "In a dress," she offers. "Like I promised."

Wearing a physician's white coat, Dr. Ramirez sits behind an office desk covered with multiple rows of neatly stacked files. Pictures of a tall, Hispanic woman and three teenage children decorate a credenza behind him, and diplomas from Emory and Johns Hopkins hang on the wall. Ty, Vanessa, and Russell wait across from him, all of them fidgeting with anxiety.

Ramirez clears his throat, picks up a file, opens it, and leans forward. "Okay," he says. "We have a couple more tests to administer today, plus we still need results from the biopsy. But this is what we know from everything we did last night."

He studies the file for a moment, rubs his hands through his hair, and faces them again. Ty reaches for Vanessa's hand on one side and Russell's on the other as Ramirez begins to talk again. A single tear rolls down Vanessa's face as she listens.

Chelsea, breathing hard now, sprints the last fifty yards up the hill, leaving Bo behind again. Reaching the crest, she stops, stretches her arms overhead, and waits as her heart rate slows. A few seconds later, Bo reaches her, huffing and puffing again, sweat pouring off his face. She gives him a minute to gather himself, then takes his hand and leads him to a clearing in the woods. A gravel driveway slopes down from there to a two-story, white-framed house with peeling paint, a sagging front porch, and a roof with shingles missing on one side.

"Isn't it amazing?" she asks as she admires the home and the view beyond it.

Bo removes his cap, rearranges his hair, puts his cap back on, and scans the property. "Does the inside need as much work as the outside?" he asks, negativity riding his voice.

"I said it's a fixer upper," she says as she grabs his hand again and strolls down the driveway. "Don't judge the book by the cover."

She leads him around the house to the backyard, where a stand of hardwood trees stretches to a ridge that overlooks Rabon in the distance. "That's my town," she stops and points with pride at Rabon. "Not exactly your style, I know, but it's actually a beautiful little village." They stand quietly for a long minute as she soaks in the view.

"It is lovely, Chelsea," Bo finally says. "Isolated, yes; tiny, certainly; inbred, no doubt. But yes, quite lovely."

"I could be happy here, Bo," she says wistfully.

He squeezes her hand. "I want happiness for you, Chelsea. I really do. But I don't see how this place works for me. For us."

She faces him, her spirit troubled by the distinctly different dreams the two of them hold. "I don't know," she says. "The thought of moving back to Atlanta? I can't deal with that right now."

"Well, you know I can't live here."

She lays her head on his shoulder and he pulls her close. She remembers all he's done for her, how he's stood by her when she desperately needed somebody. Yes, he's stubborn at times, quick to anger at others. But he's stuck with her when others disappeared, and she loves him for that. "We'll figure it out, won't we?" she says, looking up at him.

"I hope so," he says, touching her cheek. "I really do."

Coach Dub, dressed in a crisp, black suit and matching hat, stands by his apple painting in the family room, his phone to his ear as he stares out the window. "Hey, Chelsea," says Dub, leaving a message as Patrice enters and grabs her purse from a chair. "Sorry to bug you again on a Sunday, but Russell Rogers called me a little bit ago. Said Ty went into the hospital for tests late yesterday."

He pauses and rubs his eyes. "It looks bad, Chelsea. They're not certain yet, but they're saying Ty might have bone cancer." Patrice steps towards Dub and rubs his back. "Patrice and I are headed to church," continues Dub. "We'll see Ty immediately after. Call me as soon as you hear this." He hangs up, wipes his eyes, turns to the painting, and punches a hole in the apple.

"I'm so sorry," says Patrice.

Dub walks away from the easel and takes her hand. "It's a kick in the heart," he says, his voice breaking.

"If anybody can beat it," says Patrice, "Ty will."

Palmer slouches on the sofa, Dirk in the chair across from him. Two empty pop tart wrappers lay on the table between them, and an energy drink bottle and a coffee cup keep the wrappers company. The fire burns low in the hearth as Palmer strums his banjo and Dirk plucks his guitar.

"Switch with me?" asks Palmer, indicating the banjo for Dirk's guitar.

Dirk nods. They exchange instruments and play softly, Palmer's fingers quick and confident on the guitar strings.

"You're sounding strong," compliments Dirk. "With the guitar and the banjo."

"Not much else to do out here but play," says Palmer, a little sadly.

"How's the football going?"

Palmer chuckles. "I'm better at it than I am at school, but only by a whisker."

"I don't understand. As athletic as you are?"

Palmer keeps playing. "The plays confuse me, Uncle. They like a thousand-piece puzzle of a wheat field; all mashed up in my head."

"Try a simpler sport, then. Track might fit you better."

"Run round and round in a circle making left turns? Yeah, even I could handle that."

"I'm just saying." They play for another minute before Dirk speaks again. "You hear anything from Lacy?"

Palmer scowls, unhappy with the question. "She calls me some."

"How's her rehab going?"

"She's your sister," snaps Palmer, his fingers falling still on the guitar. "You should know as much as me."

"Maybe she'll come get you soon."

"Then what?" Palmer says, frustration spewing through him. "I go with her? To who knows where? For heaven knows how long? Till she's strung out again?"

"Opioids, Dude. They're tough to kick."

"Don't make excuses for her!" Palmer boils with anger now. "She does this over and over." He closes his eyes and fights against the memories of his mama, the times he put her to bed because she was too strung out to do it herself, the times she disappeared for days on end, the times... He opens his eyes and shuts down the memories.

Dirk stops playing too, throws a log onto the fire, and sits again. "I'll help you all I can, Palmer," he says. "But living with me won't cut it in the long term."

"Maybe this is as good as it gets for me," Palmer says, calming down a little. "A roof. A quiet place to play music."

"You said last night this place sucked."

Palmer starts playing again. "Yeah," he says.

"So?"

Palmer thinks of Molly and brightens a little. "Well, I did meet this girl. She works at the motel with me. She's older, a couple years maybe."

"A couple years is a lot at your age."

"I'm old enough."

"Old enough for what?"

Palmer's fingers go still on the guitar as he considers Molly—what he knows about her and what he can only sense. "I think she's a good girl," he finally says.

"Be careful with the ladies, Palmer. They are a mystery." Dirk starts playing again and Palmer's fingers tickle the strings along with him.

"I'm serious, Man. You really are getting good," says Dirk, admiring Palmer's picking. "Maybe you should try to perform somewhere—school maybe."

Palmer quickly shakes his head. "I like it just me and you."

"You afraid?"

Palmer considers the question. "What if I am?"

"It's not a crime to feel nervous," Dirk says. "Most people do at first."

"I need to save up some money for a guitar," says Palmer, changing the subject.

"Just keep that one," Dirk offers. "I'm buying me a new one."

A smile breaks out on Palmer's face. "For real?"

"I'm making a decent living these days."

"Thanks, Man. Really. Thanks."

They continue to play as the fire continues to burn.

Dressed in a dull gray gown, Ty lays in bed in a hospital room, his head propped up as he watches an NFL game on TV. Russell and Vanessa sit by him, talking quietly. The door to the room suddenly opens and Dub and Patrice walk in, both wearing their church clothes. Dub holds a football under an arm and Patrice carries a vase of flowers. Everybody hugs, holding on a little longer than normal before stepping back.

"How was church?" asks Ty as Dub lays the football on the bed.

"Preacher brought his A-game today," smiles Patrice, setting the flowers on a table. "But we missed you in the choir."

"Wish I could've been there," says Ty.

"You feeling all right?" Dub asks him.

"Ready to play again soon as they cut me loose from this place."

"That might be awhile," offers Russell. "Stay patient."

"They're running more tests," explains Vanessa, settling back in her seat. "Said they need to confirm some things."

Ty reaches for a thick, black, leather-bound book on the bedside table and hands it to Dub. "It's my Playbook," says Ty.

"Why you have it here?" asks Dub.

Ty smiles. "I keep it with me all the time, Coach."

Dub examines the book. Ecclesiastes 4:12 is stamped in silver letters on the cover. "That's a good verse," says Dub, opening the book.

"One of the best," agrees Ty as Dub flips through the pages. A diagram of an offensive play fills every page.

"The play shows every player's assignment," says Ty. "And those hand-scribbled notes, the ones on the sides of the pages?"

Dub turns the book sideways and reads the notes.

"I wrote them," continues Ty, his pride evident. "Things for the quarterback to watch for from the defense."

"What are these quotes at the bottom?" asks Dub, staring at a typed block quote stretching across the bottom of each page.

"I collect sayings I like," says Ty. "Memorize them. The ones in the book come from poets, philosophers, the scriptures."

Dub flips through several pages, then reads one of the quotes aloud. "Stand up straight and realize who you are, that you tower over your circumstances. Maya Angelou."

Dub finishes and closes the book. "Impressive, Ty."

"I started it my freshman year," Ty says proudly. "Maybe it can help Johnson get up to speed. Palmer too, I hope."

"You've always done everything first class."

"Make all the copies you need. I'll walk through it with Coach Deal, and anybody who wants my help."

Dub lays the Playbook on the table, picks up the football, and hands it to Ty. Signatures cover every side. "The pastor had folks at church sign it during the service," explains Dub.

Ty rolls the football over, slowly fingering each of the signatures. When he's finished, he wipes his eyes and clutches the football as if holding on for dear life.

Chelsea's cottage-style home perches about halfway up the hill of a long, winding road leading from the valley into the mountains. Inside, the lights burn low in the dining room and a wide window overlooks the town. A small table covered with a white tablecloth sits in the middle of the space and a woven rug covers the hardwood floors. A China cabinet fills one corner and two pictures—one of Chelsea wearing a football uniform with the number 1 on the jersey, and another of her with a tall man and woman on a hiking trail—hang on the wall over the cabinet.

Chelsea and Bo arrange plates on the table as soft music plays from her phone. A bowl of steaming spaghetti, a colorful salad, a bottle of wine, and a loaf of French bread complete the tableau.

Wearing a form-fitting blue dress, gold earrings with bold loops, and strappy black heels, Chelsea sniffs the spaghetti. "It smells fantastic," she says. "Are you Italian?"

Bo steps back. "Before we eat," he says, "I need to bring something in from the car."

"I'll put out the silverware," says Chelsea.

Bo hurries away as she pulls silverware from the cabinet and arranges it beside the plates. A few seconds later, Bo rushes back in and holds up a large, expensive picture frame.

"My law school diploma!" celebrates Chelsea. "So glad you brought it!"

"It cost a fortune to reframe it," says Bo, holding it high.

"It was pretty juvenile of you to break it in the first place."

"I wanted you to know how upset I was that you were leaving the firm."

She remembers the day: the fierce argument in her office when she told him she'd accepted a job as a football coach, his disbelief turning to dark anger, his fists clenched as he turned to the wall where the diploma hung.

"So, you punch out my diploma," she says, shaking her head in disbelief. "Real mature."

"You know me. All about the grand gesture."

She laughs and pecks him on the cheek. "Put it in the foyer for now," she says. "We'll hang it later."

He hustles out and she lights a candle in the middle of the table. Bo returns seconds later and pulls out a chair. She brushes her hair behind her ears and sits.

"I like your new hobby," he says, leaning close and fingering one of her earrings.

"I'll show you my workbench later."

"I hope it's in your bedroom."

"You're so naughty," she says with a laugh. "But yes, it's in the bedroom. Nowhere else to put it."

He walks to his chair. "Could you sell your jewelry if you wanted?"

"Probably. But that's not the point. I do it for me. Creating something— that's what I enjoy about it."

Bo pours wine into his glass and sets down the bottle. "A family," he says. "Children. Now that's creating something."

Chelsea forks spaghetti onto her plate and hands the bowl to Bo. "Someday, Bo," she says cautiously. "Like we've discussed before. I want that too. Just don't know when."

Her phone suddenly beeps. She grabs it, and hits "Ignore" before it rings a second time. The music plays again but stops once more as a phone call interrupts again. Chelsea again hits "Ignore." "Sorry," she says.

The phone beeps again.

"Enough already!" says Bo, throwing up his hands in surrender. "It's been ringing all day. Answer it, please!"

"You sure? I could just turn it off."

"Somebody obviously wants to reach you. Take the call. Put me out of my misery."

Chelsea quickly answers the phone.

"Hey, Chelsea," says Dub, his tone irritated. "I've been calling you all day!"

"What's going on, Coach?"

"You didn't listen to my messages?"

"I've worked for you for three months, Coach," she says. "You know I don't do football on Sunday."

"Meet me at my office in thirty minutes. Ty's sick."

"I'm in the middle of something," she says firmly.

"Your something will have to wait. Ty might have cancer."

Chelsea's face drops. "Cancer?" she asks, trying to comprehend what she's hearing.

"My office, Chelsea," orders Dub. "No argument."

Dub hangs up and Chelsea faces Bo, her mind racing. "I'm so sorry," she apologizes. "But I need to go."

"You're bailing on me?" His voice rises in anger.

"My quarterback might have cancer," she explains. "I need you to understand."

Bo drops his head into his hands. "I can't believe it. I haven't seen you in almost three weeks and now this."

She stands, steps toward him, and kisses him on the head. "It's an emergency, Bo, really."

He looks up and gives in. "Okay," he says. "Do what you need to do."

"Give me an hour," she says. "Let me find out what's going on."

He puts his arms around her waist and pulls her close. "I'll just finish eating and drive back to Atlanta. Let you do your thing here."

"I appreciate the spaghetti," she says, her voice hopeful that he'll understand. "And my diploma."

He stands, backs up a pace, and looks her over. "You do look fabulous," he says, playful again. "It's a shame to waste an outfit like that."

She leans into him, her head on his chest. "Football season ends soon," she offers. "I'll make it up to you then."

He kisses her head. "Scoot," he says, waving her away. "I'll clean the table before I leave."

"See you next week?" she asks.

"That's the plan."

She kisses him on the cheek.

"By the way," he says as she grabs her purse. "I'm sorry about your quarterback."

She kisses him again and rushes out the door.

Three state championship rings sit in a glass case on a cluttered desk in Dub's large office. Ty's Playbook lies beside the rings and Dub bends over it, his eyes busy as he flips through the pages. A giant video monitor covers the back wall, and a glass-fronted refrigerator filled with bottled water and energy drinks hums under the monitor. A row of chairs faces the monitor.

Coach Dub looks up from his seat as Chelsea enters, still dressed up, heels and all. "Look at you," says Dub. "All pretty in your party clothes."

"I'm not sure my attire is an appropriate subject for your comments, Coach," Chelsea teases.

He points her to a chair and she plops down. "You're right, as usual," he says. "So, let's talk about Ty."

"What's the story?"

He sighs heavily. "It's not all confirmed yet, but Dr. Ramirez believes it's bone cancer. I saw Ty's knee at the hospital after church, It's as big as a volleyball."

Chelsea grits her teeth as her emotions rise—fear, helplessness, anger. "I need to see him," she says, her instinct for action kicking in.

"Tomorrow," Dub says. "They're not allowing any more guests tonight." He picks up Ty's Playbook and hands it to her. "Ty gave it to me," he says. "Said we should make copies, use it to teach Johnson and Palmer."

"It's hard to even think about football right now," says Chelsea.

"It'll keep our minds busy," says Dub. "Least I hope it will."

Chelsea opens the Playbook and flicks through the pages, her eyes widening as she inspects it. "Wow," she exclaims. "This kid."

"He's liable to be president someday. If he beats this cancer."

Chelsea sets down the Playbook. "Cancer," she whispers. "It doesn't seem real."

"Tragedy never does."

Chelsea drops her head, and they fall silent for a few moments. Finally, Dub picks up a TV remote from his desk, points to the video screen, and hits play. "We'll have to start Johnson this week, I suppose," he says.

Images of a football scrimmage roll onto the screen. Sean Johnson, his thin body moving in a herky-jerky motion, rolls out and throws the football downfield. The pass falls five yards short of his intended receiver and a defender intercepts it. "Johnson isn't very good, Coach," says Chelsea.

"He's terrible is what he is. A stork on roller skates."

"All arms and legs," agrees Chelsea.

"He's slower than my mama on her walker and he can't throw a lick."

"On the positive side, he does know the plays," says Chelsea, trying to find something upbeat to say. "And he's paid his dues."

Dub sighs. "I know I shouldn't be so negative. Sean tries hard. And he'll play his heart out for us. But this Ty thing… I'm bummed, that's all."

"I get it, Coach. Feel the same way."

Dub clicks the remote again and brings up another play. Palmer catches a punt, darts right, then left. Three defenders chase, but Palmer leaves them in the dust, outrunning them to the endzone for a touchdown.

"Palmer just oozes speed and athleticism," marvels Dub. "But he doesn't know squat and doesn't seem to care."

"Well, we haven't given him much playing time," Chelsea says. "Maybe he's better in a game than at practice."

Dub shrugs. "Yeah, maybe. But the team doesn't know him or trust him."

"I gave him a ride home after the game last Friday," says Chelsea. "He lives in a pretty sketchy place."

"He barely speaks to the other players. And he won't look you in the eye when you talk to him."

"His confidence seems really low."

"Plus, he's missed a bunch of practices."

"I don't think he prioritizes football that much."

Dub leans back, his hands behind his head. "We start Johnson this week," he concludes. "But we work harder with Palmer, prepare him the best we can, as soon as we can, in case Johnson can't do the job."

"I'll pull Palmer out of his study hall tomorrow."

"Cram as much into his head as he can absorb."

"It's a good thing we can lose the last game and still make the playoffs."

Dub wags a finger at Chelsea. "Don't even say that, Coach. Losing is the unforgiveable sin in this town."

CHAPTER FOUR

arly arriving students fill about half the chairs in Palmer's homeroom class. Students gradually straggle in, checking their phones, talking, and laughing as they sink into their seats. Ms. Roper, a young teacher wearing stylish brown glasses and a thick black sweater, works quietly at her desk, ignoring the chaos around her.

Stepping into the room behind a couple of chatty girls, Chelsea hurries over to Ms. Roper. "Hey, how's it going?" Chelsea asks.

"Ugh," groans Roper, looking up. "It's Monday and all I remember about the weekend is a friend's birthday party that ended with tequila shots and blaring music."

"Did you have fun?"

"My friend tells me I did!"

Chelsea laughs as she quickly scans the room. "Is Palmer Norman here?"

Roper glances toward an empty seat by the back wall. "Not yet. But he's late a lot. If he shows up at all."

"Hey, Coach!" yells Don, slouching in the seat to the right of Palmer's empty chair.

"Great game Friday!" shouts Strick, in the chair behind him.

Chelsea eyes the two of them as the rest of the students fall quiet, attentive for the first time. "Have you guys seen Palmer Norman this morning?" she asks.

Don stares at Chelsea, a cocky grin on his face while Strick keys his phone. "Palmer ain't real regular, Coach," says Don. "Won't get a perfect attendance pin this year."

The class laughs as Strick speaks into his phone. "Hey, Hillbilly," he says. "Best haul your butt to school soon as you can. The hot new coach is looking for ya."

Ms. Roper stands quickly and hurries to Strick. "You know you can't talk about a teacher like that!" she barks. "Give me your phone!"

Strick grins and hands the phone over.

"Grab your things," orders Roper. "Go straight to the principal's office! You know the drill!"

Ms. Roper faces Chelsea as Strick reaches for his backpack. "What a way to start the week," she groans.

"Just let it go," offers Chelsea, not wanting to spend the next hour in Principal Roberts' office explaining what had happened. "It's not worth the effort."

"You sure?" asks Roper.

Chelsea faces Strick. "You or your brother," she glances at Don. "You ever want to play football, let me know."

Strick eyes her suspiciously as she points him back to his seat.

"I'll text you if Palmer shows up," Roper tells Chelsea.

Chelsea nods and hustles out.

A sign on a closed door about halfway down the hall reads COUNSELOR TOWE. Chelsea knocks on it as a bell rings and the hallway clears of the last arriving students. A couple seconds later, Chelsea hears a slurping sound behind the door, then a deep voice. "Come in."

She opens the door and eases into a small office filled with a large, cluttered desk. A single hard-back chair faces the desk and a much-worn leather one sits behind it. Bill Towe, a heavy-set, mid-forties man with a beard and thick glasses, fills the much-worn seat, which squeaks as he shifts and glances up from his computer screen.

"Hello, Coach Deal," Towe says as he slurps from the soft drink he holds in his meaty hand. "How can I help you this beautiful fall morning?"

Chelsea studies him for a moment, not sure of the sincerity of his question. "Has Palmer Norman called in sick today?" she finally asks.

Towe punches a few computer keys and studies the screen. "I don't see that he has," he says.

He sets down his drink, pulls his ample bottom from the chair, steps to a cabinet in the corner, pulls out a file, and flips through it. "Oh yes," he says. "Mr. Palmer Norman. A new kid with us this year."

He pushes up his glasses as he studies the file. "Okay. We're nine weeks into the school year and Mr. Norman has already missed...let me count them—" he mumbles the count before raising his eyebrows at Chelsea. "Ten days of school."

"His home situation seems a bit unsettled," says Chelsea.

Towe glances to Chelsea. "Students like Mr. Norman always have an excuse, Coach. But here's the thing. The reasons don't really matter. Missing twenty-two percent of his classes means I have a better chance of receiving the last rose on 'The Bachelorette' than this kid does of ever walking across a graduation stage."

"Unless something changes," says Chelsea, distressed at Palmer's situation but unwilling to buy into Towe's cynicism.

Towe grins. "Of course," he says. "And we both know that patterns like this change all the time." He picks up his cup. "Sarcasm intended, of course."

Fighting her instinct to slap the grin off Towe's face, Chelsea stares at him for several seconds, then stands and makes a simple request. "Please let me know if he calls in," she says.

Towe slurps his drink. "Oh, you know I will."

Palmer sits on the front steps of Dirk's house munching on a doughnut as a beat-up blue car, a strip of duct tape stuck on a cracked back window, drives into the yard and stops. Smiling widely, he stands as the driver's window rolls down and Molly pokes her head out.

"What's up, Idiot?" she asks.

Palmer eats the last of the doughnut, grabs a toolbox from the porch behind him, and heads to the car. "I appreciate you giving me a ride," he says, reaching the door.

"We can't have you missing school," grins Molly. "I'd bet a dollar that you're quite the scholar."

"I'm going to fix my motorcycle," says Palmer, ignoring her insult and opening the back door. "It broke down after the game Friday."

"You just wanted an excuse to see me."

"You didn't complain when I called you to come pick me up."

"Get in, Idiot."

Palmer sets the toolbox on the back floor and hops into the front seat beside Molly. "I don't like being called Idiot," he says.

"You like Dummy better?"

Palmer starts to speak but turns away instead and stares out the window as Molly exits the yard.

Dub sits at his desk, watching football video as Chelsea enters. He turns off the monitor, pushes out a seat with his foot, and motions Chelsea to sit. "No six-inch heels this morning?" he teases.

"You're a bad man, Coach." She smiles as she plops down.

"I hear Palmer's not in school again," says Dub.

"His attendance is terrible."

"He lives with an uncle, if I recall correctly."

"Yep. We met him when Palmer showed up for practice back in August. Palmer told me he's a musician."

"Wonder what's up with his mom and dad?"

Chelsea considers the question as she grabs a water bottle out of the fridge and sits again. "I keep a notebook," she says, swigging from the water. "Full of player profiles."

"That's smart," says Dub.

She shakes her head, not accepting the compliment. "I'm just realizing it's mostly full of crap."

Dub leans forward. "Information but not insight?"

Chelsea weighs the question and recognizes its truth. "Height, weight, forty-yard dash time, vertical leap, bench press maximums, squats. But none of it matters if you don't know the player."

"What makes him tick? Why does he play? Where he's struggling?"

Chelsea hangs her head, disgusted that she's missed the most important thing about coaching.

"So, Palmer," says Dub, pulling her thoughts back to the problem at hand.

"It must be a screwed-up family," she says, determined to know her players better in the future. "Like a lot of kids these days."

"Playing football helps one every now and again," suggests Dub. "Brings some structure, discipline, to their lives."

"I think I'll drive out to Palmer's house and check on him," Chelsea says as she stands.

"Nope," says Dub. "It should be me. You're not the only one who needs to know the kid better."

Molly's car pulls up outside the Knights' locker room and parks beside Palmer's motorcycle. "How old is that thing?' she asks, staring at the bike.

"Eleven years. But I keep it running most of the time."

"If I had a stick a dynamite, I'd blow it up for you."

"It runs better than it looks," says Palmer, reaching into the back for his toolbox.

"Except when it doesn't."

Palmer reaches for the door handle.

"Don't call me if it breaks down again," says Molly.

"You done with me already?" he asks, a little hurt by her dismissal.

"I never started with you."

"You mad at me for something?"

She reaches over and touches his shoulder. "Are you a sensitive boy?" she coos, her tone like a mother speaking to a child.

"Now you're teasing me?"

She pecks him on the cheek. "Yes!" she says. "I'm teasing! Don't take it so personal."

Totally confused, he stares at her. But she smiles and he relaxes a little.

"Go!" she orders, pointing to his door. "Fix your motorcycle. Call me if it breaks down again!"

Feeling a bit better, Palmer opens the door, climbs out, and turns back to Molly. "You working today?" he asks.

"Of course. It's my dream job. I'll be in at two."

"Me at 3."

"Don't you have football practice?

"I need to work. Not swimming in cash, and need gas money for the bike."

"Football not your thing?"

"I'm not sure I have a thing."

She blows him a kiss. "Later, Idiot."

He glares at her.

"Oh yeah." She smiles. "Later, Palmer."

"Was that so hard?" He pats the car and turns to his bike as she spins away.

At least fifteen balloons, ten flower arrangements, and several hundred get-well cards fill every unused space in Ty's hospital room. He lies in the bed while Vanessa sits in a chair beside him, her eyes on her phone as he reads the cards one at a time. He smiles every now and again as he finishes a card and lays it on his bedside table.

"Do you write a thank-you card for a get-well card?" he asks Vanessa.

She looks up, a confused scowl on her face. "I'm not sure," she says. "I'll have to google it."

Someone knocks on the door and Vanessa opens it, hugging Chelsea as she enters. "Thanks for coming, Coach," Vanessa says as she steps back.

"I came soon as I could this morning," says Chelsea, moving to Ty.

"Good to see you, Coach," says Ty.

"You too." She shifts uncomfortably, suddenly aware she has no clue what to say to a teenage boy with cancer.

"What's that?" asks Ty, pointing to something in her hands.

"Oh, yeah." She holds up a book and hands it to him. "*The Nickel Boys*. I know you like to read."

Ty checks out the cover. "Thanks, Coach. This won a Pulitzer Prize, didn't it?"

Chelsea nods, glad for something to talk about other than cancer. "You bet it did."

Vanessa points Chelsea to a chair and both sit. Chelsea focuses on Ty again. "You feeling okay today?" she asks him.

Ty lays down the book. "I feel normal except for my knee."

"They have to run a couple more tests," says Vanessa. "Then we see Dr. Ramirez again. Put a treatment plan in place."

"You have your work cut out for you, Coach," Ty says. "Johnson and Palmer."

"She's not a miracle worker," says Vanessa.

Chelsea chuckles but her mirth is short-lived as she thinks of her quarterback situation.

"I'm on board to tutor them," says Ty. "Whatever I can do."

"How well do you know Palmer?" Chelsea asks.

"Not too well," admits Ty. "He keeps pretty much to himself."

"I might want you to call him. Encourage him."

"He ditches school a lot."

"Yep. Out again today."

"I'll talk to him, Coach," Ty assures her. "But I don't know if it'll help."

Chelsea pulls out her phone. "I'm texting you his contact information."

"I'll reach out to him today."

Chelsea sends the information to Ty and the feeling hits her again. She's totally unprepared for this kind of thing. But can anyone ever be prepared for the sudden disruption—the cancer diagnosis, the divorce that strikes from the blue, the too-early death of a loved one? "Anything specific I can do for either of you right now?" she asks, pulling herself from her thoughts and looking from Vanessa to Ty.

"You can win the game Friday," says Ty.

"That would be a lot easier if you were there."

"I'll be there," he promises. "Just not in uniform."

Chelsea stands. "Get well, Ty," she says. "We really need you."

Fall leaves skitter across the country road in front of Dub's SUV as he drives toward Palmer's house. Holding up a hand against the glare of the sun, he leans sideways, hoping to see better. The Temptations sing "My Girl" on his car radio. He hits a button on his steering wheel to dial Ty's number and Ty answers almost immediately. "Good morning, Son," says Dub. "How's your knee?"

"Not ready to run a marathon," says Ty. "But the pain isn't bad today."

"Your spot is waiting for you the second you're able to play."

"Thanks, Coach. You starting Johnson this week?"

"I don't have a lot of choices."

"Any hope for Palmer?"

Dub rolls the question around in his head. "Hard to say. He ditched school again today. I'm headed to his place now. Hope to get his mind right so he can use the talent he has."

A deer darts across the road and Dub swerves the SUV, trying to miss it. "Son of a—!" he yells.

The SUV smacks into the deer, plows into a ditch, bounces out, and smashes into a tree. Dub's face bangs into the steering wheel and the air bags deploy as he falls forward, his head bloody.

"Coach?!" yells Ty through the phone. "Coach, are you okay?"

"Send an... ambulance," groans Dub, fighting to stay conscious. "Grover Road. A deer..." His voice falters as he passes out.

"Hang on, Coach!" shouts Ty. "I'm calling 911!"

The phone goes dead. Dub leans his bloody head against the driver's window, his eyes closed. A gash on his forehead oozes blood onto his nose and chin. The SUV is crushed, the driver's side mangled. Smoke rises from the hood. Dub wakes with a jerk, wipes blood from his mouth, unhooks his seat belt, and staggers out of the vehicle. Limping badly, he staggers toward the mangled deer, unmoving on the highway. Dub's left leg collapses and he falls beside the deer as the smoke from the SUV hood grows thicker. A siren wails in the distance and Dub tries to stand but topples over again.

A car zooms by but then stops, backs up, and stops again. A man jumps out and runs to Dub. "Hey!" the man yells, leaning over Dub. "Hang on! An ambulance is on the way!"

The man coughs as the smoke curls toward him and he grabs Dub by the shoulders, drags him farther from the SUV, and lays him down. "Stay with me, Coach," he whispers. "Stay with me."

Dub fights to stay awake but fails and his eyes close as his breath goes shallow. The siren wails again but Dub can't hear it anymore as he drifts away into blackness.

Approximately thirty minutes later, a black Hummer with giant tires, idles at the drive-through window of an Atlanta coffee shop. Soft jazz plays in the Hummer, a caressing sound against the plush brown leather of the upholstery.

Les Holt, a thin man in his late forties wearing a gray suit, white shirt, and black tie, waits for his coffee in the driver's seat. "Hey, Buck," Holt says calmly, his phone pressed against an ear the size of a biscuit. "You hear about Dub?"

"A wreck? Something about a deer?"

"That's the story. Ambulance brought him to the hospital just a few minutes ago."

"How bad is he?"

"Not sure yet," says Holt. "But a doctor friend at the hospital told me he didn't think it was life threatening."

"That's good to hear."

The drive-through window opens and Holt grabs his coffee, pays, and pulls onto the street. "I wonder if he'll be able to coach this week's game," he says, stopping at a redlight.

"If Dub's out, it's got to be me," says Buck, his voice hopeful, like a six-year-old wishing for a new bicycle. "Interim Head Coach?"

"You've been the Defensive Coordinator for eight years. I can't imagine the Board would choose anyone else. But you need to keep your head down. No lobbying or anything like that."

"I'm not a moron, Les."

Les thinks of a snappy comeback but decides to play nice. "You're just too aggressive sometimes, Buck. You feel me?"

"Will the Board meet tonight?" asks Buck, ignoring Holt's comment.

"It's that time of the month. Joint meeting of the Board and the Booster Club Council."

"You in my corner if I need you?"

Holt sips his coffee as the light changes and he pulls through it. "I'm your guy, Buck," he says enthusiastically. "You know that."

Buck clears his throat. "Okay. I appreciate you having my back on this."

Holt turns left and guns his Hummer onto the highway. "Just make sure your brother appreciates it."

A bright moon shines down on Rabon High School as nearly twenty-five people, including Holt, file in from the parking lot and head to the school cafeteria. They're all busy in conversation, chatting excitedly, reporting the latest gossip. Once they're inside the cafeteria, the volume drops as they find seats. Some continue to talk but in quieter tones, while others pull out phones and stare at them as if searching for updates on the accident that has the whole town buzzing.

Eight of the townsfolk—six women and two men, including Holt—take spots at a head table at the front of a small stage. Principal George Roberts, a red-faced man in his fifties with a crew cut and a pencil behind his right ear, perches dead center between the eight Board members. After a few minutes, somebody closes the cafeteria doors and Principal Roberts rises and picks up a microphone from the table. The crowd instantly falls quiet.

"All right, everybody." Roberts begins. "Good evening and welcome to the monthly meeting of our School Board and our Football Booster Club Council."

"Good evening," responds the crowd.

"I'm glad you're all here," continues Roberts. "Allows me to give everyone an update at the same time."

The crowd murmurs, leans in toward Roberts.

Chelsea, dressed in khakis, plus her Knights' jacket and baseball cap, enters the cafeteria from the back door and waits as Roberts continues.

"Let me begin by reporting what I can about Ty," Roberts says. "Though I can't be specific about his medical condition, I can say that he's unable to play football for now. So, we'll need a new quarterback, at least for a while."

A shout rings out from the back of the room. "I hear Ty's got cancer."

"I've said all I can about Ty," says Roberts.

"What about Coach Dub?!" yells the shouter.

"What about the deer?!" yells someone else. The crowd chuckles.

"Is Coach Dub okay?!" yells the first shouter.

"Hang on!" says Roberts. "One question at a time."

The crowd calms a tad and Roberts continues. "Thankfully, yes, it looks like Coach Dub will be fine. He does have injuries, but nothing critical."

Les Holt raises his hand. "Will Coach miss any games?"

Roberts turns to him. "It's too early to know," he answers, pulling his pencil from his ear and rolling it in his fingers.

"Who'll coach if he can't?" presses Holt.

"That's not applicable yet, Les," Roberts says, a touch of impatience on his face. "So, I won't speculate. We'll update everybody once we know more." He stares Holt down a moment before addressing the crowd again. "Any more questions about Ty or Dub before we hear the team report?"

The crowd shuffles restlessly for a few seconds but nobody else says anything, so Roberts looks Chelsea's way and waves her forward.

"All right," he says. "I see that Coach Chelsea Deal has arrived from practice. Come on up, Coach."

He beckons her forward and she heads his way, smiling as she threads her way through the tables. "Since Dub is out tonight," continues Roberts, "we've asked Coach Deal to give us the team update and answer a few questions for us."

The crowd leans in as Chelsea reaches the front table and removes her cap.

In Dr. Ramirez' office, Russell and Vanessa sit on either side of Ty, the three of them quietly holding hands. Dr. Ramirez rubs his fingers through his thick black hair, opens a file, and studies it for a second. Sighing, he leans forward.

"Okay," he says sadly, "I sent all the results from Ty's tests to a colleague at Johns Hopkins for a peer review, and he concurs with my diagnosis."

Ty glances at his mom and dad. Ramirez sighs, continues. "I will give it to you straight. Unfortunately, it's what I feared. An osteosarcoma. Cancer of the bone."

Ty freezes for a moment, trying to grasp what he just heard. Nobody else speaks for several seconds.

"But he's so healthy!" Vanessa says, finally breaking the silence.

"It's not what any of us want to hear," says Ramirez. "But the tests leave no doubt about the diagnosis."

Vanessa, tears in her eyes, shakes her head.

"The good news is we see no evidence that it's spread," Ramirez says hopefully.

"That's something at least," says Russell.

Ty stares from his mama to his pops, his tongue paralyzed. How do you form a word when your entire world just twisted? Ty feels like he's watching a bizarre reality show, where a character finds out he's dying, and the audience votes to predict how he'll respond when he learns the news.

"Since we've caught this early, survival rates are close to seventy percent," Ramirez offers, his tone positive.

"But thirty percent...?" Vanessa drops her head and cries harder.

"I advise you not to look at it that way, Vanessa," says Ramirez. "Doing so accomplishes nothing."

Vanessa wipes her eyes. "I'm sorry," she says. "I'm just shocked, you know."

Ramirez hands her a tissue and she brushes tears away.

"Tell us how we treat it," says Russell, his face somber but determined.

Ramirez faces Russell. "First, we use chemotherapy to shrink the tumor. Next, we do surgery to remove what's left. Last, if needed, we use radiation to make sure we've destroyed all of it."

"Let's start soon as we can," says Ty, finding his voice as he hears the treatment plan. "Beat this thing and put it behind us."

"Agreed," says Ramirez. "Chemo usually requires three to six months. We reassess, if necessary, once it's concluded. Any questions?"

Vanessa checks with Russell. "We're good for now," he says.

"I have a question," says Ty as his mind searches his body, trying to locate the cancer in his knee, to internally feel the tumor like he might feel a lump on his head if someone hit him with a hammer.

"Sure, Ty," says Ramirez. "Ask me anything."

"Can you reduce the swelling in my knee?"

Ramirez shrugs. "Not likely, but we can try."

Ty studies his hands for a moment before facing Ramirez again. "If the swelling shrinks, can I play football?"

"NO!" says Vanessa without missing a beat.

"We start the playoffs in a week, Mama," argues Ty. He turns back to Ramirez. "Any chance, Doctor? Ramirez shakes his head. "I wish I could say 'yes,' Ty. But honestly, the answer is 'no.'"

Ty bites his lip to tamp down his anger, He wants to scream, bang his head on the desk—something, anything to wake himself from the dream he's sure he's having. But he stays still and silent.

"We'll start things moving ASAP," says Ramirez, closing his file. "Schedule the first chemo treatment."

He stands and shakes Russell's hand, hugs Vanessa, then faces Ty. Grasping Ty's hand with both of his, Ramirez holds on tightly. "I will provide the best of care for you, Ty," he promises.

Ty hears the words, but they sound distant, like he's too far away to hear them. "Thank you," he nods, figuring that's the safest response.

"I will miss you on the field Friday."

"Football had to end sometime," Ty says sadly. "Just didn't expect it to end like this."

Chelsea stands on the floor in front of the head table, everyone staring at her as Roberts continues to introduce her.

"Just in case some of you have forgotten the story," Roberts explains, "I'll briefly recap how Coach Deal ended up with us at Rabon High."

He switches hands with the microphone and continues: "When last year's Offensive Coordinator bolted at the last minute for a college job, we had just two weeks to hire a new coach. Fortunately, Coach Dub remembered Ms. Deal from her one-year coaching stint at Foley High a few years ago. So, he reached out, made her an offer, and she surprised all of us and said 'yes.' So, let's give her a warm welcome as she speaks to us for the first time."

Roberts hands Chelsea the microphone and sits down as the crowd applauds.

"Hey, everybody," Chelsea begins as she places her cap on a nearby table. "I found out only a couple hours ago I was doing this, so I don't have any speech prepared."

"That's a good start!" yells the shouter from the back. People laugh.

"I agree," says Chelsea. "So, let's go straight to your questions."

"Welcome, Coach," says Holt from the table behind her. Chelsea turns to him and smiles.

"Thank you," she says.

"So," continues Holt, "it's my understanding you coached football for one year right out of college, then went to law school. Graduated and practiced law for six years. And now you've returned to coaching."

"That's right."

"What made you jump back into coaching?"

Chelsea clears her throat as she ponders the question, not sure she really knows how to answer it. "Well, I'd rather talk about the team than about me," she says, unwilling to delve too deeply into her past. "But you could say I came back because I love football, I love kids, and I love competition."

"Why did you leave your law practice?" asks Holt, not ready yet to yield the floor.

Chelsea shrugs. "People change jobs all the time. For all kinds of reasons. Some public, others not."

Holt starts to speak again but Roberts shakes his head at him, and Holt backs off.

Ginny Barnes, a young woman with heavy makeup, manicured nails, and perfect blonde hair, raises her hand at a dining table on the main floor. Chelsea points at her to speak. "We've had just one losing season in the past eight years," Ginny says. "And our offense has ranked near the top in the state during that whole time. You think you have the experience to keep the offense rolling?"

"I confess I'm still learning," says Chelsea. "But my offense at Foley performed well and I did play football back in the day. So, I have at least some of the experiences needed to lead the offense."

"You were a kicker," snickers Holt. "I'm not sure that's actually playing football." A few people chuckle but others stay quiet.

Eva Gill, a patrician, silver-haired woman in her sixties wearing a tailored gray skirt and jacket and a red ribbon in her hair, addresses Chelsea from her perch beside Roberts at the head table, "I read that you had a heck of an offense at Foley," Eva says. "Averaged over fifty points a game, didn't you?"

"That's true," says Chelsea, facing her. "We finished second in the state that year. Class 2-A, but yes."

The shouter from the back pops up again. "You had a High School All-American quarterback at Foley, didn't you? A monkey could finish second with him." A few chuckles break out again.

"He was good, that's for sure," says Chelsea, blushing a little as she faces the crowd again.

Ginny pipes up once more. "I hear that Coach Dub calls the offensive plays during our games. Is that true?"

"Yes," says Chelsea, beginning to feel like a criminal facing a hostile jury. "We work together on the game plan, but he calls most of the plays once the whistle blows."

"Did you call all the plays at Foley?" asks Holt, a sharper edge in his voice.

"Well, no coordinator calls all the plays," says Chelsea, frustrated at Holt's attitude but striving to stay calm. "On offense or defense."

Ginny interjects again. "You reckon you got hired here because you're a woman?"

Chelsea grips the microphone tighter and grits her teeth. An awkward silence falls over the room. Chelsea clears her throat and finally answers, her voice steady but terse. "Well, I'm not the one who hired me so I can't answer that."

Eva slowly stands and stares over the room, her gaze relaxed but purposeful. "Okay, friends," she says smoothly. "We're 9-0, remember? Ranked number one in the state. It seems to me that Coach Deal and the team she's helping lead are doing fine. Anybody disagree with that?"

Eva pauses, her steely hazel eyes searching the room for any dissent, but nobody else voices any. "Good," she says. "So, let's thank Coach Deal for coming tonight and let her return to her coaching while we take a ten-minute break before our official meeting begins. We all on board with that?"

Most of the crowd applauds and everyone stands as Chelsea quickly hands the microphone to Roberts.

"I don't believe we've formally met," says Eva, stepping towards Chelsea and extending a hand.

"Thanks for beating off the vultures," says Chelsea, shaking her hand. "Not exactly the friendliest bunch, is it?"

"You'll find a few jack wagons in every crowd," says Eva, handing her a card with her phone number on it. "Call me if you ever need to chat."

Dressed in his work uniform, Palmer sits cross-legged on the side of a made-up bed in a Rabon Motel room. It is clean, the trash cans emptied, the floor vacuumed, the tables dusted.

Molly lays on the bed facing him but they're not touching. "I decided I won't call you 'Idiot' anymore," says Molly.

Palmer smiles. "I do like 'Genius' better."

"Let's not go overboard."

Palmer lies down, his face no more than a foot away from Molly's.

"Did you skip football for just today?" Molly asks. "Or you done with it for good?"

Palmer shrugs. "Maybe I like music better than football. I play banjo. Guitar. Sing some too."

Molly pokes him in the ribs. "Banjo players aren't sexy."

"I said guitar too."

She pokes him again. "Banjo Boy!"

Palmer grabs a pillow and throws it at her. She jumps on him and tries to smother him with the pillow. They wrestle and he flips her over and pins her to the bed, her hands in his, stretched over her head. They're face to face, laughing. Slowly, they stop laughing and go quiet and still. Palmer lets her hands loose but keeps his legs astride her waist.

"You can kiss me if you want," whispers Molly.

"Don't call me Banjo Boy," Palmer says, a touch of hurt in his voice.

"You got a bunch of things I can't call you."

Palmer rolls off, lies down beside her, and stares at the ceiling, lost in his thoughts. People have laughed at him all his life, called him names, poked fun at him because he was poor and dumb, because his mama dipped in and out of his life—here one day, gone the next.

Molly places a hand on his chest. "You not going to kiss me?" she asks.

He shakes his head and pouts.

"Sing for me," says Molly.

"I don't sing in front of people," he whispers.

"I'm not people. I'm your girl."

Palmer slowly turns to her.

"Don't be mad when I tease you," she says. "I only tease when I like somebody."

"You like me?" The idea is a revelation to Palmer, like discovering a waterfall in a desert, and his heart rises.

"Yeah. I said it and I won't take it back."

"Say it again."

Molly touches his chin. "Sing for me and I will."

Palmer sighs, closes his eyes, and begins to sing. His voice is soft, tender, a touch mournful. Molly snuggles closer as he continues, his eyes still closed. When he finishes, he opens his eyes and stares into Molly's.

"You sing sad," says Molly.

"Tell me again you like me, and I'll be happier."

"I like you."

Palmer smiles, rolls away, and climbs off the bed.

CHAPTER FIVE

A large tray filled with bottled waters and granola bars rests in the center of an oblong table surrounded by chairs in a conference room at Rabon High School. Big windows provide a view to the east, where a brilliant sun rises on the mountains. A TV hangs from the ceiling in a corner and a clock on the wall shows 8:15.

Three men—Principal Roberts, Les Holt, and Rob Billet, a bald guy in his fifties—join six women—Eva, Ginny, and four others—at the conference table. Roberts and Holt hold water bottles. Eva wears a yellow ribbon in her hair this time, but Holt wears the same gray and black outfit he always does. An elderly man with a weathered face, a blue cap, and a shirt emblazoned with a "Phil's Plumbing" logo, sits away from the rest in a back corner.

Roberts thumps softly on the table, and everyone comes to attention. "Okay," Roberts begins, his pencil behind an ear. "Sorry to call you all back so soon after last night, but I saw Dub before daybreak this morning and he's been informed that his injuries will sideline him at least a couple of weeks." Roberts sips from his water bottle. "So, the Board needs to pick an interim head coach."

"I nominate Buck Jones," Holt quickly interjects, looking around as if daring anyone to challenge him. "He's the only logical choice."

"But he's the Defensive Coordinator," argues Billet, to Holt's surprise. "And Ty's out too. We need somebody who knows the offense to run things till Dub returns."

"What about Coach Paul?" asks Ginny. A couple of people chuckle.

"We all like Coach Paul," says Holt. "But we also know he's not head coach material."

The group nods, even Ginny, quickly accepting Holt's assessment of Coach Paul.

"I'm impressed by Coach Deal," says Eva, her tone easy, not pushing anyone in any direction.

"The offense has looked good," agrees Billet.

"She admitted last night that Dub calls the plays," says Holt, quickly on the offensive against Chelsea.

"But she puts the game plan together," counters Eva. "And the boys seem to like her."

Holt snickers. "Well, she's a good-looking young woman, and they're a bunch of teenage boys. What's not to like?"

"Let's keep this about football, please," Roberts says sternly, his pencil in hand. "Gender issues don't concern us."

"No, George," Eva counters. "We might as well face the woman thing head on. If it's between Ms. Deal and Buck, let's lay it all out there."

"Is it between those two?" asks Roberts. "Could we find an experienced coach somewhere? A retiree maybe? Hire him on a temporary basis?"

Billet shakes his head. "I don't see that working," he says. "We got one game left in the regular season. Then the playoffs. I can't imagine bringing in a new guy this late in the season."

Everybody nods agreement. Roberts shrugs and gives up the idea. "All right," he says. "We agree it's between Buck and Chelsea?"

Everyone looks around. Billet shrugs, Holt nods, and everyone joins him.

"Good," says Roberts. "At least we've narrowed it down."

The group silently weighs the options for several seconds before Ginny speaks again. "I'll be honest here," she says. "Handing the job to Coach Deal feels a little too PC for me. Like we're trying to make a statement of some kind. I prefer we leave that sort of thing to the folks in Atlanta."

"Is it a terrible thing if we give a female just a touch of preference?" asks Billet. "A lot of young girls in Rabon need to see a woman doing bold things. It's not like she'll keep the job forever."

"But we know Buck," insists Holt. "He's coached here for eight years. And he works hard. Our defense is always top of the line."

The room falls quiet for another moment and Billet grabs a granola bar, opens it, and munches. "Buck is a little too ambitious for me," he says between bites. "That year we finished 4-6, he put out feelers to see if he could steal Dub's job."

Phil the Plumber clears his throat and rises.

"You want to say something, Phil?" Roberts asks.

"I reckon I do," says Phil, removing his hat.

"He's not officially a member of the Board," protests Holt.

"And he won't vote if it comes to that," states Roberts. "But he's chair of the Booster Club and deserves our attention if he wants to speak."

Holt's giant ears redden but he quickly accepts defeat. "Okay," he says. "But keep it short, Phil." He glances at his watch. "Time is money."

Phil clears his throat again. "So, there's women coaches in the NFL these days. And they not there cause they're pretty faces. No, those NFL types don't mess around with somebody they don't think can help them win."

Holt points to his watch. "Short, Phil."

Phil eyes him but keeps talking. "The NFL hires those ladies because they make teams better. And Ms. Chelsea, she owns something—charisma, heart—call it what you want. But it's there. We can all see it if we just open our eyes. So, I figure we give Coach Chelsea a spin this next game or two, see if she impresses us." Phil raises an eyebrow at Holt, puts on his cap, and sits.

Roberts holds up eight slips of paper. "We ready to vote?"

Everybody looks to Holt. "What does Dub think?" he asks.

"Well, he's pretty banged up," Roberts says. "I haven't directly asked him."

"He knows Buck and Chelsea better than any of us," says Holt. "Shouldn't we call him, ask his opinion before we vote?"

Roberts eyes Eva. She nods, and he turns again to Holt. "That's a good suggestion, Les," he says. "Everybody good with calling Dub?"

Everyone nods and Roberts pulls out his cell phone and sets it on speaker mode.

Patrice and Chelsea sit by Dub in his hospital room. A breakfast tray filled with uneaten hospital food waits on a stand beside the bed. Dub has one leg in a cast, a bandage wrapping his head, and multiple stitches in his chin, but he's greedily finishing up a fast-food chicken biscuit as Chelsea talks.

"We have to find a backup quarterback if Palmer doesn't come back," she says as Dub hands the biscuit wrapper to Patrice.

"Sorry I didn't make it out to see him," says Dub.

A phone rings and Patrice drops the wrapper into a trash can, grabs Dub's phone off the tray, and hands it to him. Dub says hello, then listens for several seconds, his eyes widening with each moment. "Give me five minutes," he finally tells the caller. "I'll call you right back."

He hangs up and faces Patrice and Chelsea. "Well, my capacity for surprise is forever enlarged," he says.

"What's up?" asks Patrice.

"That was Principal Roberts. Seems the Board wants my opinion on whether it should be Chelsea or Buck as interim head coach."

"Me?" asks Chelsea.

"None other."

Chelsea feels like somebody just dropped a tractor on her chest and told her to drive it. "I don't want it," she protests. "Not ready for it. Don't deserve it."

"That's not exactly a confidence-building comment," says Dub.

"But it's true, right? It should be Buck." She glances at Patrice, but she offers no response.

"You have your strengths. He has his." Dub pulls himself up in the bed.

"Which one will the boys play harder for?" asks Patrice.

"Tough to say," says Dub. "Buck's a good coach and he's got a ton of experience but, well, he's also a bit of an asshat. Of course, neither of you can ever tell anybody I said that."

"But I'm a newbie!" protests Chelsea.

"True. But so far as I know, you're void of any obvious asshat tendencies."

Chelsea shakes her head, completely unpersuaded. "Some of the crowd at the meeting last night wanted to shove me into a wood-chipper," she says.

"Somebody parked a moving van in front of our house the year we went 4 and 6," says Patrice.

Dub chuckles. "Look, Chelsea, consider it from their perspective. You're an exotic creature in these parts. A woman coaching football in Rabon? Like seeing Big Foot face to face."

"I'm not sure that comparing Chelsea to Big Foot is the best analogy you could choose, dear," says Patrice.

"Forgive me," says Dub, a twinkle in his eyes. "I'm a wayward sinner, no doubt."

Chelsea walks to the window and stares out as she weighs the situation. Though not convinced she's ready, the idea of becoming head coach on an interim basis does excite her. But she doesn't feel free to admit that, not even to herself.

She turns back to Dub and Patrice. "The Board makes the final choice?" she asks.

Dub nods. "And I won't argue with them, whichever way they decide."

"I'm telling you: Don't recommend me," insists Chelsea.

"You need to call Roberts back, don't you?" Patrice asks Dub.

Dub nods and speaks directly to Chelsea. "If I recommend you and they offer you the job, will you accept it?" he asks.

Chelsea stares hard at Dub. Can she turn the opportunity down if it falls into her lap? Will she regret it if she does? "If the Board decides I'm right for the job, I'll do everything in my power to prove them correct," she finally answers. "But I want it on the record, I don't believe I'm ready."

"So noted," says Dub.

Unsure what else to say, Chelsea hugs Patrice and walks out as Dub picks up his phone.

Rabon's entire coaching staff, all dressed in matching khakis and purple shirts, surround Dub's hospital bed a few hours later. Chelsea and Paul chat quietly in one corner while Buck talks on the phone and the others jabber out and back with Dub and Patrice. Patrice hands Dub a cup of water, and he sips through a straw. A nurse steps in and looks around, a touch of disapproval in her eyes.

"I brought your pain meds," she says to Dub.

"I won't turn them down," says Dub, rising a bit.

The nurse hands him a cup which holds two pills, and he swallows them with a water chaser. The nurse checks his blood pressure. "You're limited to two visitors at a time, Coach," she says as she scans the crowded room.

Patrice nods. "I tried to tell him."

"They're just here for a short time," says Dub.

The nurse wags a finger at him. "Thirty minutes, Coach," she says. "I'll clear the room after that." She smiles, then backs out of the room as Principal Roberts enters and steps towards Dub. The noise drops a few decibels as Roberts whispers with Dub for a minute, then faces the coaches.

"Listen up, everybody," instructs Roberts.

Everyone shuts up and Roberts continues. "To repeat the good news we've all heard, Dub's going to be just fine."

"How's that good news?" jokes Buck. Everyone laughs.

"He's suffered a concussion," explains Roberts, ignoring Buck. "Internal bruising, a broken leg, eight stitches to his face."

"The stitches are an upgrade," Buck jokes again.

Roberts cuts his eyes at Buck as he continues. "Best case, Dub is back on the sideline in two weeks. Worst case, he misses the rest of the year. So, the Board had to choose an interim head coach."

Everyone, including Chelsea, glances at Buck, then back to Roberts. "The Board met earlier today," continues Roberts, "and the members took a vote."

Chelsea glances at Buck again, sees a thin smile on his face—the look of a man expecting to receive welcome news. *Good*, she thinks. *Maybe somebody already told him what he wanted to hear.*

Roberts produces a piece of paper from a shirt pocket and reads from it, his eyes down. "By a vote of five to three, the Board chose Coach Chelsea Deal to become the Interim Head Coach until Dub recovers."

The room falls dead still, Chelsea included. Roberts looks up. "Any questions?" he asks.

"It's not right," Buck quickly protests, his smile replaced by dark clouds on his brow. "I've coached here longer than anybody but Dub."

"It's not about seniority, Buck," says Roberts. "The Board—"

"The board is six women and two men!" Buck blurts out.

"It's not about gender either," counters Roberts, his tone professional. "Though it's not a bad statement to make these days. To the team, the community."

"So, it's not seniority," Buck continues, sarcasm dripping now. "And not gender. So pray tell me: What is it? I'm dying to hear the qualifications that bumped Chelsea to the head of the line."

A couple of coaches stare at Chelsea as if waiting for her to answer the question for Roberts, but she stays quiet, her tongue twisted into knots, her mind jumping all over the planet.

"I understand your feelings, Buck," offers Roberts. "But with Ty out, somebody needs to prepare a new quarterback in a hurry."

"I can coach offense," barks Buck.

"I expect you could," says Roberts. "But Coach Deal already works with

Johnson. She knows him, and the offense, better than anybody on the staff, including you."

"She's never even called a play!" Buck snaps.

Roberts chuckles slightly. "I hear she called the game-winner last week." Buck pulls off his cap and crumples the bill in his hand.

Coach Paul raises his hand. "I have a question," he says.

"Sure, Paul," encourages Roberts.

"In the locker room," starts Paul, "there's just one bathroom for the coaches. Where will she—?" Paul stops, looks down, turns red with embarrassment.

"Where does she go now?" asks Roberts, catching the drift of the question. The coaches look at Chelsea, all of them mystified.

"Mostly I just hold it," she answers calmly. "Until I get back to the school building." The room falls quiet again.

"You want to say anything else?" Roberts asks Chelsea. "Not bathroom related?"

Chelsea studies the other coaches, tries to read their faces. Will they follow her as a leader? Buck won't. But the others? Maybe. If she can prove she deserves the promotion. She turns to Roberts.

"I'm a little shocked," she says slowly. "Not sure how to respond."

Dub interjects for the first time. "Say you're stoked. Confident you can do the job."

Chelsea glances first at Buck, then at the other coaches. What can she do to win them over, even a little bit? "This promotion come with a pay bump?" she asks Roberts, an idea forming in her head.

Roberts nods. "Sure. For as long as you're head coach."

"Split it with everybody but me," she says quickly.

"I'll have to see if we can do that," Roberts says.

"I don't want your money," Buck grouses at Chelsea.

Ignoring Buck's comment, Chelsea stays focused on Roberts. "If you can't divide the pay, I don't accept the job."

Roberts raises an eyebrow. "All right. If that's what you want."

Chelsea faces the coaches. "I know I'm new here," she says, trying to express humility without seeming weak. "And I know I have less experience than anybody in this room." She looks at Buck, but his eyes face the floor, so she continues. "But

I didn't ask for this role. And honestly, I realize some of you might question the motives of those who voted for me to have it."

"Amen to that," says Buck, looking up. Roberts eyes Buck hard. Buck drops his chin again.

"I make just one promise," says Chelsea. "I promise that nobody will work harder than me for as long as I have this job."

The coaches, even Buck, face her now.

"Everybody good?" she asks.

All the coaches but Buck nod, and Chelsea steps closer to him and faces him eye to eye. For several moments, neither of them blinks, two gladiators staring at each other in a Roman Coliseum.

Buck speaks first, his tone icy. "Hang something frilly on the door when you're in the bathroom," he says.

"Lift the seat when you go," Chelsea counters. "Put it back down after you finish."

After facing off with Buck another second, she turns to the other coaches. "Anything else?" she asks. "From anybody?"

Nobody speaks. Roberts walks to her and shakes her hand. The other coaches follow, one at a time. Buck approaches last.

"Head Coach Chelsea Deal," he says. "That sure has a funny sound to it."

She extends her hand and they shake. "Couldn't agree with you more," she says.

The handshake ends and she looks around the room one more time. "Practice starts in 45 minutes," she says. "See you all on the field."

CHAPTER SIX

T wenty minutes later, Chelsea parks at the school, her heart still pounding. Hopping from her truck, she rushes into Dub's office, closes the door, and collapses against the wall. For several seconds, she scans the room, letting everything sink in. A portrait of Dub holding a "Georgia Coach of the Year" award hangs on the wall to her left, another of him on the team's shoulders after winning a state championship on the wall to her right. Rising, she steps towards Dub's desk, picks up the championship rings, examines them, and puts them back down.

Feeling a little calmer, she eases to his chair and sinks into it. A picture of Dub and Patrice in Halloween costumes stares at her from the desk—Dub dressed as a Knight, Patrice a fair maiden. Her heart settling to normalcy, Chelsea pulls out her phone, dials Bo, and reaches his voice mail.

"Hey," she says, "it's me. Long story short, they named me interim head coach today. I didn't ask for it, not sure I want it, and have no idea what to do with it. Call me after eight. I should be able to talk by then."

She hangs up and scans the room once more. Ready or not, she has to get at it. She jumps up and hurries out, down a short hallway and into her tiny office. Grabbing her whistle, she drapes it around her neck and rushes out the door and toward the football field.

Many of the players are already on the field when she reaches it, stretching, chatting, tossing a football out and back. Flags fly in the breeze on the side nearest the Knights' locker room. Chelsea pauses at the edge of the field and several players jog past her. A few say "hello" as they pass, but most just keep going.

Principal Roberts sidles up from behind and stops beside her. "You ready for this?" he asks.

Chelsea glances at the sky. "I don't know how I got here," she says.

"You mean, like bigger picture?"

She nods. "Bigger picture. Yes."

"I'd like to hear that story myself someday." Roberts says. "But right now, you need to blow your whistle and call your team together."

Chelsea glances at Roberts, smiles, puts her whistle to her lips, and blows hard.

"Bring it in!" shouts Coach Paul, as Chelsea jogs toward the Knights' logo in the center of the field. "Time to go to work!"

The team quickly gathers around Chelsea as she and the other coaches gather on the logo.

"Pipe down, everybody!" shouts Paul. "Listen up!"

Principal Roberts pushes through the circle and stands by Chelsea. The team falls quiet. "Okay, guys," starts Roberts. "You know by now that Coach Dub is hurt. But you may not have heard that the school board voted this morning for Coach Deal to be the Interim Head Coach until Dub returns."

The team shuffles, players looking at each other as Roberts turns to Chelsea.

"Coach," he says, "the field is yours." He eases back and Chelsea inhales a long breath.

"All right, gentlemen," she says, her voice quiet but not weak. "This is as new to me as it is to you."

She stares around the circle and a hundred thoughts cascade through her head—past moments, events, feelings. She fights against the emotions, shoves them down deep. *Deal with them later*, she orders herself. *Focus here and now.* She touches her whistle and speaks again. "A few things I want you to know," she says, raising her voice. "First, I need your support for this to work. We're undefeated and we want to keep it that way."

The team nods.

"Second," she says, "I plan to run practice just like Coach Dub did. No reason to change a winning formula. Right?"

The team answers quickly. "Right!"

"Third," she continues, her voice stronger now, "I care about you off the football field as much as I do on the football field. Who you are, your family, your struggles, your successes. If you need me for anything, don't hesitate to ask. Am I clear?"

They nod and she concludes. "You know the routine. We'll stretch for fifteen minutes. Break up for position work for an hour. Regroup for scrimmaging for forty-five."

Sean Johnson speaks up. "How's Ty, Coach?"

Chelsea pauses, not sure what to say. Sticks with the basics as she speaks. "As publicly announced, he does have cancer. He's out for now. I'll ask Russell and

Gary E. Parker

Vanessa for permission to bring you updates as they become available."

"Where's Palmer?" asks Johnson.

"He's out today too. That means you're the guy, Sean. So, move out front, lead the stretches! Get your team going!"

Johnson steps forward, the team spreads out in rows, and he calls out directions as they loosen up.

A pair of green dumpsters, both with rusting dents on the sides, sit in an alley near the faded back door of the Rabon Motel. The smell of oily rags mixed with day-old garbage hangs in the air. A spotted dog plods to one of the dumpsters, hikes a leg for a few seconds. then trots on past.

Wearing their motel uniforms, Palmer and Molly lean against the wall by the door as Molly pulls a long drag from a cigarette.

"You really ought to stop that," says Palmer, pointing to the cigarette. "Will make your face all leathery."

Molly exhales a plume of smoke. "Who made you my daddy?" she asks.

Palmer hesitates, not sure how to answer. One second Molly acts nice to him, the next she treats him like the dog just treated the dumpster. "I don't know much about you," he says, his tone cautious. "Except you're pretty, you work with me, and you smoke."

Molly smiles, puffs on the cigarette again. "My mama works at Walmart. My pa is a trucker. It's the great American success story."

Palmer grins a little. "That sounds like a country song."

"Maybe you should write it."

He shrugs. "Your folks do honest work."

"Poor folks' work."

"Maybe I'll meet them someday."

"Don't get ahead of yourself." Molly crushes the cigarette butt against the wall.

Palmer pauses, his feelings a little hurt. "You finish high school?" he asks, changing the subject.

"I did. Last year."

Palmer waits for more, but she offers nothing else. "My mama is in

61

court-ordered rehab," he says as if announcing the time of day. "Illegal opioids. Ninety days. Two years' probation after that."

Molly faces him. "Your mom's a druggie?"

He watches as the spotted dog turns and walks back their way.

"What about your dad?" Molly presses.

The dog stops at Palmer's feet, and he scratches him behind the ears.

"Your dad?" Molly pushes harder.

Palmer sighs. "He died when I was six."

Molly touches his shoulder. "That's dark, man."

The dog licks Palmer's hand. *No reason to cry over spilled milk*, he figures. *Or dead dads.* "What's the story with your tattoo?" he asks Molly, refocusing the conversation.

She lifts her left wrist. Points to the three Chinese symbols etched onto her skin. "My Grandma Nettie," she explains. "She loved her some Bible."

"What they mean?"

Molly points to each symbol. "Faith. Hope. Love. You got any tats?"

"No money for tats." The dog licks his hand again, then shuffles away.

"You saving your dollars to spend on me?" asks Molly.

Palmer laughs as he stands and they face each other, their chins close. "Maybe I can take you on a real date sometime," he says. "A fancy restaurant and a movie."

"Do people still go to movies?"

"Every now and again."

Molly touches his cheek. "I ain't partial to dressy places. Like to keep things simple."

Palmer leans a bit closer. "I've kissed some girls," he whispers, his nerves jangling. "But not that many."

"You truly are a babe in the woods."

"I've moved nine times. Had a job since I was twelve. Not much chance to court a lot."

"Court?" she laughs, stepping back just slightly. "What century you from?"

"Date?" he asks, his face turning red. "That better?"

Molly puts her hands on his hips and moves closer again. "You want to kiss me now?"

"I don't know," he pouts. "You gone make fun of me again."

She touches his face again. "You're handsome when you mad."

He grins. "I guess I'll kiss you now."

"Just do it before I change my mind."

On the Knights' football field, the offense and defense are huddled up for the next play of the scrimmage. The players sweat heavily, their hands on their knees, trying to catch a breath. Buck Jones huddles with the defense and Coach Paul with the offense, each of them busy coaching, calling plays. Watching intently from behind the offense, Chelsea suddenly blows her whistle, and everything stops as the players turn to her.

"Okay, gentlemen!" she yells, rushing to the middle of the team. "Every minute of this practice has sucked! But we're running three more plays and I want you to execute those plays perfectly. If the offense wins two of the three plays—gaining at least four yards per play—the defensive coaches will run ten sprints the length of the field! If the defense wins, I'll run the ten sprints!"

The players glance at each other and she repeats the plan. "Offense wins, defensive coaches run! Defense wins, I run! Everybody clear?"

The team nods and Chelsea hustles to the offensive huddle and calls a play while Buck calls it for the defense. The offense and defense face off. Johnson barks out the signals and the center snaps the ball. All three linebackers blitz Johnson, rushing at him from all angles. Two of them hit him at the same time and he drops like a stone for a loss of four yards. Chelsea blows her whistle, and the offense hustles back to the huddle while Chelsea runs toward the defense.

"Hey, Coach!" she shouts at Buck. "Hold off on the blitzes the next two plays! Johnson is just getting his feet wet. Remember?"

Buck shrugs and calls the defense into their huddle as Chelsea returns to her offense.

"Listen up!" Buck orders his defense. "We're going 47 Zoom. Three deep. Knock Johnson on his butt."

The offense and defense face each other again and Johnson calls the play. The center snaps the ball. A safety blitzes from Johnson's blind side and smacks him in the back before he throws the pass. The ball pops loose and the defense picks it up and sprints in for a touchdown. Buck and the defense go wild, whooping and jumping.

Chelsea glares at Buck and blows her whistle but says nothing to him as the team gathers around. "Okay, gentlemen," she says. "That's enough for today. But you need to know. Today's lousy effort will not do the job! We need to improve and fast! And I have sprints to run! Sean, break us down!"

Sean holds up a hand and the team gathers around him, all hands up. "Ty on three!" he shouts. "One, two, three!"

"TY!" shouts the team.

Everybody but Buck jogs away as Chelsea starts her sprints. Grinning widely, Buck stands on the sidelines and watches her run.

Fifteen minutes later, Chelsea joins the other coaches in Dub's office, her face wet with sweat. The coaches stop talking as she enters, closes the door, and plops into Dub's chair. Coach Paul tosses her a towel, and she removes her cap and wipes her face.

"That was the worst football practice I ever witnessed," starts Buck, a touch of triumph in his tone.

"I expected a bumpy ride the first day," says Chelsea.

"Our routine was fine," says Buck. "But the boys seemed unmotivated."

Chelsea picks up the monitor remote and flips on the video screen. A knock sounds on the door and Coach Paul opens it. Bo stands outside the door. Caught off guard, Chelsea quickly stands. "Bo?"

"I got your message," he says, looking at the coaches as if seeing a herd of unicorns. "Thought I'd drive up."

"Guys," stammers Chelsea. "This is Bo Burriss, my guy, my boyfriend, my..."

"Can we talk a minute?" Bo asks.

Chelsea laughs awkwardly. "Well, since you drove all this way." She turns to the coaches. "Coach Jones," she says, "lead everybody through the film."

Buck nods and Chelsea hurries out, leads Bo down the hall, and onto a portico outside. Night has fallen. "Look," starts Chelsea as she stops and faces Bo. "You coming up is a nice gesture, but I'm swamped for the next hour or so. Can you go to my place? Wait there until I'm done?"

Bo shakes his head. "I can't stay that long. Have a deposition early tomorrow. But your message. I had to see you."

"I know. Interim head coach. I'm in shock."

"How did it happen?"

"I don't have time to explain it now."

"But later you'll be even busier."

"It's only for a few weeks."

"Look, Chelsea," pleads Bo, putting a hand on her waist. "I thought this coaching gig was a phase, you know— somehow a connection with Mitchell. But give me a break. Head coach?"

"I didn't ask for it, Bo," Chelsea protests. "But I have to finish the season. We can figure things out once it's over."

"So, we're on hold. I'm on hold."

She takes his hand. "That's not the way I'd say it."

"I don't want to be selfish," he interrupts, moving his hand away. "But I'm at a loss what to do next, how to deal with all this."

Chelsea touches his arm. "I know I'm asking a lot."

"I'm holding open a spot for you at the firm open," he says. "But it won't be there forever."

Coach Paul suddenly pushes out the door and waves her back in.

"Just another minute," she tells Paul. He nods and disappears.

"I wish we could talk longer, Bo," says Chelsea, facing him again. "But I need to go. You sure you can't hang a little longer?"

"I can't," he counters. "My job is important too."

"We just need some time," she insists. "Time to situate some things, me and you."

"Go back in," Bo says, giving up. "Sorry I bothered you."

Chelsea reaches for his hand again, but he shakes his head and stalks off as she watches. Sighing, she hurries back inside and down the hall into Dub's office. Coach Paul turns off the video as she plops into Dub's chair. "Sorry, guys," she says. "Bo is. . ." she searches for the right phrase. "Too eager sometimes."

"No problem," says Paul.

Chelsea focuses on football again. "Practice really did suck," she says. "The offense especially. No rhythm at all."

Buck pulls out his phone and stares at it.

"It all boils down to quarterback play," continues Chelsea, ignoring Buck's disrespect. "And Johnson doesn't bring a lot of weapons to the battle."

Buck glances up. "Any word on what's happening with Palmer?"

"AWOL again," Chelsea notes. "I'll try to reach him tonight."

"I don't see him helping much even if he comes back," huffs Buck.

"I don't know, Buck," counters Chelsea. "You know how athletic he is."

"But he's a retard, Coach. Dumber than a fence post with a rock on top."

Chelsea sits up straighter and her eyes darken. "I don't want us talking about our players like that," she says, her tone stern.

Buck pockets his phone and stares at Chelsea. "I talk how I talk," he says. "I'm colorful." He glances at the other coaches, a smirk on his face. "And I'm too old to change."

All the coaches freeze as Chelsea tilts her head and weighs her response. It's a leadership moment, she realizes. Show any weakness and she'll lose all the coaches, not just Buck. "Okay, Buck," she says, deciding it's time to deal with his insolence, you really want to do this?"

"Do what, Coach?" he asks, feigning surprise.

"Don't fire the shot, then act all innocent on me," she says.

Buck grins. "All right, Missy. Bring it on."

"When I have differences with someone," Chelsea says, "I like to talk them out privately, one on one. But that's twice today that you've challenged me in front of these other coaches." She eyes each coach, then continues. "Now I feel like I have to respond in front of them."

Buck links his hands behind his head. "I'm all ears."

Chelsea looks around again. "I say this to all of you: If you have something to say that will help the team, please feel free to say it, whether you think I'll like it or not. But if you're trying to show me up, we have a problem. I've been put in charge of this team for now, and I plan to do that. Be. In. Charge."

She leans toward Buck. "So, which is it, Buck? You trying to help the team? Or trying to show me up?"

Buck leans forward too, until they're chin to chin. "I'm trying to help the team, Coach. If my actions or words appear to be anything else, you have mis-took my intentions."

"Glad to hear it," she says, understanding with everyone else that he's molli-
fying her but choosing to accept him at his word. "That's a reminder to everybody.
Everything we do, everything we say, should, in some way, benefit this team. We
all on board with that?" She looks coach to coach. Each one nods.

"So go home," she concludes as she leans back in her chair. "We've had a
long day."

Thirty minutes later, Chelsea pulls into the drive at Palmer's house and parks
beside an aged, black pickup truck. Dim lights are visible inside the house. Flipping
on her interior lights, Chelsea opens her player notebook and Palmer's picture and
biographical information stares back at her. She quickly scans the file, then climbs
out, walks onto the porch, and knocks. A few seconds later, a porch light turns on,
the door opens, and Dirk stands barefoot in the doorway, dressed in a pair of low-
slung jeans and tight blue tee shirt. A tattoo on his forearm reads, "Music is truth."

"Hey, Coach," he says. "You looking for Palmer, I guess."

"I tried to phone him, but he didn't answer. So, I decided to drive out."

"He's working. At the Rabon Motel."

"I didn't know he had a job."

"Has to make ends meet."

Chelsea pauses, upset that she didn't know about Palmer's job. *No wonder he
skips school and practice so often.* "Please tell him to call me soon as he can,"
she says.

Dirk steps onto the porch. "You probably already know this," he says, his tone
sympathetic, "but Palmer's not real stoked about football."

"Is he quitting?"

"You need to ask him that."

"You think that's the right decision?"

Dirk shoves his hands into his pockets. "Not really. But it's not my call to make."

A surprising sadness hits Chelsea and her heart sinks. "Is he quitting
school too?"

"I'll definitely recommend against that."

"Look," she says. "I don't know Palmer that well. But he's talented. I mean really, his speed, jumping ability, a natural throwing motion. I hate to see him—"

The sound of a motorcycle interrupts her, and they both turn as Palmer and Molly wheel up, screech to a stop, and climb off the bike.

"Hey, Coach," says Palmer, his tone nonchalant as he and Molly approach the porch.

"Hey," she responds. "You hear about Ty?"

"Nah. What's up?" Palmer and Molly reach her and stop.

"He's sick," she answers. "Cancer."

Palmer's face darkens. "That's a tough break."

Chelsea starts to say more but suddenly remembers that Ty and Palmer barely know each other. So, Ty's illness, though tragic, probably feels distant to Palmer. "We need you back on the team," she tells him.

"Johnson sucks," offers Molly.

Chelsea turns to her. "You know your football?"

"I know suck when I see it." Molly laughs briefly and Chelsea faces Palmer again.

"I think I'm done with football," he says.

"Why?" challenges Chelsea.

"Well, let me see." He counts off on his fingers, his tone flippant. "One, I don't really know anybody on the team. Two, I don't play much. Three, I can't keep the plays straight in my head. And finally, football ain't my favorite thing."

"You being a smart ass?" Dirk jumps in.

Palmer glances at him. "My bad," he says. "But really, all that is true."

"I'll help you with the plays," Chelsea says, desperate to keep him. "Ty will too."

"One more thing," says Palmer, more serious this time. "I need my job more than football."

Dirk eases around Chelsea, down the stoop to Palmer, and lays a hand on his shoulder. "I don't want to step too heavy here," he says quietly. "But you don't want to make a habit of quitting in the middle of something."

"Coach Dub had a wreck, Palmer," interjects Chelsea, eager to ally herself with Dirk. "I'm the head coach for now. I'll talk to your boss about your job. See if he can re-arrange some hours for you."

"Might be worth a try, Palmer," Dirk encourages.

Palmer drops his head and Chelsea steps to him. "Take a little walk with me?" she asks.

Palmer glances at Molly and she shrugs, so he turns back to Chelsea, and they stroll down the road. Neither of them speaks for the first thirty yards. A possum scurries across the road. Stars blink at them from above.

Chelsea finally breaks the silence. "I want what's best for you, Palmer," she says as they keep walking. "But I can't prove that unless you let me."

Palmer picks up a rock and whips it underhand into the dark.

"Twelve weeks ago, you and Dirk showed up at the end of a football practice," Chelsea continues. "Dirk asked Coach Dub to let you try out. You remember that?"

"That was Dirk's idea more than mine, but yeah, I remember."

"You didn't bring any football shoes," chuckles Chelsea.

"And your equipment guy didn't have a pair my size."

"You ran the forty-yard dash barefoot. We clocked you at 4.45. An incredible time for a high school sophomore."

"Dirk made me throw for you too."

"Dub and I could see you weren't thrilled about being there."

Palmer picks up another rock and rolls it in his hands. "It shouldn't surprise you I'm done with it now."

Chelsea stops walking, Palmer too. She faces him eye to eye. "I asked you straight up that day if you wanted to play football. Remember that?"

"I do."

"I left every door open for you to walk away."

He rolls the rock and Chelsea presses on. "For some reason that only you know, you said 'yes,' you wanted to play."

"I did." He squats and peers into the dark

She crouches beside him. "Look at me, Palmer."

He faces her but doesn't hold her gaze. She puts a hand on his shoulder, and he looks back and stays steady.

"I want you to remember that reason right now, Palmer. Why you wanted to play. If that reason still exists, you need to say 'yes' again."

Palmer rolls the rock. "I hardly ever play in a game."

"With Ty out, that could change. The job is wide open."

Palmer stares at the sky.

"This is important," Chelsea continues, pleading for his sake as much as her own. "What you decide. More important for you than me, or even the team."

"I owe you, I guess. The ride home, in the rain."

"No, Palmer. You don't owe me anything. And that's not enough reason to come back."

He stands, hesitates, whips the rock into the dark. "I'll be at practice tomorrow."

She stands with him. "You have to attend school to practice."

"I'll go back to class too."

She offers her hand, and they shake, the deal done.

Dressed in red jogging shorts and tee shirt, Ty climbs into bed as Vanessa fluffs his pillow and Russell places a cushion under his swollen knee. "I'm not a baby," Ty complains.

"Let your mama do mama things," Vanessa chides him.

"Your daddy too," laughs Russell.

Vanessa plops down beside him, Russell beside her. "Tell us, Ty," she says. "Seriously. How are you feeling?"

Ty adjusts the pillow. "It's a lot to take in, that's for real," he says.

"You scared?" asks Russell.

Ty ponders the question. "I don't know. Maybe. It doesn't seem real. Cancer is what happens to other people."

"You'll be fine," says Russell. "Just do your treatments, eat right, exercise when you feel strong enough, keep your mind positive. Nothing else matters right now but you, your soul, and your body."

"Not to argue, Pops," counters Ty, "but a couple other things do matter."

"Your health, Ty," says Vanessa. "That's it. Our only focus until you get past this."

"School matters, Mama. And my team. I plan on attending class every day I can and assisting Coach with Palmer as much as she wants."

"School sure. But Palmer? Don't waste your energy on that boy."

Ty rolls over, tired of the discussion and not wanting to argue. "I have chemo at 8 a.m." he says, dismissing Vanessa and Russell. "Please turn out the light as you leave."

Palmer leans into Molly's car window, the engine still running. "I'm glad you're sticking with football," says Molly.

"We'll see."

"Coach Deal seems cool."

"Enough about Coach Deal," he says, bending to kiss her. "I like hanging out with *you*."

"Kissing me is what you like."

Palmer grins. "I want you to come to my next game," he says.

"I'm not real fond of crowds."

"But you're my girl. I want to show you off."

She laughs. "Arm candy, baby."

He kisses her again and she drives off mid-kiss, leaving him standing with a grin on his face as she disappears around the curve.

Though pleased with Palmer's decision, an unexpected wave of loneliness washes over Chelsea as she drives home. She considers calling Bo but knows he's liable to see that as a sign to speed her way, and she doesn't have time for that. She thinks of a couple of girlfriends to call but, given all she's dealt with in the past year, she's lost track of them, and reaching out to them out of the blue makes no sense. Pulling into her driveway, a startling reality hits her—she's lived in Rabon over three months but has no friends there. She parks and checks her watch. Almost 10 p.m. On a whim, she pulls Eva's card from her pocket, stares at it for several seconds, then dials the number. Eva answers almost immediately.

"Hello, Mrs. Wilson," says Chelsea. "You still up?"

"I wondered if you'd call," says Eva.

"It's been a long day. A lot of twists and turns."

"You want to drop by for a little girl talk?"

"For the first time since I moved here, I'm feeling homesick."

"It can be lonely at the top. Not that being the interim head coach of a small-town football team is what most people think of as the top."

Chelsea chuckles before turning serious again. "It's scarier than I thought."

"Come on by if you want. Fifty-four Oak Lane. We'll have us a cup of tea."

"You're sure it's not too late?"

"I wouldn't have asked you if it was too late."

"Thanks. See you in a few."

Just over ten minutes later, Chelsea parks in front of a large, white-columned brick house at 54 Oak Lane. A long porch stretches from one side to the other and bright lights illuminate a manicured lawn and clipped shrubs. Large oaks and maples frame the lawn on both sides. Chelsea climbs out of her truck as the front door of the house opens and Eva, wearing an elegant navy robe and slippers but no ribbons in her hair, steps out.

"Welcome to my home," she says, waving Chelsea up the sidewalk. "Tea is ready."

Chelsea eases inside as Eva closes the door. A spiral staircase leads to the second floor. Hardwood floors click underfoot, and a brilliant chandelier hangs overhead. Tasteful paintings decorate the walls and portraits of a younger Eva and a handsome man in his forties looks down from the top of staircase. "What a wonderful home," says Chelsea, admiring the space.

"Jack, my late husband, oversaw the construction," Eva says proudly. "He had great taste."

She leads Chelsea through a pair of double French doors and into a study. Bookshelves line two walls, and each shelf brims with hardback books. A portrait of an older Jack dressed in skiing attire at the top of a snow-covered mountain hangs on a wall across from the bookshelves and two leather chairs face each other in front of a large bay window on the fourth. A tea pot and two cups stand on a silver tray on a table in front of the window.

Eva points Chelsea to one of the chairs. "Take a load off, dear," she says.

Chelsea sits as Eva pours tea and hands her a cup.

"Thanks," says Chelsea.

Eva steps to a liquor cabinet beneath Jack's picture, hauls out a bottle of Scotch, and pours from the bottle into her cup. "I prefer a bit of tea with my

Scotch, Coach," says Eva. "What about you?" She holds the Scotch over Chelsea's cup.

"Thank you, but 'no,'" says Chelsea. "I'm good."

Eva sits the bottle down, arranges herself in the chair across from Chelsea, and sips her "tea." Neither of them speaks for a few moments. A clock ticks in the hallway. Eva sips more tea.

"What's with the ribbons in your hair?" Chelsea begins, pushing aside the thousand thoughts banging around in her head.

Eva chuckles. "Most people don't dare to ask."

"You don't really talk that much, from what I've seen of you," says Chelsea. "But your ribbons. They're making a statement of some kind."

Eva sips tea. "There's a ribbon for everything these days," she explains. "Pink for women's breast cancer. Blue for free speech. Yellow to support the troops. You get the drift."

"And you change every day because—"

"Because it reminds me of all the needs outside my own, concerns that deserve my attention, perhaps my support."

Chelsea sips her tea. The clock ticks.

"You said you were feeling homesick," Eva says softly. "Tell me about yourself."

Chelsea stares into her cup, weighing how much to confess. "Well, I'm the interim head coach of the Rabon High Knights, at least for now," she says, not sure what Eva wants to hear.

"Yes, you are," says Eva quietly.

Chelsea waits, expecting more, but Eva stays silent.

"My starting quarterback has cancer," adds Chelsea.

"It's really sad."

Chelsea waits again but hears nothing from Eva, so she continues. "The best athlete on my team has little or no passion for football."

"I've heard."

"My defensive coordinator resents my taking the job from him."

"As I'd expect."

Chelsea pauses again. Still little to nothing from Eva. Chelsea lets her emotions out another notch. "Probably half the town hates it that Coach Dub hired a woman as a coach."

"I've noticed."

Chelsea chuckles and looks at Eva, her curiosity high. "You're quite a counselor, aren't you?" Chelsea asks.

"I hope that's true."

Chelsea again waits for Eva to elaborate but she doesn't. Chelsea sips tea again. The clock in the hallway ticks. Chelsea fights to hold back her thoughts. Eva stays silent. Chelsea speaks again. "I traded a three-hundred grand a year job to earn fifty-two thousand coaching football," she confesses. "My boyfriend believes I'm unhinged."

"I imagine so."

Chelsea stares at Eva's sphinxlike face once again. Nothing. Not a word. Chelsea places her teacup on the coaster and hangs her head. Tears suddenly slip down her cheeks. "I had a brother, Mitchell. My twin," Chelsea whispers. "And he died and I..."

She breaks into sobs. Eva slowly puts down her cup and leans towards Chelsea. "There we are, dear," Eva says soothingly as she pats Chelsea's hand. "That's what you really need to talk about."

Chelsea holds Eva's hand as the pain pours out like a waterfall, a drenching wet that soaks and washes even as it hurts.

CHAPTER SEVEN

A stone sign with the words "Rabon High School" carved into it greets scores of students as they stream into the building the next morning. Inside the doors, the high schoolers check lockers, flick through their phones, chatter, and laugh as they move toward their classes. At his locker in the hall, Palmer throws books into his backpack as Don and Strick amble up.

"Hey, Yokel. How's it hanging?" asks Don, his hair stuffed under a baseball cap as usual.

Palmer ignores him as he shoves a notebook into his backpack.

"You fix your hunk-a-junk motorcycle yet?" asks Strick, a purple lollipop in his cheek.

"Got grease under your fingernails, Yokel?" Don yanks at Palmer's hand, trying to see his fingernails, but Palmer pushes him back.

Don throws up his hands as if to surrender. "Whoa, dude," says Don. "I'm just jerking your chain."

Palmer backs off, his jaw clenched, still angry but silent.

"Treat him gentle, Don," interjects Strick. "Ain't you heard? With Ty headed to the crematorium, this boy might get to play a little come Friday night."

"Won't that be peachy?" Don mocks.

Bridget and another girl, a lanky brunette with her hair in a ponytail, stroll up beside Palmer. Bridget smiles at him. "You sure are tall," she says, her wide blue eyes admiring his frame.

"Thanks," says Palmer, eyes down.

"See that, Strick," says Don. "The girls gone be swarming on the yokel if he actually plays quarterback in a real game."

"That won't happen," says Strick, waving the lollipop around like he's directing traffic. "Johnson will play quarterback now. Ain't that right, Hillbilly?"

"I heard you can throw it through a steel wall, Hillbilly," Don picks up the banter. "Is that true? Johnson can't do that."

"Quarterback is about leadership, Don," offers Strick. "You a leader, Palmer?"

Palmer grabs a pocket calculator from his locker and Bridget steps closer. "You can lead me anywhere you want, Palmer," she teases. "I don't care if you play foot-ball or not, so long as you play with me."

Strick and Don hoot and high-five each other as Bridget and her friend giggle and stroll away.

"Bridget's way out of your league, Country Boy," says Strick, sucking on his lollipop. "But it seems she's into you for some reason."

"You get naked with Bridget, you call us," whispers Don. "We'll lend you a hand, make sure the job is done right."

Palmer closes his locker and turns to leave but Don and Strick move closer, one on each side.

"Back off!" Palmer orders, his eyes fiery.

Don and Strick stand their ground. Palmer tries to move past them, but they press in, forcing him to stop. Fed up now, he pushes Don into the wall. Strick rush-es Palmer, but he dodges him as Johnson and Swoops appear around the corner.

"Hey, Palmer," says Johnson, acting as if nothing is happening. "Time to go to class."

Strick and Don back up a few steps.

"Yo, pinheads," Swoops says in a thick British accent. "Best you leave my boy Palmer alone!"

"Or what?" Don challenges him.

Swoops forms a fist with his right hand and punches it into his left palm. "You do not want to find out," he says, stepping closer.

Strick glances at Don.

"Come on, Palmer," says Johnson.

Strick flips a middle finger at Palmer, but Johnson grabs his arm and pulls him away before Palmer can respond.

A name plate on a desk in a large, empty school office reads, "Principal Roberts." A digital display on the desk flashes pictures of Roberts: Roberts in an orange life jacket in a fishing boat; Roberts holding a hotdog at a Braves game with a heavy-set woman about his age; Roberts standing in front of Rabon High with a large group of teenagers. A large silver can filled with sharpened pencils stands by the digital display. It's the office of a middle-aged, comfortable, but out-of-shape school official, and Roberts fits the description to a "t."

Buck Jones suddenly enters the room, yanks off his cap, and plops into a chair in front of the desk. Roberts rushes in a few seconds behind him, shuts the door, and situates himself in the leather chair behind the desk.

"Okay, Buck," Roberts says, pulling a pencil from the cup. "Let's make this quick. What's on your mind?"

"Yesterday's practice was a car crash run over by a train wreck," says Buck, his hat on a knee.

"So what?" says Roberts, rolling the pencil in his fingers. "It was Coach Deal's first day. What did you expect?"

"I don't know. Something. Organization, discipline, know-how?"

"Come on, Buck," says Roberts. "I don't have time for this. If you want to report Coach Deal for something unethical, abusive, or illegal, I'm all ears. But I don't care a hoot in hell that she called you out in front of the other coaches."

"You heard about that?" Buck leans forward.

"I hear about everything. You should know that by now."

Buck leans back, trying to decide how far to push Roberts. "All right, George," he finally offers. "But listen to me on this. Something isn't right about Chelsea Deal. I feel it in my bones."

"Yeah, she's a woman. You feel that in your bones?"

Buck rearranges his hat on his knee. "Think about it, George," he argues. "Why does a woman as smart as she is—and she is smart, I can't argue that—but why does she leave a law firm where she no doubt made a boatload of money to move to our little hamlet to coach football? Seriously, why would anyone do that?"

Roberts sticks his pencil behind his ear. "I haven't really thought about it that way. I guess it is an interesting question."

"Exactly. She certainly didn't do it for the money. Her boyfriend is in Atlanta, so it's not love. And it sure isn't big-time power or control, any of your basic human motivations."

Roberts stands, pulls a file from a cabinet behind his desk, and thumbs through it. "I checked her bio when Dub first told me about her," he says. "Top grades in college and law school. Glowing recommendations. Nothing sinister anywhere. So, I signed off to hire her." Roberts puts the file back.

"If there's nothing in her official file, whatever it is must be off-line," says Buck, his eyes lit with the idea of a dark secret hiding somewhere. "A skeleton in her closet," he surmises as he warms to his conspiracy theory. "She didn't move here because she was drawn to something, but because she was running from something!"

"That's quite a leap, Buck," says Roberts. "Nothing she's done here indicates a problem of any kind."

Buck stands suddenly, his body tingling at the hint of something hidden. "I reckon I need to nose around a little," he says ominously.

"Don't do anything dumb," says Roberts.

Buck glances at his watch. Almost three p.m. "Anything I do will be for the good of the team, George."

Roberts chuckles. "Oh, yes, Buck. It's all about the team."

Chelsea and Ty sit silently in Dub's office watching video. Ty, dressed in normal clothes and appearing as healthy as a thoroughbred, sips from a water bottle as Palmer enters. "Hey," says Chelsea, pointing Palmer to a chair.

"Hey, Coach." Palmer falls into the chair and turns to Ty. "How you feeling?"

"Like I have bare feet in a pigpen," says Ty.

"You look fine," says Palmer.

"Already started chemo treatments," says Ty, putting down the water bottle.

"Shouldn't you be in the hospital or something?"

"Chemo hasn't affected me. Not yet anyway. I'm good for now."

Chelsea slides the Playbook to Palmer, and he quickly looks through it, stopping every few pages to read a moment before moving on. A couple minutes later, he closes the book and looks up. "I'll never learn all this," he complains.

Chelsea opens her copy of the Playbook. "We've got forty-five minutes before practice," she says. "Let's cover what we can."

"Page one, Palmer," says Ty.

"I'm warning you, it's a waste of time," says Palmer.

"Page one," says Ty.

Palmer shrugs and opens the Playbook back up.

"Read the quote first," instructs Ty. "Arthur Ashe."

Palmer slowly reads the quote. "A key to success is self-confidence. A key to self-confidence is preparation."

"You're the fastest guy on the team," Ty encourages. "And you can spin a football a mile. If you work hard enough, you'll eventually figure out the Playbook. Once you've done that, you'll kill it on the field."

Palmer flips through the Playbook again. "I don't know. With music, I can hear it, see it. But this?" Doubt appears on his face like fog on a mountain.

"Page one," says Chelsea. "First play. Watch this." She turns to the video and clicks the remote. Video of Ty running the page one play streams across the monitor. "It's a simple sprint out-pass," explains Chelsea. "You roll out right or left and two receivers run routes on the same side as you. If neither is open, you pull it down and run."

Palmer leans forward to concentrate, Ty on his left, Chelsea on the right.

Two and a half hours later, as the day's football practice nears its conclusion, the starting offense and defense once again line up against each other. The players brush sweat off their faces and pant for air as Johnson barks offensive signals at the line of scrimmage. Palmer stands by Chelsea, watching Johnson's every move. Johnson catches the snap and drops back. Swoops breaks open downfield, and Johnson heaves the ball toward him. Swoops stops, sprints back toward the ball, and lunges at the last second. The ball falls a few yards short.

"Follow through, Sean!" Chelsea yells. "You're leaving your elbow too high!"

The offense huddles for the next play and Chelsea grabs Palmer by the shoulder pads. "You're in," she says, pulling him close and giving him the play. "Keep it simple."

"That's not simple to me," says Palmer, his eyes blank.

"The sprint rollout. The first play we went over before practice started."

"Page one? Arthur Ashe?"

"Yeah, that one."

Though still doubtful, Palmer quickly enters the huddle and calls the play. The offense lines up against the defense. Palmer barks out the signals, receives the snap, and rolls to the right. Two receivers break open, but Palmer hesitates and doesn't throw it. Defenders close in on him, and he reverses field, breaks a tackle, gets a block from Swoops on the corner, outruns two more defenders, and crosses the goal line for a touchdown! The offense runs at him, whooping and hollering, but Chelsea isn't happy.

She races towards him, yelling all the way. "You had two receivers open, Palmer! The play says throw the ball! Run it only if the receivers aren't open!"

Palmer throws up his hands in confusion as Chelsea grabs him by the shoulder pads.

"I need you to run the play I call!" she shouts.

"I scored a touchdown!"

"When the play breaks down, yes, run it. But you need to operate the offense. Know the plays, run the plays. You clear on that?"

Completely baffled, Palmer drops his head and slumps back to the huddle.

A couple of hours later, Palmer and Dirk slouch on the sofa at their place, Palmer holding his banjo, Dirk his guitar. Two plastic trays lie on the floor with dirty paper plates and utensils on each.

"Good supper," says Dirk, sipping from a beer.

"A skillet-fried hamburger and a can of cream corn," says Palmer.

"Dinner of champions," says Dirk, setting the beer bottle on the tray and fingering his guitar.

"Maybe I can be a fry cook someday," says Palmer, jokingly content.

A fire burns in the fireplace and Dirk begins to play a country ballad on his guitar. Palmer listens a few moments, then joins him on the banjo, both sliding their fingers on the strings, a couple of pickers enjoying their craft.

"I'm playing at Georgio's this weekend," says Dirk.

"Cool. I'll try to drop by after work on Saturday," says Palmer.

Dirk strums softly. "Lacy called me today," he says.

Palmer picks the banjo but says nothing at the mention of his mama's name.

"She said she's called you a bunch a times but you don't answer," says Dirk.

Palmer's fingers snap hard and angry on the banjo strings, but he still doesn't speak.

"All right!" yells Dirk over the loud banjo. "You made your point!"

Palmer's fingers fall still and he instantly calms down.

"How was practice today?" asks Dirk, slowly chording the guitar as he changes the subject.

"I scored a touchdown," Palmer says.

"That make Coach Deal happy?"

"You would think so." Palmer props the banjo between his legs. "The play called for me to throw the ball. I ran it. Coach yelled at me."

Dirk stops playing. "Coaches are hard to please, dude. Women more so. And a woman coach? You got no chance at all."

Palmer stares into the fireplace. "The plays just mash up in my brain," he says sadly. "Can't keep straight who's doing what, who's running where."

Dirk strums the guitar again. "You ever been tested?"

"I ain't special needs," Palmer answers quickly.

"Not saying that. But, you know, for dyslexia, that sort a thing."

"In second grade, I saw a specialist, took some tests. But we moved soon after and nobody ever mentioned it again."

"Maybe we should get you checked again."

Palmer shakes his head, dead set against it. "I've muddled through school a long time, Uncle. Reckon I can survive it for another couple years."

Dirk stops playing. "Counselor Towe, from your school, called me," he says.

"Bet he was a barrel of laughs."

"You need to stop ditching school, dude. Get your mind right with your grades."

"Sure. Do my homework, pay attention in class, ask for extra credit... I heard it all before."

"I'll muster up the money for a tutor if you want."

"I already got Coach Deal and Ty on my butt," snaps Palmer, not happy with the conversation.

"Coach Deal can tutor me anytime she wants."

"Yeah, well, I'm all tutored out."

"If your grades stay in the crapper like they are now, your football days will end in a hurry."

"Like that matters to me." Palmer picks up the banjo and plays loudly again as Dirk shrugs, stands, and leaves the room.

CHAPTER EIGHT

A plastic kangaroo, at least twenty-five feet high, towers over the front of a coffee shop perched on a hill on the outskirts of Rabon. A sign over the door reads, "World's Tallest Kangaroo." Inside the building, tables and booths line three of the four walls, and a sign reading, "Hop Into Your Day With A Hot Cup of Joe-Y at Kangaroo Coffee," hangs over the serving counter. Behind the counter, a middle-aged woman in a brown apron washes down a glass display case of muffins, yogurts, and cookies. A stuffed kangaroo stands in a corner by a burning fireplace.

In a booth in the back, Buck Jones sits up tall, a muffin and coffee cup on the table. A bell over the front door tinkles and Les Holt enters—gray suit, white shirt, and black tie as usual. Holt orders a hot chocolate, ambles to Buck's booth, and slides in.

"I always wanted to ask," starts Buck, "why you wear the same outfit every day?"

"Time is money, Buck," says Holt. "Wearing the same thing means I don't waste time every morning figuring out what I want to put on."

"Don't you get tired of gray and black?"

Holt rolls his eyes. "I'm not here at 7 a.m. to debate my wardrobe with you, Buck. What you want?"

"Why didn't the Board hire me for the interim job?" asks Buck as he bites from his muffin.

The woman in the brown apron brings Holt his hot chocolate and he blows on it, then sips it as she disappears back to the counter. "I pressed all I could," he says, "but the Board voted for Chelsea."

"But *why* did the Board choose her?" presses Buck. "I can't fathom it. My defense has been in the top ten in the state ever since I showed up here. I get along with most people. No real enemies in town that I know about."

Holt tugs at one of his ears. "Rehashing the past won't help either one of us, Buck," he says. "What can I do to help you, right here, today?"

Buck leans forward. "I want you to do me a favor," he says.

"I know you want a head coaching job," says Holt. "And if I hear of anything opening up in Georgia, I'll contact you immediately."

"That's not it, Les," says Buck, shaking his head. "Why you figure a woman like Coach Deal moved from Atlanta to coach football here?"

Holt sips chocolate. "I don't know. She wants to influence a new generation of America's youth? She just loves football? Or perhaps she feels a hankering for the country life."

Buck glances side to side like a covert agent expecting a sneak attack, then lowers his voice and leans towards Holt. "Or maybe she's running from something back in Atlanta."

Holt chuckles. "That's it, Buck. She's on the lam. A drug dealer with the feds on her tail. Or the madame of a pricey escort service for the rich and famous. You've been watching too much Netflix."

"It's just fishy, that's all I'm saying." Buck leans back.

Holt finishes his chocolate. 'That's it? That's all you got?"

"You know people in Atlanta," presses Buck. "Ask around for me, find out what people say about her … you know, on the down low."

Holt laughs again as he stands, bends to Buck's ear, and whispers: "Okay, Buck. I hear the Mob has put a contract out on you. Be careful while I infiltrate the Family. And keep your eyes open."

"Mock me if you want, Les," Buck says with a pout. "But something smells wrong here."

Across town in the Cancer Treatment Center, which is adjacent to the hospital, Ty, dressed in a hideous hospital gown, lies on a table in the chemo infusion unit. Multiple tubes attach to his left arm. Vanessa waits beside him, busy on her phone. A slender, African American teenage girl with bright brown eyes enters and smiles at Ty. She wears a teal polo shirt and khaki slacks. "Either of you need anything?" she asks.

Vanessa looks up but Ty speaks first. "You're too young to be a nurse," he says.

"I'm Tanya," she says, pointing to her name tag. "A Junior Volunteer."

"We used to call them Candy Stripers, Ty," says Vanessa.

"Those awful red- and white-striped uniforms!" moans Tanya.

"Burn my memory cells now! I wore one!" laughs Vanessa.

Ty focuses on Tanya. "You don't attend my school," he says. "I'd know you if you did."

"I live over in Bishopville. This is the closest hospital. My school does this Work-Study-Grow program and I drive over a couple times a week."

"You planning to work in health care?" Vanessa asks.

"Might be a doctor. I'm doing this for some experience. To help me know if I'm up to it."

"I was a nurse," smiles Vanessa.

Dr. Ramirez steps in and interrupts them, his white coat fresh. "Hey, Ty. You hanging in there?" he asks as he checks Ty's chart hooked to the bed.

"So far so good," replies Ty.

"No side effects from the chemo?"

"Not so far."

"How bad you think the effects will be?" asks Vanessa.

"Some people don't have any," answers Ramirez. "As young and fit as Ty is, let's hope for the best. But be aware that the chemo could sicken him at any moment." Ramirez puts the chart back and faces Tanya. "I'm depending on you to keep his spirits up."

Ty grins. "She's doing an excellent job so far."

Ramirez laughs, pats Ty on the shoulder, and heads out.

The day passes quickly for Palmer. He attends school, finishes football practice, scarfs down a chicken sandwich from a fast-foot restaurant, and wheels his motorcycle to Ty's house. Quickly parking, he yanks off his helmet, throws his backpack over his shoulder, and eyes the house. *Money, money, money*, he thinks. *Must be nice.*

He climbs off his bike and heads for the porch. The door swings open before he touches the doorbell and Vanessa greets him with folded arms. "Hello, Palmer," she says coldly, not inviting him in.

"I didn't ring the bell," he says, mystified at her quick appearance.

"Your motorcycle could wake the dead." She looks past him and points to his bike.

"Oh … right."

Vanessa waits, her eyebrows lifted, as if expecting him to explain himself.

"Coach Deal said I should come by," Palmer says. "Said Ty would be expecting me. Said he would help me with the Playbook."

"He's really tired from chemo today," Vanessa counters, not yielding. "Not up to company."

Palmer shrugs. "Fine by me." He turns to leave but Russell walks to the door behind Vanessa and yells at him to stop. "Ty heard you pull up," says Russell. "Sent me to fetch you."

Palmer looks at Vanessa, then back to Russell.

"Ty made me promise to bring you to his room," Russell continues.

Vanessa glares at Russell but finally steps aside and waves Palmer in.

"Wow," Palmer says, his mouth falling open as he steps inside and stares around. "This house is way cool."

The entry way is a contemporary design with lots of windows, wide open rooms, sleek furniture. It's the home of people with the money to hire a slew of designers to act on their every decorating desire.

"Thank you," says Vanessa, softening a little.

"You design it?" asks Palmer.

Vanessa offers a small smile. "It took over a year to make it right."

Ty appears at the top of the stairs. "Move fast," he orders Palmer. "If she starts talking home design, you'll be here all night."

Palmer nods to Vanessa and Russell and heads up the stairs.

"This way," Ty says. Palmer follows him down a wide hallway and into his bedroom.

Palmer walks in slowly, his eyes wide as he takes it all in. "How did you get so rich?" he asks Ty.

Ty chuckles. "My dad played in the NFL for eight years. Was a pretty big deal back in the day."

"Oh, yeah, somebody mentioned that to me."

"You don't watch pro football?"

Palmer steps to the picture of Ty with President Obama and stares at it as he answers: "Until a few months ago, I didn't play football, care about football, talk about football, much less watch it."

"Wow," says Ty. "What kind of dude are you?"

"I don't know. A guitar-playing dude. Move-around-a-lot dude. Dumb-white-boy dude. Still trying to figure all that out."

He stares at the posters of Desmond Tutu and Martin Luther King, Jr. "It's funny," he says softly.

"What's that?" asks Ty.

Palmer waves a hand over the room. "All this. Makes me realize I never been in a black guy's house before."

Ty sits on the bed, his brow furrowed. "Come to think of it, I never been in a white dude's house."

"This day and age, you think that's weird?"

"I need to research it. How segregated are high schools after school?"

Palmer scans the room one more time as he pulls off his backpack and lifts out his Playbook. "On the field, I don't really notice color," he says. "We're all sweating together, working together."

"But here?"

"I don't know. Just a little strange, don't you think?"

Ty walks to his desk and holds up his Playbook. "Let's work on this for now. We can discuss the complexities of America's racial relationships at another time."

"Complexities? What kind of dude are you?"

Chelsea's phone dings as she parks her truck at school the next morning and checks the text. Counselor Towe: "My office ASAP. About Palmer Norman."

Immediately concerned, she hops out and hustles into the building. Some students ignore her as she hurries down the hallway while others smile and say "hello." She quickly reaches Towe's office and sticks her head in.

"Hey," he says, pointing to where she should sit. "Thanks for coming so soon." She eases into a chair as he lifts a bag of doughnuts off the floor by his desk. "Want one?" He holds up a doughnut.

"No thanks."

He yanks out a doughnut and chews off a mouthful.

"What's up?" she asks, a touch confused. "Palmer hasn't missed school since you and I talked."

Towe keys his computer and talks around the doughnut still in his cheek. "It's true, Palmer *is* showing up. But that's about it."

"What do you mean?"

Towe swallows the doughnut. "I mean he's failing three classes. Math is the worst. Plus, he seldom turns in homework, doesn't participate in class unless forced, and does as little as possible."

"So, he's not failing everything, is he?"

Towe chuckles, pulls out another doughnut, and munches as he faces Chelsea. "I love your glass half-full attitude, Coach," he says. "Mr. Norman does have an A in P.E., a C+ in English and, surprisingly enough, an A+ in Music Theory."

Chelsea smiles briefly. "He likes music."

"Well, that's sweet," answers Towe, his tone barbed. "But if he doesn't make some changes, Mr. Norman is on a definite flunk-out track."

"I'm not a fan of your sarcasm," says Chelsea, her eyes locked on Towe. "But I'll talk to Palmer."

Towe leans forward and softens a little. "Here's the thing, Coach. I see nothing in Palmer's file about any kind of learning handicap. Therefore, it must be a lack of focus. He needs to bear down, care enough to do his work."

"I'll try to motivate him," says Chelsea.

Towe leans back. "I hope he'll listen to you," he says. "Really, I do."

Chelsea stands. "He'll improve," she says. "I promise."

"Stay positive, Ms. Deal," Towe says. "I hear that'll take you places."

Chelsea grabs a doughnut from the bag and rushes out, not at all confident she can keep the promise she just made.

CHAPTER NINE

The next few days pass like a blur for Palmer. Between football practice, where he continues to make a few great plays mixed with a ton of mistakes, some feeble attempts at schoolwork, an assortment of hours worked at the motel, and music sessions with Dirk, he finds little time for anything else. About the only thing he really enjoys other than the music are his infrequent make-out sessions with Molly, usually at the motel after his work shift.

But suddenly, out of nowhere it seems to him, game day arrives. He drifts through that day, his attention scattered as he endures his classes, then works a two-hour shift at the motel. After work, he motorbikes home, where Dirk meets him on the porch, a turkey sandwich in one hand and an energy drink in the other.

"You need to hurry," Dirk says, handing him the sandwich. "Don't want to be late."

Palmer chomps into the sandwich. "I actually play tonight," he mumbles between bites. "Coach Deal put me on the kickoff return team." His phone dings and he checks. Quickly hits Ignore.

"Will be fun to see you on the field," says Dirk.

Palmer finishes the sandwich, grabs the drink, and turns back to his motorcycle.

"Remember!" he yells to Dirk. "Molly will meet you at the gate!"

His phone dings again and he again hits Ignore.

"Go!" yells Dirk.

Palmer hops onto the bike, quickly chugs down the drink, tosses the bottle to Dirk, and wheels away. Flying through pre-game traffic, he arrives at the stadium ten minutes later. Spinning through the players' gate, he speeds down the hill to the locker room, where he pulls to the side of the building and parks.

His phone dings again. Though gritting his teeth, he finally relents, yanks off his helmet, and answers the phone.

"Hey, Son." The voice on the other end is Southern, rough, and unsophisticated. "It's your mama."

"I only answered to tell you don't call me again!" he blurts.

"You don't have to be so mean."

A couple of players hustle by, wave at Palmer, and enter the locker room. Palmer steps away from the entrance. "I saved you, Mama," he says, his voice angry. "Found you, almost dead. Dug a handful of half-eaten pills out of your mouth. Shoved my fingers down your throat to make you puke up what you'd already swallowed."

"I know that, Son," Lacy argues. "But—"

Palmer interrupts her, the phone shaking in his hand. "I called 911. Held your head in my lap while I waited for the ambulance, expecting you to die any second. And you say I'm mean?"

"I'm in this god-awful place because of you! You should have just let me die!"

Palmer laughs but he's not happy. "A judge sentenced you to rehab instead of jail for a list of crimes longer than your arm. And I saved you from O.D.'ing. But somehow, I'm the bad guy!"

Chelsea steps out of the locker room, spots him, and waves him over.

"I need to go, Mama," Palmer says. "Almost game time."

"You playing football?"

"I'm hanging up, Mama."

"Come see me, Son. We need to talk."

Palmer hangs up, angrily shoves the phone into his pocket, and rushes to Chelsea.

"You're late," she growls. "That's disrespectful to the team."

Palmer starts to explain but holds his tongue and follows her into the noisy locker room. Everyone but him is already in uniform. Many of the players listen to music on headphones. Others lay on the floor, their eyes closed in concentration.

"Hurry up," Chelsea orders him. "We have to be on the field in less than fifteen minutes."

She hurries away as he rushes to his locker, quickly undresses, and slips on his pads and uniform. A tug of nerves hits his stomach as he realizes he'll play some meaningful minutes in this game. Except for a few plays in mop-up time, he's spent all his time until now on the bench, a reluctant observer, not particularly caring what happened on the field. Does he care now? Unsure how to answer that, he grabs his cleats and sits down to put them on.

Chelsea suddenly reappears and strides to the middle of the room, a football in hand. The other coaches line the walls and Coach Dub takes a spot in a wheel-chair in a corner, left leg in a cast. Coach Paul blows his whistle, and the players gather around Chelsea as Palmer laces up his shoes.

Chelsea sucks in a breath, then speaks, her tone strong. "All right, gentlemen! It's game time!" The room falls dead quiet. "It's been a crazy week," Chelsea says. "A lot of distractions. Coach Dub lost a smack-down with a deer."

The team laughs. Dub grins.

"I've never been the head coach in a game," Chelsea continues. "And I'm, well, I'm not your normal football coach."

The team laughs again as she lowers her voice. "The biggest thing of all? Ty's fighting a battle with cancer."

The team goes silent again. Palmer stares at his feet and remembers that Ty's illness, not his own abilities, has created the opportunity for him to play.

"Like I said, it's been a crazy week." Chelsea looks around the room. "But you know what, gentlemen?" Every eye stays on her. "In spite of all we've faced these past few days, I believe in these coaches," she says.

She points the football at Buck, then Paul, then the other coaches. "I believe in myself too." She pauses a moment before hitting the high note. "But you know what's most important? I believe in YOU."

Palmer stands quietly as Chelsea tosses the ball to Johnson. "I believe in Johnson." She nods toward Swoops and Johnson tosses the ball to him. "I believe in Swoops," she continues. She raises her hands and Swoops tosses her the ball. She points the ball at more players. "I believe in you. And you. And you!"

She pauses one last time, the ball over her head. "So now, each one of you. Look at the player next to you. Do you believe in him? Tell him! I believe in you! I believe in you!"

The players, Palmer included, turn to each other and shout as Chelsea commanded. "I BELIEVE IN YOU! I BELIEVE IN YOU! I BELIEVE IN YOU!"

Chelsea and the coaches lead the players out and Palmer surges with them through the door and toward the field.

The crowd stands and cheers as the team, dressed in purple pants and white jerseys with purple numbers on the back, runs onto the field. The band plays. Flags fly. The stadium announcer's voice booms through the stadium. "Welcome to Rabon High Stadium for a top-two match-up between the number-one Rabon

High Knights and the number-two Central High Longhorns!"

His heart thumping, Palmer runs with the team down the sideline. At the twenty-yard line, he rushes past Coach Dub as Patrice pushes him in his wheelchair to a spot where Russell and Vanessa wait. The crowd continues to roar as the players jump around, stretch, and pound each other on the shoulder pads.

The announcer's voice sounds again: "Ladies and Gentlemen: Please stand as Ty Rogers will now lead us in our invocation."

The crowd quietens as people stand and bow to pray. Ty's voice sounds strong to Palmer as he closes his eyes and, for a moment, feels uplifted. Nothing in his life, no matter how tough, compares to what Ty faces. But suddenly, he remembers his dad's death and his spirits drop.

Ty begins to pray.

"Dear God," prays Ty. "We believe you want the best for us. So let us give our best to you. On the field, in school, in our families. When all is good and when all is not so good. When we're healthy and when we're sick. When we lose and when we win. In your name. Amen."

The crowd cheers again and Palmer rushes onto the field with his teammates, lining up near the goal line to await the kickoff. Rubbing his hands together, he quickly glances into the stands and spots Dirk and Molly. He wants to wave but knows that's not cool. But, seeing Molly, a smile does break out inside the face guard of his helmet.

Rolling a football in her hands, Chelsea glances quickly into the crowd and spots Eva near the fifty-yard line, a blue ribbon in her hair. To her surprise, Bo sits two rows behind Eva. The grand gesture again. Showing up without asking her. Just like him. Sometimes endearing. More times, at least lately, annoying. Bo waves and she nods, then drops her eyes, her focus back on the game.

The Longhorns' kick-off sails over Palmer's head for a touchback and Chelsea waves him to the sideline beside her. Led by Johnson, the offense hustles onto the field for the first play. From that moment on, everything falls apart for the offense. Penalty flags fly over and over. Players screw up multiple plays, one player running the wrong way, another slipping on the turf, another fumbling a handoff.

Johnson overthrows some receivers, underthrows others. He gets sacked for big losses three times in the second quarter and throws an interception in the third and early in the fourth.

Exasperated, Chelsea encourages Johnson at first, hoping he'll settle down. When that doesn't work, she shifts into teaching mode, pointing out how he can fix his mistakes. After that, she yells at him a couple of times, hoping he'll respond to some tough love, but that fails too. She glances at Palmer from time to time as he stands alone on the sideline, but doesn't have the courage to put him in. *Johnson needs more time*, she assures herself. If she pulls him out too soon, she'll destroy his confidence forever.

Thankfully for her and the Knights, the defense plays tough, shutting down the Longhorns offense over and over. Buck strides up and down the sidelines, exhorting his defense, celebrating each time they make a big play. Watching him, Chelsea can't help but wonder if the Board made a mistake giving her the job.

But even the Knights' stout defense can't win the game all by itself, and early in the fourth quarter, Chelsea glances at the scoreboard to check the time left. Eleven minutes. Guests: 10. Knights: 0. Buck stands twenty feet from her, his hands on his knees, yelling at Johnson, who's lined up behind the center.

"Watch the blitz, Sean!" yells Buck. "Left-side backer! He's blitzing!"

Johnson receives the snap and rolls out. The left-side linebacker rushes him full speed and smacks him hard. The ball pops out and the linebacker scoops it up and sprints into the end zone for a touchdown. Buck cusses, throws his hat, kicks it, and turns away from the field, unable to watch the offense any longer.

Knights' fans start exiting the bleachers and Chelsea watches them go, their seatbacks under their arms, their blankets on their shoulders. With no other option, she turns to Palmer and pulls him close. "Okay," she says, her hand on his shoulder pads. "You're in for Johnson after the kickoff."

His eyes widen. "You sure?"

"We'll keep the plays simple," she says, hoping to give him confidence. "Just relax. You'll do fine."

Palmer shoves on his helmet as Chelsea walks up to Johnson. "Let's give Palmer a shot," she says, patting him on the back. "You'll get it done next time."

Johnson nods and wipes sweat away as Chelsea waves the offense over. "Okay, gentlemen," she says. "Palmer is in. Let's keep it vanilla. First play, Red right, 33, Georgia, 2 go."

After the kickoff, the offense hustles back onto the field and huddles up, Palmer in the middle. The team stares at him, and Palmer fights to swallow, his mouth drier than a bone in the desert. He slaps his helmet and tries to focus. He feels panicky, his body out of sync. He closes his eyes and struggles to calm down but fails. Shaking his head, he opens his eyes, turns to the referee, and calls time out.

Chelsea runs to the huddle.

"I can't do it!" he pants. "The play … it's all scrambled up in my brain, like an egg. Put Johnson back in."

Chelsea pulls him away from the huddle. "Palmer, it's all right," she says soothingly. "Bring it down a notch."

"I'm no good, Coach." He drops his eyes.

She pats him on the helmet. "Hey, look at me."

He obeys and she smiles. "Think of it this way," she says. "Nobody expects anything from you. Right?

Palmer shrugs. "Yeah, sure. I guess."

"If you do anything positive, it's a bonus. Correct?"

"Hadn't thought of it that way. But, sure."

"Screw up as much as you want," she says with a grin. "Low expectations."

Palmer scowls with confusion. "You insulting me, Coach?"

Chelsea pats him one last time. "Just do this. Drop straight back. The left- side receiver will sprint deep. The slot will run a slant. The right-side receiver will drag to the middle."

Palmer wipes his hands on his jersey and she offers a final word. "It's just a game, Palmer. Go play it."

The referee blows the whistle to resume play and Chelsea hustles to the side-lines as Palmer re-enters the huddle.

Swoops speaks to Palmer. "Relax, my man," he says. "You throw it, I'll catch it."

The team breaks from the huddle and lines up facing the Longhorns. Palmer barks out the count, and the center snaps the ball. Rolling out the wrong way, palmer almost knocks down his running back but avoids him at the last second. The defense closes in, and Palmer scrambles, rolls left, pivots, runs back right. His receivers stop, start, run again. Swoops breaks open fifty yards down the field.

The defense grabs for Palmer's ankles but he sidesteps them again and whips the ball through the air. It spins through the night—30, 40, 50, 60 yards. Swoops catches it in stride and runs in for a touchdown.

Palmer sprints downfield and celebrates with Swoops, jumping up and down. What's left of the home crowd goes wild.

On the sidelines, Dub, Patrice, and Russell celebrate like five-year-old kids eating cake at a birthday party, but Vanessa shakes her head.

"Palmer didn't have a clue what he was doing on that play," she says. "Just threw it up for grabs."

Dub laughs. "You see that pass? 60 yards on a dime! Pure talent!"

The extra point team runs onto the field and everybody settles down a little.

"Ty says he tries hard. Just not the sharpest knife in the drawer," says Russell.

"We can't win if luck is all we got," counters Vanessa. "I don't care how great an athlete Palmer is."

The extra point sails through the goal posts and Coach Dub leans close to Patrice. "What's up with Vanessa?" he asks.

"Mama Bear Syndrome," explains Patrice.

"I'm not following," says Dub.

"Think about it. Assuming Ty beats this cancer, Vanessa now sees Palmer as a threat for next year."

"Really?"

"She doesn't even realize it. But I have no doubt."

Less than thirty minutes later, the game ends. No more heroics from anybody, Palmer included. The stands have emptied, and the scoreboard shows the final score. Knights: 7. Guests: 17.

The Knights, Palmer near the back of the pack, trudge off the field, their heads down. Off to the side near the locker room, Buck and Roberts stand by themselves as the team slouches by.

"Tough game," Roberts consoles Buck.

"Losing the week before the playoffs start is bad mojo," grumbles Buck.

"We obviously need better quarterback play."

"Johnson is just bad. And Palmer was running around those last eleven minutes like a toddler at an Easter egg hunt."

"He did throw a great pass to Swoops," says Roberts.

"Dumb luck."

"Howitzer for an arm, though." Roberts bends to pick up an empty popcorn box.

"We can't win a playoff game with him, that's all I'm saying," says Buck. The last player straggles past them.

"I thought Palmer would be further along," admits Roberts, putting the popcorn box in a trash can. "With Coach Deal working with him every day."

"Maybe it's the coach instead of the kid."

"Easy there, Buck," says Roberts. "It's just one game and we're still headed to the playoffs."

"Experience matters, George. No way we win a championship with an inexperienced female coach at the helm."

Roberts looks around, making sure nobody heard what Buck just said. "Keep the woman comment to yourself, Buck. An inexperienced coach describes the situation without any gender references."

"Good grief, George, who spooked you?"

Roberts leans in closer. "You find out anything about her?"

Buck shrugs. "You want me to tell you if I have?"

Roberts picks up a crumpled paper cup, throwing it in the trash as he weighs his answer. "Maybe not," he finally responds. "Plausible deniability and all that."

"It's not an FBI investigation, George."

"Just let me know if you hear anything that could hurt the school."

"Yeah," says Buck. "It's all about the school."

The players, now dressed in street clothes and wearing the unfamiliar smell of defeat, drift out of the locker room, quietly greet family and friends, climb into vehicles, and drive off. Palmer, his shoulders slumped, exits beside Ty, who's on crutches. Tanya steps towards Ty, who introduces her to Palmer.

"You didn't tell me you had a girl," Palmer chides Ty.

"He doesn't have me," protests Tanya.

"I'm working on it, though," says Ty.

"I'll get my car, Playa," says Tanya. "Meet you at the gate."

Bridget and a group of girls walk up as Tanya heads off. "Hey, Palmer," says Bridget, her smile wide. "Sorry you lost."

Palmer nods, his emotions mixed. Losing sucks, but at least he played.

"Amazing throw on that touchdown," continues Bridget as she and the girls stop in front of him.

"Thanks."

"We're headed to the lookout," Bridget says. "You can see the whole town from there. Want to join us?"

Palmer glances at Ty, then steps away and waves Bridget to follow. Once they're alone, he stops. "What's with you?" he asks, suspiciously.

"Whatever do you mean?"

"You the most popular girl in our grade."

Bridget smiles and tilts her head. "I don't know about that."

"Why you talking to me so much? You mocking me?"

"No. I'd never do that," she protests, her lower lip pushed out in a pout.

"Then what's your game?" He throws up his hands, completely confused at her motives.

Bridget smiles again, gently this time, no tease in it. "I just, you know... Flirting is fun," she responds.

"But you're here." He raises a hand over his head. "And I'm—" He drops his hand below his knees.

"Really?" Her eyes sparkle under the lights. "Have you looked at yourself? Tall, blonde, and my God, your eyes. I could swim in those eyes for days."

"I don't even know what that last part means."

Bridget laughs. "I read it in a book somewhere." She touches his arm. "Come up to the mountain with me. We'll have fun. Just talk if you want."

Palmer hesitates, still not sure how to respond. Him with a girl like Bridget? Not likely. Besides, he and Molly are "a thing." "I appreciate the invite," he finally says. "But I already got a girl."

Bridget raises her eyebrows. "I didn't know."

Palmer's phone dings and he checks the text.

"By the gate in the parking lot. Molly."

He pockets the phone and faces Bridget again. "I'm flattered, Bridget, really. But... you know." He shrugs.

"Okay," she says gently. "Go on. For now, anyway. I'll get my shot with you eventually."

In a hurry now, Palmer quickly escorts Bridget back to her friends, then rejoins Ty, who's patiently waiting.

"I want you to meet Molly," he tells Ty as they move slowly away from the clubhouse. "She's out by the gate."

"You should bring her to my house," says Ty. "We'll hang out, listen to music."

"I doubt I'll like your music," says Palmer, half-joking.

"You should expand your horizons, Palmer."

"Will your mom be okay if we come over?"

"She'll put up a fuss, but I'll convince her. What else you got to do?"

"All right. So long as Molly is up for it."

Her spirits low, Chelsea texts Bo as she exits the locker room. "Meet me at the gate behind the home bleachers. Near the concession stand."

Bo immediately texts back. "Be right there."

As she walks the thirty yards to the gate, a few people speak to her but most don't, so she walks alone, a losing coach who just led Rabon to its first defeat in two years. At the gate, she brushes her hair back with her fingers and stares at her shoes. At least nobody had booed. Not that she heard anyway.

Bo rounds the bleachers, dressed in a long black coat over a blue, buttoned-down shirt, navy slacks, and black wingtips. "Hey, Head Coach Chelsea Deal!" he shouts as if greeting a celebrity.

She quickly waves him closer "Easy there," she says, smiling but not happily. "I just lost my first game as head coach."

"Yeah, sorry about that." He leans in and hugs her.

"I dread next week. Local radio is going to crucify me."

Bo eases back. "But your starting quarterback was out sick."

"People hate it when a coach makes excuses," she says.

"Your backups are pretty pathetic," he observes. "Except for the one pass that third-stringer threw."

He reaches for her hand, and she almost takes his, but exhaustion suddenly overwhelms her, and she wants nothing more than to drive home, enjoy a hot shower, and collapse into bed. But she can't do that. Not with her obligations to the Booster Club. And not with Bo there, unannounced.

She folds her arms and faces him. "You can't keep showing up without telling me, Bo," she says, hoping he'll understand.

"Oh, come on," he says. "I couldn't miss your first game as head coach."

"I know you like grand gestures. But they … I don't know …stress me out."

"Can we go somewhere and talk?" he asks. "Your place maybe?"

She weighs the idea a moment but finally shakes her head. "Our Booster Club throws a party after every home game, and I'm expected to show up. You can join me if you want."

"Kill. Me. Now."

She chuckles. "I figured that."

"What about after?"

She checks her watch. "It'll be late," she warns.

"I don't care. I want to see you."

She sighs, her bones aching with fatigue, and wishes he would take the hint and head back to Atlanta. But he shows no inclination to do that, and he did drive two hours to see her. "Okay," she finally relents. "We have a decent restaurant, Georgio's, on the town square. Meet me there in an hour. We'll eat a late dinner."

He eases closer again and touches her cheek. "Really, I'm sorry you lost."

Chelsea smiles. "I'll survive." She pecks him on the cheek. "I need to run back to the locker room and grab my backpack. See you at the restaurant."

Bo nods and she hustles away, alone, frustrated, and dreading the gathering with the Booster Club.

Dressed in blue jeans, brown boots, and a bulky white sweatshirt with the words "Truckers Roll" in red lettering on the front, Molly leans on the fence by a stadium gate, a cigarette in hand. Her hair in a ponytail, she puffs out a long plume of smoke as Don and Strick slouch by, their hats low over their eyes, their hair poking out. She braces her foot on the fence and nods to Don and Strick. They take another step, then Don stops suddenly and faces her.

"Hey," says Don. Strick stops alongside him. "You Molly, aren't you? Graduated last spring?"

"Yep," says Molly.

"Didn't you get knocked up?" sneers Strick.

"That's a idiot question," Molly says, flicking cigarette ashes to the ground.

Don and Strick high-five each other. "Yeah, that's what I heard," mocks Don. "Guy named Drew, wasn't it? Your baby daddy?"

"Leave me alone, morons," Molly orders.

Don and Strick ease closer and Molly tries to back up, but the fence blocks her escape. Strick touches her arm. She smells beer on his breath.

"You got you a rug-rat at home?" Don sneers.

Molly pushes his hand away. "I don't have a kid."

"No? Did you have The Procedure?" Don puts a hand on her waist, and she slaps it, a touch of fear rising in her throat for the first time.

Don laughs and grips her waist harder.

"Rid yourself of the little nuisance?" asks Strick.

Molly presses back into the fence and feels the metal jamming into her shoulders. She raises a boot to kick Don off, but Strick moves before she can, his hands suddenly all over her, touching her breasts, squeezing her hips and buttocks.

She kicks Don and jams her cigarette into Strick's cheek. He groans and backs up for a second. She spits in disgust, and he charges at her again, harder this time, his face scrunched up in rage. She kicks and pushes at him, desperate to fight him off, but he's on her again, squeezing her shoulders. Don grabs her too, his hands on her waist, trying to hold her still as she squirms, scratches, and kicks. Fear gushes through her and she claws at Don and Strick, her anger increasing her strength as she fights them off.

Stepping around a corner, Palmer spots Molly close to forty yards away, her back to the fence, with Don and Strick on either side of her. "Hey!" Palmer yells, not sure what's happening as he leaves Ty and runs at them.

Don and Strick drop their hands off Molly and back up as he arrives. "Maybe Palmer is her kid!" says Don, his tone relaxed, like nothing is amiss.

"Nah," says Strick, a hand covering the burned spot on his cheek. "He's a couple years too old to be her offspring."

"What's going on?" Palmer asks Molly, gently raising her chin to look into her eyes. "You all right? Did they hurt you?"

Molly bites her lip and brushes back tears. Palmer turns on Don and Strick. "What did you do to her?"

Ty hobbles up behind Palmer, Tanya next to him.

"Molly wants to hang with us, Palmer," Don says as he turns towards Molly. "Ain't that right, Little Mama? You want to spend some time with a couple grown-up men."

Molly grabs Palmer's hand and starts to walk away but Don and Strick block them.

"Come on, guys," growls Palmer, his jaw tight. "Back off."

Don laughs again. "Does Palmer know about your rug-rat, Molly?" he asks. "You share that news with him?"

Strick reaches for Molly, but she pushes him away and runs, Palmer beside her. Don lunges at her from behind and knocks her down. Her elbows bang into the asphalt.

Palmer punches Don as Molly rises and attacks Strick, her fingernails digging into his face.

"Stop it!" Ty yells, but nobody listens.

Strick throws Molly off and jumps on Palmer. Reaching the melee, Ty flings his crutch at Strick, and it bangs into his back. Don smacks Palmer in the head and Palmer grabs him and they fall, wrestling on the asphalt. Tanya screams.

Back in the coach's parking lot, Chelsea strides to her pickup with Coach Paul and Buck beside her, each of them breaking away as they reach their vehicles. She starts to unlock the truck but pauses as she hears a scream. She turns around, not sure of the scream's location. Another scream rings out.

Fixed on the sound, she sprints toward the gate, Coach Paul, and Buck behind her. Rounding the corner, she spots Palmer and Ty in the middle of a fight.

"Hey!" she yells, running hard. "Break it up!"

Strick rips Molly's sweatshirt. Ty picks up his crutch and punches Strick with it. Don shoves Palmer's face into the asphalt.

"Stop it!" yells Chelsea.

Palmer and Don roll over and over. Strick jerks Ty's crutch away, swings it, and knocks Ty down. Molly jumps on Don's back and pulls him off Palmer. Ty grabs his knee and moans as he rolls away.

Reaching the brawl, Chelsea yanks at Palmer as Buck rushes Don and Paul grabs Strick. Together, they pull the boys apart and hold them in place. Tanya helps Ty up and hands him his crutch. Still holding onto Palmer, Chelsea asks Molly. "Are you okay?"

Molly checks her elbows and knees but sees no blood. She nods. "I'm not hurt," she says.

Chelsea releases Palmer and eases closer to Molly. "Did they hurt you?" she whispers. "You know, any other way?"

Molly shakes her head, but tears start to fall on her cheeks.

Chelsea hugs her. "Come on, I'll drive you to the hospital."

Molly quickly backs up and wipes her eyes. "No hospital," she says firmly. "I'm all right."

"You sure?

"I'm fine, really," insists Molly.

Chelsea faces Don and Strick.

"It was a misunderstanding, Coach," says Don. "That's all. Sorry things got out of hand."

"He's lying!" says Palmer with a snarl. "He and Strick were all over Molly!"

Realizing things are more serious than she first thought, Chelsea faces Molly again. "I'm sorry, Molly, but a doctor needs to check you out. And I'll have to report this to the school. And the police. Let them figure out who did what."

"No!" sobs Molly, her voice frantic. "Palmer showed up before anything happened!"

"I'm obligated to report something like this, Molly."

"You can't! People will talk! Tell lies! Spread rumors! My parents ... I don't want them to know about this!" She cries again, glaring at Don and Strick.

Palmer eases towards her. "But you didn't do anything wrong," he says. "People will know that."

"People believe what they want to believe!" sobs Molly.

Chelsea glances at Buck and Paul.

"Whatever you think, Coach," says Paul. Buck stays silent.

"Please," begs Molly. "Just drop it. I'm fine."

Chelsea faces Don and Strick again and her anger rises at their smug faces. "You two. I swear. If I ever hear of you anywhere near Molly again, I'll make you regret the day you were born. You clear on that?"

"As a bell," agrees Don.

"Now get out of my sight!" orders Chelsea.

Don and Strick hurry off and Chelsea turns to Palmer. "You can't be fighting, Palmer!" she pleads. "You're already on thin ice! Something like this—no matter how it started—will go south on you in a hurry!"

Palmer stares at the ground and Chelsea shifts to Ty. "And Ty, I can't believe you're involved in this."

"Palmer is my teammate, Coach. And Molly is his girl."

Chelsea glances from person to person. Finally nods at Molly.

"Listen up," she says to the group. "Here's what we'll do. Palmer, you and Ty will drive these young women"—she points at Tanya and Molly—"straight home. No stops, no parties. And we'll keep what happened to ourselves."

"We won't report it?" asks Buck.

Chelsea looks again at Molly. Molly shakes her head.

"Molly is the victim," asserts Chelsea. "If she changes her mind, we'll report it. But otherwise, what she says carries the most weight. We clear on that?"

Everybody nods.

"Good," concludes Chelsea, waving everyone away. "That's enough excitement for one night."

The group breaks up and Chelsea heads back to her truck. Climbing in, she lays her head on the steering wheel. She's just taken a huge gamble. But what choice did she have? She raises her head, starts her truck, and hopes to heaven that what just happened never again sees the light of day.

CHAPTER TEN

Georgio's restaurant faces the town courthouse, a classic, red-brick, colonial-style building with statues of World War I and II soldiers guarding the front lawn. A fountain, with a two-foot high stone wall around it, gurgles between the two statues. A plaque attached to the stone wall reads, "Rabon Springs."

A light rain starts to fall and water drips from the helmets of the two soldiers. A sign in front of Georgio's boasts: "Quality Italian since 1924."

Chelsea, dressed now in a long brown skirt, ankle black boots, chic tan sweater, and looped gold earrings, parks about two blocks from the sign, hurries to Georgio's, and eases inside. A long, mahogany bar lines the left side of the room. People stand two deep at the bar, most of them drinking. Diners fill the rest of the place. Red-checkered cloths cover the tables, each of them full of patrons. Candles burn.

Chelsea scans the restaurant for Bo but doesn't see him. The hostess greets her. "I'm expecting someone," says Chelsea. "May I wait at the bar?"

The hostess guides her to a bar stool by the wall. A few people speak to her as she passes while others say nothing. Hearing music, she spots Dirk performing on a small stage, his music country but not twangy, soulful but not sappy. She leans closer to listen. He sees her and nods slightly as he finishes the song. The bartender, a tall young woman with brunette hair, multiple tattoos, and her hair pulled back under a green bandana, hands her a drink menu.

"What's your pleasure?" asks the bartender.

"What are your non-alcoholic options?" asks Chelsea, scanning the menu.

"Soft drink, non-alcoholic beer, and I can make most anything virgin."

"Maybe a water."

The bartender sniffs. "Will do." She grabs the menu and turns away.

Chelsea faces Dirk again as he places his guitar in a stand. "I need a short break," he tells the crowd "Back in fifteen." He brushes back his hair and strolls toward Chelsea. She checks the room for Bo again but doesn't see him.

"Tough loss tonight," Dirk says as he reaches her.

"Ain't that the truth."

The bartender brings her water, lays a napkin down, places the water glass on it, and twists away.

"I didn't know you played here," Chelsea says to Dirk. "You're good."

"You didn't hear enough to reach that conclusion."

"You're saying you're not good?" She sips her water and checks him out. Notes his rugged looks and the dimples in his cheeks.

"I like your earrings," he says, changing the subject.

"I made them myself."

"They're dangly." When he grins, his dimples make her want to smile too, but she won't let herself.

"Can I buy you a drink?" he asks.

She thinks of Bo. "I'm waiting on another man," she says.

"What kind of man makes a woman like you wait?"

"You haven't known me long enough to know what kind of woman I am."

Dirk chuckles. "You like football. Make your own earrings. Care about kids. Look good in khakis AND a skirt. What else I need to know?"

"Are you flirting with me, country singer?"

"It breaks my heart you even have to ask."

The bartender shows up and Dirk orders a beer.

"I appreciate your help with Palmer," Chelsea says, deliberately moving away from the flirtations. "You know, when he almost quit a few days ago."

Dirk shrugs. "I do what I can." His beer arrives and he tips the bottle to his lips.

"Tell me more about Palmer," says Chelsea. "I need to know everything."

The door opens and Bo walks in, his hair wet with rain. "That's my guy," she says, nodding toward Bo.

"Looks pretty corporate," says Dirk as Bo scans the crowd, obviously searching for her.

"A button-down shirt doesn't necessarily make a guy corporate," counters Chelsea.

"Wing tips do." Dirk grins again.

"How do you know he's wearing wing tips? You can't see his feet."

"I got a twenty that says he is."

"We'll continue this conversation later," she says, waving to Bo and catching his attention. "The Palmer part, I mean. Not the wing tips."

Dirk laughs. "Palmer is a good kid, Coach."

"With a cannon for an arm."

She stands to leave.

"Is it acceptable if I watch you walk away?" asks Dirk.

"It breaks my heart you even have to ask."

She turns and passes through the crowd toward Bo, just a little bit pleased to know that Dirk is watching her.

A red and black eighteen-wheel truck sits in front of a small white house on a two-lane country road. A tan car, clean but old, sits under two oak trees by a narrow front porch. Lights burn inside.

As Molly parks her car in front of the house, Palmer follows on his motorcycle. Eager to help her, he hops off his bike, opens her door, and reaches for her hand as she climbs out.

"I'm not an invalid," she says, her face dark.

"I know that. Just, you know, I want to take care of you."

They walk slowly toward the porch. "My pa is scary," she warns. "So be aware."

She opens the front door and leads Palmer into the den, where a hulking man wearing a Falcons cap, a pair of black sweatpants, and a red flannel shirt reclines in a lounge chair watching TV. A snake tattoo covers the top of his right hand. The man raises his eyes and examines Palmer head to toe. "You found one brave enough to come home with you?" he asks Molly.

"His name is Palmer," says Molly. "Palmer, this is my pa."

"Pleased to meet you, Mr. Cole," Palmer says.

"Call me Rob." Rob picks up a glass from beside his chair and swigs from what looks like a green smoothie. "You the football player?"

"I'm on the team, yes, sir," says Palmer.

Rob extends the snake-covered hand and Palmer shakes it. "How's Ty doing?" asks Rob.

"He's taking chemo. That's about all I know."

Rob swigs again from his smoothie. "You a mite young for Molly, aren't ya?"

"Palmer is wise beyond his years, Pa," offers Molly.

"Best not be too wise," says Rob, a warning riding in the words.

A woman with a glowing smile and thick dark hair sprigging out from a yellow scarf walks in from another room. She's slender and attractive but plainly dressed—a pullover blue top and black jeans. No jewelry, no makeup. Molly hugs her and Palmer notices a brief watering of Molly's eyes as she holds on for a couple of seconds.

"Well," says Mrs. Cole as Molly steps back, "that was nice."

"This is my mom," says Molly, as if Palmer doesn't already know.

"You must be Palmer," says Mrs. Cole, opening her arms for a hug.

Palmer glances at Molly. She nods, and he steps into the hug. "Yes, ma'am," he says as she embraces him. "Glad to meet you."

Mrs. Cole eases back. "Ya'll hungry?" she asks. "Be glad to fix you a sandwich or something."

"You want a smoothie?" Rob holds up his glass.

"He likes his with kale," says Mrs. Cole. "Happy to make you one."

"No, Mama," says Molly "We're good. Just going to my room. It's been a long day."

Rob points his glass at Palmer. "Don't think you spending the night here, Boy. None of that going on in my house."

"Back off, Pa," orders Molly.

"Just keep both your feet on the floor, the two of you. At all times."

Molly grabs Palmer's hand and hurriedly leads him out.

Bo and Chelsea sit at a corner table at Georgio's. A waiter pours wine for Bo, puts bread down, and scoots away.

"How was the Booster Club?" Bo asks, swirling his wine glass.

"I escaped as soon as I could."

"That much fun, huh?" He sips the wine.

"It was thoughtful of you to drive up tonight," says Chelsea, picking up a piece of bread. "Even if it was a surprise."

"I just wanted a little time with you." Bo sips his wine again and leans closer. "Where you see us headed, Chelsea?" he asks.

"That's too big a question for tonight." She butters a piece of bread, hoping he won't push her like he seems to do every time they see each other these days.

"I know," he agrees. "And I realize I shouldn't press. But I see our future and I want you to know that. I'll perform an outlandish proposal. Buy you a diamond the size of a blueberry. We'll enjoy an exotic honeymoon, then settle down, a house, green lawn, at least two little ones someday."

Chelsea sighs, her anxiety ratcheting higher, but keeps her voice calm while she speaks. "It sounds wonderful, Bo. A true fantasy."

She bites her bread to keep from saying anything else because she knows if she does, it'll come out harsh and wrong. She needs relaxation tonight, a touch of humor, something to break the tension she's faced all week, especially tonight. But Bo wants heavy, serious talk.

"It's our fantasy," Bo continues, not sensing her mood at all. "We can make it happen."

"Let me finish the playoffs," says Chelsea. "I can get a handle on things after that."

"Ah, the playoffs." Bo leans back. "Which brings me to a simple request."

She waits while he sips his wine again.

"You finish the playoffs," he says, putting down his glass, "and I do hope you win, by the way."

"You're a prince. Thank you."

He leans forward. "You're done when the playoffs end. The coaching thing, I mean. Then our fairy tale begins!"

Chelsea puts down her bread, her patience finally worn to its end. "Read the room, Bo," she says, her tone sharper than she wants. "This isn't the time for that kind of commitment. I have too many other things on my plate."

"Be reasonable, Chelsea," pleads Bo, his voice edging up a little. "You know coaching isn't your future. Tonight's game, beyond any question, should have proven that to you."

"One game?" she asks, fully angry now. "I lose one game and that proves I have no future as a coach?"

Silence falls. Bo stares at her, confusion written on his brow, as he finishes his wine. Finally, he sighs. "I put my foot in it, didn't I?" He reaches for her hand, but she pulls away. "I'm sorry, Chelsea," he apologizes. "I didn't mean that the way it came out."

The waiter suddenly returns and they both lean back as he fills Bo's wine glass and walks away.

"I don't know what my future holds, Bo," says Chelsea, working to settle herself down. "But I'm not promising to quit coaching."

"You have to let your brother go," he says gently.

"Please don't bring Mitchell into this."

"You know I'm right," he says, leaning close again, his voice soft but insistent. "This football gig? It's an offering of your life to …I don't know … give you a reason to wake up every day."

Anger flares in Chelsea again and this time she lights into him. "What's your reason to wake up, Bo? To bill a few more hours per day? To lower your golf handicap? How's that a better use of life than me coaching? How's it more noble?"

Bo places his elbows on the table and rests his chin on his hands. "I know you're afraid, Chelsea," he suggests, going amateur therapist on her. "And I understand that, given your background. But our family doesn't have to end up like yours. Broken, divorced, scattered."

"My family isn't the issue!"

Bo studies her face another few moments but then leans back and disengages. "Arguing isn't getting us anywhere."

"I keep repeating this," pleads Chelsea. "And you need to listen. I need more time. I'm not saying 'no' to you, but I'm not saying 'no' to anything else either."

Bo slowly sips his wine again, then carefully places the glass on the table. "Nobody has forever, Chelsea," he says, his tone as sharp as nails.

The rain falls heavier outside. "Is that a threat?" Chelsea asks quietly.

"No," he says tersely. "Just a fact."

Chelsea stares out the window. "I know you're angry," she says as her last ounce of energy drains away. "And it's late. I need to head home."

"We haven't even ordered," Bo says.

"I guess I'm not hungry." Chelsea rises and touches Bo's shoulder. He reaches for her hand again and this time she allows him to take it.

"Fine, Chelsea," he says, gentler again. "I hear what you're saying. You need time, so that's what I'll give you. I'll cease the grand gestures. Give you some space. Call me when you're ready to talk." He kisses her hand.

Relieved but also sad, Chelsea kisses him on the cheek, then turns and walks away, not thinking even once that he might be watching her as she leaves.

Pictures of planets and stars decorate the walls of Molly's small, square room in the back of her house. An earth globe hangs from a light in the middle of the ceiling. Molly and Palmer lie on a single bed with their shoes off, facing each other.

"Pa told you to keep both feet on the floor," Molly says with a smile.

"You gone snitch on me?"

"You make me mad, I might."

They laugh and snuggle closer.

"What about yours?" He points to her feet, both resting beside his on the bed.

She brushes his hair out of his eyes. "It's my bed," she says. "My feet belong here."

He rolls over and stares at the ceiling and she lays her head on his chest. "You sure you okay?" he asks softly. "You know, from after the game?"

"I shoved my cigarette in Strick's face," she says. "I thought he was gone cry. The ginger bastard."

"Remind me to stay on your good side. And your pa's."

They lay still and quiet for a few moments. Finally, Molly speaks: "What do you dream about, Palmer?" she asks. "You know, for your future?"

"You already know," he replies. "Music. I want to play, sing."

"Be a big star?"

"Not that so much. Just make a living from it." He turns to her and touches her chin, raising it so he can see her face. "What about you?"

She reaches to her nightstand, pulls a small remote from it, then turns off the lamp. She clicks the remote and the ceiling suddenly comes alive with a swirl of blinking stars, planets, asteroids, and comets.

Palmer gazes at the lighted universe over his head. "Wow," he says. "It's like I'm in outer space."

Molly grins. "When I was little, I wanted to be the first American female astronaut."

"Didn't a woman already do that, like a long time ago?"

Molly laughs and they face each other again. "Sally Ride," she says. "But I didn't know about her for a long time."

Palmer faces the ceiling again and stares at it for several seconds before speaking again. "Don and Strick," he says. "What did they mean? Calling you 'Mama'?"

Her body tenses beside him. "It's not important," she says dismissively.

"So why did they say it?"

Molly rolls away from him, locks her hands behind her head, and studies the ceiling. "My senior year," she starts. "This guy I dated, Andrew. Rich. Arrogant. A couple of months after we started going out, he wanted, expected, more from me than I'd give up. You know what I mean?"

Palmer nods and Molly forges ahead. "He kept pushing me. I kept saying 'no.' He eventually turned mean about it, so I ghosted him. But he told people he dumped ME because I was pregnant by another guy."

Silence falls again and Palmer lets the story sink in.

"What you thinking?" Molly finally asks.

"I don't know."

Molly touches his cheek, and he faces her again. "What happened when you never had a baby?" he asks.

"What do you think? Andrew spread the rumor that I went to a clinic."

Palmer rises on an elbow so he can see her face. "I believe you," he says softly. "But, you know, you can be honest with me. And it's okay, either way. But was there...? Did you get pregnant?"

Molly's face reddens as she quickly sits up. "Don't you dare!" she scolds Palmer. "You say you believe me, but you don't. Not really! You wouldn't ask me that if you did! You believe Don? Strick? After what happened tonight?"

Palmer panics. "Come on, Molly," he pleads. "I'm not accusing you of anything. It's just—"

Her eyes blaze. "You think I'm easy? Is that it?"

"I didn't say that."

"So why ask that idiot question?"

"I don't know," he says, his mind a jumble as he realizes he's hurt her. "This kind of stuff is new to me. I don't know what I'm supposed to say. Or do."

She climbs off the bed and stands over him, glaring. "Maybe you should leave."

"Please, Molly, just calm down. It's all right."

"No, it's not." Her eyes fill with tears. "Nothing is all right. Just leave. Now." She points toward the door.

Palmer stands slowly and reaches for her, but she backs away, still crying. He puts on his shoes and tries again to touch her, but she won't have it. "I'm sorry," he pleads again. "I'm a idiot. I didn't mean to upset you. Please don't cry."

Molly steadies herself and wipes her eyes. "I'm poor, Palmer. But that don't mean I'm cheap."

He tries to hug her again, but she pushes him away and points him to the door.

CHAPTER ELEVEN

D ining on coffee and bagels, Chelsea and Dub share a window booth in the Kangaroo Coffee Shop. A bright sun burns through the window and Chelsea points to the giant kangaroo outside. "What's with the kangaroo?" she asks.

Dub laughs. "An Aussie fellow moved here fifty-one years ago. Rabon's first foreigner, people said. Folks called him 'Roo.'"

"As in kangaroo."

Dub laughs. "Roo opened this shop and put up the giant kangaroo. Built it himself, according to local yore. The one in the corner"—Dub points to the stuffed kangaroo a few feet away—"joined us a few years later."

"That's one way to show up in a Visitor's Guide."

"This place has always thrived. So, I guess it's working." Dub lays a newspaper on the table and taps it.

"Didn't know they still printed papers," Chelsea says, picking it up as if touching a rare jewel.

"*The Rabon Reader*," says Dub. "Local News for Local Folks. Says so right there." He points to the masthead.

"Cute headline," says Chelsea, scanning the paper. "Defeat No Death Knell. Knights Get Bye."

"The loss only dropped us one notch in the state rankings."

Chelsea reads the article. "Not too tough on me," she says, a little surprised.

"Just the one line there." Dub points to a line about halfway down in the first paragraph.

"Coach Deal's inexperience showed up multiple times as she made confusing substitutions at key points in the game, especially when she inserted seldom-used Palmer Norman at quarterback while the victory still remained, at least in this reporter's opinion, within reach."

She lays the paper down. "I can't argue with that too much. When I put Palmer in, I wasn't too sure about it myself."

"Least we still have a bye week before the quarterfinal," says Dub, a bagel headed into his mouth. "Which gives you two weeks to fix your quarter-back problem."

Chelsea laughs. "So now it's my problem?"

Dub sips coffee. "The buck has to stop somewhere."

Chelsea nibbles at a bagel, her mind churning. She can't turn Johnson into Patrick Mahomes in two weeks. And Palmer? One long, lucky, touchdown pass didn't make him Tom Brady. "Who do I play?" she asks Dub. "Palmer or Johnson?"

Dub stretches an arm along the top of the booth. "Your choice. You're the head coach now."

"Come on, Dub," pleads Chelsea, desperate for his input. "I'm conflicted. I need your opinion."

"First thing," Dub orders sternly. "Stop being conflicted." His voice tightens. "And even if you are, don't say so out loud, not even to me. The team will lose confidence."

He lays both hands on the table and leans towards her. "Figure out what you want to do and just do it, come hell or high water!"

Chelsea lays down her bagel. "Last night was rougher than I expected," she confesses. "I went to the Booster Party, and Georgio's after that. Half the people I saw barely looked at me, like I had a disease or something."

"I warned you: Losing is the unforgiveable sin in this town."

"I've probably received two hundred phone calls, texts, or e-mails since last night."

"Half of them encouraging you to hang in there, half suggesting you choke to death on your whistle, or something like that."

Chelsea laughs ruefully. "A few told me in R-rated language that a woman doesn't belong on the sidelines with the Rabon High Knights."

Dub drinks coffee. "Exchange the word 'woman' for 'black man' and I can feel your pain."

She leans closer. "Really, Dub? Still?"

He shrugs. "Not that often anymore. I've won three state championships in fourteen years here. That takes some of the fire out of our less-enlightened broth-ers and sisters. But in the early days? Well, they used a different word for *black* back then."

Chelsea leans back, remembers some of the messages from the last twenty-four hours, and wonders what it must have been like for Dub. "How did you survive it?" she asks him. "Without becoming angry? Bitter?"

Dub picks up a bagel as he considers the question. "I don't know," he finally says. "I'm not an angry man by nature, I suppose. And I...well, I've always had a capacity for forgiveness. I know my own failings, so I tend to accept the failings of others."

Chelsea stares at Dub, wonder in her eyes. "Not many people can do that," she says.

"Trailblazers have to," says Dub. "Or things will blow up in your face real fast."

Chelsea weighs his words and her face brightens as a thought dawns. "I suppose I am a pioneer," she says, half in jest as she sits up straighter.

"They should put a statue of you on the town square," chuckles Dub as the mood lightens.

"I'm right proud of myself."

"As well you should be."

Chelsea breaks off a piece of bagel and turns serious again. "Any chance you'll return in time to coach the playoffs?" she asks.

"I doubt it. I'm still having some headaches. And I lose my balance now and again."

"The sooner you're back, the happier this town will be."

"You win a state championship, they'll forget I ever existed."

A couple of hours later, all the coaches are gathered in Dub's office. Coffee cups, half-empty bottles of water, and power bar wrappers are spread out all over the desk. The coaches sit in various poses around it. Video from the previous night's game plays on the monitor and the coaches focus on it, their eyes glued to the screen. A Knights' hat over her hair, Chelsea scribbles notes in a purple notebook as she studies the mistakes made in the loss. The video finally ends, and everyone leans back and stretches.

"It's win-or-go-home time, gents," says Buck. He starts to grab a water bottle but pauses first and looks at Chelsea. "And lady."

"Thank God we have a couple weeks to make adjustments," says Coach Paul.

Buck opens his water bottle, "Anybody heard when Dub's returning?" he asks.

"I ate breakfast with him this morning," Chelsea says. "He's still dealing with some concussion symptoms."

"So, we're still a ship without a captain," says Buck.

Everybody looks at Chelsea, but she decides to ignore the cut. No reason to poke the bear after a loss. Especially when his defense played lights out while her offense stunk up the field. "We all know quarterback-play is our biggest problem," she says calmly.

"Johnson should improve in the next two weeks," says Coach Paul. "Maybe we just hitch our wagon to him and see how far he can take us."

"I agree," says Buck. "Our defense will keep us in the games. Won't need much from the offense."

The other coaches nod, and Chelsea weighs their opinions for a moment. Turning the video back on, she fast-forwards to Palmer's touchdown pass and plays it. Replays it two more times. Stops the video. "You're saying we give up on that kind of talent?" she asks, looking from coach to coach.

"Not forever," says Paul. "Just for the rest of this year. No way he figures out the offense in time to help us win now."

"He might not be back next year," says Chelsea, admitting the possibility to herself for the first time.

"If we lose the quarterfinal, you might not be back next year either," says Buck.

"You're probably right," she says, grabbing a water bottle and nonchalantly opening it.

"We know you like the kid," continues Buck. "But we're football coaches, not social workers." His eyes move from coach to coach, as if tying each of them to his opinions. "We can't fix every screwed-up teenager that crosses our path."

"He's practiced a little at wide receiver," suggests Paul. "Should we play him some more there? Maybe Swoops wouldn't get double-teamed so much."

Water bottle in hand, Chelsea stands and stares out the window. Watches a hawk circle high above the trees beyond the football field, its wings arcing across the sky. The hawk suddenly dives, picking up speed, a missile with feathers zeroed in on the prey on the ground. The hawk disappears as it dips below a tree, and Chelsea can't see if it caught its prey or not. All she knows is that the hawk threw itself head-first into the attempt, holding nothing back..

She faces the coaches again, sips from her water bottle, and speaks. "Palmer will start at quarterback in the quarterfinal," she says. "Go big or go home."

Buck grunts. "Put me on the record: I think it's a mistake."

Chelsea steps over, places both palms flat on the desk, and squares her eyes up with those of the coaches. "Here's the deal, guys," she says. "We might win the quarterfinal with Johnson. But our only chance to win a state championship is to play our most talented player, and that's Palmer. We all know it." She stares them down, one at a time, challenging them to dispute her.

"You think he can learn the plays?" Paul finally asks.

Chelsea grabs the Playbook off the desk and holds it up. "If the mountain won't come to Mohammed, we'll take Mohammed to the mountain."

Paul looks at the other coaches, obviously confused. "I know I ought to understand that reference," he says as he faces Chelsea. "But you lost me."

Chelsea lays down the Playbook as Buck chuckles.

"Palmer can't learn the Playbook," explains Buck. "So, we change the Playbook to fit Palmer."

"Bingo," says Chelsea. Having made the decision, she exhales as stress rolls off her. "Okay." She stands straighter and waves her hands over the room. "Go," she orders. "Out of here, all of you. Go home, to your family, fishing, golf, whatever you do on a Saturday."

"What you gone do, Coach?" asks Paul.

Chelsea turns her cap backward and speaks wistfully. "I think I'll drive home, put some Celtic women on Pandora, light a candle, run a bubble bath, and climb in with a romance novel in hand."

Paul looks at Buck, confused again.

"She's screwing with you, Paul," chuckles Buck.

Laughing hard, Chelsea shoos everybody out, then sits down and resets the video.

Dirk and Palmer sit outside in frayed lawn chairs. In front of them is a fire burning inside an in-ground pit. Though it's a sunny day, wind whirls in every direction and the fire dips and flames with the breeze. Dirk holds the banjo this time, Palmer the guitar. "I think Molly dumped me," says Palmer, tuning the guitar.

"You think?"

"It's kind of confusing."

"Been there, done that." Dirk plucks the banjo strings.

"It's sad too," says Palmer. "For me at least." He strums the guitar and wonders what Molly is doing.

"Young love, Bro. A breakup hurts more when you're a teenager than it ever will again."

They strum their instruments for a couple minutes. Dirk finally speaks again. "I'm leaving Monday for Nashville. Rehearsals all week. An audition Friday for a big gig we hope to get."

"It turns awful quiet around here when it's just me," says Palmer, his mood sinking even deeper.

"What about friends?"

"They don't grow on trees." Palmer softly strums his guitar.

"Coach Deal cares about you," says Dirk.

"She's all right, I guess."

The fire crackles. "Georgio's booked me again," says Dirk. "For next Friday night."

Palmer stays quiet and Dirk stares at him for a few seconds, then puts the banjo aside. "I got an idea," he says. "Something that might cheer your sad ass up."

Palmer shrugs.

"Join me on stage at Georgio's. I think you're ready for an audience."

Palmer's heart jumps as he considers the notion. "That's a little scary," he says.

"Just a little?"

Palmer smiles, his mood lifting as he warms to the idea. "Would I play and sing or just play?"

"In for a penny, in for a pound," says Dirk.

Palmer imagines standing with Dirk on stage, harmonizing their favorite songs, losing himself in the music, the audience.

Dirk's phone rings. "You with me?" he asks Palmer.

Palmer smiles again as Dirk answers the phone. "Hey, Lacy," he says. "Yeah, he's here."

Palmer jumps up to leave but Dirk grabs his arm and holds him in place.

Lacy, in faded yellow pants and a green flannel shirt, slouches barefooted and makeup-less on the edge of a plain, single bed in a small room with no decorations. "I ain't gone take no for a answer this time," she warns Dirk. "Put Palmer on the phone."

She stands and peeks out a thin, rectangular window toward the mountains in the distance. Palmer comes on the line a few seconds later.

"I told you to stop bothering me," he says firmly.

"I ain't done nothing wrong this time, Son. I promise. Just want to hear your voice. We don't need to talk about nothing serious."

Palmer stays quiet, so she continues. "I won't hang up till you talk to me, Son. What you been doin'?"

"Fine, Mama. You have one minute."

"You like it there?"

"I go to school. Play football. Work. I'm living large." Sarcasm drips with every word but Lacy ignores it.

"You never took too good to school," she says.

"I'm not exactly Einstein."

"You'll finish school soon enough. Find a job after that, make some money." From her shirt pocket, Lacy pulls a cigarette and lights it. "I wish you'd visit me."

"You said we wouldn't talk serious."

"I know it'll be hard for you to come here. But you almost grown. Old enough to face what is, ugly or not."

"Your minute's up," he says, his tone still cold. "I'll put Dirk back on."

"It's lonesome here, Son." She plops back on the bed, tears rolling onto the pillow where she lays.

Palmer hands Dirk the phone and throws another log into the firepit. Dirk talks to Lacy another few seconds, then hangs up and faces Palmer.

"You need to visit her, dude," Dirk says firmly. "Soon."

"Why?"

"Well, for one thing, she's your mama. You can't stay mad at her forever."

Palmer faces Dirk, his fists clenched. "Look, Uncle, you been good to me, so I prefer not to go against you. But you don't know the junk I've been through... a lot of it caused by your sister. True, she's my mama, and that ought to mean more than blood. But blood is about all she's ever given me. So yeah, I might stay mad at her forever. And nothing you or anybody else can say will make me change on that."

"Gosh, Palmer," says Dirk. "That's the longest speech I ever heard you make."

Palmer stares into the fire. "I don't speak out everything that's inside of me."

Dirk stands up, eases over, and lays an arm across his shoulder. "Maybe you ought to say things out loud more often."

"You a therapist now?"

Dirk laughs, kneels by the fire, and warms his hands. "Here's the deal, Palmer," he says. "Seeing your mama is the price you have to pay if you want to perform with me at Georgio's. No visit with Lacy, no play at Georgio's."

Palmer stares at his shoes, feeling sadder than in a long while. "I never said I would play with you," he says, his voice barely audible over the breeze.

Dirk shrugs. "All right. Suit yourself."

The wind whips outside Ty's window, scuttling clouds across the night sky. Ty lays in a reclining chair, *The Nickel Boys* book in his hand, his crutches beside him. Vanessa enters with a tray loaded with a salad, a piece of salmon, and a bed of rice. Ty closes the book and reaches for the tray. Vanessa notices the scratches on his elbow.

"What happened there?" she asks.

"I tripped," says Ty, offering a small lie as he arranges the tray on his lap. "Not steady on my crutches yet."

"Your limp seems worse today."

"I bumped my knee when I tripped." Another lie, which is not like him at all, but he's never had to hide much from his folks and doesn't know how to do it well.

Vanessa perches on the bed and watches as he starts to eat.

"Where is Pops tonight?" he asks between bites, steering the conversation away from his injuries.

"He's speaking at a conference in Atlanta."

"He'll be home later?"

Vanessa nods and clears her throat. "This girl, Tanya," she says. "Tell me about her."

"I like her," Ty says tersely.

"I need more than that."

"What if I don't want to say more?"

Vanessa laughs. "Let's see. You drop the skinny on that girl, or you can cook your own meals, wash your own clothes, clean up your own room, live with no allowance… Should I stop or finish the list?"

"You're a hard woman, Mama," he chuckles.

"I use the tools I got," she says.

"Okay. Tanya." Ty bites into the salmon. "Her mom works as an administrator for the Bishopville schools."

"Her dad?"

"He's not part of her life from what she's said."

Vanessa wags a finger. "Tanya seems nice, Son. But you need to watch yourself. A lot of girls see you, your house, the car you drive. And they see their meal ticket."

Ty stops chewing. "That what you saw when you met Pops?"

Vanessa tilts her head. "Maybe it's what your Pops saw when he met me."

Ty chuckles. "Tanya likes to laugh, Mama. That's good for me. And she's got a pretty smile."

"That's not all she's got that's pretty."

Ty eats a bite of salad, not eager to talk to his mama about Tanya's obvious hotness. "What else you want to know about her?" he asks.

Vanessa weighs the question but then shrugs. "That will do for now. Was that so hard?"

Ty forks some salad to his mouth but doesn't respond.

"Is Palmer learning the Playbook?" Vanessa asks, changing the subject.

"Not so much yet. But we'll keep working."

"He might make a good receiver," Vanessa suggests. "He's fast enough. Once your heath returns, the two of you will make a strong combination next year."

"Next year is a long way off, Mama. We got a championship to win now."

Vanessa stands. "Just take it slow with Tanya," she says. "A mistake now can play the devil with your future."

"Go on, Mama," says Ty, dismissing her. "Let me eat in peace."

She kisses him on the cheek and walks out as Ty turns his attention back to his food.

CHAPTER TWELVE

A bell rings and students sag into their seats as the first class of the school day starts. Tired from work the previous evening, Palmer rubs his eyes as he slouches in his chair near the back of the room. The math teacher, Mr. Stone, is a slim man with long blonde hair and a flamingo-thin neck. Getting up from his desk, he steps to the chalkboard and scratches out a math problem. Half the class is paying attention and half isn't.

"All right, everybody," announces Mr. Stone, his voice perky as he faces the class. "It's Monday morning, bright and early." He claps his hands. "And what do we do every Monday morning? The thing all of us look forward to all weekend?"

Nobody speaks. "That's right!" Stone says as if everybody just answered. "We start every Monday by inviting one of you to prance on up here and solve a problem so everybody else can see how it's done. So, who's the lucky mathematician who will dazzle us today?"

Stone walks back to his desk and lifts an I-pad from it. "Okay. We're down to the N's," he announces as he studies a list on the tablet. "And that means it's Palmer Norman's turn to impress us!"

He faces the class as Palmer straightens up, his body on alert. "You da man, Palmer," Stone says as he waves Palmer up.

His nerves jangling, Palmer stands and slowly comes forward. At the board, he accepts the piece of chalk that Stone hands him and pivots to study the problem. The numbers on the board appear jumbled, a mishmash he can't fathom. He squints, focuses harder, and hopes for a miracle, but none appears. He looks back at Mr. Stone.

"Go ahead," encourages Stone. "Take your best shot."

Palmer examines the problem again, but it makes no sense—just a bunch of numbers and symbols which mean nothing to him. The chalk shakes in his fingers and his face turns red as he realizes how totally lost he is.

"Give it a shot," urges Stone. "You start and I'll guide you through it."

Palmer wants to refuse but knows he needs to try, so he nods and starts to write on the board. After a second, Mr. Stone shakes his head and Palmer erases what he's written and examines the problem again. The problem's still gibberish to him but he tries again, the chalk scratching over the board. Mr. Stone shakes his head again and Palmer stops again, the chalk in hand. "I can't," he finally mumbles.

"Yes, you can," says Stone. "We're solving for X. Remember the formula. It's a simple equation."

Palmer drops his eyes and whispers: "It ain't simple to me."

Stone eases closer. "What's that?"

"The problem ain't simple to me."

Stone sighs, his disappointment obvious, and faces the class. "Everybody listen to me," he says firmly. "I'm not trying to pick on Palmer, but this is what happens when you don't pay attention in class, when you don't do your homework, when you don't ask questions. You end up at the board and things that we've worked on, things that I've taught you, things that should be simple to you, aren't."

He faces Palmer again. "Isn't that right, Palmer? Things that should be simple … aren't?"

His body shaking, Palmer stares at his shoes, totally humiliated. He remembers other times at other classroom blackboards with other teachers, some nice, some not, but all of them the source of public embarrassment for him.

"Isn't that right?" repeats Stone. "Things that should be simple aren't."

Palmer faces Stone and his lips quiver as he whispers, "Yes."

"Say it so the class can hear you," orders Stone.

Palmer closes his eyes and tries to fight his shame and anger, but they're too strong a brew, and a lifetime of moments like this finally boil over. He whips the chalk against the wall, where it shatters into a hundred pieces. "YES!" he yells. "Things that should be simple aren't!"

Her face flustered, Chelsea hurries into Counselor Towe's office less than an hour later. Palmer's already there, his eyes down, sitting in front of Towe. A second later, Principal Roberts pops his head in also. "I need a full accounting of what happened," he orders Towe. "Before the day ends."

"I'll email everything to you," agrees Towe.

Ignoring Palmer, Roberts shakes his head at Chelsea and hurries out.

Staring hard at Palmer, Towe slurps from a soft drink and addresses him matter-of-factly. "All right. Palmer Norman. Eyes up so I can see you're listening to what I'm saying to you."

Palmer raises his head and Towe continues. "The facts are clear, so there's no reason to rehash what happened in class a little while ago. The question we must face is—what do we do about it?"

Palmer glances at Chelsea.

"You need to apologize," she says. "That's the first step."

Palmer nods. "I'm sorry, Mr. Towe. I got frustrated. It won't happen again. I promise."

"That's a good start," Towe says. "But one apology won't solve everything."

"I'll punish him," Chelsea assures Towe. "He'll run stadium steps until he pukes. And I promise that this, or anything like it, will not happen again."

"The student must take responsibility for his or her own actions," says Towe.

"I just did that," says Palmer, clenching his fists in his lap. "Took responsibility."

Towe stares at Palmer as he slurps from his drink. "Okay," he finally says, turning to his computer and clicking a few keys. "School policy states that an outburst of this type calls for first, an apology to all offended parties. Second, restitution for any destroyed objects or property. Third, twelve hours of mandatory counseling with me or a certified therapist of the student's choice. And last, we have a No-Tolerance Policy for any repeat violent offenses or any threat of a violent offense." He looks up, slurps his drink again. "Everything clear?" he asks.

Chelsea eyes Palmer and he shrugs.

"Bottom line is this," says Towe. "Mr. Norman will apologize to Mr. Stone and the math class. He will replace the piece of chalk. He will see me or someone like me for six weeks for at least two hours each week. And last, if Mr. Norman screws up again in any way, he's suspended. Done. Finished. Kaput. No school, no football, no anything. You catch my drift?"

He glances from Palmer to Chelsea, and they both nod. Towe waves a hand to dismiss them and they silently stand and leave, Palmer's shoulders slumped as they go.

When Palmer and Chelsea reach the hallway, she stops him, and they face each other. "What's up with you?" she asks, her frustration evident. "The fight on Friday night. Now this."

Palmer studies his boots.

"You hear what Mr. Towe said?" Chelsea asks. "You have no room for another mistake. If he finds out about your fight... I'm afraid to even think about it. The walls are closing in on you fast, Palmer. You get that?"

Palmer pivots to leave but Chelsea grabs his arm. "Look," she says. "I'm new here too. And I lost a football game Friday night. We're both in a tight spot right now. But we can fight through it."

Palmer pulls his arm away.

"Trust me, Palmer," pleads Chelsea. "Talk to me. About anything. Let me help you."

Palmer stares hard at her and starts to speak but then hesitates and stalks away.

A few hours later, most of the football team is on the field. Some stretch while others catch up after the weekend. A handful of stragglers drip out from the locker room, a couple moving slowly because of injuries from Friday's game. The coaches wait in the middle of the field until exactly 3:30, when Coach Paul blows his whistle and practice officially begins. The team quickly gathers around, Palmer on the edge of the group.

A football in hand, Chelsea steps forward and scans the team. Knowing the players aren't accustomed to losing, she isn't sure whether to go easy or rain hellfire and brimstone on their heads. "Okay, gentlemen," she starts, deciding to stay positive. "First thing: Last week is over. Flush it. We're not talking about it anymore."

Everyone relaxes a little as she continues. "Second, this is a bye week, so we can all rest up, recover from injuries."

The players nod, letting their guard down a little more. But Chelsea's next words jerk them quickly back to attention. "But know this," she says, her face tightening. "A bye week doesn't mean it's a 'jerk-around and waste-time' week. Or an 'act-like-an-idiot and get-in-trouble week.' Use your time wisely. We clear on that?"

The players stand straighter and Chelsea turns to Coach Paul. "Coach Paul has the schedule."

Paul holds up a stack of notecards. "Here's the outline for the week!" he shouts, handing out the cards. "Plus, we'll e-mail it to you, text it, leave you a voice mail. No excuse for you to miss anything." He faces Chelsea again.

"We'll practice light today," she says. "Harder on Tuesday, Wednesday, and Thursday. Friday and the weekend are days off. Return to the grind on Monday. Any questions?"

Nobody responds. Chelsea's eyes move from one player to the next as she stares around the circle. "Make the most of your free time, gentlemen," she says firmly. "If your body hurts, take extra treatment. If your grades suck, study more. If you're fighting with your girlfriend—well, I have no advice on how to deal with that."

The team laughs. Chelsea stops and everyone stills. "Okay." Her voice rises as she concludes. "We need to win three games to earn a championship ring that you'll wear with pride the rest of your lives. Zone in hard right now! Prepare your mind and body! Do that and nobody can stop us!"

She faces Swoops. "Swoops, break us down!"

Swoops hustles to the center of the circle. "Championship on three!" he yells.

"One, two, three! Championship!" The team shouts and breaks away, everyone headed to their practice groups.

Chelsea hurries to Palmer and tosses him the football. "Come with me," she orders.

"Where to?"

"Don't ask questions."

Palmer drops his head like a prisoner headed to death row but quickly follows her off the field, his helmet in hand.

Sitting in front of Dub's desk, Ty raises a crutch in greeting as Palmer and

Chelsea enter the office. Chelsea points Palmer to a chair beside Ty, grabs the Playbook from the desk, and drops it in front of Palmer. "Here's the deal," she tells him. "We keep working on the Playbook because you'll eventually figure it all out."

She turns and pulls three thin binders from a desk drawer and hands one to both guys. "But since we have to win the next game and Palmer is starting, we'll focus on these plays for right now." She holds up her binder.

"Whoa. Wait," Palmer says, not believing what he just heard. "I'm doing what?"

"You're starting at quarterback in the quarterfinal."

"I ain't ready for that." He lays his binder down, but Chelsea grabs it and hands it back.

"I've drawn up twelve plays," she explains. "In this binder." She points to it. "Six run plays and six passes. We've got two weeks. We'll practice these twelve until you can run them in your sleep. Open the binder."

Too shocked to argue, Palmer slowly obeys and flips through the binder. Twelve pages. Twelve plays. Palmer closes the pages and faces Chelsea. "Just twelve plays," he says. "You think I'm a moron."

"Would I make you the starter if I thought you were a moron?"

Palmer thumbs through the pages again, trying to decide what to say. *Do I even want to start? To deal with this pressure?*

Ty speaks for the first time. "We might win the next game with twelve plays," he offers cautiously. "But a championship? Not likely."

"I agree," says Chelsea. "That's why we learn the plays in here." She lifts her binder. "But also keep pounding on this." She raises the Playbook.

A bad thought enters Palmer's head. "What if I can't learn the twelve?" he asks, recalling his math class embarrassment.

"I have confidence that you can," says Chelsea.

Palmer stares hard at Chelsea. "Look," he says, fear in his voice, "what happened in math this morning? This feels the same to me. Another humiliation waiting to happen. Only it'll happen in front of thousands of people instead of a classroom. I can't. . . can't do it." He lays the binder on the desk.

"What happened in math?" asks Ty.

Palmer drops his head. "I'm a bad bet, Coach," he says to Chelsea.

"We can change that," she counters. "You, me, and Ty. Together, we can make you a good one."

"I'll quit for good this time if you try to force me," says Palmer, his mind made up.

Chelsea leans towards him. "Give it this week, Palmer," she says, her voice gentle. "If you still don't feel like you can handle it, I'll shift back to Johnson. Will let you completely off the hook."

Palmer looks at Ty, still unsure.

"I'll protect you, Palmer," Chelsea offers quietly. "I won't let what happened in math happen to you on the field. I promise you."

"I got you, Palmer," adds Ty.

"You got cancer, Ty," Palmer lashes out. "How you got anybody?"

"A week, Palmer," coaxes Chelsea, ignoring the harsh words.

Regretting his outburst at Ty, Palmer relents a little, picks up the binder, and flips through the pages once more. "Just twelve plays?" he asks.

"I promised Mr. Towe I'd punish you," says Chelsea. "But if you learn these plays, you won't run a step."

Palmer smiles slightly and looks at Ty. "Sorry, man," he apologizes. "Thanks for having my back."

"Keep your apologies," says Ty. "But learn the plays." Ty offers a fist bump and Palmer pounds back and looks at Chelsea, who holds out her fist and he bumps it too.

"Practice," says Chelsea, standing quickly. "We're already fifteen minutes late."

Ty laughs and Palmer shrugs and both follow her as she hurries out the door.

CHAPTER THIRTEEN

The next few days pass in a blur. Palmer practices hard every day, running sprints with the team, quarterbacking the scrimmages, again making some great plays but screwing up many others. He studies the binder and the Playbook, sometimes with Ty and Chelsea, other times just him and Ty, and every now and again, all on his own at home.

Because of his break-up with Molly, he works alone at the motel too, changing beds, cleaning bathrooms, vacuuming floors. He pops a school book open more regularly now, especially his math book, but quickly becomes frustrated and slams it shut. As always, his music remains the only thing he truly enjoys. He's adding more vocals to his instruments now, testing how he sounds as he plays his guitar or banjo. He wonders how he'll feel if he ever plays for an audience with Dirk, but the dread of visiting Lacy squashes that idea, and the excitement that comes with it, in a hurry.

Chelsea stays busy too, her whistle blowing at practices, her eyes turning red from watching hours of video, her fingers jotting down ideas in her notebook as she tries to figure how to beat the Knights' next opponent. At home at night, she relaxes, at least a little, at her workbench, picking gemstones, threading a necklace, hooking stones to a bracelet. Periodically, she checks her phone, searching for a call or text from Bo but finding nothing. Occasionally, she considers calling him, but always shuts the phone off before she does. To keep her stress at bay, she jogs a few miles almost every day, even as the weather turns colder.

Ty spends a lot of time in the cancer center, his chemo bag dripping poison into his body in hopes it'll kill the even-more-dangerous tumors feasting on his bones. He researches bone cancer and becomes an expert on the causes, the treatments, and the chances of living or dying. He keeps up with his studies too, unwilling to let a deadly disease shove him to second place in his quest to become valedictorian of his class.

When not studying or receiving chemo, Ty teaches Palmer the Playbook, sometimes encouraging, sometimes pushing, but always pressing on. Palmer confuses him, not because he struggles so much to learn the plays but because he tends to give up so easily, to let his frustrations defeat him. At times, Ty wants to quit on Palmer too, but he figures if he can fight cancer and not bend the knee, he can certainly keep faith with Palmer. Fortunately, in the days before the quarterfinal, Tanya shines as Ty's primary highlight. Though Palmer and the chemo grind him down, Tanya lifts him up, her laughter a tonic when he hurts the most.

Finally, the bye week passes and Friday afternoon arrives. The clock over the bar at Georgio's reads 4:17. Without a football game that night, there's no pregame traffic to fill the place, and the few people who have gathered talk quietly, without stress or hurry. Right at 4:18, a thin man in his sixties, with tan skin and eyes the color of rain, enters the front door, ambles to the bar, plops on a seat, and swivels his chair, his back to the bar. A brown, designer work-out suit fits nicely on his trim torso and a red, Atlanta United soccer cap covers most of his salt and pepper hair.

The brunette bartender, her hair pulled back in a red bandana, approaches the man from behind.

"What's up?" she asks.

The man swivels around and checks her out. "Is it always this quiet here?" he asks.

"It's not even six," the bartender counters. "And no football game tonight. What'd you expect?"

The man removes his cap and rubs his hands through his hair. "Let's do an Old-Fashioned."

"You want the cherry on top?"

"Surprise me." He swivels around again and studies the room. The bartender brings him a glass of water and places it on a coaster. Adds a bowl of trail mix beside the water. "Quaint village you have here," the man says, facing the bartender once more.

"We like it," says the bartender.

"Got a bit of a Mayberry vibe to it."

"Mayberry?"

He raises an eyebrow. "You too young for the reference?"

"I'll google it."

She mixes his drink. Sits it on another coaster. He lifts it and sips. "I hear you have a good football team."

"Had a good football team. Past tense. Got our butt kicked last week."

"Still going to the playoffs though."

"I'm not getting my hopes up about the playoffs."

The man sips his drink. "What you think about the woman coach? What's her name?"

"Coach Dumb? Coach Dull? No, it's Coach Chelsea Deal."

"You're not a fan?"

The bartender places both palms on the bar and leans forward. "We were undefeated till she took over."

"What's the word on her? Outside of football? You know, what kind of person is she? Girl Scout? Party girl? Betty Crocker?"

"Betty who?"

"Oh, come on," the man wails. "You're killing me. You got to know that one. Betty Crocker. Cake mixes? Recipes?"

"Oh yeah, Betty Crocker," remembers the bartender. "Was she a real person?"

The man raises his eyebrows. "Hell if I know."

"You should google that."

"Maybe I will." He sips his cocktail again as the bartender wipes the counter.

"Coach Deal eats here every now and again," she says. "But I've never served her a drink. Well, water, but that's all."

"No tips for serving water."

"Not from her at least. But that's all I know."

The man finishes his drink, pulls a card from his pocket and hands it over. "Sky Investigations. Sam Sky, CPI (Certified Professional Investigator). B.A. Criminal Justice." The bartender raises her eyebrows.

"Give me a call if you hear anything of note about the lovely Ms. Deal," says Sam.

The bartender stares at Sam as he slips a hundred-dollar bill under his empty glass and walks out.

His phone to his ear, Principal Roberts is perched at the head of a conference room table as Chelsea enters. Les Holt sits on one side of the table. Across from him is Eva, a white ribbon in her hair. Vanessa waits by Eva, and Phil occupies the seat opposite Roberts.

Roberts shuts off his phone, pulls out a chair for Chelsea, and hands her a bottle of water. She opens it and turns to Phil. "I've never officially met you," she says, shaking his hand.

"Phil Potter," says Roberts. "Owns fifty plumbing franchises in north Georgia. Paid for our football fieldhouse and scoreboard. We couldn't do it without Phil."

Chelsea smiles and takes her seat.

"Let's move on with it, George," says Holt. "I got places to go and people to do."

Roberts laughs. "That's funny, Les. Probably true too." He clears his throat. "All right. It's been a week since last Friday's loss, enough time for our emotions to settle some. So now, unofficially, we're here this afternoon to discuss a couple of concerns before the next game."

Everybody looks at Chelsea. "What kind of concerns?" she asks, completely blindsided by the called meeting.

"We lost last week for the first time in two years," laments Holt, instantly on the attack. "Isn't that enough of a concern for us to meet?"

"To be fair," says Vanessa, "our starting quarterback was out."

"Yes, unfortunately," says Holt. "Is Ty doing okay?"

"So far, so good," says Vanessa.

Roberts pulls a pencil from behind his ear and focuses on Chelsea again. "Are we to understand you're starting Palmer Norman in the quarterfinal next week?" he asks her.

"I believe he has the most upside, so 'yes.'" Chelsea remains on guard, even as she fights to stay calm.

"But Johnson is the steadiest," counters Holt.

"That's true," says Chelsea. "He's the most experienced."

"I hear Palmer's struggling to learn the plays," interjects Phil, his tone even.

"He is," agrees Chelsea. "But I'm scaling things back until he can get up to speed."

"Ty's working with him almost every day," interjects Vanessa.

"Is it smart to pare the Playbook down?" Holt presses Chelsea.

Chelsea pauses before she answers and tries, for the first time really, to decipher Holt. What's his angle? He obviously wanted Buck as the interim head coach. But what connects the two of them? Is it just that she's female, and both dislike that? Or is something else going on? Something she doesn't know about yet?

"I think dialing back the Playbook is the best option for now," she finally answers Holt. "I want Palmer to know enough plays to feel confident but not so many that it confuses him, sabotages our chance to win."

"I've heard he's rough around the edges," Holt notes. "Had some kind of blow up in math class?"

Chelsea balls her fists in her lap. "Yes, he had a meltdown on Monday. He and I met with Mr. Towe and ironed some things out."

Holt grunts. "You think it's wise for a kid that unstable to be leading the team into the playoffs?"

Chelsea's face reddens and, slowly opening her energy drink, she takes a sip. She can handle Holt when he comes after her, but taking pot-shots at Palmer steps beyond the pale. She speaks slowly but strongly when she responds, her eyes never leaving Holt. "Palmer isn't Ty," she concedes. "We all understand that. But to call him unstable ... that's out of bounds."

Holt lifts an eyebrow as he places both hands on the table. "Maybe it was a bad choice of words. But you're awfully intense about it. Did I hit a nerve?"

"Back away, Les," Eva interjects, verbally slapping Holt's hand. "Nobody here wants to make this personal."

Holt eyes Eva a moment but then leans back as Roberts speaks to Chelsea. "So, you're pushing your chips to the middle of the table, betting everything on Palmer Norman?"

"I am," says Chelsea, still angry at Holt but no less decisive about Palmer. "His athleticism makes us more competitive than Johnson ever could."

"What does Dub think?" asks Holt, a bit chastised but still focused.

"He won't say," answers Chelsea. "I asked him point-blank, and he said it's my decision."

"What about Buck?" asks Roberts, rolling his pencil.

"Buck disagrees with my plan."

"You believe you know, better than Buck, what's best for the team?" presses Holt, back on the attack.

Chelsea grits her teeth. "I'm not saying I know better than anybody."

"Let me get this straight," Holt pushes again. "We're laying the whole season on the line and you, with one game under your belt as head coach, are ignoring the advice of a man with over two decades of coaching experience?"

Chelsea's face turns beet-red now, but her voice stays steady as she answers. "Not ignoring it. Just not accepting it."

"You think Buck's dumb?" asks Holt, like a prosecutor interrogating a hostile witness. "That we're dumb? Because we're mountain people?"

Chelsea stares dead straight at Holt, her eyes blazing. She's had enough and her voice growls as she responds. "I'm not sure how you reach that conclusion, Les. Just because I disagree with Buck. But no, I don't think anyone here is dumb."

She glances around the table and her voice softens as she looks at Eva. "Especially not because they're mountain people," she continues. "I love it up here. This town, the beauty, the pace. I love my players—how hard they work."

The room falls quiet for a moment and Chelsea again sips her drink.

"Please forgive Les." Eva finally speaks, her tone soothing as she faces Chelsa. "He tends to get testy when we lose."

Her composure regained, Chelsea looks deliberately at each person in the room and speaks quietly but with steel in her voice. "Here's the deal," she says. "You called me into this meeting with no prior notice. And no warning of its purpose."

She eyes Holt and her anger flares again. "You interrogate me like I've committed a crime." She looks back at the others. "So, I'll give it to you straight. The Board hired me for this job. And I'm doing what I think is best for the team. Your choices are clear—either choose another coach or stand down and let me do what you hired me to do."

Everybody falls dead still. Holt glances at Roberts like a drowning man hoping for a life jacket. But Roberts stays silent. After a few seconds, Eva clears her throat. "Anybody else have something in their craw they want to spit out?" she asks. "Anything else they want to ask Coach Deal? Say to her?"

Nobody speaks.

"All right," says Eva. "I suggest we end this meeting and let Coach Deal return to her duties."

Nobody objects, so Eva stands and everyone else follows, the room still silent. Chelsea rushes out without a word and Eva quickly follows. When Chelsea reaches the hallway, Eva calls to her. "Slow down, Coach," she says. "Anger won't fix anything."

Chelsea turns, her eyes hot. "I'm way past anger, Eva. I'm. . ." She slaps the wall with both hands.

"Meet me in the park in fifteen minutes," says Eva. "The bench by the pond. We'll feed the ducks and watch the sun go down."

Chelsea slaps the wall again. "I'm in no mood to feed ducks!"

"I'll bring the bread. You'll enjoy it ... I promise."

Chelsea slaps the wall a third time, turns, and hurries away.

Back in the conference room, Vanessa, Phil, and Roberts stand around the table. "That went south in a hurry," says Phil.

"She is feisty," says Roberts. "Maybe that's a good thing."

Holt glances at his watch. "One more thing, before I forget: I didn't mention it in the meeting because I don't know the details, but I've heard that a fight broke out after the game last week."

"A fight breaks out after almost every game," says Phil.

Everybody chuckles for a second, but Holt quickly shuts them down. "A fight involving Palmer." Holt stares at Vanessa. "And Ty."

"Ty?" asks Vanessa.

"I'm gathering more information, but yes. Palmer's girlfriend got mixed up in something. Palmer jumped in to protect her, and Ty backed him up."

Vanessa wags a finger at no one in particular. "I knew from the jump that Palmer was trouble."

"Trailer-park trash," says Holt.

"That's a little harsh, Les," says Phil.

Holt shrugs.

"Nobody filed a report on a fight," says Roberts.

"I don't expect anybody will," says Holt. "Chelsea swore everybody to secrecy."

"Chelsea was there?" asks Vanessa.

"She broke it up," says Holt. "Told everybody to keep their mouths shut."

"That's a serious charge, Les," says Phil, his face dark.

"We have protocols on fighting," says Roberts, his tone somber. "If Chelsea knew about this and didn't report it, that's a serious breach of policy."

"Who told you about this, Les?" asks Phil.

Holt shakes his head. "I'm not at liberty to say."

"This stays here for now," Roberts instructs everyone. "Until I can dig around some, find out what actually happened."

"I agree," Vanessa jumps in. "Something like this could spin in a lot of directions if the rumor mill cranks up."

Roberts turns to Les. "Like I said, leave this with me. You clear on that, Les? No shenanigans from you."

"My lips are sealed."

"That's it," concludes Roberts. "I'll find out what happened, and we'll meet again if needed."

Less than an hour later, Vanessa hauls a load of groceries to the counter in her kitchen and starts putting them away. Ty limps in, crutches under his arms.

"How was chemo today?" Vanessa asks.

"Same as usual. Tanya drove me."

"Don't let that girl hook her claws into you."

"She's coming over in a few minutes," Ty says, ignoring Vanessa's warning.

"Claws, Ty. Avoid them at all costs."

"I'm starving. Can you scramble some eggs?"

Vanessa points him to a chair as she pulls eggs from the fridge and a pan from a cabinet. "What's this I hear about a fight last Friday night?"

"What?"

"I know about the fight, Ty," says Vanessa as she pours olive oil into the pan. "You and Palmer." She cracks the eggs, pours them into the pan, throws some mushrooms and spinach in, puts the pan on the stove.

"Nobody was hurt," says Ty, minimizing what happened. "Nothing to worry about."

"You lied to me about tripping. The scrapes on your elbows."

"I'm sorry, Mama. It didn't seem important. No reason to bother you."

"I hear Coach Deal swore everyone to secrecy."

"She asked Molly what she wanted, and Molly insisted that we say nothing."

Vanessa grabs orange juice from the fridge, pours a glass, and hands it to Ty. "I want you to steer clear of Palmer from now on," she says.

"What you mean?"

"He's not good for you. You can work with him here or at school. But no more socializing."

"I'm seventeen-years-old, Mama," argues Ty, asserting himself a bit. "Too old for you to pick my friends for me."

Vanessa flips the eggs. "Your friends reflect who you are, Ty. You know that. And Palmer is... well, he's not the kind of friend you need. He's—"

"He's what, Mama?" Ty turns defensive. "He's poor? Academically challenged? From a bad family? White?"

Vanessa dumps the eggs onto a plate, which she slides to Ty. "Help him learn the Playbook. But that's it! Don't argue with me anymore!" She points to the eggs and storms out.

Eva sits on a two-person bench by a pond the size of a small-town airfield. A gaggle of ducks floats near the shore a few feet from the bench. Eva tears pieces of bread off a loaf and tosses them to the ducks. Dressed in khaki slacks and a green sweater but no jacket, Chelsea walks up beside her. Eva pats the bench and hands her a piece of bread. Chelsea plops down and throws bread to the ducks. "Glad you could join me," Eva says quietly.

Chelsea breaks off more bread and tries to relax. "It's a gorgeous afternoon."

"Supposed to freeze soon after dark." Eva tosses bread.

"You grow up in Rabon?" asks Chelsea, her mood slowly adjusting to Eva's.

Eva nods. "Left after I became a nurse, joined the Navy."

"When did you move back?"

"After I retired, Jack and I started a medical supply business. We moved here to set it up. Over twenty-five years ago."

"How long since Jack passed?"

"Nine years."

Chelsea tosses another piece of bread. "How'd you get interested in football?"

"Jack played in college. When we moved here, we both became involved. In a town like this, football creates identity—a tribe if you will. And you find more integration—racial, economic, gender—at a football game than anywhere else, churches and schools included."

Chelsea stares at the sun dropping on the horizon. "I never thought of it that way."

They both throw bread at the ducks, their motions synchronized. "What's the story with Les Holt?" Chelsea asks.

Eva chuckles. "He's the president of the largest sports equipment and apparel firm in the Southeast. Every sport you can imagine. Hundreds of millions a year in revenue, and he makes bank on every piece sold."

"And he supports Buck because..."

Eva chuckles again. "Buck introduced him to his little brother Roger, the head coach over at Tech, years ago. And Roger—"

"Wait a second." Chelsea sits up straighter. "Roger Jones is Buck's little brother?"

Eva nods and waves away a duck that's walked too close.

"That explains so much!" says Chelsea, her eyes wide.

"Exactly. Buck connected Holt to Roger and Roger started doing ads for Holt's company. Holt rode that relationship to millions in sales and straight to his company's penthouse office."

"Everybody enjoys a cut of the pie." Chelsea leans back, glad to know the connection.

"To stay on Roger's good side, Holt plugs Buck every chance he can."

"He doesn't hate me because I'm a woman!" Chelsea says, surprised at the finding. "Holt promotes Buck because that's his hook-up!"

"Don't give him too much credit," laughs Eva. "I expect it's a little bit of both."

"That giant Hummer he drives?"

Eva chuckles again. "You know what they say about a man who drives a big car."

They laugh together and throw more bread to the ducks.

Suddenly feeling sick, Ty stretches out in his bed as Tanya walks in. He groans slightly, puts a hand on his stomach, rolls sideways, and moans louder. Tanya rushes over.

"What's wrong?" she asks.

"In the bathroom, under the sink, there's a tray they gave me in case this happens."

Tanya runs for the tray as Ty moans again. Seconds later, she returns just in time for him to retch into the tray. When he's finished, she runs back to the bathroom, quickly returns with a wet cloth, and wipes his face as he balls up in pain.

"I understand now," he groans.

"What?"

"Why some people refuse to do chemo." He closes his eyes and fights the pain.

"I'll get your mama," she says.

He throws up again as she rushes out.

Her hands empty of bread, Chelsea stands from the bench and walks to the water's edge. Eva joins her as she stares into the pond.

"I don't have any friends here," Chelsea says wistfully.

"Friends take time," counsels Eva.

"If we lose the quarterfinal, I don't think I'll have any more of that."

"Rabon folks do like to win."

"Does half the town hate me?"

Eva tosses her last piece of bread to the ducks. "In the water, Chelsea. What do you see?" Eva points to the pond.

Confused by Eva's question, Chelsea peers into the pond. "Ducks," she answers. "Breadcrumbs."

"Look closer."

Chelsea obeys but still doesn't understand. "Algae? Scattered leaves?"

"Your reflection?"

Chelsea tilts her head at an angle to catch the dying rays of the sun. "Sure. I see that too."

"Do you like what you see?"

Chelsea stares at her face in the water and ponders the question. "I don't know," she responds slowly. "Sometimes. Most days, yes, I'm okay with me."

Eva stays quiet as the ducks drift away on the water, the last of the bread having disappeared into their stomachs. When she speaks, her words fall quietly, soothingly. "So long as *you* like what you see, then what other people think doesn't matter a damn bit."

CHAPTER FOURTEEN

The early dinner crowd at Georgio's chats quietly as people order their salads and sip from their wine glasses. With no football game to amp them up, they're more subdued than usual, their emotions set at a lower voltage. On the stage, Dirk sets up his microphone, then adjusts two small spotlights facing him. As he stoops to pull his guitar from its case, his phone dings with a text and he checks it.

"Hey, it's Chelsea. Where are you?"

Dirk quickly texts back. "At Georgio's. Setting up to play tonight."

Another text dings and he reads it. "You got a minute?"

He responds. "Yup."

Chelsea replies. "I'll be there in a few."

Parked in a white Tesla on the street across from the duck pond, Sam Sky snaps pictures with a long-range lens as Chelsea puts her phone away and climbs into her truck. Pulling a pork rind from a bag on the passenger seat, he waits a few seconds as Chelsea starts her truck and drives away. Contentedly chewing the pork rind, he sets the camera down, grabs another pork rind, and follows as Chelsea pilots the truck toward town.

Rushing through Georgio's front door a few minutes later, Chelsea immediately spots Dirk hauling an amplifier to the platform. Quickly greeting the few people who speak to her, she hustles over to him.

"Hey," he says, putting down the amplifier. "I got fifteen minutes."

"Can we walk outside? I'll make it quick."

Dirk picks up a faded brown bomber jacket from the corner of the stage and slips it on. "That's not warm enough," he says, indicating Chelsea's outfit. "Try this." He pulls a blue scarf off a wall hook behind the stage and wraps it around her neck.

"Thanks," she says.

"I can't let you freeze."

Snuggled warmly in his Tesla, Sam Sky snaps pictures as Chelsea and Dirk exit Georgio's and walk into the cold. Chelsea pulls Dirk's scarf tighter as they amble to the Rabon Springs fountain and stop. Sam keeps clicking as they stand close and stare into the water.

Finally satisfied, Sam puts down the camera, pops another pork rind, and picks up his phone. "Hey," he says. "I've been here since yesterday. Think I have enough."

"You've finished your other work too? All of it?" asks a man on the other end.

"Every nook, every cranny."

"What's your assessment?"

"Everything checks out, just like we expected."

"Good to hear. Meet me in two hours at the office."

"Can do."

"One more thing."

"Yep?"

"What's a cranny?"

"A man of your pedigree should know that." Sam hangs up, starts the car, and drives slowly down the street and heads out of town.

Chelsea shivers as she stares into the water spraying from the fountain. "Eva told me it was going to freeze after dark."

"I like the cold. Makes me feel alive. Want my jacket?"

"I'll survive with just your scarf." She lifts it up and around her chin and ears.

"I think it looks better on me."

She pokes him in the ribs.

"Sit?" he asks, pointing to the ledge around the fountain.

"Sure."

They ease down, their bodies close. "I don't know how much Palmer tells you," Chelsea begins.

"He tends to keep his words spare."

"Did he mention the episode in his math class? The fight after the Longhorn game?"

Dirk shakes his head. "Mr. Towe left me a message to call him. I figured it was grades again. Didn't call back."

"Here's the short version." Chelsea pours out the story, her tone concerned as she lays everything out. Dirk watches her as she talks, notes her fear for Palmer, her desire for him to find his way off the path he's following. When she's finished, she folds her hands in her lap and stares into the fountain.

"Sounds like he's had a rough time of it lately," Dirk says quietly.

"That's an understatement."

"I wish I could do more to help him."

"He just seems so alone."

Dirk pushes back his hair. "I'm headed back to Nashville on Monday. My band got a good gig. Might last a couple months, maybe a lot longer."

Chelsea faces him. "Any way you can postpone that?"

Dirk shakes his head. "Wish I could. But if I don't play, I don't get paid, and Palmer and I both end up on the street. Or the state puts him into foster care."

"He needs support right now," counters Chelsea. "Where's his mom? Dad? Other family?"

Dirk faces her. "That's not in his files?"

"The files have his grades and whatever he or a parent or social worker report to us."

"I wasn't aware." Dirk checks his watch. "I'd like to tell you his backstory, but I have to go back inside. Can you come back later? I'll take a long break, fill you in on everything I know."

"I can make that work."

They stand and head back to Georgio's. At the door, they stop, and Dirk unwraps his scarf from her neck. "Didn't think I'd forget this, did you?"

"You could've used it as an excuse to see me again."

Dirk playfully slaps the wall. "Man, I'm slipping. Didn't think of that."
"See you later," she says.
"I'm watching you walk away."
She waves at him without looking back.

Soft jazz is playing inside Holt's Hummer as he wheels around a mountain curve. Smoke floats around his face as he puffs a cigar. His phone rings and he taps a button on the steering wheel and answers the call. "Hey, Chief," says Holt. "How's it hanging?"

"It's a beautiful night in Atlanta," says Chief. "Dinner at the Chop House before heading to the theater. I think it's *Nutcracker* night."

"Big city life," says Holt. "God, how I hated it."

Chief laughs. "On your lawyer friend. Chelsea Deal. I talked to a guy who retained her former law firm for some work a while back."

Holt knocks cigar ashes into the ashtray. "What's the down and dirty?"

"This might be worth a face-to-face."

"You heard something juicy?"

"Not *National Enquirer* scandal, but juicy enough for Rabon, I expect."

Holt pulls to a redlight. "How's your schedule Monday?" he asks, his adrenaline high with excitement.

"Golf in the afternoon if the weather cooperates."

"Atlanta Country Club?"

"Tee time at one o'clock. Bring some of those high-dollar cigars you like."

Holt laughs. "You hand me something I can use, and I'll buy you a whole box of high-dollar cigars." He clicks off, and puffs happily on his cigar before pulling through the green light ahead.

People fill every seat in Georgio's. Silverware clinks and servers hustle here and there. The noise from the dinner conversations creates a warm buzz. Though it's cold outside, everyone feels snug and comfortable, eating and drinking to their heart's content. The clock on the back wall shows 9:29.

Dirk and Palmer are performing on-stage, Dirk singing lead, Palmer back-up. Both play guitars as they belt out a Luke Combs tune. They're simply dressed—blue jeans and flannel shirts. Bridget and a couple of her friends, sitting at the table directly in front of Palmer, lead the applause as the song ends.

Smiling widely, Dirk wipes his face and thanks the crowd. "Appreciate that nice applause. It's cool to be with you again."

He turns and points to Palmer. "I have my nephew Palmer with me tonight. He's pretty good, huh?" The crowd applauds again, and Bridgett whoops it up along with her friends.

The front door opens and Chelsea enters, wearing a black wool coat and a red scarf around her neck. Dirk immediately spots her and speaks again to the crowd. "I have an idea," he says. "Since I'm thirsty and Palmer's ready to try it solo, I think I'll leave it with him and find myself a beer!"

He waves Palmer to the center microphone, but Palmer shakes his head. Dirk turns to the crowd again. "What you think? He ready to go it alone?"

Bridget and her friends stand and clap and the crowd joins in, whistling its approval. Dirk motions to Palmer again and his face turns red.

"Come on!" Dirk shouts over the crowd. "Give the people what they want!"

Palmer glances at Bridget as the crowd keeps clapping and she jumps up and down. Giving up, Palmer steps to the center of the stage. Dirk raises the microphone, pats Palmer on the back, and eases off the platform.

Giving himself a moment to calm down, Palmer adjusts his guitar strap and clears his throat. "So, uh, this is unexpected," he stammers. "I, uh, didn't know I'd be on my own tonight. But uh, this is what they call my debut." He fiddles a moment with the microphone.

At the back of the room Dirk and Chelsea ease onto bar stools. She unwraps her scarf and Dirk helps her remove her coat.

"This is, uh, the original version of 'Me and Bobby McGee,'" says Palmer. "Kris Kristofferson wrote it." He clears his throat again.

Dirk and Chelsea face Palmer as he begins to play, then sing. From the first note, it's magical. The audience falls quiet, immediately enthralled. Bridget and her friends, silent for once, watch in open-mouthed amazement.

Chelsea's eyes widen as she listens. "Wow!" she says. "He's amazing."

"I knew he was good," agrees Dirk, his eyes fixed on Palmer. "But I had no idea he was this good."

"It's like he's done it a thousand times."

"Maybe he will before he's done."

They listen quietly for a long minute, both entranced. "I wish he was this smooth at quarterback," Chelsea finally whispers.

"Maybe he will be before he's done."

Chelsea leans closer. "I hate to leave this, but is there a place where we can talk?" she asks.

"I bought a new truck this week."

"I thought you were a starving musician."

"Things are looking up a little."

"A new truck works fine."

Principal Roberts, in a light jacket but no hat, and slippers minus socks, walks a tiny dog around a circle in the front yard of his red-brick ranch home. The dog sniffs a bush, a tree, another bush, another tree. "Come on, Tab," urges Roberts. "We do this every night. You should know what tree you want to use by now. I'm freezing my nuggets off out here."

Tab sniffs, runs, reaches the biggest tree in the yard, a thick oak, and lifts a leg. Roberts' phone rings and he quickly answers, his fingers numb in the cold. "Hey, Buck," he says. "What's happening?"

"I been thinking."

"Good to know. About what?"

"I understand you've heard about the fisticuffs that Palmer got into last week."

"Holt mentioned a rumor today, yes. But I haven't had a chance to do any digging yet."

"What if I can point you to an eyewitness?"

"Protocol would demand that I talk to that eyewitness." Tab puts his front paws on Roberts' knee and whines.

"Ask Coach Paul if he knows anything about it," instructs Buck.

"Coach Paul?" Roberts scratches Tab between the ears.

"It's come to my attention he might have been there. Helped Chelsea break it up."

"Paul's a straight arrow, Buck. Can't imagine he's kept this to himself."

"He's up Chelsea's skirt, George. Too gob-smacked by her to do anything but what she wants him to do."

"I like Paul, Buck. Would hate for this to blow back on him."

"Yeah, well, just so it doesn't blow back on me or you."

"Roger that." Roberts hangs up and leads Tab back into the house.

The wind whirls outside as Dirk and Chelsea climb into his truck. Christmas lights illuminate the wreaths wrapped around the streetlights on the square. Dirk turns on the truck and its heater.

"Nice," says Chelsea, admiring the interior. "Leather seats and everything." She rubs the seats. "I love that new truck smell."

"You don't have a male companion tonight?"

"We're here to talk about Palmer," she says quickly, not wanting to veer off track. "Not the whereabouts of my male companion."

"It was worth a shot."

Chelsea laughs before turning serious. "About Palmer. What's his story?"

Dirk adjusts the heater and faces her. "Okay. First, I do believe he has a learning issue, but I don't know what. He says he was assessed years ago, but he's murky about the results."

"You think he'll talk to me about it?"

"Not likely. He's got trust issues, especially with women."

"Mama troubles?"

"Oh, God yes. My sister, Lacy. Addicted to opioids. At least one suicide attempt. Several petty crimes. Has another fifty days or so in court-ordered rehab. Probation to follow."

Chelsea pauses to let the information sink in, then continues. "What about his dad?"

Dirk drops his head. Something bangs on the truck. Dirk turns. Palmer is there, standing by his door. Dirk rolls down the window.

"You left me in there by myself!" accuses Palmer.

"You were doing great! Give me another minute?"

Palmer glares at Chelsea, his eyes hot.

"A minute," insists Dirk.

Pivoting quickly, Palmer stalks off as Dirk rolls the window back up.

"What happened to Palmer's dad?" asks Chelsea.

Bridget and her friends stand between Palmer and the door as he reaches Georgio's front porch.

"You're amazing, Palmer," coos Bridget, her blue eyes bright in the porch light.

"Thanks." Palmer tries to step past her but she blocks his way. "I need to go back inside," he says.

Bridget doesn't move. "I hear you're single now."

"Yeah, I guess." He stares at his shoes, confused by seeing Dirk and Chelsea together, and worried what Dirk might be telling her.

"You scared of me, Palmer?" asks Bridget, easing closer.

He shakes his head as Bridget fingers a button on his shirt. "Maybe you should be."

"I need to go," insists Palmer. "Back on stage."

Bridget hands him a napkin smudged with lipstick and points to a phone number on it. "Call me. For real. It'll be fun."

She and her friends giggle and run down the steps as Palmer pockets the napkin and rushes through the door.

Dirk stares at his steering wheel as wind whips around his truck. "Lacy shot Palmer's dad," he says softly. "Killed him. Palmer was six."

"Poor kid. No wonder he seems angry most of the time."

Dirk faces Chelsea. "Lacy claims it was accidental. But I don't think it matters to Palmer either way."

"It's a wonder he's not in jail or something. Dealing with all of that. It's tough to hear, much less live through."

"You can't tell him I told you."

Chelsea puts a hand on his. "I'll help him, Dirk. I promise. Any way I can."

An Atlanta building at least fifty stories high and decked out with Christmas lights and red bows looms over an almost-empty parking lot. Pulling into a space near the building, Sam parks his Tesla, hops out, hustles to a side entrance, scans his thumb over a security pad, steps inside to an elevator, and punches the button to the top floor. At the top, he leaves the elevator and strides into an office complex at the end of the hall. Plush sofas, hardwood floors, and chic lighting dominate the lobby. A large clock with a sun-dial face reads 9:55.

Reggie Tillis, an immaculately groomed, athletically slender man in his mid-forties dressed in a tailored, pin-striped suit, greets Sam with a handshake and ushers him into an interior office. The ultra-modern furniture in the office matches that in the lobby: a standing desk, all-glass, ergonomic seating, a small coffee-maker, and a gleaming beverage cooler in a corner. A wall of windows overlooks the city. A picture of Reggie wearing a University of Michigan football uniform and standing on the field at the Rose Bowl hangs on one wall. A picture of Reggie with Roger Goodell, the National Football League Commissioner, in business suits in Mercedes-Benz Stadium, fills another.

Sam hands Reggie a thumb-drive and Reggie quickly inserts it into a laptop on his desk. Sam walks to the fridge, pulls out two bottles of coconut water, and hands one to Reggie as he studies the information on the laptop. Sam sits, sips water, waits. Finally, Reggie looks up and nods. "I agree," he says.

"Do we move on her now?"

Reggie glides to the window and stares out. "Not yet. Our timing must be perfect. We don't want to spook her."

"I don't think she's a woman who's easily spooked."

"The thing with her brother?"

"That's the touchstone. The leverage."

Reggie faces Sam. "Let's not think of it that way. Call it the wellspring—that's better. The source."

"When do we push the button?"

"Soon, Sam, really soon."

They shake hands again and Sam heads out and down the hall, the coconut water still in his hands.

CHAPTER FIFTEEN

A sign on the wall behind the cash register reads, "Patty's Pancake House." A picture, hanging by the sign, shows a buxom, red-headed woman in a brown apron holding a giant spatula. A fire burns in a stone fireplace on the back wall. A stuffed deer head with a Christmas wreath hanging around its neck stares down from above the fireplace.

Principal Roberts sits with Coach Paul in the booth nearest the fireplace, both of them with pancakes and eggs on their plates. Paul smothers his pancakes with molasses while Roberts spreads butter on his.

"Thanks for meeting on such short notice," says Roberts. "I know it's your first Saturday off since the season started."

Paul eats pancakes as Roberts continues. "I need to ask you about something that's a little delicate."

Paul looks up, his mouth full. "I'm an open book, George. What's up?"

Roberts leans closer. "I've been told you were present at a fight after the Longhorn game. Palmer Norman got into a scrape, and you and Chelsea broke it up."

Paul pours more molasses on his pancakes. "If such a thing did happen, and I'm not saying it did, but if it did, wouldn't I or Coach Deal have reported it? As we're bound by policy to do?"

"Perhaps you and Coach Deal forgot to report it but have since remembered the policy and will now turn in the report by Monday."

Paul eats another bite of pancakes. "If we do know of this fight, and I'm not saying we do, I suspect that Buck and Ty were there too. And if we report this hypothetical scrape, we'll have to note their presence in said filing."

Roberts eats a bite of eggs. "That would also put Buck in jeopardy for failing to follow policy," he says.

"It would put Ty at the scene as a combatant as well. Vanessa and Russell would certainly not appreciate that turn of events."

Roberts weighs his words carefully as he voices them. "This is a more complicated situation than I imagined."

"Perhaps you need to discuss this further with whoever mentioned this alleged incident to you."

Paul pours more syrup on his pancakes.

"That sounds like a reasonable suggestion," Roberts agrees. "No use stirring the waters any more than necessary."

Dressed in faded blue jeans and the same flannel shirt he wore the previous night, Palmer slouches on the sofa and stuffs his feet into his boots. Standing, he yanks a brown jacket off a hook by the fireplace and pulls it on. Finally, he lifts his backpack off the sofa and drapes it over his shoulder.

Stepping in from the kitchen, Dirk tosses him a heated pop tart. Palmer catches it and takes a bite.

"You made the right decision," says Dirk.

"A devil's bargain I'll regret soon enough."

"That attitude is exactly what you need today," Dirk says. "No extra charge for the sarcasm."

"You're quite the jokester, Uncle." Palmer bites into the pop tart again. "But you know this won't go well."

"It'll go as well as you let it."

Palmer shakes his head. "Me and Mama… it's all screwed up."

"That's in the past, kid. Doesn't have to haunt us forever."

Palmer finishes the pop tart. "I'll be back this afternoon," he says.

"You call Lacy to let her know you're coming?"

"Yep. It was a short conversation."

"Catch." Dirk tosses a set of keys to Palmer. "It's cold today. Drive my old truck."

Palmer pockets the keys. "Thanks."

"It's permanently yours, dude—the truck."

"Seriously?"

"Be nice to your mama."

"Like she's always been to me?"

Palmer eases to the door and out.

Strings of bright, white Christmas lights hang on the eaves of a small but attractive mountain house. Red wreaths decorate rounded windows on the front. Bundled in a hunting jacket, sweatpants, and a Knights cap pulled low over his eyes, Coach Paul steps onto the front steps of the porch where a plastic Santa Clause smiles at him, his cheeks lit by a light inside the plastic.

Paul punches the doorbell and steps back half a step. Moments later, the door opens and Buck, holding a cup of coffee and wearing a thick black bathrobe and slippers, appears. "This is a surprise," says Buck, sipping his coffee.

"I ought to punch you right in the mouth," Paul says, his jaw clenched.

Buck steps onto the porch and closes the door. "What's got you all riled up today?" he asks.

"You're a conniver, Buck."

Buck chuckles. "Conniver? That's the best you can come up with? People usually take the Lord's name in vain when they're insulting me."

"You told Roberts about the fight!"

Buck sips coffee. "Oh, that."

The door opens and a little boy sticks his head out. "Pee Paw," the boy says, "come back in. We're playing trains."

Buck pats the boy on the head. "I'll be right there." The boy ducks back inside and Buck turns to Paul again.

"Pee Paw?" asks Paul, surprised at the endearment.

Buck shrugs and sips coffee again. "Where were we?"

"You told Roberts about the fight," says Paul, his anger rising again. "Pointed the finger at me and Chelsea but conveniently forgot to mention your presence."

"I didn't directly say I wasn't there," shrugs Buck, not the least bit defensive. "And Roberts didn't directly ask."

Paul jerks off his cap and squeezes the bill. "You want to know why you didn't get the interim job, Buck?" he growls.

Buck pulls the belt tighter around his robe but doesn't speak.

"Me and the other coaches—all of us—we went to Eva and others on the

Board," says Paul. "Told them none of us trusted you."

Buck eyes him closely. "That was a sneaky thing to do, Paul. Didn't know you had it in you."

"We lobbied against you! To be honest, I felt bad about it until this morning. But you've shown me I was right. You're a prick and always will be!"

"I didn't know you felt that way, Paul."

"Well, I do. You selfish … you selfish—"

Buck tips his cup and pours coffee onto Paul's shoes. "I think 'son of a bitch' is the phrase you're searching for," he says.

Paul swats Buck across the chest with his cap. "I ought to whip your sorry butt!"

"Maybe you could ask Eva to help you with that."

The door opens again and a mid-forties woman holding a spotted cat pokes her head out.

"Patches is crying for you," says the woman. She holds the cat out and Buck embraces it.

"You're a cat guy?" asks Paul, more disbelief written on his face.

Buck laughs. "Get the hell off my porch, Paul. Before I take offense and kick your ass all the way to the stadium."

Paul turns, smacks Santa Claus with his cap, shoves it back on, and stomps off as Buck returns to his house.

Vanessa strides into Ty's bedroom, a tray in her hands, Russell behind her. Still in his pajamas, Ty lays in bed, sedated but not asleep, a throw-up tray beside him. His pajamas hang loosely—cloth on skin and bones. Dr. Ramirez stands beside him, a blood pressure gauge at the ready.

"We really appreciate you driving out here," Vanessa says to Ramirez. "He started throwing up again last night. We wanted to take him to the hospital, but he wouldn't let us. Said he wanted to stay home."

"Glad to come," says Ramirez. "But he will have to return to the hospital if his condition worsens. We can monitor him better there, make sure he's hydrated. You know the drill."

"Will this be a permanent thing now?" asks Russell. "The chemo making him sick?"

"Hard to say," explains Ramirez. "Chemo can be a yo-yo for some. Feel better today, worse tomorrow, better the next day."

"So tomorrow he might be fine?" asks Vanessa.

"That's certainly our hope," says Ramirez. He packs the blood pressure gauge into a black bag on the floor, shuts the bag, and hugs Vanessa. "I'll check with you again this afternoon," he says. "Call if you need me before then."

"Thanks again," says Vanessa.

"I'll walk you out," says Russell.

Russell heads out the door with Ramirez as Vanessa turns to Ty and gently nudges his shoulder. "How you feelin', son?" she asks.

Ty speaks in a whisper, his eyes closed. "Like a day-old diaper on a newborn baby."

"You're still funny." She sits down beside him.

"At least I'm home," he says. "I hate the hospital."

"It's a lovely day, Son. Warmed up a lot since daylight. Want to sit by the pool later? I'll wrap you up real tight in blankets, let you feel the sun on your face."

"I'm too tired," he says, his eyes still closed.

Vanessa gently touches his hand. "I'm so sorry, Ty. But you need to keep fighting this."

"It hurts, Mama. Every move I make. I just want to sleep."

She wipes her eyes. "You can't just give up."

He pulls his covers tighter, like he's climbing deeper into a cave. Vanessa sits silently and watches as his chest rises and falls with each breath.

Dub sits by his easel in the family room, his paintbrush busy on an avocado. The doorbell rings. "Hey, Patrice!" Dub yells. "Could you please answer the door?"

"Sure, honey!" she calls from the kitchen.

Dub dabs paint. A couple minutes later, Patrice leads Buck in. "I'll bring you guys some coffee," she offers as Buck walks over to Dub and stares at the painting.

"Thanks, honey," says Dub.

"Is this what retirement will be?" Buck asks Dub. "Avocado painting?"

"It's this or golf."

"You swing a golf club like a blind man with the hiccups."

"Thus, the avocado." Dub lays down the brush and faces Buck. "Painting is about perspective, Buck. Seeing things through a clear eye."

"Some folks say life is the same."

Dub chuckles. "That's some pretty deep thinking for a football coach."

Patrice brings in two cups of coffee. "You boys need anything else, you're on your own," she declares as she hands the coffee to them. "I have things to do." She kisses Dub on the head and walks out as Buck sits down beside Dub.

"You didn't come here to discuss my artistic endeavors, Buck," says Dub, placing his coffee on the table beside him. "What's on your mind?"

Buck sips his coffee. "Are you coaching again this year?" he asks Dub. "If the doctor gives the okay and we somehow win the quarterfinal?"

"Spit out what you came to say, Buck."

Buck pulls out an envelope and hands it to Dub. "My resignation. If you're not comin' back, I'm done after the quarterfinal."

Dub grunts, his displeasure written all over his face. "You'd quit on the boys? Even if they win?"

"It's not my preference. But I figure it this way: If we win next Friday, Coach Deal will be the toast of Rabon, the heir apparent for when you hang up your whistle. All my years here will have been for nothing."

Dub lays the envelope in his lap and eyes Buck. "Is it because she's a woman?" he asks.

Buck stares at the avocado again. "That's why they promoted her, isn't it? Good PR for the district. Shows we woke, and all that. It's just wrong, Dub, and you know it." He turns from the painting and stares at Dub.

"What about me, Buck?" Dub asks gently. "Am I here because the district is *woke*?"

Buck sips his coffee, both men's eyes locked on the other. "We're coaches, Dub," says Buck, a touch of respect in his tone. "You and me. Our blood runs the same color. And that color is the color of our team's uniform."

Dub picks up his coffee cup and speaks slowly, almost reverently as he defends Chelsea. "She played ball, Buck. Ran sprints in ninety-five-degree heat. Lifted weights. Practiced at six a.m. No different than a boy. And her one-year coaching gig before she came here? Her offense averaged fifty-three a game. Fifty-three! Hell, we're lucky to score twenty-eight."

Dub puts his coffee down and continues. "So yes, she's a woman. But she's a coach too. Her blood runs the same color as yours and mine."

Buck stares at Dub, a wry smile on his face. "That's quite a speech," he says. "You should start a side gig. Be a preacher or something."

"I can spin a few syllables when the situation calls for it."

Buck slowly rises, arranging his coffee cup on a coaster on the table. "I appreciate your time," he says, his tone conclusive, like a man saying goodbye at a train station.

"The world changes, Buck," says Dub. "No man ever steps into the same river in the same place twice. We either swim with the current or it leaves us behind."

"It just seems like I've run out my string here," Buck says, a touch sadly.

Dub pulls himself up and extends his hand. "You'd know that better than me," he says. They shake hands, each of them acknowledging the past they've shared with the firm grip of their fingers.

"What happens if we lose the quarterfinal?" Dub asks as the handshake breaks off.

"That would create an interesting conundrum," concedes Buck.

They pause a moment as the thought runs through both their heads. Buck breaks the quiet. "This conversation," he says. "Can you keep it between us for now?"

Dub nods and Buck pivots to leave but then suddenly stops, his back to Dub. "I hate that I need to ask you this," he says. "But I have to know."

Dub picks up his paint brush, faces his avocado, and speaks softly, like a parent offering bad news to a child.

"I recommended Chelsea, Buck."

"All right then." Buck walks out without another word as Dub dabs some more paint on the avocado.

Wearing a Georgia Bulldog apron over black shorts and a red sweatshirt, Russell grills three omelets in a large pan. As the omelets simmer, he hauls blueberries and yogurt out of the fridge. Quietly entering without his notice, Vanessa steps up behind him and slides her arms around his waist. "My man," she purrs. "Sexy in his apron."

Russell turns and kisses her. "Brunch is almost ready."

She smiles, backs away, and pulls plates and silverware from the cabinets. "Ty is really frail this morning," she says as she arranges the table.

"We knew he'd have hard days," says Russell.

"I'm worried about him."

"Maybe we should force him to go back to the hospital."

"He wants to stay home."

Russell lifts the omelets off the stove and slides them onto the plates. "He's just worn out," he says as he and Vanessa sit. "Puking since yesterday."

"I feel like it's more than that. Like he's lost his will to fight or something."

Russell tastes his omelet as Vanessa stares at her plate, the omelet growing cold as her eyes water. "It's just… I've never seen him like this."

Russell reaches for her hand. "We're doing everything we can."

She pulls her hand away. "We've been too easy on him. Pampered him his whole life."

"Maybe. But why not? No reason for him to grow up like we did."

Vanessa wipes her eyes and her face firms up. "I think we've made him soft. And this cancer… he won't beat it without some grit in his gut."

"Ty's got plenty of grit, Vanessa."

She stands, hands on her hips, her face set as she suddenly reaches a conclusion. "We need to take a trip," she declares.

"What are you talking about?"

"Home, Russell. We need to take Ty home."

Palmer parks his truck in front of a plain three-story brick building. A sign in front reads: "Sunrise Treatment Center." For several seconds, he just sits there, wrapped in dread. A man and two little girls hurry past his truck and disappear through the front door. Unable to put it off any longer, Palmer climbs out, zips up his jacket tight, and trudges toward the door.

Ty wakes as Vanessa strides into his room. He smiles weakly but doesn't speak as she hurriedly pulls clothes from his dresser. Russell appears at the door and stops, like he's afraid to enter when Vanessa's on a mission.

"Put these on," Vanessa orders Ty, dropping the clothes on the bed.

"No, Mama," whispers Ty. "Let me rest."

"We're taking a little trip." Her tone leaves no room for debate, but Ty tries anyway.

"I'm too sick," he insists.

"It's time, Ty."

He tries to rise. "What are you doing?" he asks.

"You need a reminder, Son." Vanessa yanks his bed covers off, grabs shoes from his closet, and drops them by his bed.

Ty looks at Russell. "Dad?"

Russell shakes his head. "Your mama wants us to take a drive."

"Where?"

"To a place you've never been. A place I never wanted you to see."

Palmer slowly approaches a freckle-faced, female security guard sitting behind a metal desk inside Sunrise Treatment Center. A set of double doors waits behind the guard as she eyes him up and down. "You have an appointment?" she asks.

"1:30 with Lacy Norman."

The guard checks a computer screen. "Show me some identification."

Palmer produces his driver's license. The guard examines it and hands it back. "You Ms. Norman's son?"

"Yes."

The guard waves him through a security scanner, then leads him through the double doors to a large, open room on the other side. A plastic Christmas tree decorated with shiny ornaments fills one corner. People sit at various gathering spaces—on sofas and chairs, and around tables. Palmer spots a man and his little girls in front of a gas-burning fireplace. A woman with long dark hair is holding a girl on each knee.

"Stay right here," orders the guard. "I'll bring your mother out."

Palmer moves toward a small table and two chairs in a corner. A checkerboard sits on the table, all the pieces in place. The guard reappears, Lacy beside her. Palmer waits as Lacy spots him and hurries his way.

The guard heads back through the doors and Lacy tries to hug him but he wants nothing to do with that, so he stays still, and the hug is awkward. Lacy quickly backs away.

"I got us a table," says Palmer, pointing to the checkerboard.

They sit. Lacy reaches for his hands and Palmer lets her hold them.

"I'm so happy you drove up," says Lacy, smiling.

"I can't stay long," Palmer says sullenly. "I got a shift at the motel starting at four."

Lacy looks him over, pride in her eyes. "You look like a man. Growing up so fast."

Palmer pulls his hands away.

"Tell me everything," encourages Lacy. "Your grades, football, work. You got a girl, I bet. How could you not? Look at you, so tall, those eyes, just like your—"

"Like Dad?" Palmer straightens at the thought, not happy that Lacy has mentioned his dad.

"Sorry, Son," she says. "I know that's a hard topic."

He leans back and tries to settle down but finds it tough. Lacy picks at a fingernail and silence falls for a few seconds.

"I be out of here soon," Lacy finally says. "Then a month in the halfway center."

"What happens after that?" Palmer challenges.

"I don't know. I'll find a job, rent us a place."

"I'm doing okay, Mama. Where I am." Palmer folds his arms and stares at her, determined to keep his distance.

"Maybe Dirk will put me up for a while," suggests Lacy. "Let me stay with the two of you."

Palmer grits his teeth and almost growls. "What if I don't want that?" he asks.

Ty's eyes are closed, his head leaning into a pillow in the back seat of Russell's car. His throw-up tray sits on the seat beside him as Vanessa drives, Russell beside her. She turns off a highway, speeds through a green light, passes blocks of seedy convenience stores, run-down houses, and fences with barbed wire on top. Graffiti covers a couple of old bridges and a string of empty, dilapidated buildings.

Ty opens his eyes. "How much longer?" he asks. "I'm feeling sick."

"Not much further," soothes Russell. "Just rest."

For another few minutes, Vanessa speeds through the broken neighborhood—rows of unkempt yards and houses with broken windows and sagging porches. Finally, she turns right and pulls into a sprawling collection of old, multi-level apartment buildings. Shattered windows stare at them, like mouths with teeth knocked out. More graffiti covers many of the doors.

African American teenagers fill two asphalt basketball courts in the center of the apartments, and a mix of older people sit, stand, and walk across the dirt areas around them. Many in the crowd hold beer bottles while others drink from brown bags with the tops of liquor bottles poking out. A couple of older men stand by a grill, smoke pouring from it. Another man staggers to the steps on one of the buildings, passes out, falls, and doesn't get up. A gaggle of men roll dice beside a barrel fire, and a handful of younger girls jump rope close by.

Vanessa parks a couple hundred feet from the basketball courts and reaches for Russell's hand. For a minute or so, they sit quietly, eyes darting here and there, watching everything all at once.

"I don't feel good," says Ty.

"We won't stay long," Russell assures him.

"This place looks dangerous," says Ty.

"It *is* dangerous," says Russell. "Has been for a long time."

Lacy tries to hold Palmer's hand again, but he pushes it away. "I got nowhere else to go, Son," she says, her eyes filling. "Nobody left but you and Dirk."

"You bring me misery every time you show up," Palmer says, anger in his tone.

"That's a rude thing to say, Son."

"Tell me where I'm wrong, Mama!" he snaps. "Remind me of a time when things were good with you around." He scowls at her, challenging her with his eyes.

"You think you too good for me now?" Her tears disappear as she fights back. "Is that it? You a big football player now? Singing with Dirk? You 'Mr. Big Man in Town' now?"

"No, Mama," he explains, as much to himself as to her. "That's not it. I'm just trying, I don't know, to find some solid ground—somewhere to stand."

"Rabon is that place?"

"I ain't sure. But at least it's quiet there. Low-key, safe."

Lacy grunts. "There ain't nowhere in this world that's safe, Son. You got to scratch and claw no matter where you are. That's the truth of it, and you old enough now to hear it plain."

For several seconds, Palmer stares at the checkerboard before leaning close and facing Lacy. "All right, Mama," he says, deciding to say something he never thought he would admit. "You want some truth? Try this. I was there, outside your bedroom door, the night you shot Dad. I saw it all."

A couple of teenage boys walk by Russell's Aston Martin and head toward the basketball courts. They glance back after they're past the car and eye Vanessa, Russell, and Ty.

"What are we doing here?" asks Ty.

"Take a good look," orders Vanessa.

The two teenagers reach a group of other guys by the courts, turn around, and stare at Russell's car.

"I wanted you to see where your dad and I grew up," says Vanessa.

"Here?"

"Yes," says Russell.

"You never told me," says Ty.

"You never asked."

Ty falls quiet, his mind jumbled.

"I lived in that building." Vanessa points left. "Your father in that one." She points right.

The teenagers at the basketball courts point at them. An older man hands the teenagers a bottle.

"Those guys, Mama," says Ty, indicating the teenagers.

"Don't stare at them, Ty," advises Russell. "You look them in the eye, they see it as disrespect."

"We fought our way out," explains Vanessa. "Your dad, his football, he worked so hard, sacrificed so much."

"What do you see, Ty?" asks Russell.

"Can we please go home?" pleads Ty. "I'm so tired."

Russell twists to face him. "You need to see, Ty. Really look. We won't leave until you do."

Ty coughs, then sits up straight and wills himself to focus. He sees the broken windows, the graffiti, the passed-out man, the barrel fire, the teenage boys now striding their way. "Poverty," he says. "I see poverty."

"What else?" presses Russell.

"Devastation? Apocalypse?"

"Dig deeper."

Hesitant to say anything more, Ty watches the boys striding toward them, the old man limping along behind. "I don't know," he groans. "Hopelessness? History?"

"Our history," agrees Russell. "Your mama's and mine. Yours too. Where you're from. Your people's history most of all. This is where we've all been for way too long."

The teenagers step closer, their faces threatening. Vanessa starts the car and Russell faces forward again.

The boys yell at them. "What you want? What you lookin' for?"

One of them picks up a rock and rushes their way.

"Get us out of here, Vanessa," urges Russell.

Vanessa whips the car around, hits the accelerator, and wheels away from the apartments, the teenagers cussing at them in her rear-view mirror.

"We fought, Ty," she says, her jaw tight. "Me and your dad. We fought our way out of there."

Russell faces Ty again. "We need you to fight too, Son. That's the blood in you. No matter how sick you get, how low you feel, you never quit, never give up. Not if you want to survive."

Ty lays his head back onto the pillow as the Aston Martin speeds down the street.

"Something woke me that night," continues Palmer, eyes looking straight at Lacy. "I heard noises, so I walked down the hall. Stopped at the door. Saw you and Dad. Him with the gun in his hand."

Palmer lowers his head, his eyes on the checkerboard, his heart churning. He's held this in for so long, he feels like he'll die if he doesn't tell the story now. Keeping what he knows caged up won't kill him with an explosion, but it's a death just the same, slowly chewing him up from the inside until he's a shell, with no life left. So, this is the time. Say it out loud, no matter who it hurts or what damage it causes.

"Dad was waving the gun around, talking out of his head," he remembers.

"He had nightmares, Son. They got really bad that last year."

"You kept begging him to give you the gun."

"He finally did," she said. "It took a while, but I talked him down like I'd done lots of times in the past."

Palmer talks slower, still finding the memories hard to voice. "I saw him give you the gun, Mama. It was over, I thought. I walked away."

"That's not the end of the story."

"I know," he recounts, his voice quicker now. "You killed him within seconds. I heard the gunshot halfway down the hall. Ran back to your room, saw him, and the blood, on the floor, the gun in your hand!"

"No, listen to me! You didn't see—"

"Stop lying!" he shouts, jumping up. "You shot him! I know what happened!" Palmer flips the checkerboard, and the pieces fly in every direction. Rushing away, he escapes the room before the last piece rolls to a stop by the woman with the two little girls.

CHAPTER SIXTEEN

S tained glass windows with rounded arches decorate both walls on the inside of a tall, steepled church. Rows of white pews stretch from the back to the front and a carpeted aisle runs down the center. A mahogany pulpit sits on a rostrum above the pews and a large silver cross hangs high on the wall behind the pulpit.

An interracial congregation fills the pews. About half the men in the crowd wear suits with dress shirts and ties, while others wear a variety of attire— everything from blue jeans and flannel shirts to khakis and sport coats. Coach Dub and Patrice sit halfway down the aisle on the right side, Dub on the aisle seat, his injured leg stretched out.

Holding Patrice's hand, Dub smiles at Ty, who sits in his wheelchair on the rostrum beside the pulpit. A blanket covers Ty's legs and he wears a dark suit, white shirt, and blue bow tie. Vanessa and Russell watch Ty from seats in the first pew, Tanya beside them, all dressed in their Sunday best.

Reverend Jeremiah Rose, a tall, regal man in his fifties, with silver hair and trim beard, stands at the pulpit, a microphone in hand. "As most of you know," he intones, "Ty Rodgers, one of our own and the quarterback for our beloved Knights, faces a mighty foe right now."

The crowd murmurs, "Oh yes, a mighty foe."

"Cancer," Rose says, turning to Ty. "Cancer."

The congregation falls quiet for a moment. Rose walks to Ty and puts a hand on his back. "A few weeks ago, before we knew about Ty's illness, I asked him if he would read our scripture today, and he said he would."

The congregation applauds. Once the members are quiet again, Rose continues. "To be honest, once I heard about Ty's sickness, I figured he would back out of that reading. But you know what?"

"What?" calls the congregation.

"Ty said he wanted to keep his commitment to me! And to you!"

The crowd applauds again and Rose pats Ty on the back. "We thank you for your example, Ty. You've given us a wonderful example of what commitment means."

The congregation applauds a final time and Rose hands Ty the microphone and steps away.

"Like Pastor said," starts Ty, his voice hoarse as he addresses the congregation, "I'm not at the top of my game right now. But I was reminded just yesterday that we can't give up hope when life knocks us down."

"Don't give up hope," says the congregation.

"I want to read a verse that means a lot to me right now," continues Ty. "It's God talking to Isaiah."

He pulls a Bible from under his blanket, opens it, clears his throat, and reads: "And God says, Fear not, for I am with you; be not dismayed, for I am your God; I will strengthen you, I will help you." Amen.

The crowd applauds again, and the choir starts singing as Ty closes the Bible and bows his head.

Dressed in black pants and a blue football jersey with the number 1, in white, on the front and back, Chelsea pilots her pickup around a curve and passes a road sign designating the town limit of Cuwalla, Tennessee. Another mile down the road, she drives past a red barn on her right and turns left. A minute later, she reaches a crossroads and spots a stone sign pointing to the North Lake Cemetery. Braking slowly, she pulls onto a gravel road leading into the cemetery, then parks, climbs out, and looks around. Nothing moves except a light breeze.

Walking quietly, Chelsea ambles down a row of tombstones until she reaches a bare oak tree. For several seconds, she stands there, her eyes staring past the oak to the blue sky above. The breeze fingers her hair, and she brushes it back, walks another twenty strides, and reaches a tombstone near a split-rail fence. There she stops, eases down, sits on the grave, and inhales deeply.

A couple minutes later, she hears a car approach from the road and turns to face the parking area as a black sedan pulls up beside her truck. A middle-aged woman climbs out of the sedan and gazes her way.

"Hey, Mama!" yells Chelsea, waving her hand. "I'm already here!"

Her mama smiles and walks toward her. She's wearing a flowing multi-colored skirt and a tan pullover sweater, and her thick hair hangs in gray curls on her shoulders. Chelsea hugs her as they come together, a long embrace, with eyes closed and a touch of unspoken sadness connecting them.

"Have a seat," says Chelsea, disengaging and pointing to the grave. "I saved you a spot."

Her mama sits and Chelsea joins her. "Thanks for letting me know you were coming," Mama says.

"I visit every year on the anniversary," says Chelsea, a note of melancholy in her voice. "Fourteen years in a row."

"It's two years since I last saw you, though."

"I know. At Dad's funeral."

"I miss him," says Mama.

Chelsea turns to the tombstone at the head of the grave where she sits and reads the inscription: "MITCHELL DEAL. LOVING SON, BROTHER, AND TEAMMATE."

"I miss them both," Chelsea says as she wipes her eyes.

"I know."

Chelsea sighs and turns back to her mama. "You doing all right these days?" she asks.

"Good enough, I suppose. Running the art gallery. Staying busy. You?"

A chipmunk darts in front of them. "I'm not at the law firm anymore," Chelsea replies.

"How are you making a living?"

Chelsea chuckles. "I'm coaching football again."

Mama laughs too. "Good heavens, girl. But I can't say I'm surprised."

Chelsea stares at the sky. "You think Dad would be proud of me?"

"Your father coached for thirty-four years, Chelsea. Probably expected Mitchell, not you, to follow him."

"Well, being a woman is a bit of a hindrance in the football coaching arena."

Mama laughs again, picks up a stick, and rolls it in her hands. The chipmunk runs back across the grave.

"What you think, Mama?" Chelsea asks. "If Mitchell hadn't died? You and Dad... all of us... Still together or not?"

Mama stares at her stick. "It's hard to say," she muses. "Your dad built a wall after Mitchell's passing. Closed himself off. Shut everybody else out."

"Walls can be easy to build," says Chelsea, feeling lonelier than she's felt in a long time.

"But hell to tear down." Mama gently digs her stick into the ground. "After your dad left, I barely heard from him again. Kind of like you."

"I'm sorry, Mama. But I don't know. Calling you, seeing you. It pushes all the hurt back up again. Feels easier not to call."

The stick stills in Mama's hands. "A family is like a sweater, I think," she says softly. "One thread pulls loose and, if you don't fix it pretty fast, the whole thing eventually falls apart."

Chelsea weighs the words but says nothing as Mama again pokes the grass with her stick.

"You still fit in your jersey," Mama says, pointing the stick at Chelsea. "You should feel good about that."

Chelsea looks down at her number. "The good old Rockets. I miss those days."

"Things were simpler then, I guess."

Chelsea leans against the gravestone and closes her eyes. "Me and Mitchell," she murmurs. "Not a lot of responsibility. Nobody really criticizing us. Just hang out, dream of the future."

Mama looks closely at her. "Sounds like you're dealing with some things."

Chelsea opens her eyes and wipes tears away, her emotions rawer by the minute. "I told myself I wouldn't do this again this year, you know? It's been such a long time."

"So, what's going on?" Mama asks.

Chelsea gathers herself. "A lot of questions to answer, Mama. Will I, should I marry a guy at my old law firm? Should I keep coaching or return to the law firm? Will my starting quarterback beat his cancer or die? Simple things like that."

"Goodness, girl. That's a plateful. No wonder you're such a wreck."

Chelsea smiles a little. "There's this kid, Mama. He's tall, with amazing athletic talent. But he's from a hard-scrabble family, no advantages. Plus, he suffers from a learning disability of some kind. I want to help him but, honestly, I'm scared to death I can't."

"Like you couldn't help Mitchell?"

Chelsea wipes her eyes a third time, stands, lays both hands on top of Mitchell's gravestone, and softly rubs the polished stone, as if soothing a baby. "I know I need to move past it, Mama," she sighs. "Need to realize that sometimes—maybe most of the time—there's not a damn thing you can do."

Mama stands too, tosses away her stick, and places her hands beside Chelsea's on the gravestone. There they stand, both of them silent as the breeze blows gently through their hair and the noonday sun lightens the darkness on their faces.

The noon bells ring out at Ty's church and, ten minutes later, the front doors open and the congregation pours out. Some of the attendees exit the grounds quickly while others linger on the front lawn to chat, laugh, and catch up with one another. An extensive line forms in front of Ty in his wheelchair on the sidewalk as worshippers seek him out to offer hugs, handshakes, and prayers.

After a few minutes, Dr. Ramirez joins the well-wishers waiting to see Ty. A heavy-set woman behind him asks Ramirez what to do about her sore foot and he answers as best he can as the line slowly moves forward. As he gets near Ty, Vanessa spots him and waves him forward to her and Russell.

"May we speak privately for a moment?" the doctor asks quietly.

"Sure," says Vanessa.

Russell pushes Ty a few feet off the sidewalk, momentarily away from the few remaining congregants.

"Okay," says Ramirez, "I planned to bring you up to date in the office tomorrow, but since we're all here, I see no need to wait."

Vanessa holds onto the back of Ty's wheelchair. "We got the scans back, after the chemo last week," says Ramirez.

"What did they show?" asks Russell, his brow dark.

"I can't sugarcoat it," says Ramirez. "The cancer has spread. We found another tumor, on the left ankle."

Vanessa starts crying.

"It's all right, Mama," Ty soothes. "We fight it. Like you said."

"Exactly," encourages Ramirez. "We keep treating it, same plan as before. Next chemo dose is tomorrow. If we don't see the progress we want soon, we consider something else, some new therapies that are showing great promise."

"What kind of new therapies?" asks Vanessa.

"We'll discuss them later," says Ramirez, "if it becomes necessary." He glances at Russell first, then back to Ty and Vanessa. They all nod, their faces determined. "I know this isn't the news we wanted," says Ramirez. "But these things happen." He pats Ty on the shoulder. "See you tomorrow."

"I'll be there."

Ramirez hugs Vanessa and walks away.

"Let's go home," says Ty. "I'm really tired."

Russell pushes his wheelchair toward the parking lot as Vanessa follows. "I'll call Coach Deal," says Russell. "Let her know you can't meet Palmer today."

"Don't do that," says Ty.

"I forbid you to waste any more energy on that boy!" orders Vanessa. "And I'm tired of arguing with you about it!"

"I'm not dead, Mama," counters Ty. "And Palmer's not ready. So, I'm not quitting until I am. Or he is."

"You just said you were tired," argues Russell.

"I am. But I'm not quitting on Palmer or Coach. No more discussion."

A thin moon hangs in the sky outside and the fireplace burns low in the front room as Palmer plays guitar on the sofa. The lamp casts shadows on the table. Dirk brings in a packed travel bag and guitar case and places both by the front door.

"What time you leavin' tomorrow?" Palmer asks, his fingers busy on the guitar.

"Before sun-up. I have rehearsal in the afternoon."

Palmer stops strumming and points to Dirk's guitar case. "Want to play awhile?"

"You gone tell me about your visit with Lacy?"

"Maybe you should ask her about it," says Palmer.

Dirk pulls his guitar from the case.

"There's this girl," says Palmer, eager to change the subject. "Bridget. She gave me her number."

Dirk steps to the hearth, props a foot up, and strums his guitar. "The blonde at Georgio's the other night?"

Palmer nods.

"You and Molly done for good?"

Palmer shrugs. "I've called her, texted, tried to talk to her at the motel. But she ain't responding."

"I don't know this Bridget girl. But my advice? Stay cautious with that one."

Palmer grins. "She likes me. And she's popular."

Dirk's fingers go still on the guitar.

"I get it. She's a honey and she's hot for your bones. But you might not be ready for a girl like that."

Palmer shrugs, not ready to accept Dirk's opinion. "I don't know, Uncle. She may be a tease, but she also seems nice."

"She dresses like she's got money."

"I heard her folks own the strip mall south of town."

Dirk strums his guitar again. "So, look," he says. "With girls? How … you know … how experienced are you?"

"I been in a bunch of sex ed classes at school." Palmer stares at his guitar strings, his fingers lightly moving on them.

"That's not what I'm asking."

Palmer grins. "You gone fill me in? Teach me the birds and the bees?"

"I don't know. But your dad's not around, so—"

"I never been with a girl, Uncle. If that's what you asking."

Dirk stops strumming and sits on the hearth. "So, you know, the bases. Which ones you been on?"

"First and second, mostly. Third a couple of times. Wasn't sure what to do while I was there, but—"

"You been online much?"

"I don't own a computer, so 'no.'"

"Ah, right, no computer. I should have thought of that. So, no home plate yet?"

Palmer stops strumming the guitar. "Are we still talking about sex?"

Dirk laughs and Palmer continues. "I been outside of home plate once or twice, but never, you know, landed there."

"Well, you did just turn sixteen."

Palmer strums his guitar again, not sure what else to say but not ready to drop the subject either. "Some guys at school brag a lot. Say they've scored a bunch of times. Embarrasses me a little, to be honest, being such a dud in comparison to them."

"Guys lie, dude. Don't feel bad because you're still innocent."

"I've just, you know, tried to respect girls."

"That attitude will carry you far in the long run. Girls get really starry-eyed when a man treats them well."

"I wonder how experienced Bridget is."

Dirk chuckles. "That girl might lead you around the bases a lot faster than you ever knew you could run."

Palmer's eyes widen. "That might be fun."

Dirk stands, his head shaking. "Might be trouble is what it might be."

Palmer grins and lays his guitar down, his mind busy thinking about Bridget as Dirk picks up his bag and leaves.

An NFL game plays on the TV in the family room, but Dub flips it off as Patrice enters and hands him a beer.

"Yesterday," Patrice says as she sits on the sofa. "Buck's unexpected visit. What was that about?"

Dub sips from his beer. "I'm not supposed to tell anybody."

"You've never kept a secret from me, dear. Not once in thirty-five years. Can't go silent on me now."

Dub places his beer on a coaster. "Promise me," he says, "you will lock it in the vault and throw away the key."

"You know I always have."

He picks up his beer and takes a swig. "Buck might quit after the quarterfinal."

"Wow!" exclaims Patrice. "That's a twist I didn't expect."

"I figured he might leave eventually. But not during the playoffs."

"Maybe we shouldn't be that surprised. He's been passed over."

Dub stands, hobbles to the window, and stares into the dark. "If Chelsea was a man, she'd be on a college staff in a couple years," he says quietly. "Maybe a head coach someday."

"If Chelsea was a man, she'd have to stop wearing those pretty earrings she makes."

"These days, maybe not." They laugh as Dub limps back to Patrice and eases down beside her. "Look," he says, taking her hand. "What if I wanted to quit? You know, retire?"

Patrice lifts her eyebrows. "I figured you for a lifer."

"Thirty-one coaching years *is* a life."

"What would you do with yourself all day?"
"I'm still ruminating on that."

Patrice smiles. "You have your painting."

"Maybe I could try golf again."

"You have your painting."

They laugh again as Dub shakes his head. "I'll tell you one thing: Once I retire, I'm never painting a fruit or vegetable again."

Double-dormer windows frame the four-poster bed in the center of Chelsea's bedroom. A ten-foot ceiling hovers above. A desk with a laptop computer sitting on it faces the back wall. Her law school diploma hangs over the desk.

Dressed in warm green pajamas and fuzzy night slippers, Chelsea perches on the edge of an ergonomic chair, her body leaning over a small work table by one of the windows. Little boxes of gemstones, jewelry chains, and hooks fill one corner of the table, and a picture of her and Mitchell, both in football uniforms, hangs on the wall above it.

Chelsea threads a thin chain through a hook and holds it up for closer examination. Her phone rings and she checks it. A text from Bo.

"Got your text," Bo says. "Can talk now, if you want."

She lays down the chain and stares at the text for several seconds. Finally, she sighs and calls Bo.

"Hey," he says, answering quickly.

"Thanks for responding."

"It's Sunday night. What else do I have to do?"

"I don't know," Chelsea says, standing and staring out the window. "Prepare for a deposition, work out at the gym, hook up with some other woman."

"I did all that yesterday."

"Cute."

"I try. What's up?"

Chelsea lays down on the bed. "I've been thinking," she says. "Maybe I was a jerk the last time we saw each other."

"Surely not."

"I want to thank you for backing off, giving me space."

The phone falls silent and Chelsea rolls onto her stomach, her elbows propped on the bed.

"Look," Bo says, "I confess I want you for myself, and I want you now. But I also want what's best for you. So, as much as it contradicts my basic nature, I'm trying to stay patient. You're spinning a lot of plates right now and your timeline is different than mine."

"I appreciate that more than you'll ever know."

"You're welcome."

She rolls back over. "What if I come to Atlanta next Saturday night?" she asks on a whim. "Make up for my recent lack of attention to you."

"I like where this is going."

"I'm not making any promises about the future, just so you understand. But we've invested almost two years in each other."

Bo stays quiet a few seconds. "One question," he finally says.

"Ask away."

"Why now?" he asks. "What's changed since I saw you?"

Chelsea stares at the ceiling, not sure she wants to reveal too much but realizing she owes him at least a hint of an explanation.

"I saw Mama," she says, leaving out that she also visited Mitchell's grave. "Maybe I need to leave some things behind. Give some other things a chance to move forward."

"Wow," offers Bo. "If I was a therapist, I'd say it sounds like you've had a breakthrough."

"I don't know if I'd go that far. But, yeah, I'm rethinking a few things."

"I'll make reservations at The Empire."

Chelsea rolls to the side of the bed. "I'll buy some new heels," she announces, her mood suddenly lighter.

"Now you're just teasing me."

"You treat me right, I might slip them off for you before the night is over."

"I won't be able to sleep tonight thinking about that."

"Down boy. Talk to you soon." Chelsea hangs up, walks back to her work table, and picks up the chain, a light smile on her face.

CHAPTER SEVENTEEN

A bright sun shines on Holt as he watches Chief line up a putt on the eighteenth green. Chief, a bald, thick-chested man dressed in bright red pants and a shirt that looks like some kid fingerpainted it with multiple colors, puffs on a cigar as he steps to the ball.

"Double the bet!" shouts Holt, hoping to break Chief's concentration.

Chief grins, blows out a plume of smoke, and knocks the ball smack into the center of the hole.

"Damn," says Holt.

Chief chuckles and turns to Holt to shake hands. "You played well today," he says as he blows smoke into Holt's face.

"Don't patronize me," grouses Holt as they amble towards the golf cart. "You won 640 bucks off me."

"Pocket change to a man of your means."

They drop their putters into their golf bags, hop into the golf cart, and head toward the club house. "You're buying drinks," says Holt.

A couple of minutes later, they step off the cart and into the club restaurant. Giant windows rise to the ceiling, framing a rustic bar and grill in the dining room. Rich brown beams cross the ceiling and wooden fans and lights complete the décor. The sun glistens off a lake not far away. Holt and Chief remove their caps as they plop down at a table overlooking the lake. A waitress approaches and they quickly order sandwiches and cocktails.

"How long we been playing golf together, Chief?" asks Holt.

"Ten, twelve years?"

Holt grunts and hands over the $640.00. "Have I ever won any money off you?"

Chief laughs as he pockets the cash. "I hope I die before you ever do."

The waitress brings their cocktails, and they nod approvingly as they taste them.

"Well, down to business," says Chief, placing his cocktail on the table. "And I have to say, your Coach Deal is an intriguing woman."

"I'm all ears."

Chief chuckles and points to Holt's giant ears. "You shouldn't use that phrase, Les. I mean, for God's sake, you're carrying manhole covers on your head."

"At least I have hair."

Chief laughs again, pulls out his phone, finds an e-mail, and forwards it to Holt.

Sipping his cocktail, Holt quickly reads the email, his eyes widening by the second. "How did you find this?" he asks when he's finished, his voice tinged with shock.

"Never you mind about that. Question is, what will you do with it?"

Holt puts down his phone and eyes Chief. "I'm not sure," he says, sipping his beverage.

"You could blow her world up in your little town."

Holt nods as he considers the possibilities. "It's just leverage for now," he decides. "Maybe I'll use it, maybe I won't."

"It's good though."

"Way better than good."

Their sandwiches arrive. "Tell me this, Les," says Chief, chewing on the sandwich. "What's your beef with this woman?"

Les takes another drink as he weighs the question. Thinks back to the first time he met Chelsea. He liked her after that first encounter, a social gathering at a Booster Club meeting right after Dub hired her as his offensive coordinator. Thought to himself then: *I might hire this woman if I needed a lawyer. But as a football coach? Not a chance in hell.*

"I don't know," Holt says, addressing Chief query. "The Rabon School Board passed over a friend of mine to hire her as the interim head coach."

"You're loyal to a friend. Admirable."

Holt swallows a bite of sandwich. "Well, the woman thing too. Affirmative action, the politically correct mob running amuck. I mean, a female football coach in Rabon? What's the world coming to?"

"Its senses maybe?" Chief shrugs.

Surprised by the response, Holt puts down his sandwich. "You voting Democrat now?" he asks Chief.

Chief chuckles before turning serious again. "I have two daughters, Les. What if one of them wanted to coach football? Who am I to say she shouldn't ... or couldn't?"

Holt sips his cocktail. "I need to get out of Atlanta before that kind of thinking rubs off on me."

"What if this woman wins a championship for you?"

Holt smiles at the possibility, as unlikely as it is. "I'll congratulate her and send her something pink for Christmas."

Chief laughs and raises his glass as if to toast. "That's some Grade-A sexism right there, my friend!"

"It's a joke, Chief! A joke!"

His eyes closed, Ty lays in his bed at home, an IV in his arm. Russell and Vanessa read their phones in chairs beside him, the TV on mute across from them. Russell's phone rings and he quickly answers. "Okay," he says. "We're in Ty's room. Come on in."

Russell walks out to the top of the stairs and waves Dr. Ramirez up. A folder under his arm, Ramirez hurries upstairs and follows Russell into Ty's bedroom.

"We do appreciate you making these house calls," Vanessa says as she stands and hugs Ramirez.

"It's way beyond the call of duty," agrees Russell.

Ramirez smiles. "Just get me tickets if the Falcons make the playoffs."

Russell laughs. "Fat chance of that happening."

Ramirez chuckles again and steps to Ty as he opens his eyes. "You feeling any better today?" Ramirez asks.

"Better than the last day or so."

"That's good. As I said, you can be miserable today but fine tomorrow. It varies, person to person, treatment to treatment."

"I just want to stay out of the hospital."

"As long as you're not any worse, you can stay right here." Ramirez turns back to Vanessa and Russell. "Can we talk outside a minute?" he asks.

Vanessa and Russell glance at each other. "Sure," says Russell.

Ty closes his eyes again and Ramirez leads Russell and Vanessa out and down the hall beyond Ty's room.

"Here's the deal," starts Ramirez after they stop walking. "Since Ty is a little stronger, I want to up his chemo dose this afternoon at the infusion center. It might make the nausea worse, but I think it's worth trying."

"And you're doing this why?" asks Russell.

Ramirez opens his folder and pulls out a scan image. "Because we've found a third spot."

Flags flap in the wind as the football team and coaches huddle around Chelsea before practice starts. She tosses up a football and catches it as it falls. "Okay, gentlemen," she begins. "We've had a week off. Everyone should be rested and ready to go."

She looks around as the team nods. "It's every cliché in the book," she continues. "Do or die. Backs against the wall. Survive and advance."

She faces Palmer. "Palmer will start at quarterback this week," she announces. "And we're planning to win with just twelve plays on offense."

"Twelve plays?" asks Buck, his brow furrowed in surprise.

"Twelve plays," Chelsea responds confidently.

"Good God Almighty!" Buck exclaims.

Chelsea ignores the outburst and tosses the football to Swoops. "Swoops, lead the warmup!"

Swoops barks out the instructions and the team lines up in rows across the field.

About three hours later, Palmer and Chelsea sit quietly in Dub's office as he studies the Playbook and she watches game video. The wall clock shows 8:30. Yawning, Palmer leans back and stretches. "This stuff is killing me," he says.

"You had a good practice today," Chelsea says. "You're improving."

Palmer grabs two water bottles from the fridge, hands one to Chelsea, and plops down again. "Dirk's back in Nashville," he says.

Chelsea opens her water bottle. "You miss him when he's away?"

Palmer weighs the question. "I been alone a lot in my life. It ain't the worst thing."

Chelsea drinks water. "I meant to tell you," she says. "You were outstanding at Georgio's the other night."

Palmer grins. "They hired me for a regular gig. Twelve dollars an hour, plus tips."

Chelsea studies him closely. "I believe that's the first time I've ever seen you smile," she observes. "You should do it more often."

Palmer picks up the Playbook and flips a page.

"You like music more than football, don't you?" Chelsea asks softly.

"With music, it's just me and my guitar," Palmer explains. "But football? I have to trust everybody on the field ... Have to connect what I'm doing with what they're doing."

"That's hard for you, isn't it? Trusting people."

Palmer sits up straighter, instantly suspicious. "What did Dirk tell you?"

Chelsea's phone beeps and she checks it, holds a hand up to Palmer, and answers the phone. "Hey, Russell, what's up?"

"It's Ty, Coach. Not good news. He's taken a turn for the worse and we're back at the hospital. He wants to see you. And Palmer. Come now."

Ty is resting in bed, his eyes swollen and his face puffy. Vanessa hovers beside him as Russell meets Palmer and Chelsea at the door and ushers them into the room. "They increased his chemo a few hours ago," Russell quickly informs them. "He had a terrible reaction to it."

He steps aside and Chelsea hurries to hug Vanessa while Palmer hangs back. Ty struggles to raise himself up but is too weak and sags back down. Chelsea quickly moves to Ty.

"Hey," she starts. "Bad day, huh?"

Ty smiles weakly. Chelsea turns to Palmer and waves him over. He reluctantly steps closer as Vanessa and Russell wait by the wall. "You look like somebody beat you up," he tells Ty.

"If I had a choice, I'd choose the beating over chemo." Ty coughs and his body shakes. After a few moments, he settles a little and speaks again, his voice weak. "Mama, Pops, I need a few minutes alone with Coach and Palmer."

"Okay," says Vanessa. "We'll be right outside." She leads Russell out and Ty turns to Palmer.

"It's time you got your mind right with the Playbook," he says.

"I've tried, Ty," answers Palmer. "But I ain't smart like you."

Ty's eyes brighten a bit, like he just took a shot of adrenaline. "That's busting an old stereotype, right there," he grins. "Black kid smarter than a white boy."

He offers a weak fist pump and Palmer returns it. "White boy faster than a black kid," retorts Palmer.

"Black kid richer than a white boy."

"You guys shouldn't be joking that way," interjects Chelsea. "Might get us all in trouble."

They laugh but another cough hits Ty and everyone turns serious again. "This cancer has a mind of its own," Ty manages to say. "I don't know if I'll beat it."

Unsure what to say, Palmer stares at his shoes as Ty continues. "I tell you this, though. If I go down, I don't want my last memory to be watching you screw up a play to lose us a championship."

Palmer looks back up. "I don't know what else to do, man. The more I study, the more mixed up I seem to get."

"I've thought about your situation, Palmer," says Chelsea. Talked with Mr. Towe. What about doing some testing, see—"

Palmer raises a hand to stop her. "I see Mr. Towe twice a week already. Don't need more time with him."

"But testing might help you," she says. "If we can diagnose the problem, we might find a treatment for it, something to make learning easier for you."

Palmer shakes his head. "What's the good of hanging a label on me? How will that help me learn the Playbook before Friday?"

Chelsea glances at Ty, back to Palmer. "You're right," she admits. "Nothing we can do between now and Friday. But what about next year? The rest of your life?"

"I'll study more," says Palmer. "But no testing."

Chelsea starts to speak again but then sighs and gives up.

"All right," Ty says. "We'll just work harder. Longer. Till it's done."

Palmer leans closer to Ty. "You still up for that? As sick as you are?"

Ty coughs and closes his eyes. "That's what I wanted to tell you, man. It's ride-or-die time, Palmer. Me and you."

Back at her house thirty minutes later, Chelsea parks her truck and leans back. Totally exhausted, she feels helpless, unable to do anything for Ty or Palmer. Her phone rings and she checks Caller-ID, then quickly answers. "Hey, Russell," she says. "Ty hanging in there?"

"Yeah, nothing new since you left. But here's the thing: Vanessa and I talked. Ty can't work with Palmer anymore."

Chelsea rubs her eyes. "I'm a little surprised," she says. "After what Ty just said to me and Palmer."

"He's too fragile, Chelsea. Needs to conserve his energy. We're taking him out of school too."

"He seems to enjoy coaching Palmer."

"This isn't a debate. Our minds are made up."

Chelsea starts to argue but realizes she shouldn't. Vanessa and Russell are just protecting their son, like all good parents would do. "You know I want what's best for Ty," she says. "If you and Vanessa feel sure of this, I'm on board. I'll let Palmer know."

"No hard feelings, Chelsea. We have to do whatever we can to help Ty win this war."

"I understand."

"And Chelsea, one more thing: Don't mention to Ty that I called you."

"If that's what you want."

"It's what we want."

Palmer slouches on his sofa with a tray in his lap. A hotdog, a bag of chips, and a glass of water sit on the tray. The Playbook lays open beside him, but he ignores it as he bites into the hot dog and chews. Seeing Ty so sick bothers him, forces him to remember his dad, the only other person he's cared about who died before his time.

He swigs from the water and eats another bite of hotdog. Other than Ty and Coach Deal, he's got no close friends in Rabon. But can he really call them friends? If he suddenly died in a motorcycle accident, who wound attend his funeral? Dirk and his mama if they let her out of rehab. But who else?

He finishes the hotdog. Stupid thoughts, he decides. He won't live in Rabon forever. Truth is, he might not live here longer than a few more months. So, what difference does it make if he doesn't know anybody here? He's spent most of his life alone, so nothing has changed.

Wanting to keep his promise to Ty and Coach, he sets his tray on the floor, picks up the Playbook, flips to a play, and studies it for a minute. But the diagram makes no sense, just a jumble of X's and O's darting this way and that.

Frustrated, he slams the Playbook shut and stares around the empty room. Suddenly, he wants to talk to somebody, anybody, to not be alone with his crazy thoughts. He grabs his phone, clicks through his contacts, finds Molly's number, and texts her.

"Hey. Me again. Playing at Georgio's on the weekends now. You should come. I quit the motel, so I won't see you there anymore. Miss you." He sends the text but receives no response.

CHAPTER EIGHTEEN

The pace of life in Rabon intensifies as the quarterfinal game approaches. Townspeople hustle about quicker, their blood charged as they prepare for the much-anticipated gridiron battle. Local radio talk shows dissect every angle of the forthcoming game, cutting up the negative and positive possibilities like a butcher carving a filet mignon, each slice made thinner and thinner as they whittle away at it.

Conversations in restaurants, business offices, and beauty salons spout opinion after opinion on what to expect in the game. The verdict splits pretty evenly on the chances of a Knights' victory, especially with that woman coach leading the team and Ty too sick to play. Christmas decorations suddenly appear everywhere on the streets, but only because it's the season, not because the birth of the baby Jesus somehow takes precedence over the upcoming football contest.

The football team, caught up in the town's enthusiasm, practices harder every afternoon, the offense running the same twelve plays over and over, Palmer at quarterback most of the time. Buck guns the defensive pressure up a notch, throwing every trick in the book at Palmer as the week slips by. Palmer and Chelsea study the Playbook after practice until all hours of the night, the two of them in Dub's office, watching film, discussing plays.

Though Ty is still managing to avoid another hospital stay, his chemo treatments knock him down even more and he retches, coughs, and hurts worse and worse every day. But he still fights back, pushing himself to limits he didn't know he could cross. Vanessa, Russell, and Tanya care for him around the clock, their hands holding his, their voices encouraging him to hold on, their spirits working to lift him up. Sadly, though, as the week rolls forward, his strength ebbs lower and lower.

Buck and Holt meet at Kangaroo Coffee early in the morning on two separate days, sliding into a back booth both times and whispering to each other as if trading international secrets. The afternoon after the second meeting, Buck and Principal Roberts talk behind the locker room after football practice. Buck carries most of the conversation while Roberts rolls a pencil in his fingers. The morning after that, Dub shows up in Principal Roberts' office, a crutch under his arm, and a worried scowl on his face. He and Roberts discuss something for close to an hour, then Dub shakes his head and leaves in a huff.

On Thursday night, an hour or so after football practice, Palmer holds a math book in his lap at home, his eyes on an equation he can't figure out. Working hard, he scratches numbers on a yellow legal pad, his fingers busy as his mind grinds away, trying to decipher the problem. Sadly, though, the equation won't yield to his sincere but confused efforts. Stymied, he tosses the book to the floor and leans back on the sofa.

His phone buzzes and, grateful to escape the schoolwork, he quickly answers. "Hey, Ty," he says. "How you feelin'?"

"Where have you been?" Ty grouses, his voice a little stronger than Palmer expected. "I haven't seen you all week."

"Hold on, dude," says Palmer, surprised by Ty's outburst. "Don't lay that on me. Coach said you'd gone downhill. Said you were too sick to keep working with me."

"Where did she get that idea? I haven't talked to Coach."

Palmer tries to figure it out. A realization hits him. "Your folks," he suggests. "Maybe they said something to Coach."

"Damn!" says Ty.

"What happened to Saint Ty?" teases Palmer.

"It had to be my mama. She drives me crazy sometimes."

"Welcome to my world."

Ty falls quiet for a moment.

"What you thinking?" asks Palmer.

"You got the Playbook memorized yet?"

Palmer laughs. "You beat your cancer yet?"

"Get your butt over here."

"It's past eight, man. You need your rest."

"I feel a little better today. Dr. Ramirez said this could happen."

"What about your folks? They don't want me bothering you."

"See you in twenty minutes. I'll deal with them."

Principal Roberts slouches at his office desk, Chelsea across from him. Dub sits in the corner, a crutch by his chair. Roberts faces Chelsea, a pencil, as always, in his fingers. "Big game tomorrow night," he begins. "We ready?"

"I feel good about it," Chelsea says firmly.

"Can we win with just twelve plays?"

"Our opponent won't be expecting it. If our defense shuts down their offense like I expect, twelve could be enough."

Roberts rolls the pencil. Chelsea checks the time on her phone. "Why are we here, George?" she asks, her impatience visible.

Roberts leans forward. "I'll cut to the chase."

Chelsea senses a shoe about to drop.

"As you know," Roberts says, "Buck resents you getting the interim job over him."

"He's made that plain. But he's doing an excellent job with the defense."

Roberts glances first at Dub, then back to Chelsea. "Here's the plot twist you don't know about. Dub here," he points the pencil at Dub. "Well, after he's recovered, he's not returning as coach. This year or next."

Chelsea rocks back in her seat. "What?"

Roberts points his pencil at Dub and Chelsea faces him.

"My accident has given me time to do some pondering," explains Dub. "Patrice and I ... we have things we want to do. And I'm tired of the pressure. You know how that is."

Chelsea stays quiet as emotions boil. Surprise followed by fear accompanied by a touch of excitement.

"With Dub retired, the head job will be up for grabs," Roberts adds, jerking Chelsea out of her thoughts.

"Okay," she nods as she turns back to Roberts. "With Dub gone, it'll be me or Buck as head coach next year."

"Bingo," says Roberts. "Unless Nick Saban decides to coach at Rabon High, it will no doubt be either you or Buck."

"So, a lot rides on the game tomorrow night."

Roberts chuckles. "As you're aware, some people in town believe the Board rushed the choice on you. They're suggesting there was a whiff of reverse gender preference in that decision and they're not happy. And the loss in your first game didn't help any."

"I see their point," agrees Chelsea. "About the loss, anyway."

"Here's the deal," continues Roberts. "The Board needs a win this week to validate their choice. If that happens, it's ninety-nine percent certain they'll offer you the permanent job. If you want it."

"If we lose, it will definitely go to Buck?"

"You're so smart. But one more surprise. You win this week and Buck resigns after the game."

Chelsea sits up straighter. "I didn't see that coming."

"My reaction exactly," says Dub.

"I want him to stay until the season's over," says Chelsea, weighing the downside of Buck bailing on the team. "He's a pain at times, but we need his defensive expertise."

"I know," sighs Roberts. But he wants to start looking ASAP for a head coaching position."

Chelsea faces Dub. "Can you talk to him?" she asks.

"I already tried. He said his mind is made up."

"So that's it?" asks Chelsea. "We just let him walk?"

"He'll stay if I promise him your job," says Roberts. "But other than that, he's done if we win."

"I never took him to be a quitter," says Chelsea, her mind busy with how to handle this turn of events.

Dub pulls himself up and situates his crutch. Chelsea also rises and shakes Dub's hand. "I admire you, Coach," she says. "And all you've done."

"It's been the kids, Chelsea. And coaches like you."

"Female coaches?" she teases.

"Stop busting my chops," Dubs says with a laugh. "And go knock some heads tomorrow night."

Vanessa opens the front door and waves Palmer in, but she's anything but friendly. "You know Russell and I don't want you here," she says. "Ty's too sick to tutor you anymore."

"No disrespect, ma'am," counters Palmer. "But Ty asked me to come."

"It's not his decision."

Palmer drops his head.

"Parents protect their kids, Palmer," continues Vanessa. "It's in the job description."

"Some parents do."

Ty appears in his wheelchair at the top of the stairs. He's lost more weight. "Leave him alone, Mama!" Ty shouts. "Come on up, Palmer!"

Palmer hesitates but Vanessa waves him past. "It's 8:30, Ty!" she shouts back. "One hour, no more."

Close to two hours later, Palmer sits at Ty's desk, his head in his hands, the Playbook open in front of him. Ty rests on his bed, his Playbook beside him as he props himself up on the headboard. Palmer slams the Playbook closed and leans back. "I'm toast," he exhales. "Done."

Ty holds up his Playbook. "Study thirty more minutes. You can leave after that. I promise."

"Come on, man," sighs Palmer, frustrated to the point of breaking. "We been over these plays a hundred times. And they're still as muddy in my mind as ever. I'm finished. It's just not happening."

"You just give up?"

Palmer shrugs. "I'm tired of this."

Ty suddenly coughs, a wracking sound that rolls through his body like a choppy wave. He turns over and Palmer grabs a water glass off the table and hands it to him. Ty, slowly drinking, settles down again.

Palmer fluffs his pillow. "You know what's funny?" Palmer asks, his voice gentle as he backs up and sits at Ty's feet. "I've started remembering some of your quotes. It's weird. They pop up while I'm playing my guitar. Still can't keep the plays straight but I can see your corny quotes in my head."

"My quotes aren't corny," says Ty, taking a shallow breath.

"Dude, some of them are."

Ty smiles weakly.

"But some of them I really like," concedes Palmer.

"Name one."

Palmer closes his eyes, and a quote appears in his head. "'If you are going through Hell, keep going.' —Winston Churchill, page 54 of the Playbook."

"That's cool, man. Another one."

"'Woe to him who is alone when he falls and has not another to lift him up. Though a man might prevail against one who is alone, two will withstand him—a threefold cord is not quickly broken.' Ecclesiastes, Playbook page 31."

"That's a long one. My favorite right now. You, me, and Coach Deal. A three-fold cord."

Palmer opens his eyes. "Is it weird, Ty? One white, one black, one female?"

Ty chuckles. "Seems to me that's how it ought to be."

"Man, you like a Gandhi or something." They bump fists.

"I better scoot," says Palmer, "Before your mom shoots me."

"She knows when she's beat," says Ty.

"You coming to the game?"

"Like I said, me and you, ride or die."

Ty closes his eyes. Palmer pulls the covers over him and quietly exits the room.

CHAPTER NINETEEN

F riday night blows in windy and cold. People dressed in winter gear pack Rabon High Stadium under dazzling lights. The Knights wear purple, the Eagles white. Sam Sky and Reggie Tillis sit near the fifty-yard line, Sam with binoculars, Reggie eating popcorn with gloved hands.

Bundled in a brown leather coat and purple wool hat, Bridget stands with her girlfriends near the cheerleaders. Eva, Phil, and Principal Roberts drink hot chocolate on the fifty-yard line, just a few rows in front of Sam and Reggie. Ty, covered in blankets in his wheelchair, and accompanied by Vanessa, Tanya, and Russell, watches with the team near the bench.

The stadium announcer reports the starting lineup, his voice blasting over the noisy crowd. "A new quarterback will start for the Knights tonight!" he thunders. "Sophomore Palmer Norman will guide the offense for this quarterfinal contest!"

The crowd applauds in approval and, a couple of minutes later, after the kickoff soars high and deep into the end zone, Palmer leads the offense onto the field. Rubbing his hands together to warm them up, he huddles the team at the twenty-five-yard line. "Okay," he says, his breath short, but more excited than panicked this time. "Here we go. First play. Max protection right. Roll out right. Left post. Right corner. On two."

The team claps and breaks the huddle and Palmer lines up in a shotgun formation. The defense shifts. The center snaps the ball. Palmer moves too early and fumbles the ball, but quickly picks it up and sprints right. A defender dives at his feet, but Palmer leaps over him and spots Swoops racing down the left sideline. Two defenders cover Swoops, but Palmer throws the ball anyway. It zips like a frozen rope forty yards across the field. One defensive back slips and falls, and Swoops out-jumps the second one, snatches the pass out of the air, and sprints downfield, outrunning the defense for a touchdown.

"TOUCHDOWN KNIGHTS!" booms the announcer. The crowd roars and the Knights' sideline celebrates. Screaming like a banshee, Palmer sprints to Ty and they fist-bump three times, both grinning ear to ear.

"Twelve plays, baby!" shouts Palmer. "Twelve plays!"

Standing in her tiny room at the Sunrise Treatment Center, Lacy slips on a denim jacket, puts a frayed, stained backpack over her shoulders, grabs a pack of cigarettes from a nightstand, and looks around. The room is bare—no evidence she's ever been there.

At the door, she peeks out. Seeing no one in either direction, she quietly sneaks into the hall. After checking left and right, she hustles to a door marked "Stairs," and pushes it open. Still moving quietly, Lacy hurries down to the basement. At the bottom, she sees an emergency exit, pushes through it, and runs into the dark as the alarm sounds behind her.

More than two hours later, the fans in Rabon High Stadium are on their feet, their cold breath puffing in and out like gray smoke. On the field, Palmer lines up under center on the Knights' own 6-yard line. The scoreboard shows the score: Knights: 10. Guests: 7. Fourth Quarter. Five minutes left.

The stadium announcer roars. "It's third down! Nine yards to go for the Knights!"

Palmer yells out the signals as he scans the defense. Nerves rush through his body and his fingers tingle. A mistake now, so deep in his own territory, might cost his team the game. He hesitates and almost calls a time-out but knows he can't waste one this close to the final whistle.

He squeezes his fists to settle the tingling and barks out the snap count. The ball zips back to him and he rolls right, a running back trailing him. Just before he reaches the line of scrimmage, he pitches the ball to the back, who turns upfield. A defender hits the ball carrier from the side and the ball pops straight up.

Acting on instinct, Palmer stretches toward the ball and almost falls, but a defender hits him in the back and knocks him forward. Palmer manages to snag the ball in mid-air. Another defender smacks him from the side, and he almost drops the ball but hangs on at the last second, jerks the ball to his chest, and sprints straight ahead. A third defender dives at his knees but he bangs through him, reverses field, sees green grass ahead, and zooms toward it.

The fans scream as he sprints to the fifty, then the forty, his long legs eating up the turf. He rushes past the thirty, cuts back against the last defender, and runs into the end zone for a ninety-four-yard touchdown to clinch the victory.

Close to sixty miles away, Lacy wearily drops her backpack on the bed in a plain, cut-rate motel room. A dingy yellow spread covers the bed. A small TV sits on a dresser. A miniature refrigerator hums in the corner.

Stepping to the window, Lacy looks out at a dim sign: "Asheville City Motel. $89.00." She rubs her tired eyes, unsure what to do next. Nobody knows where she is, or that she's a drug addict with less than fifty dollars in her pocket.

Seeing no other option, she sags onto the bed, pulls out a flip phone, and studies it for a long minute. After rubbing her eyes again, she punches in a number. A phone rings on the other side of the call and she almost hangs up but doesn't. Dirk's voicemail answers.

"Hey, Dirk," she sobs. "Please call me. I got nowhere else to go. I'm headed to Nashville to see you tomorrow."

Almost forty-five minutes later, the echoes of a home victory have subsided in Rabon High Stadium and most of the fans have left. The scoreboard reads: Knights: 17. Eagles: 7. Many of the players and coaches remain on the field, their celebration not quite over. On the sidelines, Buck strides over to Roberts and they chat for a couple of minutes. Then Buck shakes Roberts' hand and walks away.

Worn out from the game and at least a thousand pats on the back, Chelsea shakes the last hand offered to her and faces the scoreboard for one last glorious look at the score. Smiling, she pivots toward the locker room and spots Palmer, who's surrounded by a gaggle of girls near mid-field. Bridget holds him by the elbow, a broad grin on her face, as several of her friends take selfies with him.

Concerned for reasons she doesn't take time to identify, Chelsea hustles over to Palmer and the girls part to let her through. "Hey," she says, pulling Palmer aside. "Great game."

"Thanks."

She glances at Bridget and leans in closer. "Don't be out late, Palmer."

"I'm playing at Georgio's soon as I can get there," he says.

"Straight home when you finish at Georgio's," she insists. "You need your rest. We're back in the Playbook tomorrow."

"No days off?"

"Straight home." She glances at Bridget again, pats Palmer on the shoulder pads, and heads toward the locker room. Roberts meets her by the door.

"Congrats, Coach," he smiles. "Two wins to a championship."

"The job's mine now? If I want it?"

Roberts drops his eyes. "Yeah, you know. We'll see what happens."

Her antenna flashes a warning. Something isn't right. "You're hedging, George. What's the problem?"

Roberts leans close. "Meet me for breakfast tomorrow. Kangaroo Coffee. Seven a.m."

"That's early."

"Early is good."

He pivots and hurries off before she can question him further. A sense of dread suddenly courses through her veins. Though she can't explain why, she senses something dark about to fall on her head.

The clock over the bar at Georgio's reads 12:25. The place is empty except for Palmer packing up his guitar, Bridget on her phone at the front table, and the clean-up staff finishing their work. "There's a party!" Bridget suddenly exclaims, her face beaming. "On the lake!"

"I'm really fried," Palmer says.

Bridget hurries to him as he collects his tips from the jar on the edge of the stage. "You're the hero tonight!" she encourages. "Come for an hour. Celebrate a little."

Without warning, the front door pops open and Chelsea hustles inside. "The kitchen's closed, Coach," says Palmer.

"I'm not here to eat," she says, hurrying over. "Can we talk a second? Privately?" She glances at Bridget, then back to Palmer.

"I'll visit the ladies' room," says Bridget.

"Thanks," says Chelsea.

Bridget prances away as Palmer unhooks the microphone and starts wrapping the electrical cord around it. "You checkin' up on me?" he asks Chelsea.

"Dirk called me a few minutes ago," she answers.

"He say when he's coming home?"

"He said your mom is driving his way."

Palmer scowls but doesn't speak as he puts the microphone into a small cabinet behind the stage.

"I know about her rehab," says Chelsea.

Trying to ignore Chelsea's news, Palmer picks up his guitar.

"Dirk believes she'll visit you after she leaves him," says Chelsea.

"She needs to leave me alone."

He glances toward the ladies' restroom, but Bridget is nowhere to be seen.

"She's your mom, Palmer," argues Chelsea. "Might be good for you to make peace with her."

A sense of claustrophobia hits Palmer, like walls closing in, and he turns on Chelsea. "You don't know what's good for me," he says, his resentment boiling over. "I'll deal with my mama without your help."

Chelsea backs up half a step. "You're right. It's not my place. I apologize. But I want good things for you, Palmer. Please believe that."

Eager to leave, Palmer glances toward the bathroom again. Still no Bridget. He changes the subject. "You and Dirk an item now?" he asks Chelsea.

"Nothing like that."

"Why's he calling you and not me?"

"He … we … talked about you. Care about you. That okay?"

Bridget finally reappears.

"I want what's best for you," Chelsea says again.

Palmer grabs Bridget's hand and heads to the front door, Chelsea trailing. He pushes the door open and turns to Chelsea.

"Talk to Dirk all you want. But my mama and me, that's between us. It's not your business."

Scores of cars line the street in front of the lake house, an A-frame, chalet-style building within fifty feet of the water's edge. Music blares from the backyard overlooking the water, and Bridget hangs onto Palmer's hand as they stride toward the sound. Rounding the corner, Palmer sees a huge crowd of teenagers stretching from the back of the house all the way to the lake. Friends shout at Bridget and high-five Palmer as they make their way into the throng.

Near the water's edge, a huge bonfire licks flames to the sky. Cups and bottles cover a picnic table a few feet from the bonfire. Several teenagers stand on a dock jutting into the lake, while a couple others jump into the water, scream against the cold, and quickly swim back to the dock. Multiple couples around the bonfire make out, some in lounge chairs, others standing up. One guy is passed out on the grass by the picnic table, a purple and white cap on his head but no shirt or shoes.

. A guy with a feather tattoo on his neck hands Palmer a beer and slaps him on the back. "Palmer is da man!" the guy yells.

A girl Palmer vaguely recognizes from math class offers him a joint but he declines. Within seconds, he and Bridget reach the bonfire, and a circle quickly forms around them, everybody high-fiving, bumping fists, whooping over the music.

"You were zipping, dude!" a teenager yells at Palmer. "I mean, flying. Ninety-four effing yards for a touchdown! A Knight on the loose!"

Palmer lifts his beer over his head in celebration and others join him. Somebody turns the music up and the noise ratchets higher. Palmer's ears ring from the raucous sounds. He faces Bridget and she throws her head back and laughs as she jumps up and down, the music pounding, the crowd going berserk.

Soft classical music plays as Chelsea lies in bed and stares at her ceiling. Unable to sleep, her mind zig-zags from one thought to another. Why does Roberts want to see her? Did she do the right thing calling Bo? Can Palmer handle more plays as he preps for the game next week? How much will Buck's resignation affect the defense?

Sitting up, she wraps the covers around her shoulders, shuffles into the kitchen, heats up some tea, sits down at the table, and sips from her mug. But that doesn't help. Her mind drifts to Roberts again and she concludes that he knows something.

Still holding her mug, she steps to the window and stares out. If Roberts knows the wrong thing, her just-won victory won't matter much after breakfast. But how could he know?

Her mind clouded, she slumps back to her bedroom, picks up her phone, puts it down, picks it back up again, and finally texts. "Roberts wants to meet at seven a.m. tomorrow. Any idea what's up?"

She sends it to Eva, turns out the light, hops back into bed, and stares again at the ceiling.

The crowd at the lake house keeps growing bigger and louder. Kids slam whiskey shots at the picnic table. The guy with the feather tattoo strips naked on the dock and whoops to the heavens before plunging into the cold water. Palmer and Bridget lay on lounge chairs by the fire, their hands intertwined. Palmer drinks half his beer and sets the bottle on the ground. Bridget tugs his hand, and he faces her. "You having fun?!" she yells over the chaos.

"You're pretty!" he shouts.

She leans over and kisses him just as Swoops and Johnson appear behind them. "Isn't this romantic?!" Swoops shouts, pushing his face between Palmer and Bridget.

Palmer laughs and pushes Swoops away, but Swoops and Johnson plop down, one at the bottom of Palmer's chair, the other on Bridget's.

"Swoops!" yells Palmer. "I been meaning to ask: That accent of yours..."

"It's Ethiopian, my strong-armed Caucasian friend!" shouts Swoops. "By way of Great Britain."

"So, how does an Ethiopian with a British accent end up in Rabon?"

"My father is a professor at the university satellite in Bishopville."

Bridget's lanky brunette friend suddenly appears with a guitar in her hand and

Bridget jumps up and hugs her. The brunette speaks into Bridget's ear and Bridget nods, hops up on the picnic table, and shouts to the crowd. "Hey, hey, hey!"

The crowd quiets a little but not enough, so Bridget yells louder and the noise level drops some more. The brunette hands Bridget the guitar, somebody whistles, and the crowd falls silent enough for everyone to hear Bridget.

"Who wants to hear Palmer play this guitar?" she shouts, holding it over her head. The crowd whoops and Bridget turns to Palmer, but he shakes his head.

"Come on, Palmer!" she pleads. "Give the people what they want!"

He rises and tries to pull her off the table, but she laughs and pushes him away. The crowd begins to chant. "Palmer! Palmer! Palmer!" The chant booms across the water.

Bridget jumps down and hands Palmer the guitar. Swoops and Johnson clear the cups and bottles, then grab Palmer and force him onto the table. The swimmers on the dock, the kids slamming shots, the lovers making out—everybody stops and watches as Palmer stands still for several seconds, staring at the crowd below him.

Swoops leans towards Johnson. "Is he actually any good?" he asks.

"I've heard he is."

"Do it, Palmer!" somebody yells from the dock.

Palmer shakes his head at Bridget. "Do it, Palmer!" she shouts.

Palmer's fingers slowly begin to strum the guitar. The crowd falls completely silent. Palmer tunes the guitar a little as he gazes from one teenager to the next. "Ya'll sure about this?!" he yells.

"Do it, Palmer!" they shout.

He clears his throat. "All right, I guess."

He quietly strums the guitar another few seconds as the crowd holds its breath. He faces Bridget and smiles. Then he hits the guitar strings hard and starts to sing, his voice raw and raucous. "I got friends in low places, where the whiskey drowns and the beer chases..."

The crowd erupts, whooping, chest-bumping, screaming. Everyone loves it— everyone except Don and Strick, who are standing in the shadows not far from the picnic table.

Chelsea's phone dings. After fumbling for a moment, she finds it on her bedside table, and picks it up.

"I have no idea about the meeting," reads the text. "But you coached a great game. Now go to sleep!"

Chelsea puts down the phone and rolls over, her eyes open, still staring at the ceiling.

The crowd cheers again as Palmer hits the last note of the song, hops off the table, and hands Bridget the guitar. People pat him on the back and high-five him.

Swoops slaps Johnson on the shoulder. "The boy is brilliant!"

Palmer bends to Bridget and takes her hand. "I'm going home."

She smiles ear to ear as they leave the bonfire and stroll back through the crowd. In the shadows at the side of the house, he stops, pulls her close, and kisses her. For a moment, everything disappears except Bridget, her smell, her warmth.

A noise sounds behind him and Palmer turns as Don and Strick appear from the shadows. He drops his hands off Bridget and faces them, his fists instantly clenched. He smells liquor and pushes Bridget behind him as Don and Strick stomp closer.

"Well, look here, Strick," says Don. "It's our old friend Yokel. Ain't he the bell of the ball tonight."

"He's upgraded his trollop, Don," says Strick, leering at Bridget.

"He's a star now, Strick. Gets the pick of the female litter."

"Don't talk about Bridget that way," says Palmer, steel in his voice.

"You such a gentleman, Palmer," says Strick as he edges even closer. "Sticking up for your trollop like always."

Bridget steps beside Palmer.

"I like Bridget better than his last one, Strick," says Don. "Blondes over brunettes any day of the week."

"Back away," Palmer orders. "I don't need no more trouble."

"I hear you on Mr. Towe's naughty list." Strick laughs. "One more screw- up and your hero days will flush right down the toilet."

Palmer grabs Bridget's hand and tries to push past them, but Don grabs his arm and whirls him around. Palmer knocks Don away, swings at Strick, and hits him in the face. Bridget screams as Don and Strick jump on Palmer, their fists busy as he fights to break loose. Bridget smacks Don in the back, but her blow has little impact.

Swoops and Johnson suddenly appear from the back of the house. "Hey!" yells Swoops, sprinting at them. "That's enough!"

Don and Strick quickly drop their fists and back off as Swoops and Johnson stop beside them. "You all right?" Johnson asks Bridgett.

She nods and Swoops yells at Strick and Don: "You messin' with my quarterback and his girl?"

Don quickly shakes his head. "Nah, man. No big deal."

"Move your asses out of here!" orders Swoops. "And if I see you within twenty feet of these two again, I'll make it my life's purpose to whip your butts at least once a day every day until graduation. We clear?"

"Clear," nods Strick.

"Go!" shouts Swoops.

Don and Strick obey immediately and hustle away.

Palmer grabs Bridget's hand and they rush toward the street with Swoops and Johnson following.

"What happened back there?" Swoops asks Palmer.

"Nothing," says Palmer, still leading Bridget. "We're fine."

They reach his truck and Palmer yanks open the passenger-side door for Bridget.

"You sure?" asks Johnson as Palmer climbs in.

Palmer starts the truck and drives away, leaving Swoops and Johnson on the street in front of the lake house.

CHAPTER TWENTY

With all but two seats filled in Kangaroo Coffee, the hum of conversation buzzes in the air. A little girl wearing red sneakers and screaming at the top of her lungs runs past Chelsea as she enters and a young woman wearing what looks to be blue flannel pajamas chases after her. Many in the café crowd smile at Chelsea as she removes her jacket and orders coffee.

She spots Roberts in a back corner booth as she waits for coffee. He appears at ease as she watches him, normal. Her coffee appears and she picks it up, threads her way through the crowd, and sits down across from Roberts. Muffins and hot chocolate sit on the table in front of him.

"It's cold out there today," she says, arranging herself in her seat, her hands wrapped around the coffee cup.

"You're in the mountains in November," Roberts says. "What did you expect?"

Chelsea sips her coffee as Roberts bites into a muffin. "Congrats on last night," he says as he chews. "Big win. You should feel proud."

"I'm proud of the team. Palmer played especially well."

"Absolutely. Gutsy call on that. Starting him."

"Thanks. He is talented."

Roberts bites his muffin again and sucks in a breath. "About the job." He shifts in his seat.

"Sure. Right to it."

Roberts shrugs.

"I have to admit I'm curious what's going on," says Chelsea, understating by a mile the anxiety she's feeling.

Roberts pulls a folded piece of paper from his pocket, lays it on the table, and stares at it. "I have a few questions I need to ask you."

Chelsea blows on her coffee. Roberts unfolds the paper and looks up. "Before I start, this is just between you and me as far as I'm concerned. And I hope it stays that way."

Chelsea shrugs. "Good by me."

Roberts drops his eyes again, studying the paper as if he's about to read a death sentence. "I need to know," he starts with a quivery voice, "did you spend two weeks in an alcohol rehab facility about fifteen months ago?"

Chelsea sits her coffee cup down and fights to stay calm. "I did," she says, her tone even.

"Did you participate in approximately six months of therapy following your rehab?"

The little girl in red shoes screams past their table, the woman in flannel pajamas in pursuit.

"Yes," Chelsea answers Roberts, her heart notching higher with each question.

"Did you take a sixty-day leave of absence from your law firm in the past twelve months?"

Chelsea places both hands on the table, her face turning as red as the little girl's shoes. "I did."

"Was that because of a recurrence of the alcohol problem you had previously?"

"No, it was not." Anger boils in Chelsea now, fury that someone has invaded her privacy and leaked this information to Roberts. But worse than that, Roberts now threatens her with the results of that invasion.

"Have you ever been ticketed for a DUI?" asks Roberts, continuing the interrogation.

Chelsea jerks the paper from Robert's hand and crumples it up. He looks up, his face also red. "I'm sorry, Coach," he says. "But I must ask these questions. Nothing personal, and I'm not trying to hurt you. But I have to do my job."

He reaches for the paper and Chelsea slowly hands it back. "Okay," he sighs. "Have you ever been charged with a DUI?"

"If I have, it would be in any standard background check," Chelsea answers, her tone a little calmer as she realizes she can't avoid what's happening.

"Have you?" Roberts presses.

Chelsea gives in. "No. Never."

Roberts exhales slowly. "Good. I'm almost done. Do you consume alcohol on a frequent basis now?"

Resigned to the questions, Chelsea decides to end the ordeal as quickly as possible. "No," she says.

"Do you consume alcohol at all now?"

Everything she just decided flies out the window. Some questions just don't deserve a response. "I don't think that's pertinent," she says, teeth gritted. "What I do, if it's legal, which drinking is, is my private business."

Roberts tilts his head. "We can investigate that issue if you want. But we'll find out, either way."

Chelsea sighs, accepts his logic, and yields again. "No," she responds. "I haven't taken a drink of any kind of alcohol in over fifteen months."

Roberts exhales, pockets the paper, and bites his muffin as if he and Chelsea have been discussing the weather.

"I'm interested to know who provided you this information," Chelsea says, her lawyer mode kicking in.

"That's not important right now," says Roberts.

"I can't face my accuser?"

"This is not an official inquiry, Coach. From everything I've seen, you've conducted yourself with the utmost professionalism since you arrived at Rabon High."

Chelsea stares out the window as old memories wash up and old fears come alive again. "What's the endgame here?" she asks Roberts. "You threaten to release this information if I don't resign?"

Roberts finishes his muffin and leans back. "I have no endgame, Chelsea. Believe that or not. But, as the principal of the school where you work, I'm required to do my due diligence. There's nothing here that disqualifies you from working at my school. True, it will embarrass all of us if this becomes public knowledge. But, in what I currently know, I see no cause for termination."

"I just have to hope that whoever brought this to you chooses to keep it quiet?"

"That seems to be the size of it."

Struggling to keep her emotions steady, Chelsea leans across the table and drops her voice to a whisper. "Whose side are you on, George?"

Roberts drinks the last of his hot chocolate, stands, and lays his hands on the table. "Enjoy your day, Coach," he says. "And let's win again next week. That would be a blessing for all of us."

Biting her tongue, Chelsea watches him leave, her coffee growing cold as she fears what will happen next.

A few hours later, Palmer's phone dings and he rolls over in bed, slowly wakes up, and checks the time: 10:46. He picks up the phone and reads a text from Bridget. "U up?" she asks.

He texts back. "Barely."

"Big night last night."

"Glad we won."

"My folks are out of town tonight. Come over later?"

"You sure?" he texts.

"Just me and you."

He pauses a moment, excitement building. Does she mean what he thinks she means? His fingers shake as he texts back: "Will do."

"I'm with my posse till ten. Come after that."

"Yup."

Palmer puts down the phone and lays in bed for a long minute, a big smile on his face. Finally, he rolls out and grabs his clothes to dress, his mind racing with what the night might bring.

Wearing winter jogging gear and maintaining a steady stride, Chelsea runs up a hill about four miles from her house. A vulture flies overhead against a gray sky, then dives toward the ground. Chelsea reaches a ridge in the road, stops, and checks her fitness app: "4.1 miles. 8:37 minutes per mile." She grabs a water bottle from her hydration belt, drinks from it, and puts it back. Looking down at Rabon in the valley, she pulls out her phone and keys it. It rings four times before Eva answers.

"Hey," says Chelsea.

"What's up?" asks Eva.

"Sorry I texted you so late last night."

"Say what you need to say, Chelsea."

'You deserve a heads-up. I have some baggage."

Vanessa steps back as Palmer enters her front door just after lunch. "Good game last night," Vanessa says.

"Thanks."

"You can't stay long."

"I just need a few minutes. Not here to study."

Vanessa nods. "Go on up. Tanya's with him."

Palmer hustles up the stairs and into Ty's room. Ty sits up in bed, Tanya in a chair beside him, showing him a video on her phone. "You two look cozy," Palmer says.

"Show him, Tanya," says Ty.

"It's for your eyes only," she says.

Ty reaches to grab her phone, but she pulls it away and hops up.

"Come on," Ty pleads. "It was a public event. People at the meet saw it."

Palmer reaches for the phone and the two of them laugh as they wrestle for it.

"Let him see it," pleads Ty. "Do it for me. I'm sick."

Tanya fights for the phone another few seconds but finally gives up. "All right, Palmer," she pants. "Pay me ten dollars and you can watch it."

"I'll pay you twenty to see it again," says Ty.

Palmer quickly watches the video. Tanya, wearing a snug blue leotard, is performing a balance beam routine at a gymnastics competition.

"It's from yesterday," Tanya explains. "Ty's been begging me to video a meet."

"Wow," says Palmer. "I'm impressed. You have such classic form on the beam."

"It's my form that impresses you?" asks Tanya, teasing him.

"He knows more about Calculus than he does about gymnastics form," says Ty. "Which means he knows nothing about it."

"Amen, Brother," agrees Palmer, handing Tanya's phone back to her. "But yes, I can see you're good at … whatever you call it."

"That leotard makes her look fine," a smiling Ty says.

"I make that leotard look fine," counters Tanya.

"I agree with you both," says Palmer.

Tanya glances at her watch. "Gotta go," she says.

"Text me that video," orders Ty. "It lifts my spirits."

"Not the only thing it lifts," teases Palmer.

Tanya throws a pillow at him.

"Sorry," Palmer says. "No disrespect. It was just too easy."

Tanya kisses Ty, smacks Palmer on the shoulder, and heads out the door.

Palmer turns to Ty. "You seem stronger today," he says.

"Holding the grim reaper off for the moment."

"You should have been at the party last night. It was jumping."

"I heard Don and Strick showed up."

"Swoops or Johnson tell you?"

"They're my boys. Keep me in the loop."

Palmer plops down on the bed beside Ty. "Have any idea where Strick and Don live?" he asks.

"Why you want to know?"

"This is twice, Ty. The way they talk about girls, what they did to Molly..."

"Report it to the police."

"Molly will hate me if I do that. And last night, Johnson and Swoops showed up before anything happened. Nothing the police can do."

"Don't get any ideas, Palmer. They're not worth it."

"Somebody needs to cut them down a notch or two."

"And you're the man to do that?"

"You gone tell me where they live or not?"

"Not."

"I thought you had my back."

Ty stares him down.

"Suit yourself," says Palmer, still determined but not wanting to hassle Ty any longer. "I'll ask somebody else."

"It's a mistake, Palmer. Whatever you're thinking."

"Some things a guy just has to do. They've been after me since I showed up here."

Ty reaches for a water cup on his bedside table and sucks down a swallow. "Okay," he says, giving into Palmer. "I feel you. They live on Pineview Street. Don't know the house number. But the place is green—lime green. You can't miss it."

Palmer stands. "I appreciate it."

"Don't do something stupid, dude. Promise me."

"Tanya is legit," says Palmer, revealing nothing of his plans. "Don't mess that up."

At 7:30 that evening, Chelsea and Bo eat at a quiet table beside a fireplace in one of Atlanta's most romantic restaurants. A violinist plays in a corner. A small fountain trickles water into a cistern by the door. Servers in white shirts, black pants, and ties, bustle about. Bo sips wine, Chelsea sparkling water.

"I have to admit it," says Chelsea, glancing around, "you can't find a place like this in Rabon."

Bo points to the new red heels on her foot closest to him. "You can't buy shoes like that in Rabon either."

She raises the foot and arches her ankle. "I take it you like them."

"Mercy."

They laugh. "This is nice," says Bo, looking at Chelsea again.

A server approaches, places bread on the table, and quietly leaves.

"Yes, Bo, this is nice," says Chelsea.

"You sounded different last Sunday when you called."

"A lot has happened since I saw you."

"Bad? Good?"

"We won the quarterfinal last night." She smiles at the memory.

"Yes. I checked it out online. Your first win as a head coach. No doubt you're now the Queen of Rabon." He holds up his wine glass. "To victory," he toasts.

She raises her water glass and they clink glasses.

Clearing her throat, Chelsea sets her glass down and leans closer to Bo. "Somebody found out," she says calmly, belying the hurt churning in her stomach.

"Found out what?"

"My rehab. The leave of absence. The therapy."

A scowl darkens Bo's face, and he doesn't speak for a minute. Chelsea leans back, takes a drink of water, and waits.

"That's all confidential," Bo finally says.

"It's supposed to be," agrees Chelsea. "And only a few people know about it. You, me, my therapist, Human Resources at the firm, the rehab center. I didn't even tell my mom."

Bo, finishing his wine, rubs his chin.

"My principal came to me with a bunch of questions," Chelsea explains, her voice tinged with anger. "Wouldn't say who told him. Doesn't know what the source will do with what he knows."

"That's nuts, Chelsea."

She bites into a piece of bread as her emotions boil. "I'm trying to decipher who would reveal this—what their motives are. Do they just want to hurt me? Get me fired? Force me to stop coaching?" She suddenly feels desperate, like someone is tightening a noose around her neck and she's fighting to claw it off.

"They can't fire you for any of that!" Bo argues. "Nothing you did is a crime!"

"They don't need a crime!" Chelsea says, her voice rising with frustration. "Just the rumor that the new coach, a woman no less, is a drunk!"

"But you're clean now—don't drink at all!"

"You know that, and I know that, but people in Rabon will hear a totally different story. If this leaks, I'll have to quit and leave town in shame." She drops her head as the server arrives but Bo waves him off and he quickly disappears.

"Maybe it's a sign," Bo suggests. "You belong in Atlanta, with me at the firm. Take this as a chance to leave before anything blows up. Don't give them the satisfaction of forcing you out."

Chelsea faces Bo and shakes her head, the idea of giving up not an option. "That's exactly what they want me to do. Tuck tail and run. Make it easy for them."

Bo reaches for her hand. "So what?" he soothes. "Who cares what they want you to do? You're bigger than all that. Bigger than all of them, too."

She pulls her hand away. "I hoped we could enjoy tonight," she says, sadly. "But, after Roberts put me through the third degree, I need to ask you a question I know you won't like."

"I'm an open book, Chelsea."

She sighs, locks her hands in her lap, and eyes him straight on. "Did you do it, Bo?" she asks.

He rocks back as if shot but doesn't answer.

"You have motive and opportunity," she says.

Bo finally shakes his head. "I can't believe you'd ask me that. Yes, I want you back in Atlanta. But, as God is my witness, I'd never do anything to hurt you. Please tell me you know that."

Chelsea's eyes stay locked on him, her senses testing his sincerity. Yes, he had motive and opportunity. But would he go so far as to humiliate her like this? She leans forward and touches his hand. "I believe you, Bo," she finally concludes. "But, as you keep telling me, I'm a lawyer. I had to ask."

His window down, Palmer parks his truck about fifty yards up the street from a dirty, lime-green house. He's dressed in his best clothes—a collared blue shirt, a recently bought pair of khaki slacks, and the only shoes he owns that don't have scuffs. A streetlight burns overhead and a dim bulb on the porch of the lime-green house illuminates the scruffy yard. A yellow tarp covers a section of the roof nearest Palmer, and a couple of mongrel dogs lie near the steps. Three beat-up cars sit parked on a patch of thin grass. Palmer checks his phone. Almost ten.

The front door of the house opens, and Don and Strick suddenly hustle out and down the steps. An old man in tattered overalls trails them, a beer bottle in one hand and a cigarette in the other. The old man cusses loudly as Don and Strick head to one of the cars. "Git your sorry butts on out of here!" shouts the man. "And don't come back for all I care!"

The dogs rise and start barking as Don and Strick jump into the car. A woman appears at the door and yells at the old man. "Leave the boys be, Red!" snarls the woman. "They not worth the aggravation."

Don starts the car and quickly backs it up, almost running over Red. Cursing, Red hurls his beer bottle at the car, and it bangs off the trunk as the car peels onto the street.

"I'm changing the locks on the house, you ungrateful bastards!" Red shouts.

Don flips Red off and Red returns the finger as the car disappears around a corner.

"Come on, Red!" calls the woman. "Your supper is gone be cold!"

Red retrieves the beer bottle as the dogs fall silent and lie back down. Sucking the last drops left in the bottle, Red pulls himself slowly up the steps and back into the house.

Watching from his truck, Palmer waits until Red disappears through the door before starting the engine and driving off.

About ten minutes later, Palmer parks his truck in a circular stone driveway of a home on the opposite side of town. Evenly spaced spruce pines curve around the front of the house and strings of white Christmas lights twinkle from the branches of the pines. The house, an English-style country manor made of brick and stone, sits on a flat front yard covered with dark green grass.

For a couple of minutes, Palmer stays still and stares at the grandeur of the estate. He feels out of place, like one of the mongrel dogs at Red's house suddenly showing up at the Westminster Dog Show. He almost starts the truck to drive away but then his phone dings and he checks the text.

"You close?" asks Bridget.

"Here," he answers.

"Yay!" texts Bridget.

Though still feeling out of place, Palmer climbs out of his truck and heads toward the front door. A second later, the door flings open and Bridget, dressed in tight black leggings and a buttoned-up purple Knights' sweater, sprints out and jumps into his arms. Laughing together, they twirl around and around until Palmer feels dizzy and they drop and roll in the grass.

Catching her breath, Bridget grabs Palmer's hand and leads him quickly inside, up the stairs, and into a bedroom. Falling onto her bed, she yanks Palmer close, and he topples on top of her. "I'm so happy you came!" Bridget pants, her face red with excitement.

She rolls on top of him, her legs astride his waist, and kisses him. Her phone dings on a table by the bed but she ignores it and lays down on top of him. The phone dings again and she grabs it to turn it off but then sees the number, rolls off Palmer, and answers. "Hey, Sis," she says quickly, "It's been a minute."

"Mom told me to check on you."

Palmer sits up and scans the room. High, arched windows with a sitting area under them. A giant TV on one wall. An aquarium with several multi-colored fish on another. A computer on an elegant desk. Hardwood floors with a plush rug under the bed.

"I don't need a chaperone," says Bridget, her face a pout.

"Mom said you've been seeing a football player."

Palmer eases to the side of the bed and puts his feet on the floor.

"I answered because you never call," Bridget tells her sister. "But I'm hanging up now."

"Bridget!"

Bridget beeps off, slams down the phone, and turns to Palmer. "Where were we?"

Without facing her, he steps to the windows and stares out.

"What's wrong?" she asks, concern in her voice.

He turns to her again. "It's just. . . your house, your yard, this room." He waves a hand over the space.

"What about it?" asks Bridget.

"Compared to where I live? You're the princess in the castle and I'm a serf in the mud hut."

"Nobody is comparing, Palmer."

He faces the window again and looks out. In the past few weeks, he's entered two homes where he feels like an intruder, like a "rube," as Don and Strick would say. Nothing has prepared him for it and, deep in his gut, he knows he doesn't belong.

Bridget eases from the bed and hugs him from behind. "Last night," she whispers. "You stood up for me."

She kisses his back and Palmer turns to her and speaks quietly, almost reverently. "I don't remember much about my dad," he says. "Just bits and pieces. But I never heard him cuss around my mama. And he lit a candle on the dinner table every night. Said it made every supper with mama romantic. Before the war, he. . ."

Bridget rises to her tip-toes, kisses him, slowly eases him back to the bed, where she promptly settles. He kicks off his shoes as she reaches for him again. He kisses her on the neck as she unbuttons his shirt.

"Get undressed," she whispers as she starts to undo her sweater.

His head spinning, Palmer turns his back to her and hurries to obey, tossing aside his shirt and unzipping his khakis. She tosses her leggings to the floor beside his shirt.

"I need to tell you," he says as his pants come off. "I never—"

"Never?"

Still in his underwear, he hesitates as his face flushes with embarrassment. "Never," he repeats. "So, you know..."

"Neither have I," Bridget giggles as she slides under the covers.

He turns around, totally surprised. "But you—"

"Tease a lot? Yes. But that's as far as I've ever gone. Until I met you, I never really wanted to. . .you know, be with a guy all the way."

Her phone dings again but she ignores it. Dings a third time. Keeping herself covered, she grabs the phone and turns it off.

Palmer sits on the edge of the bed.

"Come on," says Bridget, pulling back the bedcovers on his side. He doesn't move.

"What's wrong now?" she asks.

"I don't know. The fact that you're a—"

"Virgin?"

"Yeah. It makes me feel weird."

"It's not a disease," she teases as she sits up, the covers pulled up to her chin. "It's the first time for both of us. That makes it even more romantic."

He puts his face in his hands, his emotions torn. "There's this other girl," he says quietly.

"Molly."

"Yeah."

"But you broke up with her."

He looks back at Bridget. "After the Longhorn game, Don and Strick... They... mistreated her."

"So, last night, when they showed up at the lake—"

"Molly is the brunette they mentioned. Me and Ty, we got there before it went too far with Molly, but last night, them doing what they did, it all boiled up in me again."

"You in love with Molly?" Bridget asks.

"I'm sixteen," whispers Palmer. "How do I know? But I handled things real bad with her. I hurt her."

He leans closer to Bridget, his eyes locked on hers. "I don't want to hurt anybody else."

"You want to be with me, Palmer? Here? Completely? In this bed?"

"You know I do," he says eagerly. "But I'm mixed up. Not sure we should ... at least not yet."

Bridget lays down and he stretches out beside her, he outside the covers, she under them. "I didn't know guys like you still existed," she says dreamily as she puts her head on his chest.

"Guys like me?"

"Kind. Innocent. Honorable."

"An idiot. A twit."

"A twit?" She raises her head and stares at him.

"A word I remember from English class. A foolish person."

"You're definitely that." She lays on his chest again and they both fall silent.

Palmer's mind swirls. He knows what most guys would do and he's no different than the rest. But something holds him back. Molly? Or memories of his dad and the respect he showed women? Or is it just fear? He and Bridget live in two different worlds, and no matter how much he wants to change that, he knows he can't. He touches her hair, his fingers gentle. "I can't believe the serf is not ravaging the princess," he says softly.

"Ravaging?"

"I guess I remember two words from English."

"It's your loss." She tickles him and he tickles her back. Then they wrestle, rolling over and over on the bed.

CHAPTER TWENTY-ONE

The pre-game buzz in Rabon notches higher and higher as the week runs by. With the football team preparing for the semi-finals, everything else in town drops in importance. Local merchants, gas stations, and restaurants show their support for the Knights with neon signs, giant posters, and handwritten notes scratched on lunch boards advertising the daily specials.

Tyler receives chemo every morning and he and Palmer study the Playbook every night he feels up to it. Palmer visits Counselor Towe on Tuesday and Thursday during his study hall and Chelsea pushes him harder than anyone else at practice every afternoon. At night, when he's not with Ty, he visits with Bridget, making out most of the time but working on some math as well.

On Thursday night, he's in Coach Dub's office with Ty again, poring over the Playbook. Ty reclines in Dub's chair, a blanket on his legs. Worn out from the day, Palmer closes the Playbook, picks up a football, and tosses it up and down. "Your mama's gone kill you for being out so late," he tells Ty.

"I can't stay in the house all the time."

"Tanya coming to drive you home?"

"Yep."

Palmer tosses the football to him.

"You nervous?" Ty asks. "Semi-final is just two days away." He tosses the ball back to Palmer.

"Football has never been a big a deal to me," Palmer says. "So, no, not too nervous."

"The crowd will be huge!"

"You trying to make me nervous?" He flips the ball back to Ty.

"I wish I could play."

"I wish you could too."

They laugh. Ty throws the ball to Palmer, and he grips it hard in his large hands. "I also wish the Playbook made sense to me."

"You're so close," encourages Ty. "I bet it will hit you all at once, like a puzzle snapping together."

Palmer lays the ball in his lap. "I have Rapid Automatic Naming Dyslexia," he says as if on auto-pilot. "My brain gets letters and numbers all tangled up, like a spider web. When you read something, you understand it two to three times faster than me. And a chart? A graph? A diagram of a football play? Throw one of those in front of me and I'm as lost as a yellow marble in a wheat field."

Ty eyes widen. "You've known this all along?" he asks.

Palmer shrugs. "I've known it most of my life."

"Why you telling me now?"

Palmer weighs the question, thinking of all the schools he's attended, all the houses he's lived in, all the people who have appeared and disappeared in his life before he even learned their names. "I don't know," he says to Ty. "I haven't had a friend in a long time. Maybe never."

"We're friends?" Ty smiles as he asks.

"Racial reconciliation, Bro."

"You paying me reparations?"

Palmer reaches into his pocket. Hands Ty a couple of quarters. "It's all I got."

Palmer stands, lays the ball on the desk, and hugs Ty. Doesn't see Chelsea walk into the office behind them.

"Isn't this cozy?" chuckles Chelsea.

Palmer and Ty quickly disengage and face her. "Don't even ask, Coach," says Ty.

"Saturday night, guys," she says. "Just be ready for the game Saturday night."

Forty-eight hours later and Saturday night has not only arrived, but the game is almost over. Sadly, Palmer and the Knights have looked anything but ready. The scoreboard shows the dismal story. Fourth Quarter: 21 seconds left. Knights: 0. Guests: 7.

The home fans are jammed into the Rabon High bleachers even tighter than normal. Not a seat or an aisle is unfilled. And, even with a season-ending loss staring them in the face, nobody has departed. Dressed for the awful weather— thirty-nine degrees amidst a steady drizzle—the spectators hang in there, unwilling to give up.

The Knights, their white jerseys heavy with mud, possess the ball at mid-field.

Chelsea and the other coaches yell from the sidelines. Tension rides the air on the field and in the stands. The stadium announcer booms the situation. "It's third down! Six yards to go for a first!"

Palmer, slathered in mud and breathing hard, calls the play in the huddle. "Split Right. Scat Right. 343. 1 go."

The huddle breaks and the offense lines up. The defense, wearing black and gold, shouts signals and players shift. The center snaps the ball. Palmer rolls out, slips on the wet grass, and almost falls. A defender hits him, driving his left shoulder into the ground. Another defender falls on him, crushing him under his weight. He lays on the ground, moaning, as pain shivers through his left shoulder and down to his ribs.

Chelsea yells for a time-out and the offense sprints to her on the sideline, Palmer trailing, his left arm limp. A trainer rushes to him and starts massaging his shoulder. Palmer grunts in pain and Chelsea steps to him. "How bad is it?" she asks.

"It's fine. I can play."

Chelsea glances at the trainer, who shakes his head. "Raise your left hand over your head," she instructs Palmer.

Palmer lifts his arm and groans again as it reaches shoulder height.

Chelsea turns to Johnson standing a couple feet away. "Johnson," she commands. "You're in."

"My right arm is fine!" protests Palmer. "I can play, Coach!"

"We've run the same twelve plays the whole game," Chelsea explains as Johnson buckles his chin strap. "They know we have to pass here. If you're in, that limits us to six plays. Plus, you're hurt. So, let's give Sean this last shot. See if we can fool 'em." She glances at the scoreboard. Six seconds left.

She leans to Johnson and gives him the play as Palmer trudges off, slams his helmet to the ground, and plops onto the bench. He looks down the sideline to where Ty usually sits and hangs his head. Ty isn't there. Russell, Vanessa, and Tanya are missing too.

The referee blows his whistle for play to resume and Palmer glances into the stands, looking for Bridget but doesn't see her. Wondering where she is, his eyes search left to right. No Bridget. From the corner of his eye, he spots Molly, sitting beside a well-dressed, older guy, the two of them snuggled close under a blanket.

The offense runs back onto the field and Palmer picks up his helmet, fights off the temptation to look back at Molly, and focuses on the game again. The stadium announcer makes a brief announcement, no roar in his voice this time: "Johnson in for Norman."

The offense lines up. The center snaps the ball to Johnson, and he laterals to a running back. The back sprints to the right, then pitches the ball to Swoops running left on a reverse. Apparently out of the play now, Johnson drifts to the right and the defense ignores him. Swoops suddenly slows down, stops, and raises his arm to pass. In that brief second, Johnson turns on his top speed and sprints downfield. No defender is within twenty yards.

Swoops throws the ball across the field and Johnson catches it in stride and runs toward the goal line. A defensive back chases, his legs churning, and it looks for a second like he'll catch Johnson. But Johnson has too big a lead and lunges across the goal line for a touchdown as the clock runs out. The Knights' crowd explodes with joy.

Chelsea jumps up and down on the sideline, holds two fingers to the sky, and shouts over and over. "Two! Two! Two! Go for two!"

Johnson calmly looks to Chelsea, and she offers him a polite curtsy, as if she's a ballerina acknowledging the audience applause . Johnson quickly offers a thumbs up, the sign that he's clear on the play she's called.

A hush falls on the Rabon side of the stadium while the guests' side screams and bangs on the bleachers, hoping the noise will bother the offense. Breathing hard, Johnson calls the play at the line of scrimmage, receives the snap, and runs right as fast as he can. The offense's tight end, lined up on the left side of the line, fakes a block, then rumbles to the left corner of the end zone. At the last second, Johnson turns and lofts a perfect across-the-field pass to the tight end for the two-point conversion. Pandemonium erupts as the Knights win 8 to 7.

Thirty minutes later, the on-field party continues in the Knights' locker room as music blasts away and players and coaches dance. In his wheelchair in a corner, Dub chews on an unlit cigar while Chelsea and Paul swing around and around like spinning tops. Dizziness overcomes Paul and he falls backwards onto the floor.

Catching her breath, Chelsea grabs a football, climbs onto a chair, and motions for everyone to quiet down. It takes a minute, but everybody eventually stops talking and focuses on her. "They wanted me to stay on the field to do media!" she shouts. "But I said 'no.' I wanted to celebrate with you!"

The players roar again.

"I'm so proud of how you kept fighting," she yells. "Defense? Amazing. No quit in you. Thanks to Coach Paul for leading the defense this week!"

The team cheers. "Defense! Defense! Defense!"

"Talk about no quit!" cheers Chelsea. "Sean Johnson, game ball!" She tosses him the ball and the team cheers again. "Johnson! Johnson! Johnson!"

"One more game, gentlemen!" yells Chelsea. "The biggest game of your lives. We stick together, we'll win it all!"

The team erupts one last time while Palmer stands quietly in the corner, his helmet in his hands.

About an hour later, a light breeze blows after-game litter across the parking lot outside the locker room. Most everyone—fans, players, and coaches—have finally left, worn out from tension, relief, and celebration. The drizzle continues to fall.

Sitting in her pickup, the engine running and the windshield wipers swishing, Chelsea relaxes, her emotions spent. She leans back and allows herself to enjoy the moment. What a night! She breathes deeply one more time. She's going to coach in a championship game. Who would have thought it? She smiles, flips on her headlights, and almost drives off, but Roberts suddenly appears in front of her, running in a half-waddle, his hands waving for her to stop. She almost laughs but holds back and rolls down her window.

"Great game, Coach," says Roberts, fighting to catch his breath.

"Is the job mine yet?" she asks, surprising herself with the pointed question.

Roberts leans closer, still panting. "Huge news, Chelsea. You're blowing up. I took a call right after the game. ESPN wants to interview you ASAP. We're setting up an Instagram profile for you, and an X account. Time to do some branding."

"The job?"

"After the championship game. We'll firm things up when it's over."

"That other thing we talked about?"

"Nothing new from the other party. So, no worries."

The sound of a motorcycle roars from behind them and Chelsea turns as Palmer pulls up.

"Get some rest," Roberts orders Chelsea.

She nods and Roberts hustles away as Palmer rolls up to Chelsea's window.

"Where's your truck?" Chelsea asks.

"My motorcycle uses less gas."

"How's your shoulder?"

"Sore. But the trainer said it looked okay. Nothing torn or broken."

"Make sure to ice it when you get home. We'll check it again tomorrow."

"Am I starting the championship game?"

"Let's talk tomorrow. Meeting at six."

"Am I starting?" Palmer insists.

The rain falls harder. Chelsea hesitates, knowing if she answers the wrong way, it will crush Palmer, kill the confidence he gained by winning the quarterfinal. But she can't lie to him either—not now, not ever. As much as he already distrusts women, a lie is the last thing he needs to hear from her. "I don't know," she finally answers. "It's the championship. I don't see how we can win running the same twelve plays."

Palmer stares at her like he wants to say something, and she almost turns her truck off to talk to him, but he shakes his head, revs his bike, and speeds off before she can. Watching him go, Chelsea senses she just screwed up, that a connection she should have made will forever remain out of reach. Frustrated, she pounds her hands on the steering wheel and the joy of the night's victory seeps quickly away.

CHAPTER TWENTY-TWO

A t Georgio's, the after-game crowd presses in tighter than stuffing in a turkey. Everybody talks loudly, reliving the final plays of the victory. Strangers buy new friends a beer and toast the win. Somebody throws a Knights' cap into the air and people dive for it. Christmas decorations brighten the festive mood into something bordering on sheer bliss.

Palmer performs in the corner, but the louder-than-normal noise muffles his music. He scans the crowd as he plays, searching for Bridget, but doesn't find her. Out of the corner of his eye, he sees the front door open, and Molly enters, her date right behind her. His heart drops but he keeps playing as the hostess leads Molly and her male companion past him to the only empty table, which is a few feet from the stage.

The date pulls out Molly's chair, helps her remove her coat, and whispers in her ear as she sits. She's dolled up, wearing full make-up, her hair cut shorter and professionally styled.

Palmer's face clouds as he watches them, but he finishes the song, and the room quiets a little. Palmer leans into the mike: "I'll be back in just a few," he says.

Molly smiles at him as he lays down his guitar, but he wants nothing to do with her, so he turns away and heads toward the restroom. Moving quickly, Molly rises and rushes after him. He stops and pivots around. "Leave me alone," he snarls, his face flushed.

"Is your shoulder all right?"

"What do you care?'

Molly drops her head.

"I thought you hated crowds,' continues Palmer. "Restaurants. Dressing up."

"It wasn't my choice to eat here."

"He made you come?" he challenges her, growing angrier by the second. "The Molly I knew didn't let nobody make her do nothing she didn't want to do."

Molly looks up. "He just … he wanted to bring me somewhere nice."

"So did I but you said 'no.' Reckon you were embarrassed to be seen with me."

"That's not true. I just liked it me and you, by ourselves, the two of us."

Palmer grunts and glances at Molly's date, who's shoving a bread stick into his mouth. "Who is he?"

"Just a guy. Drew. Nobody really."

Palmer's anger spews full blast. "Andrew? Your rich boy? The liar?"

Molly tries to explain. "He's on Christmas break. He reached out."

"Snagged yourself a college boy, did you?"

"He's matured a lot. He apologized, for, you know, what happened before."

"I apologized too." Palmer is almost shouting now and a couple of diners glance in his direction.

"Bring it down a notch," Molly pleads. "Drew's not important. Besides, you're with Bridget now."

Palmer settles a little. "I see her some, yes."

"Where is she tonight?"

Palmer shrugs. "It's not your concern."

"She's a party girl, Palmer. Everybody knows it."

He leans closer, his voice a tad quieter, but still full of venom. "You my mama now?"

Molly glances back at Drew, who's now watching them. "I'm sorry," says Molly.

Drew stands and walks their way.

"That night at my house," continues Molly. "I was mad at Don and Strick. But took it out on you."

Drew puts an arm around Molly but speaks to Palmer. "You playing your banjo tonight?"

Palmer glares at Molly but addresses Drew. "I only play banjo for special people."

"Did you bring your banjo?" Drew says. "I'd like to hear it, Banjo Boy."

Palmer grabs Drew's shirt with one hand and balls his other into a fist.

"Let it go, Palmer!" pleads Molly, touching his arm. "People are watching!"

Palmer glances around. The people nearest them have stopped eating, their eyes on him, Molly, and Drew. Palmer drops his hand from Drew and stomps away.

A couple of hours later, Georgio's is closed. Only a few cars remain on the town square. A light drizzle continues to fall. In the parking lot, Palmer is strapping his guitar case to his motorcycle when his phone rings. "Hey, Ty," he gruffly answers.

Ty coughs. "Sorry I couldn't make the game."

"I banged up my shoulder."

"I heard it on the radio. Are you okay?"

"Why you calling so late, Ty?" Palmer asks, his patience thin.

"Do I need a reason?"

"I'm done, man. I played awful. Johnson should start the championship game."

"This isn't about who starts the next game. It's about you. It's about what kind of person you want to be."

"Everybody is a therapist these days."

"A least I don't give up."

"What I do ain't for you to decide."

Ty coughs hard and long. "I called to tell you I'm back in the hospital. Been awful sick all day."

Palmer pauses, unhappy with himself for dumping on Ty. "Sorry, man," he apologizes. "I'm a jerk sometimes."

"You don't sound good, Palmer."

"No worries. I'm fine."

"No, you're not."

"I appreciate you, Ty. Take care of yourself."

Palmer hangs up, climbs onto his bike, and peels away into the darkness.

An old car sits empty beside Palmer's truck as he pulls up to his house and parks his bike. Careful with his shoulder, he climbs off and peeks inside the car. Sees nothing to indicate its owner. Growing suspicious, he unhooks his guitar, hurries through the rain, and into the house.

As Palmer enters, Lacy gets up from the sofa. "I figured it was you," he says tersely as he stops by the open door. "Hoped I was wrong."

"Sorry to just show up, Son," says Lacy. "But you don't answer my calls."

"You done with rehab?" he asks, closing the door.

"That place not doing me any good. And the way you left when you visited, I needed to see you."

Palmer eases the guitar case to the floor, his anxiety spiking. "Where you been the past few days?"

"I had to tidy up a few things."

"What does that mean?"

She shakes her head. "Nothing that concerns you."

"The police looking for you?"

"I don't expect I'm their top priority. But yeah, I broke my sentence requirements."

Palmer stares at his shoes, not sure what to say. One thing he knows for sure, though. He can't live in the same house or the same town as his mama. He faces Lacy again. "What you want, Mama?" His voice sounds like cold steel.

"I know you doing good here. Regular Renaissance man. I'm not gone mess that up. I'm telling you clear."

"Intentions are one thing, Mama. What you do is another."

She takes a small step towards him. "I saw Dirk. He's open to me staying here awhile. I want you, us, to be together. A family, as best as we can make it." She steps closer, but he raises a hand to stop her, determined to shut her down, to kill the idea of living with him before it can draw a full breath.

"I ain't a child anymore," he growls. "You can't just waltz in here, expect me to do what you say."

"I know, Son. You're all growed up. But still, I'm your mama."

His face turns darker. "You killed Dad! That forfeits your mama card! Don't you understand that?"

Lacy wipes tears. "You need to believe me, Son. I didn't mean it. It just happened. "

"Stop it!" he shouts, his anger boiling. "I saw it … remember? It's done. And we're done. You live your life, I live mine." He jerks open the front door and waves for her to leave. She reaches for him, but he pushes her away and backs up.

"I'm sorry, Son," cries Lacy. "For all I did, didn't do, that hurt you."

He points to the open door, his body rigid, unflinching. Rain drips off the door to the floor.

"I ain't leaving!" she shouts, "Got nowhere else to go!"

Palmer stays still, unyielding. "If you stay, I go," he says.

Lacy moves toward him again, but he yanks the door completely open and rain blows in on him.

"I'm sorry, Son," cries Lacy.

"Don't call me 'Son' again."

Lacy drops her head into her hands and wails as rain drips off the door. When she finally looks up, she sighs, nods, and picks up her jacket off the sofa.

Palmer digs into his pocket as she slips the jacket on and hands her his tip money as she moves to the door.

"Bye, Palmer," says Lacy, her eyes down.

Still silent, he holds the door open as she walks slowly past him and out into the rain.

The clock in Ty's hospital room shows 1:33. Ty is asleep, the bed covers pulled tightly to his chin. Nobody else is in the room. Moving quietly, Palmer slowly pokes his head around the corner and creeps over to Ty. Bending to the bed, he gently shakes Ty awake.

"Hey, man," Ty whispers, his voice groggy.

"Where your folks?" asks Palmer.

"Pops is out of town. Mama ... I don't know. Bathroom? A snack?"

Palmer grabs the wheelchair in the corner.

"What time is it?" whispers Ty.

"It's late," says Palmer, rolling the wheelchair to the bed.

"What you doing?" asks Ty.

"We're going on a little road trip."

"You crazy, man."

Palmer leans towards Ty, wraps him in the bedcovers, and lifts him out of bed.

"Stop it, Palmer," objects Ty. "I'm too sick."

Palmer ignores his protests and eases him into the wheelchair. "My bad hanging up on you earlier."

"I can't do this. Put me back in bed."

"Relax, man," insists Palmer. "You in my hands now."

Too tired to argue, Ty closes his eyes as Palmer grabs a pillow and slides it behind his back.

"Okay," murmurs Ty. "Where we going?"

"Complexities, man. You said we'd discuss them someday."

"My mama will have your head for this."

Ignoring Ty's threat, Palmer wheels him out of the room and down the hallway.

The rain has stopped, and stars peek down on the parking lot as Palmer wraps the covers tighter around Ty and lifts him into his truck. Using the pillow as a cushion, he carefully lays Ty's head against the seat and shuts the door.

"Take me back inside," pleads Ty as he closes his eyes.

"Just rest." Palmer quickly shuts the door, hauls the wheelchair into the truck bed, and jumps into the driver's seat.

Neither of them speak as Palmer drives up the mountain toward the overlook. Though he's never been there, he's heard it's the spot where tourists go for the best view of Rabon Valley. And, according to the rumor mill, it's a favorite hookup place for teenagers like him. Palmer glances at Ty as he drives, but Ty's eyes stay closed, so he leaves him alone.

About fifteen minutes later, they reach the overlook and Palmer backs the truck up to the edge, so the rear faces the valley. Turning off the truck, he hops out, unloads the wheelchair, and turns it to face the cliffs. Finally, he opens the passenger door, gently shakes Ty awake, carries him to the wheelchair, and pushes it close to the precipice.

"One more thing," Palmer whispers as Ty's eyes stay closed. "Borrowed from my uncle Dirk."

He grabs a six pack of beer from the cab, returns to Ty, and shakes him gently. Ty finally wakes and inhales a deep breath. "What are we doing here?"

Palmer climbs onto the tailgate, opens two beers, and hands one to Ty. The moon watches them now, the sky bright.

"Now we can talk," says Palmer.

Ty raises up slightly. "I always knew white people were nut jobs," he says, his voice weak.

Palmer waves at the sky and the town square below, the latter outlined in Christmas lights. "Complexities, Bro," he says quietly as he tastes the beer. "Night and day. Men and Women. White, black, brown, and yellow. Life and Death. Complexities. A long list of complexities."

Ty chuckles, seems to gather a bit of strength, and sips from his beer. "I don't really like beer," he says, his face wrinkling against the flavor.

"I've heard you have to develop a taste for it."

"We're supposed to drink something we don't like until we eventually like it?" Palmer swallows a big guzzle and his face scrunches. "Sounds stupid to me too. I mean, what's the charm?"

They laugh. Ty hands Palmer his beer and he sets both bottles in the truck bed.

"I think I'm leaving Rabon," says Palmer, as if announcing he planned to brush his teeth before bed.

"That's foolish talk," Ty says quickly.

"I'm a pretty good guitar player," observes Palmer, building his case for leaving. "Sing okay too. Think that's my best shot to make something of myself."

"Skipping out now is a bad move."

"I stink at football. Molly has hooked up with another guy. Bridget didn't show tonight, and I have no clue why. My grades remain in the crapper and my junkie mama now says she's gone move in with me and Dirk."

"Cry me a river," says Ty. "I got cancer."

Palmer chuckles but not happily. "Well, yeah, I guess cancer trumps everything in the 'my-life-sucks' department."

"Don't leave, dude. I need you," pleads Ty.

Palmer stares at the moon. "I don't know," he says. "Everything is piling up on me."

Ty looks at the stars. "What you feeling right now?" he asks, facing Palmer.

Palmer studies his feet dangling off the tailgate. "Everything. Nothing. Sad. Afraid. Alone."

"You're not alone, dude."

Palmer faces Ty. "Just how sick are you?" Palmer asks.

"Well," says Ty, "death is a genuine possibility."

Palmer picks up his beer again and takes a drink. "You scared?"

"I'd be lying if I said I wasn't."

"You don't act scared."

"Hand me my beer."

Palmer hands the beer to Ty and he sips.

"My fear is silent, man," says Ty. "It can't speak unless I let it, and I decided from the jump to hold it down."

They fall quiet. Stare at the sky.

"What you think happens after we die?" Palmer asks, swallowing another drink of beer.

"That's a deep question for a country boy."

"You rubbin' off on me, I guess."

They both sip beer.

"Hard to say, on your question," says Ty, his voice stronger as he warms to the topic. "My folks, they believe in traditional things—the Lord, life after death, heaven, hell, all of that."

"You?"

"Maybe. Sometimes. I mean, we're all made of matter and energy."

"If you say so."

"Matter and energy are just two sides of the same coin. And energy never dies. It just takes different forms."

"So?" Palmer looks at Ty again, focused, interested.

"The energy that makes us who we are—the spirit, the soul, the essence of us—whatever you call it, that survives past this life."

"Hard to imagine how."

Ty sips beer again. "Think of a baby in the womb, Palmer," he says. "No way that baby can imagine what this life is like. So how can we imagine what the next life will be like?"

Palmer stares at the sky again, his feet swinging. "That's pretty heavy stuff for a jock," he says.

"Well," replies Ty, "I'm a philosopher at heart." Ty sips the beer one more time, makes a face, and hands the bottle back to Palmer. "Yeah, really," he says. "What's the big deal with beer?"

They laugh for a long minute before growing quiet again. "Guess I need to take you back before the cops find me," Palmer finally says, jumping off the gate.

"One more thing before we leave," says Ty.

"What's that?" Palmer faces Ty.

"The race thing. It's not really so complex."

Palmer empties Ty's beer bottle, then his. "That's not what I hear," he says.

"In that next life?"

Palmer turns back to Ty, both serious now. "Yeah?" Palmer asks.

"I don't see how race can matter at all."

Palmer bends to Ty, extending a hand, and they shake as the stars twinkle above them.

CHAPTER TWENTY-THREE

P atrice leads Chelsea, dressed in a tweedy, gray-and-white plaid jacket, tailored black slacks, and black pumps, into the family room, where Dub, his leg up, works at his easel, his fingers busily painting an old tractor.

"Look who's come to visit," chirps Patrice.

"Hey, young lady," Dub greets Chelsea. "Forgive me for not standing up."

"That's the least of the things you need my forgiveness for," teases Chelsea.

"I almost commented on your professional outfit but thought better of it," smiles Dub.

"I knew you were teachable," grins Chelsea.

"Coffee, Chelsea? Tea?" Patrice asks.

"Tea would be great. Can I help you get it?"

Patrice smiles. "Not at all. You're the head coach who just won us a semi-final game. I'll be right back."

Dub lays down his paint brush as Patrice exits and Chelsea steps closer to examine his work. "I heard you were painting avocados these days," she says, a smile still on her face.

"Nah," says Dub. "I'm on to manly things now." He points her to a chair and she sits. "What brings you to my humble abode on a Sunday?" asks Dub, his eyes twinkling.

Chelsea leans forward. "I heard a rumor that Conway High has hired Buck as a consultant," she says, turning quickly to business.

"I thought you didn't do football on Sunday," says Dub.

"Yeah, well, I'm sitting in the head chair now."

Dub nods. "It's different, isn't it?"

"Completely." Patrice brings in her tea. "Thank you," says Chelsea.

"Anytime," says Patrice. She looks at Dub. "I'll let you two talk." She smiles and leaves the room.

"I'm aware of Buck's new gig," Dub says as Chelsea sips tea.

"Is that even legal?" she asks. "Him going to work for the team we're facing in a championship game?"

"It's a gray area, I expect. But you probably can't stop it this late."

"What a Judas!"

"Buck knows your twelve plays and how to stop them," Dub reminds Chelsea.

"You think he'll back-stab us like that? Tell them what he knows?"

Dub chuckles. "We're not writing him a paycheck anymore. So yes, I have no doubt he'll spill every bean in his pockets."

"Which leads me to my quarterback dilemma."

Dub smiles. "Johnson did the job last night."

"Not to minimize his heroics," counters Chelsea, "but he caught one pass and threw another one twenty-five yards. Buck knows Sean can't throw the ball accurately over forty yards."

"But Johnson knew the plays that allowed him to do what he did," says Dub.

"Could we rotate him and Palmer?"

"That'll just confuse your offense," advises Dub. "And Conway will adjust based on which quarterback is in."

Chelsea holds her tea in her lap. "I want you to coach the defense for the championship game," she says.

Dub picks up his paint brush and dabs at the tractor. "Not sure I'm physically up to it," he says.

"I need you, Dub. Simple as that."

"Coach Paul did an excellent job with the defense last night."

"True. But I need your experience this last game. It'll make the team more confident."

Dub examines the tractor painting. "I hear Roberts is still waffling on giving you the job on a permanent basis."

Chelsea chuckles. "He won't commit to me as the head coach, but he wants me to do some branding. Seems I'm good PR for the school right now."

Dub laughs. "Roberts wouldn't know branding if it bit him in his hindquarters."

Chelsea sips tea again and her voice softens. "If Roberts doesn't hire me for next year, I suppose I can just move back to Atlanta, go back to my law firm."

Dub points his paintbrush at her. "I don't believe for a second that's where your heart is."

Chelsea stares at him, admires his gentle but firm ways, his humble wisdom, his willingness to stick his neck out for her. "You're a perceptive man, Coach," she says finally.

"Call me Dr. Phil." He lays down his brush.

"We don't always get to follow our heart," she says. "Do we?"

"I reckon not."

Chelsea sighs and shifts her thoughts back to football. "I wish Palmer loved football," she says.

"Like you do? Like your brother did?"

Chelsea sips tea, her emotions suddenly raw. "I have a soft spot for quarterbacks," she says.

"I'm sure there's a good reason for that."

She puts down the teacup and wipes her eyes.

"You want to talk about it?" asks Dub.

Chelsea weighs the idea but shakes her head. "Can't," she says. "Hurts too much."

Dub reaches for her hand, and she lets him take it. "I need to get going," she says. "Big game coming up."

Dub nods slowly. "Be careful with Palmer," he advises. "He's riddled with cracks. But he's the best pure talent I've ever seen."

He pulls himself up and balances on the table as Chelsea also stands. Dub opens his arms, she steps to him, and they embrace.

"I'm almost certain that hugging a female colleague is against policy, Coach," whispers Chelsea as a tear rolls down each cheek.

"I'm retiring," Dub counters. "I can hug whoever the hell I want."

The fireplace in Palmer's house is burning low. A couple of empty pizza boxes rest on the floor, three empty bottles of water by them. Palmer, dressed in gray sweats, sits on the hearth and calls Dirk. "Hey, man," he says when Dirk answers. "You hear about the game last night?"

"No, dude, sorry. We played till almost three a.m. Fell into bed after, slept late. You know the drill. You win?"

"Yeah, but no thanks to me. Coach Deal benched me."

"Don't sweat it," encourages Dirk. "Play better next time."

"You think I can make a living playing music?"

"That's a strange question out of nowhere."

"Seriously, what you think?"

"A living? Yeah. Being a star … that's a whole different animal. Takes talent, which you have, plus a whole lotta luck."

"What if I come live with you, find myself a band, a place to play music?"

"That's a bad idea, Palmer."

"I'm old enough to drop out of school if I want."

"The music business eats most people up, dude. Then spits 'em out."

Palmer stands, picks up the pizza boxes, and throws them into the fireplace. "I ain't cut out for football," he says.

"No problem. Quit after the season. But finish school before you even think about Nashville."

Palmer watches the pizza boxes blaze up. "You still playing at the Wildhorse?" he asks Dirk.

"You sounding weird, man. What you thinking?"

"I don't know. But maybe Rabon's not the place for me."

"That's idiot talk. You show up here now, you're not living with me."

"Mama dropped by."

The phone falls quiet for a moment. Finally, Dirk speaks. "I figured she would."

"I can't stay here. Not if she's around."

"She's my sister, dude. You want me to leave her on the street?"

Palmer props a foot on the hearth, closes his eyes, opens them again. "What's gone happen when she screws up again?" he asks, anger flaring like the pizza boxes in the fireplace. "Or the cops show up looking for her? You know how bad that'll be for me? How embarrassing?"

"We'll figure something out. Just don't go off half-cocked and do something stupid."

The pizza boxes disintegrate into ashes and the momentary blaze drops to a low, smoky ebb. "I appreciate you, Dirk," says Palmer. "How you took me in."

"Whoa. Slow down, Kid. Don't—"

His mind suddenly made up, Palmer hangs up, picks up the empty bottles and carries them to the kitchen, where he tosses them into the trash can. Pivoting, he hurries back to the front room, folds up a blanket on the sofa, and lays it neatly across the back. Walks to the front window and stares out. It's almost dark. He pulls out his phone and locates his Contact List. Deletes Coach Dub, Ty, Chelsea, Lacy.

He brings up Bridget's number and calls her. No answer. He leaves a voice-mail. "Hey, sorry you couldn't make Georgio's last night." He turns around, stares at the fire, continues. "Look, me and you, I don't know. You might not see me for a while, maybe a long time. So, us, you shouldn't wait around. I like your teasing. You're not what people think you are. Bye."

He hangs up and deletes her number. Brings up Molly's. Pauses. Deletes that one too.

Turning off the video in Dub's office, Chelsea checks her phone: 6:21. She calls Palmer but no answer. Worried, she calls Ty, but Vanessa picks up. "Hey," says Chelsea.

"Congrats on the game," says Vanessa. "Sorry we couldn't be there."

"How's Ty?"

"He's back in the hospital."

"Sorry to hear that. I'll visit soon as I can. Do you know if he's heard from Palmer today?" She tries to keep her voice steady but doesn't quite succeed.

"Ty's been asleep since this morning. Don't think he's heard from anybody."

"If Palmer contacts him, let me know immediately."

"What's going on?"

Chelsea voices her fear. "Palmer didn't show up for our six o'clock meeting. Something is wrong. I can feel it."

"He snuck Ty out of the hospital late last night. Drove him up the mountain for some guy talk."

"That's crazy."

"He's getting a piece of my mind when I see him, and it won't be the pretty part!"

"Palmer's girlfriend," says Chelsea, feeling more panicked by the second. "Any idea how I can reach her?"

"Molly or Bridget?"

"I have Bridget's number, but not Molly's."

"Reckon she still works at the motel?"

"I'll check there," says Chelsea. "Anything I can do to help Ty?"

"Win Saturday. A championship will lift his spirits better than anything I can imagine."

Vaness beeps off and Chelsea tries Palmer again but gets no answer. She tries Dirk. Also no answer. Her heart in her throat, she pockets her phone and hustles out.

The living room at Palmer's place is clean. The floor swept. A fresh stack of wood on the hearth. The fire is out, the fireplace cleared of ashes. His guitar case and a small gym bag sit by the door.

His mind set, Palmer slips on his jacket, throws his backpack over his shoulder, and takes a 360 degree turn around the room. A touch of nostalgia hits him, and he sighs. Though here only four months, the place had started to feel a little like a home, a spot to hunker down in, at least until he finished high school.

Thoughts of Molly flit through his head, then memories of Bridget and Dirk. Finally, he thinks of Ty and Coach Deal. Good people, he concludes, but no more permanent than a log in a fire. Here one moment but vanished the next, like so many others he's met in his life. He glances around one last time, then picks up his guitar and gym bag and heads out the door.

In the yard, he loads his belongings into his truck, then walks to his motorcycle. Careful with his shoulder, he pushes the bike up the front steps, parks it on the porch, and pauses for a second. Is he really doing this? Setting his jaw, he pats the motorcycle seat, then runs to the truck, hops in, and pulls out of the yard, the wheels kicking up gravel as he speeds away.

Less than a half hour later, Chelsea parks in Palmer's front yard, jumps out of her truck, and hustles to the dark porch. She sees his motorcycle, pushes past it, and bangs on the door. No answer. She knocks again but instinctively knows it's futile. The house is empty.

She keys her phone as she hurries back to her truck. "Palmer's gone, Dub," she laments as soon as he answers. "He missed our six o'clock meeting. I'm at his house. It's dark—empty dark."

"Stay calm," advises Dub. "Teenage boys slide off the rails sometimes. Do crazy things. Doesn't mean he's disappeared for good."

Chelsea climbs into her truck. "He left his motorcycle, Dub. I'm telling you, I feel it in my gut. Last night, the last time I saw him, I blew him off. He's got nobody and, when I should've been there for him, I screwed up."

"It's all right, Chelsea," soothes Dub. "I'm here. Tell me what you need."

"I'm going to find Palmer. If I'm not available for practice tomorrow, handle that for me."

"That will confuse the team," Dub warns.

"It doesn't matter. This is bigger than football. I won't be able to live with myself if something happens to Palmer and I just stood by and did nothing."

"You want help looking for him?

Chelsea lays her head on the steering wheel, her mind racing, trying to figure out where to start searching.

"Chelsea?" Dub asks.

"Handle practice if I'm not there," she repeats. "That's what I need from you."

"Okay then. I got your back. Do what you need to do."

Chelsea hangs up, starts the truck, and calls Bridget as she wheels down the road. To her surprise, Bridget answers almost immediately. "Hey, Bridget. This is Coach Deal. Have you seen Palmer today?"

"Nope. But he left me a weird voice message a little bit ago. Said I might not see him for a while."

"Did you break up with him?"

"No! But my folks grounded me. No phone, no games, no parties. I didn't see him last night and had no way to tell him why I didn't show up."

"The message he left ... did he say where he was going?"

"No. You think he's okay?"

"Just let me know if he contacts you."

241

Air pods jammed into her ears, Molly vacuums the motel lobby, burrowing the vacuum under a sofa. Bouncing a bit with the music, she picks up a dirty sandal left beside a coffee table.

Chelsea enters the lobby, spots her, and hurries over. "Hey, Molly!" she yells as she touches her shoulder.

Molly jumps at the touch, turns, and removes an air pod. "Hey, Coach," she says. "What's up?"

"You heard from Palmer lately?" asks Chelsea, her concern clear in her voice.

Molly turns off the vacuum. "We're not together anymore."

"I know," says Chelsea. "But I'm worried about him. He missed our study session tonight. I called him but he didn't answer. I drove to his house. No sign of him. I think he's left Rabon."

Molly drops her eyes. "I talked to him for a couple minutes last night. At Georgio's after the game. He was upset and I made it worse."

Chelsea puts a hand on Molly's shoulder and Molly raises her eyes. "Where do you think he would go?" asks Chelsea, urgency permeating her voice.

"His new girl's house? Bridget?"

"I already talked to her. He's not there."

"Nashville? To stay with Dirk?"

"I've tried to reach Dirk but no luck."

Molly thinks a second. "Palmer told me once that Dirk plays sometimes at a bar called the Wildhorse," she finally offers.

"I'll call there."

Chelsea turns to leave but Molly grabs her arm. "If you go to Nashville, I'm riding with you," says Molly.

"But you're not with Palmer anymore."

"Maybe I should be. If you go, let me tag along."

"I'll see," says Chelsea, backing away. "But no promises." She rushes off as Molly watches her, the vacuum still quiet in her hand.

Her hair in a ponytail and her eyes red, Lacy pulls her beat-up car into the parking lot of a dive bar in a seedy part of Nashville. A row of lights burns over the bar's entrance, illuminating a sign for Honky Tonk Heaven. Worn out from lack of sleep, and the almost four-hour drive from Rabon to here, Lacy lays her head on the steering wheel and deals with second thoughts. She's come to this place to see if she can score a fix. But another part of knows she should run from this skanky place as fast as her trashy car will take her.

She thinks of Palmer pointing her to the door. Just as she deserved, she decides. She's no good to him or anybody else. She's a failure, a screw-up, a burden. Resigned to her fate, she pulls her jacket tighter, climbs out of the car, and walks toward the bar. Two guys stand by the front door. Lacy pulls a cigarette from her jacket. "Got a light?" she asks.

The tallest man, an unshaven middle-aged guy wearing a dirty baseball cap and a Tennessee Titans sweatshirt, lights her cigarette. "I'm Flip," says the man.

Lacy puffs her cigarette.

"You all by your lonesome?" Flip asks, eyeing her top to toes.

"Not looking for company tonight," answers Lacy.

"Pretty lady like you ought to always have company," says Flip, a smirk on his face.

"You got party favors if I choose to accept your company?"

"You like a particular party favor?"

"Miss Emma, China Girl, Ox. They're all favorites."

"You offering cash for these favors? Or, you know, me and you, all night?" Flip leers at her again.

Lacy pulls cash from a pocket. "I ain't for sale. If I party with you, it's 'cause I choose to do it, not 'cause you bought me."

The second man, a short guy with a bad combover of his reddish hair, chuckles. "The lady's got scruples, Flip."

Flip points to an alley past the building and Lacy follows him as he heads that way, the other guy trailing. In the alley, Flip stops and turns to Lacy, a pistol now in hand. "I'm plumb out of party favors, lady," he says. "But I'll take that cash just the same." He points at Lacy's money as the short guy blocks the alley.

"Come on, man," pleads Lacy. "Play fair."

"Fair is what you make it, lady."

Lacy tries to back up, but the other guy stands in her way.

Flip reaches for the money and Lacy fights him off, but he punches her in the face, and she drops. The money scatters.

Not giving up, Lacy latches onto Flip's leg, but the short guy pulls her off. She stands and rushes Flip again, but he throws her against the wall, and she bangs her head and falls again.

Grabbing the money, Flip tosses a few dollars at her and walks away. Her lip bloody, Lacy lays in the alley, tears running down her face.

CHAPTER TWENTY-FOUR

The sun rises as a steady stream of vehicles pull up to the gas pumps of Gerty's Gas and Go service station. Many of the drivers run inside to buy coffee, doughnuts, or microwaved sandwiches as their tanks fill up. Everyone is in a hurry. Jobs and schools await on a chilly Monday morning. Horns honk, engines rev, and music pours out of car doors and windows.

Behind a green dumpster on the backside of the gas station, Palmer slumbers in his truck bed, a sleeping bag stretched out to cover his long body. A toboggan cap is pulled tightly on his head and cloth gloves cover his hands. A blue jay perches on the edge of the dumpster, its eyes on Palmer, chirping as if trying to wake him up. A trash truck rumbles to the dumpster and the blue jay flies away. The truck's hydraulic arm embraces the dumpster and dumps its contents into the truck bin, but Palmer continues to sleep.

A couple minutes later, the truck pulls away and Gerty, an older woman wearing a blue vest and saggy black pants, hauls a trash bag from the station's back door to the dumpster. As she tosses the trash in, she spots Palmer and steps closer. "Hey!" she yells at him, her voice shrill. "Wake up!"

Somehow, Palmer is still asleep.

Gerty bangs a fist on the tailgate of his truck. "I said wake up!"

Palmer rolls over and rubs his eyes.

"This ain't no Holiday Inn!" shouts Gerty. "You can't be sleeping here!"

"Sorry," says Palmer, sitting up. "I'll get moving." He rolls up his sleeping bag and hops out as Gerty examines him a little closer.

"How old are you, boy?" she asks.

Palmer ignores the question and opens the truck door.

"Where are your folks?" Gerty presses.

"Where am I, exactly?" Palmer asks, facing her as he removes his gloves.

"Should I call the cops?"

Palmer shoves his gloves into a pocket as he considers how to respond. "No disrespect, ma'am," he finally says, "but I'd just as soon move along."

Gerty eyes him. "You don't look harmful," she says, her face softening.

"I'm not," agrees Palmer.

Gerty pulls a pack of cheese crackers from her vest and tosses it to him. "You a few miles outside Jackson, Mississippi, son."

"How far to Austin, Texas?" Palmer asks, relaxing a little.

"Your mama know where you are?"

Palmer pulls off his cap but doesn't answer.

"What's your name?" presses Gerty.

"Don't call the police," he says. "I'm leaving."

"I ain't on no first-name basis with the police."

"Name is Palmer Norman," he offers.

"You gone play music in Austin, Palmer Norman?"

Palmer smiles a little and Gerty does too.

"Willie Nelson started there," he says. "Reckon I can too."

"You gone be a big star?"

Palmer smiles again and Gerty reaches back into her vest, produces a pack of beef jerky, and throws it to him.

"All right," she finally concludes. "Go get famous, Palmer Norman. One day I'll tell folks you slept behind my dumpster!"

Palmer climbs into his truck and smiles back at Gerty. "Thank you, Gerty." He points to her nametag on the vest and she grins. He pockets the jerky, starts the truck, and rolls off, Gerty watching as he disappears past the dumpster.

Flags fly in a steady breeze directly in front of Rabon High School. Several camera crews have set up in and around the flag area and production vans line the curb up and down the street. An ESPN crew is set to film first while others wait for their turn in front of the flags.

Sandra Brinner, an early-thirties ESPN correspondent with a model's face and a gymnast's body, smiles happily and raises her microphone to just below chin level as her producer counts down. Nothing better than getting a jump-start on the competition. A red scarf wraps around Brinner's neck and her white teeth line up straight and perfect, like a picket fence in a Norman Rockwell painting.

"Good afternoon." Brinner beams at the camera as her producer points for her to begin. "It's lunchtime at Rabon High School in the mountains of North Georgia and I'm here to introduce you to a remarkable woman. Her name is Chelsea Deal and she's the first female coach to ever lead a boys' high school football team to a state championship game. We've requested an interview with Coach Deal but, to our surprise, nobody seems able to locate her!"

Brinner raises a well-groomed eyebrow at the unexplained mystery of the missing Coach Deal and quickly continues. "For reasons yet to be explained, Ms. Deal is absent from school today and practice is scheduled to start in about four hours. We'll talk with her and bring you that interview as soon as we can track her down! This is Sandra Brinner with ESPN."

A country road zips by under the wheels of her pickup as Chelsea wolfs down a fast-food burger. Molly eats French fries beside her and washes them down with a soda. Both women stay quiet, focused on their own thoughts. Chelsea's phone beeps and she quickly hits the answer button on her steering wheel.

"Hey, Chelsea," barks Principal Roberts. "You have to stop whatever you're doing, turn around wherever you are, run every speed limit sign you see, and get back here right now!"

Chelsea bites her lip before she answers but doesn't give in. "No can do, sir," she says. "I'm going to find Palmer, like I said on the voice message I left you this morning. I arranged a substitute for my classes and Dub will manage practice for me."

"Listen to me," insists Roberts, his voice desperate. "The media showed up like a pack of hyenas this morning. I can see cameras right now outside my window and my phone is exploding. Everyone wants to interview you, but you're MIA and I have no answer when they ask where you are!"

"That branding you mentioned... I guess it's working."

"Don't be flippant, Coach!" Roberts shouts.

Chelsea glances at Molly and whispers a silent "Yikes!"

Molly grins as Chelsea responds to Roberts. "Sorry, sir. My bad."

"What do you suggest I tell the media?" asks Roberts. "Our quarterback has gone AWOL and you're tracking him down?"

"Sounds about right to me."

"Come on, Chelsea, I'm not joking!" Roberts grouses. "If we say anything about Palmer, that will lead to questions about him. They'll find out about his grades, the math class meltdown, his family situation. Who knows what else? You know what I'm talking about. Not good for you, me, or anybody else."

Chelsea looks at Molly again and Molly vigorously shakes her head. Chelsea knows why. The assault after the Longhorn game. Questions about Palmer might reveal it all to the media. Not a good outcome for anyone. Chelsea, shifting in her seat, speaks again to Roberts. "I don't have a choice on this, George. Tell the media I'm sick. Or took a mental health day. I don't care how you spin it."

"Tell them she's suffering from menstrual cramps!" Molly yells.

"Who was that?" asks Roberts.

Chelsea glares at Molly and waves her off. "Don't worry about it," she advises Roberts.

"This is serious, Chelsea," says Roberts. "Not a laughing matter. Good publicity helps us all. Bad publicity? Not so much."

"I understand, George. And I swear I'm doing everything possible to resolve the situation with Palmer and return to Rabon. I'll be back by tomorrow. Hold the media off until then."

She hangs up and faces Molly. "Menstrual cramps?"

"Not a laughing matter!" yells Molly.

"Come on, Molly." A smile breaks out on Chelsea's face, but she tries to hold it back.

"Your time of the month!" yells Molly. "Tell them that! No football coach ever said that before!"

Chelsea and Molly both laugh hysterically now, Chelsea slapping the steering wheel with both hands as Molly doubles over, her whole body shaking. Chelsea turns on some music, which blasts through the speakers as they slowly stop giggling.

Lacy, still wearing the same clothes from the previous night, rolls over in her motel bed and stares into the mirror hanging over the TV. She sees a bruise on her right cheek, plus a puffy black eye. She touches the scrape, winces, and sits up. A clock on the table shows 1:48. She slowly reaches for her phone, lies back on the bed, and makes a call.

"Hey, Dirk," she says, her voice weak. "I have to go back."

"Back where?"

Lacy wipes tears. "Rehab."

"Where are you now?"

"Here. Nashville."

Dirk exhales. "I thought you were going to Rabon?" He sounds agitated.

"I did. But Palmer said I couldn't stay there." Lacy stands, steps to the mirror, wipes tears away. "I'm asking you to drive me back to rehab," she continues.

"Why can't you take yourself?"

"I know you mad at me, Dirk. And I lay no fault on you for it. But I need you with me to make sure I don't change my mind." She bites her lip to shut off tears.

"God, Lacy," says Dirk, complete frustration in his voice. "I'm so tired of this."

"I know, Dirk. I got no right to ask you again."

"I've heard all this before, Lacy."

She cries again, harder now, sobbing into the phone. "I been a bad mama, Dirk. A bad sister. All my sins done caught up with me. And I know you got no cause to trust me. But you the only person I know to call."

"If I do it, Lacy, you're spending your last nickel with me," Dirk threatens. "Nothing left in the bank if this goes bad."

"I'm hanging on by a fingernail here. I swear on Palmer's life, I'll get better this time or die trying."

Silence falls for several seconds. Lacy walks to the window and stares out, her heart thumping. If Dirk says no, she's dead in the water. No one else to call. Nowhere to go. She pulls out the few dollars in her pocket and wonders if she can sell her car for enough to...well ... to buy enough junk to put herself down for good.

Dirk finally speaks. "All right," he says. "One last time. But I'm done if you screw up again."

Lacy sags back onto the bed, sucks in a breath, and wipes her eyes again.

"I can't come till tomorrow," says Dirk. "Can you stay out of trouble for twenty-four hours? Stay where you are until I call you back?"

"Whatever you say. I won't go nowhere, do nothing bad."

"Good. I'm cutting off my phone the rest of the day so I can get some things finished."

"I'll not bother you no more today. I promise."

"Text me the address."

Wires hook Ty to multiple monitors in his hospital room. His clothes hang loose on him, like a giant cape on a pygmy's skeleton. His cheekbones poke through his skin and his mouth gapes open as he sleeps. Russell and Vanessa stand by the door with Dr. Ramirez.

"It's like a switch has turned off in him," mourns Vanessa. "He acted a little stronger the past few days, but this morning—he can't seem to stay awake and can barely move."

"It happens with some patients when we increase their chemo dosage," explains Ramirez, almost whispering. "The chemo saturates the body to the point where the body's organs react against it."

"The cure becomes worse than the disease?" asks Russell.

"In some cases, yes."

"But he seemed to be holding his own before," Vanessa protests.

Ramirez drops his head. "No one can explain it," he says sadly. "But with the tumors still spreading, we had no choice but to do what we did."

"What's the plan now?" asks Russell.

Ramirez faces him eye to eye. "We need to shut down the chemo. Immediately. No more treatments."

"All of it?"

Ramirez nods and Vanessa erupts into tears.

"We can't just give up," says Russell, putting an arm around Vanessa.

"I agree. We wait a few days," says Ramirez. "If he responds, he'll recover some strength. Then we try another chemo treatment."

Vanessa leans into Russell. "What do you mean, if he responds?" asks Russell.

Ramirez rubs his face. "Not everybody does."

"My boy is not going to die!" wails Vanessa, stepping towards Ramirez, her face close to his, challenging him to argue with her.

"We all love Ty," says Ramirez, his voice soft. "I assure you we're doing everything we possibly can."

Russell gently pulls Vanessa back as Ramirez pivots and walks away.

Chelsea and Molly aren't laughing anymore. Empty fast-food bags sit on the floor at Molly's feet as their pickup passes a sign: "135 miles to Nashville."

"I appreciate you letting me ride with you," says Molly.

"I know you care for Palmer. And I don't mind the company."

"Sorry I kept you from leaving as early as you wanted."

Chelsea shrugs. "We all have jobs. And if Palmer is with Dirk, a few hours won't matter one way or the other."

Molly stares out the window. "Let's say we find him," she says. "How will you convince him to come back?"

"I might need your help with that."

"What if that don't work? We're not exactly. . .well, he's really mad at me."

Chelsea reaches for Molly's hand. "One step at a time, Molly."

"He's had it rough, you know."

Chelsea passes a large truck. "Why did y'all break up anyway?" she asks.

"Because we're both idiots."

"Been there, done that."

Darkness slowly falls in Austin as Palmer points his truck around a curve and spots a long wooden building dead ahead. A wide porch fronts the building, and a flat roof covers it. A sign out front reads: "The Busted Spoke."

Palmer wheels into a parking spot just up the street and parks, climbs out, and stretches, his bones weary from the almost ten-hour drive. People of all ages hustle in and out of the Busted Spoke as night closes in and streetlights blink on. The people wear wide belts with shiny buckles and cowboy hats and boots. Music blasts out when the front door opens, and is still audible when it closes. A big crowd of folks sit in rocking chairs on the lighted front porch, laughing and drinking beer.

After watching for several minutes, Palmer gathers his courage, opens his door, grabs his guitar case, and strolls up the sidewalk. At the bottom of the porch, he hesitates and reconsiders what he's about to do. Is he ready for this? He sets his guitar on the ground and sucks in a breath. Should he turn around and head back to Rabon with his tail tucked between his legs? Probably. Or at least get some sleep and then come back? He picks up his guitar and almost turns around. But then he stops. *Nothing in Rabon for me. And no reason to wait. Better to fail here and now than to never have tried.*

Setting his jaw, he stands up straighter, walks onto the porch, past the crowd and through the front door of The Busted Spoke. Once inside, he stops and stares. Even though it's just past six on a Monday night, the place is popping. Waiters and waitresses hurry out and back, trays loaded with food, beer, and wine. Scores of folks hang out at a long wood bar covered with beer bottles. A group near the back slams back whisky shots. A band plays on a stage on the far side of the room and people dance on a square, polished wood floor.

Palmer soaks it all in, his emotions on overload, shocked that he's actually there. He's imagined this moment for years but never let himself dream it would actually happen. For a few seconds, his nerves jump on him again and he almost falters. But the raucous band stops him. Focusing hard, he listens to the vocalist's voice, watches the guitarist's fingers on his instrument. *Smooth*, he decides. But not necessarily better than him and Dirk. Encouraged by this, he regains his courage, pushes back his hair, and steps to the reception counter.

A hostess, dressed in blue jeans, a white blouse with a ruffled neckline, and brown cowboy boots, quickly greets him. She's early twenties with bright brown eyes, a face like a country singer, and lips made for kissing. "Seating for two?" she asks with a wide smile.

Palmer looks around. "Two?"

The hostess points to his guitar case. "Around here, a guitar is almost as important as a person."

He grins. "Uh, no, sorry. My name is Palmer Norman. I'd like to see the manager."

"I bet you play that guitar pretty good."

Palmer grins, getting more comfortable by the second as adrenaline rushes through him. "Some people say I do. I got a regular gig where I play, back in

Georgia." He places a hand on the counter.

"Musicians show up here every day asking for an audition," says the hostess, a bit of warning in her tone.

"Five minutes with your manager. That's all I ask."

The hostess wags a finger at him. "I got strict orders," she says. "No walk-in musicians. Shoo." She waves him away.

Palmer starts to argue but she dismisses him again and he slouches out, his head down, his momentary confidence shattered.

A cup of coffee in one hand, Chelsea stands on Broadway Street in Nashville and punches off her phone with the other.

"No luck?" asks Molly, standing beside her with a smoothie in her hand.

Chelsea shakes her head, unlocks her truck, and both climb back in. Molly slurps on her smoothie while Chelsea sips her coffee. A sign for the Wildhorse bar blinks on and off across the street and people stroll both ways on the sidewalk in front of it, but no one goes inside.

"I can't believe this," says Molly, staring at the Wildhorse. "Their web page says they open at 6:30."

"I can't believe we've been in Nashville three hours, and Dirk hasn't called me back. I've left enough messages."

Molly places her smoothie in a cup holder and stretches. "What if Dirk doesn't play here anymore?"

"He'll eventually call me back." Chelsea adjusts the rearview mirror so she can see herself and applies a touch of lipstick.

"Palmer has to be with him," Molly says, trying to assure them both.

"If he's not, we've driven a long way for nothing," Chelsea says as she smooths down her hair and moistens her lips.

Molly stares at her a minute, then speaks as if she's just discovered gold. "You got a thing for Dirk!"

"Not at all," argues Chelsea. "I'm attached already. Or I was. We haven't talked much lately."

"Dirk is hot."

"Hot or not, he should have called me back by now." Chelsea turns away from the mirror.

"Guys are such idiots," says Molly.

"You sure use the word 'idiot' a lot," observes Chelsea.

"It fits a lot of situations."

"Dirk is an idiot for not calling me back. Yes, I see what you mean."

They laugh and Chelsea calls Dirk again. To her surprise, he answers this time.

"Hey, Coach," he says nonchalantly. "Sorry I haven't returned your calls. Been crazy busy."

"I left you at least ten messages!" she scolds.

"Like I said, sorry. Played till late last night. Turned my phone off to get some sleep, then rehearsals this afternoon."

"I need to talk to Palmer," she says sternly to Dirk.

"I assume you've called him."

"He's not answering his phone. Like his uncle."

"You couldn't resist, could you?"

"It was too easy."

"You're forgiven," Dirk says. "But still, if you want to talk to Palmer and can't get him on the phone, drive out to the house."

"You didn't listen to any of my messages?"

"No. Saw you called but didn't listen to the messages."

Chelsea bites her lip to keep from boiling over. "I can't go see Palmer at your house because he's with you!" she blurts..

"What makes you think that?"

The same hostess greets Palmer as he enters the Busted Spoke a second time. "What's it been, Georgia Boy?" asks the hostess with a wide grin. "An hour?"

"I hoped you'd be gone," Palmer says, grinning only slightly.

"That's no way to charm a girl."

Palmer leans over the counter and begs her with his eyes. "Please. Five minutes. Let me play."

"You're not shy, I give you that."

"Usually I am."

"How old are you?"

"Music don't know a age."

The hostess smiles. "That's a good answer. But still 'no.'"

Palmer starts to push harder but she presses a finger to his lips to shush him. He walks out, his heart sinking a second time.

Dirk, Chelsea, and Molly sit in a booth in a small café. Food waits on the table in front of them, but no one eats. Dirk holds his phone to his ear and leaves a message. "Hey, Palmer," he says. "Call me. We need to talk." He hangs up and texts Palmer the same message.

"Where else could he go?" Chelsea asks.

"It's not your problem," says Dirk. "You've done all you can. Now you need to drive home and prepare your team for the game this weekend."

Chelsea stares out the window. "I can't just give up on him," she says.

"He'll call me sooner or later," Dirk assures her. "And I'll order him back to Rabon. I'll let you know when he'll arrive."

"You think he's somewhere else here in Nashville?" asks Chelsea.

"I doubt it. He'd come to me if he was in town."

"He's all alone, wherever he is," Molly says sadly.

Dirk waves off her concern. "He's been alone a lot in his life. He can handle himself."

They all fall quiet. Chelsea drinks from a water glass. "Where else would he go?" she asks as she puts the glass back on the table.

"It's all about his music," says Dirk. "He thinks he's ready to make a living from it."

"If not Nashville, then—"

"Austin!" exclaims Dirk. "We talked about it more than once. The best places for starry-eyed musicians to make it are Nashville or Austin. Since he's not here, I'd bet my last dollar he's there. And I know exactly where he'll go when he gets there!"

"I don't have time to fly to Austin!" declares Chelsea.

"Me either," agrees Dirk. "I'm driving his mama back to rehab tomorrow. Scooting back here to play immediately after."

"His mama?"

Dirk waves her off. "I'll explain later."

"I'll go to Austin," pipes in Molly. "It needs to be me."

Palmer steps into the Busted Spoke a third time and the hostess laughs when she sees him. "You're not a quitter," she says. "I admire that."

"What time do you leave?" he asks hopefully.

"My replacement is a dude the size of a beer truck and he, unlike me, won't give two hoots that you're cute."

"Come on, five minutes," Palmer pleads, desperation in his voice. "I drove all night and day from Georgia to play here! Have a heart."

The hostess sighs, checks her watch, places both hands on the counter, and leans close to Palmer. "Okay, Georgia Boy," she finally says. "I'm a pushover for tall blondes with blue eyes. It just happens to be my break time." She grabs Palmer by the hand, leads him past the bar, across the dance floor, and through a kitchen.

"Where's the manager?" asks Palmer, still pushing for what he drove to Austin to do.

"Shush," says the hostess. "Trust me."

She opens a door behind the kitchen and pulls him into a large room filled with spare chairs, tables, assorted pieces of cleaning equipment, and boxes of beer glasses. A broken microphone stands in one corner, several empty beer kegs in another. The hostess pulls out a chair, flips it around, and straddles it. "Stand there," she orders, pointing to an open spot about ten feet from her. "You got one song. Impress me."

"What about the manager?" Palmer asks again.

"Five minutes, Georgia Boy. You want to perform or not?"

Though still frustrated he's not playing for the manager, Palmer realizes this is his only shot, so he quickly pulls out his guitar and straps it over his shoulder. "Just so you know," he says, clearing his throat, "I slept in the back of a truck last night."

"You gone perform or make excuses? I said impress me."

Palmer closes his eyes, shakes out his hands and shoulders, strums the guitar a few moments, inhales deeply, and begins to sing. From the first note, it's soulful, gritty, and pure, his voice and guitar flowing together, the rhythm in sync, like a newlywed couple gently making love on their honeymoon.

The hostess leans in, seduced by his sound. She smiles to herself, obviously charmed far past what she expected. When Palmer plays the last note, she almost tips forward in the chair, but quickly pulls it back as he opens his eyes.

"Well done, Georgia Boy," she whispers as she stands and applauds. "Really good."

"Thank you," he says, grinning slightly.

She steps to him and hands him a business card.

"You'll let me see the manager?" asks Palmer.

"You're not ready yet," says the hostess. "But don't give up. Get some more seasoning, a year or two. Grow up a bit. Call me after that." She taps the business card he's holding.

"What about the manager?" he presses.

She laughs softly and touches his arm. "Look at the card, Georgia Boy. I am the manager."

Dirk and Molly stand by the driver's window of Chelsea's pickup. "In the morning, I'll put Molly on the first plane to Austin," promises Dirk. "And I'll keep calling Palmer until he answers."

"What if you don't reach him by the time Molly lands?" asks Chelsea.

"Molly will head to the Busted Spoke to find him. I bet a new pair of boots he'll badger somebody there until they listen to him play."

Still stoked, Palmer pilots his truck down a tree-lined street a few miles from the Busted Spoke, his eyes searching for a spot to sleep overnight. Large brick houses with flat lawns and paved driveways lay out on both sides of the street for blocks and blocks and it seems he'll never reach the end of them. Finally, he sees a high-steepled, white-brick church on a corner, and pulls into the parking lot and around to the back.

Driving slowly, he reaches a grove of trees in a secluded corner, parks, and climbs out. A grassy spot beckons a few yards away. After scanning the area to make sure he's alone, Palmer pulls his sleeping bag from the truck, stretches it out on the ground, lays down, and checks his phone.

He sees multiple calls from Dirk but ignores them. His stomach rumbles and he pulls Gerty's jerky from a pocket, unwraps it, and bites off a big chew as he stares at the stars. A tan cat strides by, stops, and eyes him. Palmer sits up. The cat creeps closer and Palmer picks it up and scratches it behind the ears.

"You by your lonesome too, buddy?" he asks the cat as he bites from the jerky. The cat purrs. Palmer gazes into the sky again. A shooting star streaks by.

"I had this friend one time," Palmer confides to the cat, his voice soft. "She would've loved to see that star fly by."

The cat stretches out on his chest.

"Where you live, buddy?" Palmer asks the cat. The cat meows. "Don't know, huh," says Palmer as loneliness engulfs him. "I know the feeling."

The cat purrs again and Palmer feeds him the last of the jerky, climbs into his sleeping bag, and stares at the sky as the cat watches him from its perch on his stomach.

The giant kangaroo in front of the coffee shop watches as Holt pulls his Hummer into the empty parking lot and turns off the radio. A second later, the door opens and Buck climbs in. "It's freezing out here," grumbles Buck as he blows on his hands. "I hear we might get snow this week."

"I didn't meet you this time of night to discuss the weather," grouses Holt.

Buck grunts as he faces him. "Who peed in your Cheerios?"

"You asked for this meeting," replies Holt, not at all pleased. "And I'm here. Speak your piece."

"All right," says Buck. "I see your girl is a media darling now."

Holt pulls a wrapped cigar from his console. "We should have expected it," he says. "A pretty woman achieving something unprecedented in a man's world. For the media, it's better than sex."

"Yeah, well, maybe we should point them in a different direction. You know, shape the narrative, as they say."

"That's a low thought, Buck, even for you."

"I'm not the one that went to rehab for a drinking problem," says Buck. "Don't you think the public deserves to know that Chelsea isn't the innocent doll that everybody is painting her to be? All we're doing is telling them the truth."

Holt unwraps the cigar but doesn't speak. After a few seconds, Buck extends an envelope toward him.

"You're not a coach at Rabon anymore," says Holt, unwilling to accept the envelope.

"The public has a right to know," Buck insists, again pushing the envelope at Holt.

Holt reaches for the envelope but quickly stops, his loyalties divided. "I can't do it, Buck. It's a step too far, even for me."

Buck's voice becomes sinister, threatening. "My brother will be sad to hear it, Les."

"Probably," says Holt, not backing down. "But I'm hoping he'll understand."

Buck reaches into Holt's console, pulls out a wrapped cigar, and sniffs it. "One thing about you, Les," he says admiringly. "You do cultivate the finer things in life."

"I enjoy my pleasures … like everyone else."

Buck's voice turns to steel. "My brother is not a forgiving man, Les. In case you didn't know."

"I understand the threat, Buck. You've made it perfectly clear." Holt points to Buck's door. "Have a good evening."

"Suit yourself. Just don't say I didn't warn you."

Holt points to the door again. Buck pockets the envelope and climbs out, the cigar in hand as he slams the door and stalks away.

CHAPTER TWENTY-FIVE

The next morning, with Lacy sitting quietly in his truck, Dirk leaves Palmer another brief voice message.

"Hey," says Dirk, passing a *Welcome to North Carolina* sign. "Molly is flying to Austin to bring you home. Hope I guessed right and you're there. Call me soon as you hear this." He hangs up.

"I need to see Palmer soon as you find him," says Lacy.

"What he does once I find him is his business."

Lacy stares out the window. "I could end up in prison this time."

Dirk exhales with exasperation. "I already told you: I called your rehab center. They checked with law enforcement, who said if you return to Sunrise today, they'll let sleeping dogs lie. But if you dip out again, they'll find you and send you straight to jail."

Sandra Brinner, dressed in a tight black skirt and bright green sweater, looks out of a dormer window on the third floor of Barbara's Bed and Breakfast, a large, white-framed house with a wrap-around porch and a row of hollies in the yard. Brinner holds a phone in one hand and a piece of paper with a typed message in the other. She starts talking as soon as a man answers on the other end. "Hey, Derrick," she says, her voice quick with excitement. "Quite the tip we received last night about Coach Deal!"

"Heck of a twist," agrees Derrick. "What's the best angle now that we know about this tasty backstory?"

Brinner holds up the paper. "We have to use it. Right?"

Derrick chuckles. "I love that you're still naive enough to ask."

"Two positive ways to go," says Brinner. "Coach Deal is the history-making, All-American golden girl leading her team to a championship game. Or she's the gritty, courageous history-making woman who's overcome a drinking problem to lead her team to a championship game."

"Or a third, more negative option," counters Derrick. "She's the booze-soaked, former lawyer with enough baggage to crush a freight train who shouldn't be allowed to lead a bunch of impressionable high school boys into anything, much less a championship game."

Brinner pauses, her brow furrowed. "We don't want to shape it that way, do we?"

"Which story captures the most eyeballs?" asks Derrick. "That's the only question we need to ask."

Brinner walks away from the window, lays the paper on the bed, and stares at it as she considers the choices. "I think we should go with the courageous woman overcoming the drinking problem," she suggests. "That gives us the 'female succeeding in a man's world' story. It's richer and deeper, with more heart."

"The booze-soaked lawyer sounds juicy to me," counters Derrick. "Scandal captures a lot of attention."

Brinner weighs how best to guide Derrick to where she wants him to go. "Sure," she notes. "Scandal rocks. But here's the thing."

She stalks to the window again and stares out. "Do we kick a woman while she's down? Or lift her up for what she's overcome? Seems like people want the positive story, at least right now, when it's about a woman. Later, we can always fall back on the booze-soaked angle if we want, once we've worn the legs off the courageous woman narrative."

Derrick hesitates a moment.

"I feel like I'm right on this one, Derrick," adds Brinner.

Derrick gives in. "Okay," he says. "You're closer to it than me. Choose the angle you think best."

Impressed with her powers of persuasion, Brinner smiles. "One last thing," she says. "Why would someone bring confidential information like this to us? What's the informer's motive?"

"Dislike of a woman coach?" suggests Derrick. "Somebody who wants her job? An opponent who wants to distract her before the championship?"

"Maybe that's a story too," says Brinner. "A mysterious tipster with a hidden motive leaks confidential information. That might be a criminal offense, too. I'll see if I can smoke this person out."

"Sounds good. A second thread to pull. But focus on Deal for now. Push somebody, pay somebody, sleep with somebody. I don't care what it takes, but set up an interview with her today! If that doesn't happen, post the story without an interview, ASAP."

"Will do." Brinner hangs up and plops on the bed, her excitement rising. Yes, she desperately craves an interview with Chelsea Deal. But she also wants to find the snake that's after Chelsea, a snake whose head she plans to cut off before she closes shop in this quaint little burg called Rabon.

Her coat pulled tight and her eyes darting out and back across the terminal, Molly hurries through the crowded airport in Austin. Pictures of longhorn cattle stare at her from the wall on the left while photos of oil wells do the same on the right. People wearing all manner of denim jeans, outlandish cowboy hats, and sharp-toed boots hustle here and there. A cart carrying an elderly woman almost runs her over as she rounds a corner. Electronic signs overhead offer all sorts of confounding directions, and a cowboy performing a rope trick draws a crowd ahead.

Dazed and confused, she spots an exit sign and hustles as fast as she can toward it.

Munching on the crackers from Gerty, Palmer ties up his sleeping bag and lays it in his truck while his cat friend follows. Finished with the crackers, he pulls out his phone. Sees more messages from Dirk. Opens the most recent one and listens. "Hey," says Dirk. "Molly is flying to Austin today."

The cat paws at his feet and Palmer squats to scratch its ears as he listens to the rest of Dirk's message. "Are you surprised?" he asks the cat as he puts the phone away. The cat yawns.

Palmer picks up the cat, scratches it one last time, gingerly places it on the ground, and climbs into his truck. He reaches to start the engine but suddenly pauses, pulls out his phone, and calls Dirk. "What time will Molly land?" he asks the moment Dirk answers.

"Are you in Austin?"

"Why's she coming?"

"Why you think, kid? We're all looking for you."

"Who's we?"

"Me, Molly, Chelsea, Ty, your teammates, the folks at Georgio's, that stray dog that walks by our porch sometimes."

"You should add comedy to your show."

"Molly will meet you in about an hour at the Busted Spoke."

Palmer spots the cat stalking into the trees. "What if I don't show up?" he asks, unsure whether he wants to see Molly or not.

"I'll personally fly to Austin and kick your butt from there into Christmas."

Though weary to the bone, Chelsea hides out in Dub's office and stares at more video of Conway High's defense. To reach the championship, this tough, veteran group shut out their opponents in both the quarterfinal and semi-final—a truly amazing feat. Her phone beeps every fifteen minutes or so but she ignores it, just as she has for most of the past twenty-four hours. She picks up a crimson binder marked "Conway Defensive Tendencies" and flips it open.

Her phone beeps again. She eyes the number just as Roberts rushes in, his face flush, his eyes as round as silver dollars.

"It's out, Chelsea!" he exclaims, his voice panicky.

"What?" She lays down the binder, already knowing the answer but trying to remain calm.

Roberts hands her his phone. Points to the story on screen from the ESPN app. "That reporter, Sandra Brinner," he pants. "The one that's tried since yesterday to set up an interview with you!"

Chelsea eyes the headline: "The Knights' Queen and Fifteen Days in Exile."

"Your alcohol rehab!" blurts Roberts. "Must be twenty media vans outside. More on the way. You should have given Brinner that interview!"

"You really think that would have made a difference?" Chelsea hands Roberts his phone, leans back, and battles to think clearly. Everything runs together in her head. Worries about Palmer. Frustration with the media. Anger at whoever spilled her private information. Not to mention how to score against Conway's stout defense.

Her phone buzzes again but she doesn't answer.

"Your phone!" Roberts points to it on the desk like it's a bomb with one second left on a timer. "Answer it!

Chelsea leans over and shuts the phone off.

"What are you ... we ... going to do?" Roberts pleads. "Talk to me!"

Chelsea picks up the binder again. "I don't know about you," she says as she flips to the first page, "but I'm going to figure out a way to score some points against Conway High."

Under a brilliant but cold sun, Molly eases onto a bench in front of the Busted Spoke and tries to relax. Having traveled out of Georgia less than ten times in her life, the combination of her first flight and the bustle of the airport have fried her brain and jangled her nerves. Her eyes dart all over the place, landing everywhere and nowhere at the same time. Feeling cold, she snuggles into her coat and waits. Though Dirk has called and told her he'd finally reached Palmer, she has no assurances he'll show up.

Unsure what she'll say if Palmer does come, she takes a deep breath and raises her face to the sun.

"You gettin' a tan?" It's Palmer's voice from behind her, so she quickly turns around. Walking slowly, he moves to the bench and sits down beside her.

"You snuck up on me," she says.

"Truck's back there." He points to it about thirty yards behind the bench.

"I would have heard you if you were on your motorcycle."

"Too far and too cold to ride a motorcycle," he says.

"But a motorcycle is sexy."

He laughs and props a leg on the bench. 'You a long way from Rabon," he says, staring at the Busted Spoke.

"I never flew on a plane before," she says.

"I still haven't," says Palmer. "Was it scary?" He faces her.

She shrugs. "Yeah. But scary can be all right, I guess."

He stares at his hands and falls silent.

"The woman beside me on the plane had a comfort parrot," says Molly.

Palmer chuckles. "At least it wasn't a snake."

They watch a dirty pickup truck pull up and four guys climb out, three in cowboy hats, all in boots.

"I'm here to bring you home," Molly says quietly.

Palmer points to the men as they amble down the street. "I like hats like that. Boots too. Maybe this is my home."

"We all miss you," Molly counters.

"I realized something last night," says Palmer, still watching the men. "All by myself. Staring at the stars."

She turns to him. "What's that?"

"The universe is a big place."

"Now that's a revelation."

He pokes her in the side and smiles. "I saw a shooting star. Thought of you."

She touches his hand. "That's sweet."

He stares at the ground. "You want to stay here with me? We could get us a place maybe. Just the two of us."

"What about Bridget?"

He smiles. "She's fun. Not loose like everybody thinks. But she ain't you."

Molly lays a hand on his back. "You know *ain't* ain't a good word, don't ya?" she asks, grinning.

He laughs. "You come a long way to tell me that."

She loops her arm in his and turns serious again. "We're too young to set up house together, Palmer," she says gently. "Maybe someday, years from now. Who knows? But not now."

He picks up a small rock and rolls it in his hands. "I don't know if I can go back."

"You only been gone a couple days. It's not the end of the world."

He stands, looks toward the Busted Spoke, and remembers why he left Rabon. Feels the same feelings again. "What am I going back for?" he asks. "To live with my mama?"

"Your mama is headed back to rehab."

He tosses the rock from one hand to the other. "I didn't know that. Hope it helps her this time."

He tosses the rock again. "I'm free here," he says. "Nobody forcing me to do anything."

"Aren't you sad too? At least a little, leaving Rabon like you did?"

He rolls the rock in his hands. "I guess so. What little bit of home I know lives in Rabon."

"Dirk wants you back," encourages Molly. "Chelsea too. Even if you don't play football no more. Me and her drove to Nashville to look for you."

Sitting down again, Palmer fingers Molly's tattoo. "You there if I go back? Me and you?"

"We need to talk about some things. Take it real slow. But yeah, I'm there." She lays her head on his shoulder.

A bus pulls up and a line of people pile off and scatter. "I'm coming back here one day," says Palmer. "I performed for the manager." He pulls out the business card and examines it as if studying a diamond. "She said I needed more experience," he says, handing the card to Molly. "Then come back."

Molly inspects the card. "The future's bright for you, Palmer. I got no doubt. For now, though, let's go home."

Palmer smiles and pockets the card.

Roberts sits at the head of the conference table with Phil and Holt on his right and Eva and Chelsea to his left. Chelsea wears her coach's gear—khaki pants, Knights' jersey, whistle around her neck. "We all know the situation," Roberts begins without preliminaries. "The question is, how do we respond?"

"It's not really that bad, what's been reported," says Holt, surprisingly at ease, his tone matter of fact. "Makes Coach seem kind of heroic, overcoming her struggle with alcohol, all of that."

"Not so bad for you maybe," says Chelsea, unsure what Holt is up to but not trusting him an inch.

"If it ends now, it'll probably be all right," Roberts says, agreeing with Holt.

"We'll have to make a statement to the media," says Phil.

"I agree," says Eva. "The media is like a fire. Cut the oxygen off and it dies quickly. We provide a short statement of support for our coach and move on." She opens a notebook and pulls out a piece of paper.

"Something like this," she suggests, staring at the paper. "All medical information about an employee at Rabon High School is, and will remain, confidential. Ms. Deal is our head football coach. We're proud of her for all she's faced and overcome in her past and we're happy for her in all that she's accomplished during her short tenure at Rabon High. We fully support her and our team as we face a tough opponent this weekend in our quest for a state championship." She lays the statement on the table.

"I like that," Roberts says. "But I'm afraid the media will demand more."

"What else can they find?" questions Phil. "Putting out the statement will pull the rug out from under 'em. And the game is just four days away. If somethin' pops up after that, we handle it as it comes."

Roberts turns to Holt. "Anything else from you, Les?" he asks.

"Whatever you feel works best."

Roberts turns to Chelsea. "Coach? What are you thinking?"

Considering an option no one else has mentioned, Chelsea doesn't speak for several seconds. But finally, she places both hands on the table and leans forward. "I could resign," she offers.

Everybody sits up ramrod straight.

"I don't see that as an option," Eva says.

"Why not?" asks Chelsea. "It immediately deflates the media balloon. Removes the spotlight on the school and the team."

"It hurts you, Chelsea," Eva continues, pressing her argument. "Will make you look guilty. And for what? An illness? You can't quit because of this. You just can't."

"It might be the wisest thing," Chelsea counters, warming to the idea as she voices it. "It'll remove me as a distraction and give the boys best chance to win." A sense of relief suddenly washes over her. Now that the story is out, why not put everything behind her for the last time? Return to Atlanta and lose herself in the anonymity of the city?

"Maybe Dub will step back in if you resign," says Holt, interrupting Chelsea's thoughts.

Nobody responds for a long minute. Then Roberts speaks, his message and tone seemingly offering no room for dissent. "I see no reason for you to resign, Chelsea." He stares hard at her. "And I won't accept it if you do."

Chelsea opens her mouth to argue but Eva puts a hand on hers and she stays quiet.

"I can understand why you want to bail," Eva says softly. "Drive your truck—your life—out of our little hamlet. God knows we haven't made things easy for you here." She glares at Holt, and he drops his head. Eva focuses on Chelsea again.

"But I'm asking you to remember your team. They've played hard for you, made sacrifices for you. As I see it, they won't have a snowball's chance in hell if you don't coach in the championship. I think you owe it to the boys to see this through to the end, one way or the other. I believe you'll regret it if you don't."

She pats Chelsea's hand and leans back, finished.

Chelsea bites her lip, her momentary relief shifting into uncertainty. "I don't know, Eva."

Phil clears his throat. "Adversity, Coach," he says.

She looks at him, confused but ready to listen.

"You figure out who's a winner and who's a loser," he says, "by watching what they do when adversity bites them on the ass. Do they turn tail and run? Or do they stand and fight?" He stops and the room falls dead quiet.

Chelsea stares at her hands. Does she want to quit because she feels it's best for the team? Or best for herself? Is Phil right? If she resigns, is she running from a fight? Will she regret it later, as Eva said? She looks up and exhales. "Okay," she sighs. "I won't resign, at least not now. But, for the record, I reserve the right to do so if things jump the rails any more than they already have."

"So noted," says Roberts, slapping a hand on the table. "I'll put out the statement as Eva wrote it."

He faces Chelsea. "Get back to your team, Coach. Keep your eye on the prize. Somebody will win a championship Saturday and we're counting on you to make sure it's us."

A couple hours later, the football team quietly gathers around Chelsea on the field. Dub, on his crutches, stands beside her. She holds a football under her arm and her whistle hangs around her neck. "Okay, gentlemen," she says, starting slowly. "I'm sure you've all seen the news. So, here's the skinny. Yes, I did a rehab stint for an alcohol problem I had some time ago. And I saw a therapist for a while after that. But I don't drink anything now. And I'm still your coach. And we have a game to play on Saturday. Any questions?"

Nobody speaks.

"Great," says Chelsea. "If any of you want to talk privately about any of this, let me know and we'll set up a time to do it."

She rolls the football in her hand. "I want to thank Coach Dub for handling things yesterday!"

While the team glances at Dub, Chelsea waits a second before continuing. "I also want you to know why I missed practice. In case you haven't heard, Palmer left Rabon this weekend. I was worried about him, so I took off to find him. And here's the thing: I'd do the same for any of you."

She rolls the football again and forges ahead. "I care about all of you. Some folks say that means I'm not tough enough … that, because I'm a woman, I'm too soft to be a good coach. But I don't agree."

She tosses the ball to Dub. "You know why I don't agree?" she asks.

The team waits for her to finish. "I don't agree because I played the game. I got hit and did some hitting. No, not like a linebacker hits. Fact is, when I played, folks said I hit like a girl. And it was true!"

The team laughs and Chelsea speaks again, louder as she nears a conclusion. "I like to compete, gentlemen. Just like you. So, let's prepare to compete this Saturday! Us against them! Hit or be hit! Knock the other guy on his butt or get knocked on yours!"

Music suddenly blares from the stadium speakers. As the players start cheering and jumping up and down, pumping themselves up for the Saturday night battle to come, Chelsea and the other coaches join in.

Palmer's truck is parked on a gravel road behind a thicket of bushes a couple hundred feet from the highway. Daylight hovers but darkness waits close by. Palmer and Molly sit in his truck bed, their backs propped against the side. A bare oak tree hangs overhead. Palmer's sleeping bag wraps around Molly, protecting her against the chilly air. He hands her a bottle of water and an apple from his backpack. "Eat that," Palmer says. "Then we'll sleep awhile if we can. Maybe twelve hours more to drive tonight."

He pulls out a second apple and munches as he hops down, grabs his guitar from inside the truck, returns to his spot by Molly, and starts to strum. "I wonder if Coach Deal will let me back on the team," he asks.

"Do you want that?" asks Molly, snacking on her apple.

"I don't know. Sometimes I love football. Sometimes I don't."

"You love music all the time," she says as she throws away the apple core and snuggles deeper into the sleeping bag.

Palmer closes his eyes as he strums the guitar. A quote from the Playbook appears in his head. "Why do you go away?'" he whispers the quote. "So that you can see the place you came from with new eyes. Tom Pratchett, Playbook, page 77."

"What's that?" asks Molly, her voice sleepy.

Palmer thinks of Ty and his mood sinks. "It's a quote from Ty's Playbook. It's crazy. I remember most of the quotes now." His eyes stay closed, and he starts to hum as his fingers play. Behind the quote, a hazy play also appears. Blurry players running and blocking.

Palmer slows down his thoughts and focuses on the play as he continues to hum. To his surprise, the play clears up even more and a couple seconds later, he sees it all: X's, O's, players now clearly moving, shifting. Exactly who does what and where!

He sees another quote and softly speaks it. "Alone we can do so little; together we can do so much. Helen Keller, Playbook page 19." Again, he focuses, and the play appears behind the quote, in rhythm to his music. Every move, every player.

Molly mumbles beside him, her breathing slowed as she drifts toward sleep.

Palmer's fingers fall still, and he opens his eyes. "I can see the plays!" He speaks with wonder, like he's just seen an elephant appear out of thin air on the word of a magician.

Molly glances up at him.

"It was all a jumble before," Palmer explains. "But now, it's like, remember the quote, hear the music, and everything falls into place!"

"That's nice." Molly closes her eyes.

Palmer shuts his eyes also and just hums this time, no guitar. He sees another quote *and* another play. He smiles, lays down his guitar, and snuggles by Molly as the stars twinkle at him.

Chelsea jogs at a steady pace down the country road that leads to her house. A reflector on her runner's vest brightens as a car speeds around her. She checks her fitness watch: Thirty-six minutes. She picks up her pace as she runs down the hill about half a mile from her front door. Her legs churn, her arms pump. A burst of energy surges through her and she imagines she's escaping— running past her house and out of Rabon, totally evading the eye of the storm. At the thought, her body hits top speed, and she almost decides to escape. Pack her things now and get the hell out of Dodge.

As she reaches the bottom of the hill, her adrenaline drops and she remembers Eva's words: "Your team needs you." She can't run from that. The team trumps her personal wishes. Always has, always will.

She slows down as she passes the last curve in the road and sees her house. Bo's car sits on the street in front of it.

She stops immediately. Though far from the top of the list of people she doesn't want to see, the idea of talking to him right now perturbs her. She's just not up to it. But he's here, so she has no choice but to deal with him. Steeling her emotions, she trudges toward his car, and he climbs out as she reaches the yard.

"Hey," he says, offering an uncertain wave as she stops.

"You said no more pop-ins," she says softly.

"I saw the news, Chelsea. I had to come. I'm so sorry."

Alone in his Hummer, Holt fidgets with an unlit cigar as he waits in a dark alley behind Patty's Pancake House. Soft jazz plays but it's not doing much to soothe his tightly wound nerves. He spots Buck hurrying up behind the vehicle and hits the unlock button on the passenger door. Buck hops in and Holt turns down the music. "Not a word about the weather," he warns Buck as he glances at his watch. "I'm in a hurry."

"The alcoholic coach story took an unexpected turn," grouses Buck. "They're painting Deal as the most amazing American woman since Mother Teresa! And yes, I know Mother Teresa wasn't an American! But still!"

"It's the law of unintended consequences," says Holt.

Buck slams the dashboard in frustration. "It's B.S.!" he shouts.

"You fired your best shot, Buck," counters Holt, anxious to end the conversation and head home. "It's time now to abandon ship."

"What you think will happen if she loses the championship? With Dub retiring, will they open the job search? Or still just hand it to her on a silver platter?"

"The lottery is up to nine-hundred and seventy million dollars, Buck," Holt says slowly as he pulls a second cigar from his console and unwraps it.

"So?"

"The odds of winning it are one in three-hundred and two million."

"What's your point?"

Holt hands a cigar to Buck. "You bailed on us, Buck. Even if Chelsea loses and the Board conducts an open search for a replacement, I have a better chance of winning the lottery than you do of ever serving as the head football coach at Rabon High."

Buck stares at his cigar. "That's what I figured," Buck says with resignation.

Holt rolls his cigar in his fingers but doesn't light it. "If you already figured that, why this meeting?"

Buck chuckles a little and faces Holt. "I got one more bullet in the chamber, my friend. And I need you to pull the trigger on it."

Holt drops his eyes, already guessing Buck's next move. "The fight," he says.

"Think about it!" declares Buck, his excitement rising as he outlines his story. "A young woman is sexually assaulted. A fight breaks out. A coach stops the fight. But—and here's the juicy part—" His voice notches higher. "The coach covers everything up! To protect her quarterback, she orders everybody to keep it quiet and the victim never gets a chance for justice against her attackers!"

"That's not exactly the story you first reported to me," argues Holt.

"It's all in the lens you see it through. Nothing in what I just said is necessarily untrue."

"But the coach didn't report it because the victim didn't want it reported!" Holt's voice rises, surprising himself as he defends Chelsea. "It had nothing to do with protecting her quarterback!"

"If the media wants to clarify all that, they certainly have the right to do so."

"You hate Coach Deal that much?" Holt's tone softens as he tries to understand.

"It's not hate," says Buck. "She took a job I deserved. That's all. This is a competition. Let the best coach win."

"This could bring Roberts down too."

Buck shrugs. "So what? Collateral damage. Maybe a new principal doesn't know the lottery odds and hires me once Chelsea tucks tail and runs back to Atlanta."

"I already turned you down once, Buck. I won't carry your water on this one either."

"I can't risk this getting traced back to me. So, I'm asking for your help."

"My answer is firm: I won't do it."

"I'm offering you one last chance to make things right with me and Roger."

Holt pulls a match from his pocket and lights his cigar, then Buck's. "I'm a Knight, Buck," he says, his voice strong. "Would wear purple underwear if the Mrs. would allow it. And we play Conway on Saturday night. You're the enemy now. You're dead to me."

Buck stares hard at him for several seconds as he puffs his cigar.

"Enjoy that," Holt says, pointing at Buck's cigar. "It's your last one from me."

Buck shakes his head, climbs out, and walks away.

Chelsea and Bo stand by a granite bar in her kitchen. She fills two glasses with ice from the refrigerator, pours water on the ice, hands one glass to Bo and drinks from the other. "I appreciate your concern, Bo," she says. "But I'm hanging in there. Really. I'm fine."

"You're a strong woman, Chelsea. I've never doubted that. But this... it must be especially tough."

She pulls out two bar stools. "I've had easier days," she admits. "But who knows? Perhaps it's good that everything became public. Maybe I needed this to help me move past my history."

Bo drinks from his water. "The last time I saw you," he says. "At the Empire."

"My new heels."

He smiles briefly. "You asked me if I had tipped off anyone about your rehab."

"I'm sorry, Bo. Bad form on my part."

"I haven't contacted you since that night."

"We both needed some space."

"I've thought a lot about that night. And I finally came to a hurtful realization." He places his glass on the bar. "You don't trust me, Chelsea. And that's a killer in a relationship."

She stares at the ice in her glass as Bo continues. "This morning, when the news about you hit the media, who did you call? Contact?"

Chelsea considers the question and realizes the answer says something she doesn't want to confess but can't escape. "Nobody," she finally admits. "I was too busy trying to keep my head above water."

"Think about that, Chelsea," says Bo. "The national media reveals confidential information about you to the entire world and you reach out to nobody."

She drops her head, recognizing her aloneness in a way she's never understood until now. Mitchell is dead. Her father too. Her mother available but almost never seen. No close friends from college, law school, or her previous employment.

"What kind of person tries to deal with all that by themselves?" Bo asks.

Chelsea tears up. She has no answer to Bo's question. At least none she wants to admit, especially to herself. She wipes her eyes as Bo presses harder.

"What does that say about you? About us?" he asks.

Chelsea finally finds her voice again. "What do you want me to do, Bo? Apologize? I can do that."

He shakes his head, takes her hands, and kisses her fingers. "No, Chelsea. I'm not here for an apology."

"Then what, Bo? What can I say? Do?"

"Nothing," he says gently. "It's done. I'm done. We're done."

He drops her hands and stands. She remains silent. "I wish the best for you, Chelsea," he says. "I really do. You deserve it. But I deserve something too. And you're not able to provide it for me."

He stares at her for several long moments, obviously waiting for a response, but she's too numb to offer one. Finally, he kisses her on the cheek and walks out.

She leans on the bar as he leaves, her water glass still in hand.

CHAPTER TWENTY-SIX

Though worn out by the drive home, Palmer eases into Ty's hospital room on Wednesday morning and finds him alone, propped up in bed.

"Where you been?" asks Ty, his voice weak.

Palmer pulls up a chair, plops down, and sighs heavily. "I took a road trip."

"You look like roadkill."

"You got no room to talk."

Ty tries to laugh but a hard wracking cough shakes his whole body.

"I'm sorry, man," Palmer says after Ty's cough subsides. "The way I skipped out."

"You should be sorry. Ghosting everybody like you did."

Palmer rubs his eyes and sits up straighter. "What can I do to make it up to you?"

Ty clears his throat. "Go see Coach." He points to a water cup on a table and Palmer hands it to him. "Beg her to take you back."

"I doubt she'll do that. It's the second time I quit."

"I want you to try," insists Ty, drinking water through a straw.

"One thing is good, I guess," says Palmer. "I can see the plays now. Like a dance, with music. I see the quotes, I hear the music, and the plays come alive."

"My corny quotes, too?" Ty hands Palmer the cup and closes his eyes. "All those hours we studied together finally paid off. I promised you it would."

"I'll ask Coach," says Palmer. "But I ain't. . . am not optimistic."

Ty opens his eyes again. "What time is it?"

"You got somewhere you gotta be?"

"School, Palmer. You. Now."

Palmer nods, fist-bumps Ty, and hurries out.

Thirty-minutes later, Palmer knocks on Coach Dub's office door and Chelsea waves him in.

"Hey," she says, pointing him to a seat across from hers. "Glad you made it home safely."

"Thanks." He sits on the edge of the chair, his palms sweaty, nerves eating away at him. "I went to see Ty first," he says.

"Good," she says. "He any better today?"

"Seemed tired. But hanging in." Palmer stares at his shoes.

"You need to check in with Counselor Towe," Chelsea says, her tone neutral. "Do whatever he asks. No room for another error, no matter how small."

Palmer works to slow his heartbeat. He wants to stand, to run, to forget what he promised Ty.

"Anything else?" asks Chelsea.

Palmer hesitates but knows he can't escape, not if he really wants back on the team. "I'm sorry, Coach," he finally says, plunging into the deep end of what he came to confess. "Disappearing like I did. And I appreciate, you know, how you came looking for me." He faces her, not sure what else to say.

"Lots of people care about you, Palmer."

He leans forward, elbows on his knees. "I know I don't deserve it," he says hesitantly. "But I want back on the team. If you'll let me."

"Tell me why you want to come back."

He shrugs. "For Ty. He asked me to do it."

"That's not good enough." A hint of frustration tinges her voice.

Palmer drops his head again, and thinks a moment, trying to decipher what she wants to hear. "Like Dirk said, quitting is a bad habit to fall into."

"Look at me, Palmer," Chelsea orders. He raises his eyes. "That's still not good enough."

Palmer props his chin on his hands and tries to figure out what to say next.

"This shouldn't be about Ty or Dirk," Chelsea says. "It has to be about you. Why do *you* want to come back?"

Palmer closes his eyes again and hopes he'll disappear but knows he won't. Nobody has ever asked him a question like this, and nothing in his life has prepared him to answer it.

"I don't know," he finally says.

"I can't take you back until you do." Chelsea, rocking forward, almost stands to leave, but Palmer holds up a hand to stop her. She drops back into her chair.

"Okay," he says, speaking slowly as he searches for the words, "I been alone a long time. Since I was six or so. After my dad passed, mama just... slipped away. To a dark place. I basically took care of myself from then on. That's my story."

He looks at Chelsea, back to the floor, then talks again, as much to himself as to Chelsea. "In Austin, by myself, it dawned on me, I guess for the first time, how I need other people. Dirk, Molly, Ty. You. A team, you could say. Somebody I can count on, somebody who can count on me."

He pauses again.

"Go on, Palmer," encourages Chelsea, her tone softer. "Finish what you need to say."

He bites his lip. Spits out the last of it. "That's why I want to come back. To be part of something, connected to something, someone, bigger than me." His voice trails off and his eyes water.

Chelsea rises and puts a hand on his shoulder. "That's good," she soothes. "That's what I wanted to hear."

"I've quit on you twice, Coach," he says, his voice cracking. "I don't deserve to come back."

"Learn the lesson, Palmer. That's all any of us can do."

"I need to apologize to the team too." He looks up and wipes his eyes.

Chelsea nods. "You can speak to them before practice today. I'll let them decide if you can come back."

That afternoon, after a day of sneaking around school to avoid Roberts and the media, Chelsea stands with Palmer in the middle of the football field.

"You ready?" she asks him.

"As much as I'll ever be."

Chelsea pats him on the back, puts her whistle to her lips, and blows long and hard. The team gathers around her and Palmer. "Listen up, gentlemen," Chelsea starts. "Palmer wants to say something."

Palmer faces the team, his heart pounding. "Okay," he begins. "Last week, I screwed up. Some hard things happened to me, and I bailed. I'm sorry."

He pauses to compose himself. "I want to be with you this last game. I know

I don't deserve to, but without a team, a family—"

He drops his eyes and stops as Chelsea quickly pulls her phone from a pocket and keys in a number.

"I have somebody here who wants to speak on Palmer's behalf," she says. "Ty?" she speaks into the phone, which she puts on "speaker."

Ty's voice sounds weak but it's loud enough for the team to hear. "Hey, guys," he calls. "Wish I was there. But I have better things to do."

The team laughs. Ty continues: "Palmer made a mistake. I'm asking you to forgive him. I believe in second chances. Hope you do too." He stops.

"Thanks, Ty," says Chelsea.

The phone beeps off.

"Gentlemen," says Chelsea, facing the team again. "It's up to you. We let Palmer back on the team or not?"

Nobody moves. Palmer holds his breath. Chelsea eyes her team, waiting, hoping. Johnson raises his hand. "I agree with Ty," he says. "I believe in second chances."

Another second passes, then Swoops raises his hand. "I believe in second chances too, Coach," he says.

Another hand goes up, another and another, and soon they're all in the air and the team begins to chant: "Palmer, Palmer, Palmer!"

Forty-five minutes later, the offense and defense face off in a scrimmage, with Johnson running the offense. Palmer, now in uniform, stands close to Chelsea as she ducks into the huddle and calls the offensive play. "Run I form, 34 blast. 2 go," she says.

Johnson nods and Chelsea steps back beside Palmer. Palmer closes his eyes and sees a quote. "You miss 100 percent of the shots you don't take…Wayne Gretzky, Playbook page 9." Palmer hums softly and sees the play running behind the quote. He opens his eyes, and the offense runs the play exactly as he saw it. He grins as the offense huddles up again and Chelsea calls another play.

Palmer closes his eyes, sees a quote, and hums. The play appears in his head, and he opens his eyes and grins again. Chelsea sees the smile as she resumes her spot beside him.

"Wipe that grin off your face, Palmer!" she commands. "We have a title game in three days!"

Dressed in a pair of Christmas red pajamas, Sandra Brinner stands at the window in her room at Betty's Bed and Breakfast. Rabon Valley stretches out below, lit up with Christmas lights. Though exhausted from a busy day, nothing about Brinner even suggests that. Not her eyes, not her posture, not her energy. Her phone buzzes and she notes the time as she answers— 9:09 p.m. "Hey, Derrick," she says, her voice perky as ever.

"I have Legal on the line with us," Derrick quickly states. "They're concerned about this latest bombshell."

"Like I told you a few hours ago," explains Brinner, "I found another envelope at my door this afternoon. The note inside detailed a fight after a football game at Rabon High a few weeks ago. Gave the place, date, time, cause, and people involved. Included the accusation of a cover-up that followed."

"You have any independent confirmation of the story?" asks Derrick.

"No. I've nosed around all day. Asked discreet questions like you instructed. Tried to track down the people named in the note. But can't reach any of them. No corroboration."

"We can't afford to be wrong on this one, Sandra," warns Derrick. "Too many people involved. Too many potential landmines."

"And lawsuits." She plops onto the bed. "What's the move?"

"Hold tight for now. Give us overnight to figure some things out. I'll call you back in the morning."

Standing in Dirk's kitchen, Palmer flips a burger out of a sizzling frying pan and drops it onto the bottom half of a bun sitting on a paper plate on the counter. Slaps mustard, lettuce, and a slab of American cheese on top. Grabs a soft drink from the fridge and a paper towel from a rack beside it. Puts everything on a tray, hurries to the front room, flops onto the sofa, and starts chowing down. Halfway through the burger, the front door opens, and Dirk steps inside, his travel bag in hand.

"I thought you were playing a gig all weekend," says Palmer, his mouth full.

"I hear there's a big football game Saturday. Some kid named Johnson is starting at quarterback. I can't miss that." Dirk lays his bag on the floor and ambles to the fireplace to warm his hands.

"Again with the comedy." Palmer stands, high-fives Dirk, and steps in for a bro hug.

"How's Chelsea?" Dirk asks, stepping back and throwing a log on the fire. "I caught something in the news about a stint in rehab?" He plops down on the hearth, his back to the fire.

"That's the story," says Palmer as he sits again. "She seems all right, though. Let me rejoin the team."

"Glad to hear that. I need to call her."

"I bet she's dying to hear from you." Palmer chomps on another bite of burger.

"She has a number of attractive features, you know."

"I got ten bucks that say she won't let you within fifty feet of her attractive features."

Dirk laughs. "You got mustard on your chin, ladies' man."

Palmer wipes the mustard off.

"How's Molly?" asks Dirk.

"She's good. Still recovering from her flight, I think."

"Bridget?"

"Ain't seen her since I returned. Hoping we can talk tomorrow at school."

Dirk steps to his bag and pulls a computer out. "I bought this for you. For schoolwork." He hands the computer to Palmer.

"Great," says Palmer, sarcastically. "Now I got no excuse when I miss an assignment."

"Remember, it's for schoolwork only. Not that other stuff—you know."

"The bases?" Palmer says, chuckling.

"Exactly."

Palmer takes a swig of his soft drink.

"That burger smells mighty good," says Dirk.

"Come on," says Palmer. "I'll fry you one." He jumps up and they head to the kitchen together.

♦

Roberts stands by his office desk, an ear glued to his phone. "Hey, Eva. FYI: That ESPN reporter was nosing around the school all afternoon."

"That's her job, George."

"She's not asking about Chelsea's rehab anymore." He picks up a pencil and rolls it in his fingers.

"What *is* she asking about?"

"Nothing specific."

"Why does that worry you?"

"I guess it shouldn't." He rolls the pencil again.

Eva clears her throat. "I've known you seventeen years, George. You're worried about something."

"I don't know if I should say." He walks to the front of his desk and settles on the edge.

"Put your pencil down, George. And tell me about the other shoe you're afraid Brinner is about to drop."

Roberts parks his pencil on the ear opposite the phone. No part of him wants to say what he knows, but Eva deserves to hear the whole truth. "Remember that Friday we talked to Chelsea?" he asks. "A week after the Longhorn loss?"

"The day I wanted to slap Les? Yes, I do recall that."

"Well, after you and Chelsea left, Les told us about a fight..."

CHAPTER TWENTY-SEVEN

Dressed in tight tan slacks, a form-fitting white sweater, and a long, Christmas-green coat, Sandra Brinner peers into the bathroom mirror and puts the last touch on her high-gloss red lipstick. When her phone buzzes, she arranges the lipstick on the counter and answers the call. "You're calling early this morning, Derrick. What's the word?"

"Legal noticed something last night," Derrick says, jumping right in. "A name listed in the note. An attendee at the fight who's no longer connected to Rabon High."

"I know," says Brinner, again pleased with herself. "Buck Jones. Story here is he bugged out the week after Coach Deal won the quarterfinal."

"Legal assumes, without confirmation, that he's the one who sent you both notes," concludes Derrick.

Brinner steps into the bedroom and pulls a pair of ankle-high black boots from the closet. "Why the cloak and dagger?" she asks, edging onto the bed as she tries to puzzle it all out. "No name in the first note. But several names, including his, in the second. Why not leave his out?"

"My suspicion?" asks Derrick. "Jones anonymously sent the note about the alcoholism. Figured that would take Deal down. But when that didn't work, he dropped us another envelope. Throws his last punch. And this time he doesn't care whether or not we find out who our source is. Maybe assumes we'll find out anyway once we investigate."

"That makes sense," Brinner agrees. "He's burned his bridges at Rabon. Looking for revenge now."

"You sitting down?" asks Derrick.

"Should I be?"

"Legal called Jones early this morning, Sandra. He's willing to do an interview with you!"

"You're kidding!" Brinner quickly stands and paces to the window as her heart ticks higher.

"I swear on my mother's grave."

"He confess to sending the notes?"

"Nope. But he admits to being at the fight. Says he wants to speak the truth."

"He must really hate Chelsea Deal."

"Either way, we don't care. You interview him. Legal will vet the video to see if we have enough to reveal the assault story and not get sued."

"Jones is just one source," Brinner cautions. "He could say anything. Shouldn't we have corroboration before we start wrecking lives?"

"Or he could be telling the unvarnished truth. Deal might have covered the whole thing up."

Brinner turns from the window. "I hate to think that. But yes, she might have."

"Interview Jones. Send us the video. We'll figure it out from there."

A line of cars almost a quarter-mile long slowly makes its way to the front of Rabon High, where each car stops and lets out a student who slowly slouches into the building. Darting around the cars, Palmer wheels his motorcycle into the parking lot, parks, climbs off, and removes his helmet. To his right, he spots Bridget exiting her car a couple rows over. "Hey!" he yells. "Bridget!"

She grins widely. "Hey, Prince!" she yells, running his way, her arms wide. "I missed you!"

She reaches him and they hug. "I'm so glad you're back!" she says, slowly breaking off the embrace.

"You're not mad at me?" he asks in surprise. "The way I bugged out?"

She puffs her lips into a pout. "A little. But you're the one missing out on this." She throws out a hip and slaps it. Smiles again.

Palmer shakes his head. "I should've climbed under the covers with you when I had the chance."

"You be nice and maybe I'll give you another shot at it."

She kisses him on the cheek. "Go to class, Palmer. I don't want you to flunk out because of me."

Hours later, after surviving his classes and enduring a highly unpleasant scolding from Counselor Towe, Palmer changes into his practice uniform, joins the rest of the team on the football field, and starts stretching. After a few minutes, Coach Paul blows his whistle and everyone hustles over to him and Chelsea in the middle of the field.

"All right, gentlemen," Chelsea begins without fanfare. "We're two days away from the championship! I need you focused today! Zoned in!" She turns to Coach Paul.

"We leave for Atlanta at three p.m.," Paul announces. "Game at eight. Be here, ready to go by two. No parties Friday night. No girlfriends. Save your energy."

He faces Chelsea. "We're scrimmaging now!" she orders. "Offense against defense! Fourth-and-two drill! Offense, huddle with me! Coach Paul, huddle the defense!"

The offense and defense hurry to their separate sides of the fifty-yard line and Chelsea turns to Palmer. "I want you to start us off today," she says quietly. "Run a couple plays. Johnson will come back in after that."

Palmer freezes for a moment, too shocked to act, but Chelsea motions him to the huddle and he steps in. "What's the play?" he asks her.

"Pro, 927, T flat. 1 go."

Palmer rubs his hands on his pants. "Let's run a different one, Coach," he suggests.

"It's one of the twelve you know," answers Chelsea. "Run it."

"I can call anything in the Playbook now," Palmer argues.

"Be grateful you're out here, Palmer," Chelsea advises, her brow furrowed. "And run the play I call."

Too scared to push any harder, Palmer nods and the offense sets up at the line of scrimmage. For the first time ever, Palmer feels almost confident as he takes the snap from center and runs the play, a short pass that he completes to a tight end. The offense huddles again and Chelsea calls another of the twelve plays. Palmer handles it too, throwing a perfect spiral to Swoops over fifty yards downfield for a touchdown.

"Great job, Palmer!" yells Chelsea as the offense celebrates.

"That's it?" he asks, hoping for more.

"I said two plays."

Palmer starts to argue but knows he's still on thin ice. Dropping his eyes, he steps aside.

"Johnson," Chelsea calls, turning to Sean. "You're back in."

Two cameras, set up in the parlor of Betty's Bed and Breakfast, focus on two cushioned chairs, one facing a stone fireplace, the other directly across from it. Wood burns in the fireplace, giving the room a warm, holiday glow. Dark cloth covers the six windows and the double French doors leading from the parlor into the lobby, effectively blocking out any onlookers. Deep in professional mode, Sandra Brinner wordlessly points Buck to the chair across from the fireplace and he obliges her silent order. Pleased, she places herself exactly in the center of her chair, framed perfectly by the glowing fireplace behind her.

Smiling, but not in an over-the-top way, Brinner leans towards Buck and speaks in a smooth, neutral tone. "When we start the filming, I'll briefly introduce you, then move straight into a series of questions related to the incident we're investigating. I'll film a fuller intro to the story later, to establish the context, plus do a short conclusion to wrap up any loose ends."

"You won't edit my words to make them say what you want them to say, will you?" asks Buck.

"No, Coach. I don't operate that way."

Buck shrugs, cool as the bottom of a pillow. "Lots of deceptive editing these days," he says.

A sound technician checks the microphone attached to Buck's shirt.

"You signed paperwork, didn't you?" Brinner asks.

Buck nods.

"All the legal stuff is covered there," she says. "You want to read through everything again before we start?"

"Nah," says Buck as the sound guy backs away. "I'm good."

"Good deal," Brinner says. "You ready to roll?"

"Time for kickoff," says Buck, a little grin on his face.

"Great." Brinner smiles again and nods to her producer. He points to his camera team and starts a countdown. "Three, two, one."

"I'm in Rabon, Georgia again," Brinner begins, looking warmly at the camera in front of her. "Talking with Coach Buck Jones, the former Defensive Coordinator for the Rabon High Knights. We asked Coach Jones for this interview because we believe he can shed some light on a disturbing incident that allegedly involved Coach Chelsea Deal and two of her football players."

Brinner turns to Buck. "So, Coach Jones, let's confirm this to start. Did you formerly work as a coach at Rabon High with Coach Chelsea Deal?"

"Yes," Buck says confidently. "I coached for eight years at Rabon High."

"Were you coaching on the night of November 11 of this year?"

"I was, yes."

"Did you witness a fight on school property right after the Rabon High football game that night?"

"I did, yes." Buck's voice comes out smooth and steady.

Brinner's easy tone shifts to stern. "Did two male students from Rabon High School sexually assault a young woman just prior to that fight?"

"I didn't actually witness the assault," says Buck. "And I'm not a lawyer so I can't exactly define what makes an attack a sexual assault. But I was told that an assault did occur, and I did see how upset the young woman was right after the alleged assault and the fight that followed."

"Did this young woman's boyfriend intervene to stop this assault?"

"Yes. I saw her boyfriend fighting two other young men near the gate behind the football locker room and, after I helped break up the fight, I was told that an assault was the cause of the fight."

"Was this young woman's boyfriend named Palmer Norman, a sometime starting quarterback for the Rabon Knights?"

Buck rubs his hands together as if about to open a Christmas present. "Yes."

Brinner's speaking pace slows as she moves to the crux of her questions. "Was Coach Chelsea Deal at the scene of this fight on the night of November 11?"

Buck nods vigorously. "Yes, she arrived at the scene at almost the same moment I did, and we both intervened to stop the fight."

Brinner shifts in her chair. "Now these questions become tougher, Coach Jones."

"I'll just say what I saw and did," Buck responds.

"Did Coach Deal report this alleged assault and the fight that followed to school authorities, as she is required by policy to do?"

Buck shakes his head as if greatly disturbed by Chelsea's negligence. "No, she did not. In fact, she told everyone present to keep quiet about what happened."

"Do you have any idea why she told all of you to stay silent about this horrible chain of events?"

Buck bows his head over his hands, positioned together as if in prayer. When he speaks again, he's solemn, seemingly shaken by the truth he must now reveal. "I can't say for sure what was in Coach Deal's heart, but it seemed to me she wanted to protect Palmer Norman, her quarterback, a disturbed but talented kid for whom she obviously has great affection. Palmer was already in trouble, seeing a counselor in fact, due to a previous violent outburst at school. So—and I'm certain of this—Coach Deal believed that another incident would get Palmer suspended. Keep him from playing any more football."

Brinner glances at her notes, clears her throat, stares back at Buck. "Coach Jones," she starts, "here's the toughest question of all. And I want you to be perfectly honest with me."

She pauses dramatically and seconds tick before she continues. "Coach Jones, do you see this as a cover-up of a sexual assault, perpetuated by Coach Chelsea Deal?"

Buck shifts in his seat and his voice seems to quiver as he speaks. But his eyes sparkle as he lays out the charge. "I hate to say it, but yes, I do," he whispers. "I believe Coach Deal deliberately covered up a sexual assault to protect Palmer Norman."

Brinner leans forward. "Why did you wait until now to come forward?"

Buck sits up ramrod straight and stares into the camera. "It was no secret that I wanted the head coaching job that the School Board gave Coach Deal. I was afraid if I came forward, people would say I was just jealous she got the job instead of me."

"You left your position at Rabon soon after this alleged assault, didn't you?"

"Yes."

"Why did you leave, Coach Jones? Was it because you didn't like working for a woman? A woman that you believed had unfairly received a job that should have rightfully been yours?"

Buck rubs his hands together as he stares into the camera with steely eyes. "I left because two thugs assaulted a nice young woman, and my conscience wouldn't let me work any longer with a coach who ordered me to cover that up."

Brinner leans back, her notes in her lap. "Thank you, Coach Jones," she concludes. "I'm certain our audience is grateful for your willingness to tell this painful story."

Brinner motions to her camera team and they immediately stop filming.

"When you expect to show this?" asks Buck, quickly standing.

"We should be ready by nine tomorrow morning."

Buck unhooks his microphone and lays it on the chair.

"You're the one who sent me the notes. Right?" Brinner asks Buck.

Buck chuckles, shrugs, and walks away.

A bright fire blazes in the makeshift firepit behind Dirk's house. Stars twinkle above and a string of lights runs from the back of the house to a telephone pole at the edge of the yard. Plamer and Dirk sit in their lawn chairs close to the fire, Dirk's fingers busy with his guitar, Palmer's plucking his banjo as they play a bluesy tune together. A bag of marshmallows sits on the end of Palmer's chair and Molly, situated on a tree stump beside him, roasts one hanging at the end of a straightened metal coat-hanger.

"Hey, Banjo Boy," she teases Palmer. "You want me to toast you a marshmallow?"

He grabs a marshmallow and throws it at her as Russell's car pulls up and Tanya hops out of the driver's side.

"Hey!" Palmer calls to her as he stands and lays the banjo in his chair. "This is a surprise."

Ignoring him, Tanya runs around the car and opens the passenger door.

"What you doing here?" Palmer asks as he sees Ty.

"He wanted to see how the other half lives," says Tanya.

"The poor half? The white half?" teases Palmer as he hurries to the car.

Ty smiles but his eyes sag deep in their sockets and his cheekbones poke sharply against his skin. Tanya walks to the back of the car and opens the trunk as Chelsea's truck pulls up.

"We having a convention or something?" Palmer asks Dirk as he pulls Ty's wheelchair from the trunk.

Chelsea steps out, dressed in a wool vest over a long-sleeved green blouse, a flowing beige skirt, and a necklace made of several cut stones.

"I invited Coach over," says Dirk.

"I went to see Ty," says Chelsea, walking toward Dirk. "Told him I was coming over here, and he wanted to join me."

"His mama will have a stroke when she finds out," warns Palmer as he pushes the wheelchair towards Ty.

"Not this time," says Tanya. "I asked permission. She said it wouldn't hurt Ty to leave the hospital for a while."

"I'll grab a couple more chairs," says Dirk, laying his guitar aside.

"I'll help," says Chelsea.

They hustle away as Palmer helps Ty into the wheelchair.

"Put him close to the fire," Tanya says as she grabs a blanket from the back seat.

Moving slowly across the uneven ground, Palmer pushes Ty to the edge of the firepit and Tanya positions the blanket over his lap.

"You warm enough?" she asks Ty.

"Toasty," he says softly.

Dirk and Chelsea stroll back from the house, Dirk with two folding chairs and Chelsea with coat hangers for everybody. "Sit," orders Dirk, stationing the chairs around the fire.

Everybody but Molly takes a spot, Chelsea by Dirk, Palmer and Tanya on either side of Ty. Molly hands out marshmallows and Chelsea straightens out the coat hangers. A couple minutes later, everybody but Ty holds a marshmallow over the fire—Tanya holds Ty's for him.

"We need some chocolate," says Chelsea as her marshmallow flames and she blows it out.

"Some graham crackers too," suggests Tanya as she hands a toasted marshmallow to Ty.

"I like my marshmallows plain," says Dirk. "Burned black on the outside and gooey white on the inside."

Tanya leans back in her chair, crosses her ankles close to the fire, and puts her feet up.

"No socks?" Molly asks, pointing to Tanya's ankles.

Tanya lifts her right leg and points to a tattoo right above the ankle. "My first one," she says.

Molly and Chelsea lean closer. The tattoo flickers in the light of the fire. A small, black female fist with red fingernails.

"What is it?" asks Chelsea.

"You go, girl," Molly says, grinning at Tanya.

Tanya leans back. "A femme fist."

"I'm dating a revolutionary," says Ty, his voice soft but tinged with humor.

Everybody laughs. Toasts their marshmallows.

Dirk picks up his guitar and turns to Chelsea. "You wearing a new necklace?"

Chelsea holds it up so he can see. "Finished it last week."

"What about your guy?" Molly asks, leaning to look at the necklace.

"He's not my guy anymore."

"You too famous for him now?" Molly teases.

"I'm too famous for 'me' now," says Chelsea.

"Have they shown up at your house yet?" asks Dirk.

"Please, God, don't let that happen!" begs Chelsea.

Dirk strums his guitar, a satisfied grin on his face. Palmer grabs his banjo and gently tweaks the strings.

"My pa is coming home from Alabama tomorrow," says Molly. "Driving me and Mama to the game Saturday."

"Now I'm nervous," says Palmer. "Not that I'm likely to play any."

"I think my pa likes you," says Molly.

"I'm not sure he likes anybody," counters Palmer.

"He might let you keep just one foot on the floor next time you visit us," teases Molly.

Palmer throws a marshmallow at her.

Dirk faces Palmer. "Saturday is *your* dad's birthday," he says.

"With the game and all, I can't go. We'll drive up there Sunday."

"You've visited his grave on his birthday every year since he died."

"Let's talk about it later."

"I think you should go," Molly says, jumping in.

"We don't leave for Atlanta until three," notes Chelsea.

Palmer glances at Molly, then Chelsea and Dirk. "This some kind of conspiracy?"

"We can leave at daybreak," says Dirk. "An hour to get over there. Stay thirty minutes. An hour back. Plenty of time before you gotta be at the bus."

Palmer drops his eyes. Visiting his dad's grave always hurts. Like scratching a scab until it bleeds again. But he's never missed his dad's birthday. Even at his mama's worst, she always saw to it that he made it to the grave on that day.

He faces Dirk. "I'll consider it," he says. "And I'll decide by morning."

Dirk nods and Palmer picks at his banjo again. Tanya toasts another marshmallow and hands it to Ty. Dirk throws a couple pieces of wood on the fire. Quiet falls over the group for several moments.

"This is nice," Ty says, his voice barely a whisper.

"I'm glad you here, man," says Palmer.

"It's peaceful," agrees Ty.

Palmer softly plays the banjo.

"That banjo, man," Ty says.

"You like it?" asks Palmer.

"No way, dude. That banjo's got to go."

CHAPTER TWENTY-EIGHT

R oberts, Eva, Phil, Holt, and Chelsea are all gathered in the school conference room the next morning, each staring at the TV. Nobody speaks. The
granola bars and bottled water in the middle of the table are untouched.
The pencil behind Roberts' ear is broken. Sandra Brinner suddenly appears on the
screen with the Rabon High football stadium behind her.

"She called me thirty minutes ago," Roberts sighs, pointing to Brinner. "Told
me what she planned to do."

He faces Chelsea, his eyes sad. "I begged her to hold off until I talked to you,
but she said she couldn't."

"She left me several messages last night," says Chelsea. "But she didn't say
anything about this."

"Maybe you should have called her back," accuses Holt.

Chelsea bites her tongue and says nothing, her eyes fixed on Brinner. A long
black coat covers her body, from her stylish gray boots to a bright green scarf
tucked around her neck.

"Good morning," she starts, a bright smile revealing her perfect teeth. "I'm
Sandra Brinner, ESPN Sports, and I've been in Rabon, Georgia this week, reporting on the remarkable story of Coach Chelsea Deal, the first woman to lead a high
school football team into a state championship game. I've told you previously
about her brave victory overcoming an alcohol addiction."

Brinner starts walking toward the stadium, the cameras fixed on her. "Today,
I'm adding another CHAPTER to Coach Deal's saga. Unfortunately, it's a darker
CHAPTER, one that chronicles the sad tale of a coach being accused of covering-up a sexual assault that occurred right here, in this picturesque football stadium in the heart of the Blue Ridge Mountains."

Brinner stops and gestures toward the stadium. "Late yesterday, I spoke with
Buck Jones, a former coach with Chelsea Deal on the Rabon High staff, and he
laid out for us the facts of a most-distressing story."

The screen flips to Buck Jones, sitting in the parlor in Betty's Bed and
Breakfast.

Ty sleeps under a stack of bedcovers. Russell sits beside him. Ty looks frailer than ever, his face thin and sharp, as if the bones under his skin have decided to break out. A thin crack in his lower lip bleeds a little.

Russell stares at the overhead TV, but his mind drifts and wanders. Mostly, he feels helpless, a dad with no way to protect his son. He glances at Ty and wants to weep but pushes back the sadness. Ty needs him to stay strong, Vanessa too.

He stares back at the TV and Buck Jones' face suddenly appears. Quickly standing, Russell turns up the volume and listens for several seconds. "Hey, Ty," he says as he nudges him. "You need to wake up and see this."

Ty stirs, opens his eyes, and watches Jones. "He's twisting everything," he protests weakly as Buck tells his story. "Everything."

Ty closes his eyes again, his limited strength exhausted.

Eva's face turns purple with anger as she watches the end of Buck's interview and Roberts turns off the TV.

"That back-stabbing, two-faced, weasel-eyed, son of a bitch!" she growls.

Everyone stares at Eva, their jaws dropping in shock.

"What?" says Eva. "I was in the Navy!"

"We're hip-deep in sewage with no boots on," moans Roberts.

"For the record," says Chelsea, "I didn't file a report because the young woman begged me not to. I asked her twice."

"You confident all the witnesses but Buck will confirm that?" asks Phil.

"The boys who assaulted the young woman will deny it happened at all. But yes, the others will confirm."

"No one really matters but the victim," says Eva. "If she backs you up, the media will aim the spotlight on her, and you'll most likely fall off their radar."

"We'll need the district's lawyer to take statements from everyone involved," he says as he faces Chelsea. "And, I hate to say it, but we'll have to suspend you until the matter is settled."

"Suspension?" asks Phil, surprised.

"Standard procedure, Phil,' says Roberts. "When an allegation like this comes to light, the accused is automatically suspended until resolution of the accusation."

"But the victim hasn't accused Coach of anything!"

"Procedure, Phil. I must follow it to the letter."

"You must cover your backside is more like it." Phil yanks off his cap and throws it on the table in disgust.

Roberts faces Chelsea again. "No contact with the young woman, Coach. You can't, in any way, appear to influence a victim."

"I don't plan to influence anybody," says Chelsea, still processing what she's just watched. In one way, Buck's actions aren't a surprise. A man with no core doesn't mind bending the truth to fit the story he wants to tell. She tries to put herself in his shoes. Did she cause him to do this? Did she treat him unfairly? Obviously, they had conflicts. But they were both coaches. Didn't he respect that, at least a little? But no, she suddenly realizes. In Buck's mind, he was wronged. Reason enough to destroy her if he can.

"Who'll coach tomorrow night?" asks Holt, turning to the practicalities of the situation.

"I'll ask Dub to step in," says Roberts. "Has to be him or Paul."

"I hope nobody leaks the victim's name," says Chelsea, thinking of Molly.

"I'll draft a statement for the media," Eva sighs. "God, this just breaks my heart."

They all stand except Chelsea, who remains at the table, her hands steepled in front of her face.

Eva turns to her. "Coach? What's on your mind?"

Chelsea looks up, her eyes clear. "It's time I cashed in my right to resign."

"I won't let you do it," counters Eva.

"I know the young woman," explains Chelsea. "You said it yourself. If she comes forward, the spotlight will land on her. That'll scare her to death."

"We'll support her," continues Eva. "Whatever she needs."

"My resignation is what she needs. What the school and the team need too. It'll remove the distractions—the embarrassment I've become."

Eva moves close to Chelsea, placing a hand on her shoulder. "I beg you,

Chelsea. Don't decide something this important in the heat of the moment. Take the rest of the day. Weigh it."

"I'm with Eva," declares Roberts. "Don't rush this."

"I agree," says Phil.

Eva looks to Holt.

"Oddly enough, I also agree," he says.

Chelsea closes her eyes for several long seconds as she considers her options. Whatever happens, she will protect Molly. That's job one. She opens her eyes and stands. "I'll hold off until the end of the day. But you need to know that unless something changes my mind, I'm done by this evening."

"Reconvene here at 7:30," commands Roberts. "Keep your heads down until then."

Palmer works on a math problem at his desk in class. His phone vibrates in his pocket, but he ignores it and concentrates again on the equation. His phone vibrates again. He carefully pulls his phone out and sees a text from Ty.

"This is Russell. Come to hospital! Now!"

Palmer texts back. "In math."

A text quickly responds. "Tell Mr. Stone that Ty is dying."

Palmer jumps up, hurries to Mr. Stone, and shows him the text.

"I shouldn't let you go," says Stone. You're improving but still on the line between passing or failing."

"E-mail me some extra credit problems. I'll do them. I promise!"

"You better." Stone waves Palmer away. He grabs his backpack and hustles out. In the hallway, he calls Ty, but Russell answers.

"You see the news?" Russell asks.

"I've been in math."

"Buck Jones did an interview. Trashed Coach Deal. Said she covered up that fight—what happened to Molly."

"I'm on the way."

Pocketing his phone, he rushes down the hall and out to his motorcycle in the parking lot. Ten minutes later, after whipping through town at breakneck speed, he parks the bike, sprints into the hospital, and pounds up the stairs, too impatient to wait on an elevator. Russell and Vanessa stand as he enters the room and hurries to Ty.

"It's BS, man," Ty says weakly.

"But it's serious BS," says Russell. "A thing like this can ruin a person, innocent or not."

"Coach Jones is a prick," says Ty .

"You have to do something, Palmer!" blurts Vanessa.

"Me?"

"Convince Molly to tell what happened!"

"I don't know," says Palmer, instantly concerned for Molly. "Don and Strick have made up stories about her before. They'll do it again—say all kinds of bad things about her."

"Convince him, Ty," orders Vanessa. "Without Molly's statement, Coach is toast."

"Molly's tight... with Coach," whispers Ty. "She'll do it for her."

Palmer's mind swirls. He wants to help Chelsea but can't without putting Molly at risk. "I'll ask Molly," he finally agrees. "But I won't pressure her. That'll make her lock down."

When Ty cough, Vanessa gives him water and rubs lotion on his lips.

"You also have to tell the team what happened," Russell orders Palmer.

"Coach Paul can do that. He was there."

"But you're a player," insists Russell. "It makes a difference coming from a player."

"They won't pay much attention to me," argues Palmer.

"They will on this," insists Russell.

Ty tries to speak but starts coughing instead, his body heaving with effort.

"Back to class, Palmer," says Vanessa. "You know what's necessary. Get Molly to do the right thing."

Palmer touches Ty's shoulder, but he coughs hard again, and Palmer pivots and hurries out. Rushing down the hallway and out the exit, Palmer calls Molly but receives no answer. In the parking lot, he sees gray clouds gathering, pushed by a whipping wind. At his motorcycle, a few flakes of snow float down. He calls Molly again, but again no response. He leaves a message, climbs onto his cycle, and calls Dirk.

"Somebody needs to put a beat-down on Coach Jones!" he shouts when Dirk answers.

"I tried to reach Chelsea," says Dirk. "Any idea where she is?"

"They probably told her to go dark."

"Molly will clear this up. Right?"

"I haven't talked to her yet."

Palmer hangs up, starts his bike, and speeds back toward school as snow continues to fall.

Pictures of Molly and Mrs. Cole are glued to the center of the steering wheel inside the cab of Rob Cole's eighteen-wheel truck. Country music plays on the radio. Windshield wipers flip out and back, pushing away falling snow as Rob pilots his truck down a snaky mountain road. At least an inch of white already covers the ground. Rob slurps a green smoothie.

The road straightens a little and the horn from a car behind him honks as the car pulls out to pass. Rob slows and the car zooms up on his left. Another car suddenly appears around a curve just a quarter-mile ahead. Rob touches the brakes. Swerving at the last second to miss the oncoming car, the passing car swerves to the right, just inches in front of Rob's fender. Rob brakes harder. The horn from the oncoming car blares.

Rob's truck slides sideways as the two cars barely miss each other. He jerks his foot off the brakes, but the truck continues to slip on the icy road. Rob fights to straighten the truck, but it's got a mind of its own. The truck swerves to the right and the front bumper cracks through the guard rail on the shoulder of the road and side-swipes a thick oak tree.

Rob's chin bounces on the edge of the steering wheel. Blood spurts but the blow doesn't knock him unconscious. The truck jolts forward, not fast now but still moving, its hood pointed down the slope of the mountain. The truck bangs through a couple of slender trees and Rob's nose smacks hard into the pictures of Molly and her mama. Blood flows as the truck gradually rolls to a stop about thirty feet off the road, its grill pointed down the hill.

Though blood pours from his nose and chin, Rob yanks off his seatbelt, kicks open the door, and fights to climb out. But the angle of the truck on the mountain makes that impossible. A car stops on the road above him. Rob tries again to crawl out but suddenly feels dizzy and passes out, his head rolling back on his shoulders and one leg dangling from the truck.

A man's head appears from the road above. His phone presses to his ear as he calls 911.

Still hiding from the press, Chelsea sits in Dub's office and stares at video of Conway's offense. She starts to scribble some notes but she's too distracted, so she throws the pen down and leans back, her hands behind her head. A second later, a man wearing a black suit and carrying a beat-up brown briefcase pokes his head through the door.

"Hello, Coach Deal," says the black-suited man, his voice tinted with formality. "I'm Ralph Pierce. From the school district's legal department. I need to take your statement regarding the incident on the night of November 11, immediately following the football game."

Chelsea stands, quickly shakes hands with Pierce, and points him to a chair. They both sit. Pierce pulls a legal pad from his briefcase and a phone from his pocket and hits the record button.

An ambulance stops on the road above Rob's truck. Two men grab a gurney from the back and gingerly ease their way down the slope to Rob. When they reach him, he opens his eyes and tries to speak but no words can be heard. The EMTs quickly cover him with a Mylar blanket and check his vital signs. He raises his hand and opens his mouth but blood bubbles on his lips and he blacks out again as two more EMTs slide down the mountain with a stretcher held between them.

A few hours later, a light snow is falling on the Rabon High football field as Coach Paul blows his whistle, and the team quickly forms a circle around him. He removes his hat as they settle.

"I'll keep this brief," he says. "I'm sure you've heard the news. I'm the interim coach for now, while the powers that be straighten this mess out. As to the accusations against Coach Deal, I was with her that night. The young woman involved specifically said she wanted everyone to keep quiet about what happened. That's the truth."

He turns to Palmer, and he steps up beside him. "Coach Paul is right," Palmer says, his voice quivering a little. "Coach Deal did what she did to protect the victim. That's it. Coach cares about people more than anybody I know. She's shown that to all of us."

The players nod and Coach Paul steps forward again. "The championship game is tomorrow," he says. "Let's have a great final practice to prepare for it."

Dressed in khakis and a thick maroon sweater, Chelsea sits at her work table at home, a rope necklace in one hand and several multi-colored beads in the other. Snow falls outside her window and gas logs burn in the fireplace. Her doorbell rings and she puts down the necklace and beads, steps into the living room, and peeks out the window. A white Tesla sits in her driveway, but she sees no signs of any media.

When the doorbell rings again, she moves to the peephole and stares out. Two men stand on her porch: an older guy with salt and pepper hair, dressed in a long black coat, a gray scarf, and black gloves; and another man she recognizes from her days as a lawyer.

Cautious but also curious, she slowly opens the door. The older man quickly removes a glove and extends a hand. "Hello, Coach Deal," he says as pleasantly as if greeting a potential buyer at a used car sales showroom. "I'm Sam Sky and this is—"

"I know who he is," says Chelsea, focused on Tillis. "Reggie Tillis, the best-known plaintiff's lawyer in the Southeast." She eyes Tillis carefully, noting his tailored, three-button suit, white shirt, and crisp blue tie.

"May we come in for a minute?" Reggie shivers. "I obviously didn't wear the proper attire for this weather and I'm freezing my biscuits off out here."

"Give me a hint what this is about," says Chelsea, not yet ready to let them in her house.

"A little suspicious, are we?" asks Sam.

"You watched any sports news lately?"

Sam chuckles. "I see your point."

Reggie blows on his hands. "I beg you, in the name of all that's holy, let us inside, please."

Chelsea glances up and down the road. Sees nothing except the Tesla. "You have fifteen minutes," she says, finally yielding. "I have a lot happening right now." She stands back and lets them enter.

Alone in her study, Eva pours tea and scotch into a teacup, sits down in a cushioned chair by the window, sips her brew, and watches the snow fall. After a few minutes, she places the cup on a coaster on a side table and unties the gold ribbon in her hair. Standing, she lays the ribbon by the coaster, picks up her phone, and punches in Chelsea's number.

"Hello, Chelsea," she says sadly when she reaches voicemail. "I know you have a difficult decision to make, and you know what I prefer you do. We need you in Rabon. All of us. But I want you to do what you feel will make you happy."

She pauses, gathers herself, and continues. "Whichever way this unfolds, please know I'll always have tea in my kettle for you. Blessings, my dear girl. Call me if you need a listening ear." Eva hangs up, pours a touch more scotch into her tea, sits back down, and stares out the window as the snow begins to cover the ground.

Chelsea, Sam, and Reggie assemble on chairs in a semi-circle in the living room. Chelsea studies the men's faces, trying to determine the motive for their sudden appearance but sees nothing she can read. Sam lays his coat over the arm of his chair, clears his throat, and speaks first. "How are you doing, Coach?" he asks. "With everything that's happening?"

"I don't want to be rude," says Chelsea, "but I don't know you. Why would I reveal anything to you about how I'm doing?" She looks at Reggie, obviously the leader of the two, and asks: "Who's your client in this?"

Reggie glances at Sam, and back to Chelsea. "We're not here about a client," says Reggie, a slight grin on his face. "We're here about you."

"You want to be my lawyer?"

Reggie grins so big it's almost a giggle. "Not at all, Ms. Deal. We want to hire you as one of ours."

Chelsea rocks back a little, her mind racing. "I'm confused," she confesses.

Reggie stands, buttons his suit coat, and begins to speak as if to a jury. "You have a unique blend of experiences and skills, Ms. Deal. You've played football, you've coached football, you have connections in football. *And* you're a highly skilled lawyer, from an excellent law school, with a sterling reputation among clients, judges, and fellow employees."

He pauses and Chelsea jumps in. "I'm still not following."

"Wait for it," says Sam, building the suspense.

Palmer stands on the sidelines beside Coach Paul, both watching Johnson call the offensive signals. The center snaps the ball, and the offense runs the play at half-speed. Johnson whips the ball to Swoops on a short pass. He snags it and sprints up field.

The lawyer Pierce suddenly appears behind Paul and whispers in his ear. Paul nods and turns to Palmer. "Me and you, kid. We need to give our statements." Palmer starts to argue but realizes he can't, under the circumstances, so he sucks in a breath and follows Paul and Pierce toward the locker room.

Reggie Tillis speaks clearly as he lays out his case to Chelsea, his bearing as confident as a king before his court. "My firm will soon open a new division," he announces. "That division will focus entirely on plaintiffs who need representation because of sports injuries. Are you aware, Ms. Deal, that over 500,000 football injuries occur each year? Add lacrosse, soccer, wrestling, and all the other sports, and it's an avalanche of mammoth proportions."

"I'm aware that sports bring risks," says Chelsea, not yet comprehending Reggie's endgame.

"Are you also aware that no law firm in America specializes specifically in this field and that literally thousands of cases need quality representation."

"It is, indeed," adds Sam. "A target-rich environment."

Reggie cuts his eyes at Sam as he continues. "Badly maintained fields, Ms. Deal. Faulty equipment, especially football helmets, poorly trained medical staff, a lack of clear, national standards for workouts and practices, abusive coaches... The causes stretch to the heavens. It's a wonder anybody survives in any sports arena."

"Lots of lawyers handle personal injury cases," asserts Chelsea.

"Agreed," says Reggie. "But, as I noted, none handles only sports injury cases. None have the expertise we believe is needed."

"Bottom-line it for her, Reggie," suggests Sam, a twinkle in his eyes. "She's on a tight schedule."

"Ms. Deal," says Reggie, his voice rising to close the pitch, "I'm here to offer you a job as the lead attorney for the ten-lawyer Southern office we plan to establish in Atlanta. An office that will handle *only* sports injury cases. An office what will develop a specialty to a degree unparalleled in the field of jurisprudence." Reggie stops, unbuttons his coat, and looks to Sam.

Chelsea stays seated, her mind rushing, not sure how to respond.

Sam pulls a piece of paper from a pocket and hands it to her. "We'll start you at that figure," he points to a number on the paper. "I suspect it's ten times what you make now. Plus, we'll provide you with a car, expense account, and a country club membership. You know the drill. A full partner in the firm from the jump."

Chelsea stares at the number on the paper. "You're offering me a job."

"See, Reggie," chuckles Sam. "I told you she was quick on the uptake."

Still trying to find her footing, Chelsea looks up. "If you do what you're saying, it could destroy sports," she suggests. "With plaintiffs suing at every turn."

"Or it could make sports better," argues Sam. "Safer."

"We plan to donate half our profits back to the sports," explains Reggie, excitement in his voice. "Head trauma research, equipment innovation, especially helmets. We'll make donations to install safer fields for schools in poor communities, offer grants to pay for medical staff for schools that can't afford it."

Chelsea pauses, now intrigued by the offer. Reggie's perspective makes some sense to her and she especially appreciates the monetary investment in safer conditions for players. "I don't know what to say," she finally says.

"We don't expect a decision right now," says Reggie. "Think about it a couple days. Reach out to us after the championship."

She puts her hands in her lap. "Answer me this," she says, still confused. "You know about the accusations I'm dealing with right now."

"Of course," says Reggie.

"So, why are you making me this offer?"

Reggie glances at Sam and they both smile.

"We've done our due diligence, Coach," says Sam as he stands. "We know who you are."

Chelsea inhales slowly, a sense of relief washing over her. Though still not clear about her feelings, she recognizes the offer for what it is—a lifeboat in the middle of stormy seas. Though not overly religious, this feels almost providential. She exhales, stands, and shakes hands with Sam and Reggie. Sam puts on his gloves and Reggie bows at the waist as if about to back away from royalty.

Chelsea ushers them to the door in silence, then watches as they climb into Sam's Tesla and drive away in the snow. Turning back into her house, she looks again at the paper in her hand, folds it, and slips it into her pocket.

CHAPTER TWENTY-NINE

S itting in front of his locker after practice, Palmer slips off his shoulder pads and drops them into his locker. For a few seconds, he sits and tries to figure out what to do next. Other players around him shower and dress, and a couple pat him on the back as they head out the door. Finally, with no clear plan in mind, he changes clothes without showering, pulls out his phone, and sees a text from Molly. "Call me ASAP," she says. "My pa had an accident in Alabama. He's okay, but me and Mama are headed over there."

Palmer quickly tries to call her but gets no answer. He leaves a message. "You hear about Coach Deal? Call me! Also, I'm glad your dad is all right."

Dressed in gray runner's pants and a yellow reflecting vest, Chelsea jogs through falling snow down the dark road in front of her house. Sweat pours off her face as she powers over a narrow bridge, then up a slope. At the top of the ridge, she stops on an overlook, pulls water from her pack, and swigs a long drink.

Voices in her head clamor for attention—Eva asking her to stay, Tillis offering her a job, Buck accusing her of covering up a sexual assault. Though not exactly sure what she wants to say, she pulls out her phone, taps in Palmer's number, reaches his voicemail, and pauses. Snow swirls around her face and it tickles a little, so she leans her head back and, for just a moment, she's a little girl again, excited about snow landing on her cheeks. Suddenly, the voices in her head go quiet and the only thing she hears is her own heartbeat. It thumps strong and clear, and she knows what she needs to do.

"Hey, Palmer," she says, leaving a message. "I don't know what you've said to Molly. But don't ask her to come forward on my behalf. She's been through enough. I'm fine just walking away."

Feeling an overwhelming sense of peace, she puts her phone away and lifts her head again. Snow falls on her cheeks and she smiles as she raises her arms to embrace it.

Palmer drops his backpack into a chair and collapses onto the couch as Dirk enters from the kitchen, a ham and cheese sandwich in each hand. "Hey, man," says Dirk. "You hanging in there? With all that's going on?" He hands a sandwich to Palmer and sits on the hearth.

"Let me see," says Palmer, chomping into the sandwich. "Coach Deal is suspended. Molly is in Alabama with her pa, who's been in a wreck. I'm freaked out wondering if I passed math so I can play in the game tomorrow. And, oh yeah, my best bud Ty lies on his death bed. Just another day in paradise." He bites again into the sandwich.

"How are your grades, other than math?"

"Passing everything else...barely, but I'll take it."

Dirk bites into his sandwich. "I still can't reach Chelsea," he mumbles, his mouth full.

"She left me a message a little while ago. Doesn't want Molly to do anything. Said she would just resign."

"I hate to see her stop coaching."

"Me too." Palmer swallows a bite of ham and cheese. "I don't think Molly even knows yet."

"She'll do the right thing once she does."

Palmer hesitates. "I don't know," he finally says. "She's feisty with people she knows but way shy in public. With Coach Deal letting her off the hook..." He shrugs and finishes the sandwich.

"Keep calling her. Tell her what's going on. At least give her the option."

Palmer grabs his guitar from its stand in the corner and strums it. "The game doesn't seem real important right now," he says.

"Roger that."

"Life can go off the rails in a hurry."

Dirk finishes his sandwich. "You said a mouthful there, kid."

Chelsea pulls into the school parking lot right at 7:25 and quickly spots media vans, camera lights, and a noisy crowd near the front entrance. Thinking fast, she steers away from the scrum and around to the back of the school. She parks there, hops out, and rushes to the door before anyone sees her. Careful at every turn in the hallway, she quickly slips inside the conference room, where she finds everyone in place. To her surprise, Dub is there too, leaning on a crutch by the window, watching the snow as it continues to fall.

Roberts shoves a pencil behind his ear as Chelsea takes a seat and Dub turns to the group. "Here's the deal," Roberts begins. "Legal has taken statements from everyone except Don and Strick. They're refusing to cooperate."

"Can the police make them talk?" asks Holt.

Roberts shakes his head. "I made a call," he says. "Unless the young woman makes an accusation, the police won't get involved."

"What about the young woman?" asks Eva. "Anybody reach her?"

"There are no secrets in Rabon," says Holt. "So, we can stop pretending we don't know her name."

"At least the media hasn't publicly identified her yet," says Eva.

"Legal hasn't been able to make contact with her," says Roberts.

The room falls quiet for a moment and Chelsea decides it's time to put everyone out of their misery. "Don't try to reach Molly again," she orders Roberts. "I've made my decision."

Eva's face falls. Holt's ears seem to grow bigger. Phil removes his cap and covers his face with it. Dub leans forward on his crutch.

"The team needs you, Coach," Dub says softly.

"Molly is more important," says Chelsea.

"Maybe she wants to tell her side of the story."

"If so, fine," says Chelsea, not relenting an inch. "But I won't ask her to do it for me."

"You're worth fighting for," continues Dub. "Everybody in this room believes that." Dub looks at Holt.

"What? Yes! I'm with you!" agrees Holt.

Chelsea pushes her chair back and stands. "I moved here to coach football,"

she says, relief flooding her body as she speaks, all the stress seeping out, like water through a sieve. "I wanted to make a difference for young people. But this?
This is not what I signed up for." Her eyes move from one person to the next and
land on Eva last. "I've weighed things every way I know how," she concludes, her
voice breaking as she finishes. "And I've decided the price for me to keep coaching is too high for Molly to pay." Tears fall now, from her eyes and Eva's. Phil
wipes his cheeks with his cap.

"We can't talk you out of it?" asks Roberts.

Chelsea shakes her head. Dub hobbles over and pats her on the back. Eva
starts to speak but stops and drops her eyes. Phil slowly puts his cap back on.

"What about the press?" asks Holt, breaking the quiet. "Somebody will need
to issue a statement."

"I need to tidy up a few things tonight," says Chelsea. "I'll speak to them at
noon tomorrow."

Eva sighs and stands. "We'll respect Chelsea's decision," she says softly. "If
word seeps out before her press conference tomorrow, I'll personally track down
the leaker and cut out his tongue. We clear?"

Everybody nods.

The fireplace burns high as Dirk plays his guitar and Palmer works on math
problems on his new computer. A knock clacks on the door and Dirk looks at
Palmer, who shrugs. Dirk stands, ambles to the door, and opens it. Chelsea waits
on the porch, snow in her hair. "The press found my house," she says quietly. "So,
I'm looking for a fire to sit by. Maybe a marshmallow to roast."

"You came to the right place," says Dirk, ushering her in. "So long as you're
not particular about the company."

"Hey, Coach," says Palmer as he emails his homework to Mr. Stone.

"I need a beer," says Dirk. He looks at Chelsea. "And a fizzy water for the
lady." He steps out.

"I left a million messages for Molly," says Palmer. "She'll call back. I know
she will."

"Thanks for trying," says Chelsea, sitting on the hearth. "But I'm good."

"She's in Alabama. Her dad had a wreck."

Dirk returns, hands Chelsea the water, and sits on the hearth beside her. Palmer's phone buzzes. "Hey, Mr. Rogers," he answers quickly. "How's Ty?"

"Weaker by the minute," says Russell. "It's tearing us up."

"Wish I could do something," Palmer says.

"Swoops and Johnson, some others from the team just left the hospital," says Russell. "They're saying the team won't play tomorrow if Chelsea doesn't coach."

"What?!" Palmer jumps up and faces Dirk and Chelsea.

"The players plan to boycott the game if they don't let Chelsea coach," explains Russell.

"Coach Deal is here!" blurts Palmer.

"Can you put your phone on speaker?"

Palmer hits the speaker button and holds up his phone.

"Chelsea," says Russell, "I just told Palmer: The kids say they won't play tomorrow for any coach but you."

"Don't let them do that, Russell," Chelsea pleads, taking the phone from Palmer. "It'll just escalate the media circus. Tell Ty to make them play!"

"Ty agrees with them," says Russell.

"I'm done, Russell!" insists Chelsea. "Of my own accord, I'm packing it in. It's best for everybody."

"If that's your choice, fine. But you'll need to tell the team, face to face. Otherwise, I can't predict what they'll do."

Chelsea turns and stares into the fire as she weighs her options,

Wanting to do something but not sure what, Palmer walks to her and stops at her side. A second later, Dirk joins them, Chelsea in the middle.

"Okay, Russell," Chelsea finally says. "Gather the team at the middle school football field at eleven in the morning. Swear them all to secrecy about time and place. I don't want any media."

"Will do."

Chelsea hangs up and hands the phone to Palmer. "You can stay here tonight if you want," Palmer tells Chelsea. "Avoid the media."

Chelsea glances at Dirk and he laughs. "Don't look at me," he says. "I didn't tell him to say that."

"But can I?" she asks Dirk. "I'll sleep on the sofa."

"You can sleep in my bed if you want," says Dirk. "Course, I'll be there too."

"Good try. The sofa will do fine."

Chelsea faces Palmer again. "I appreciate you trying to reach Molly," she says.

"I'm sorry, Coach," says Palmer. "After all that's happened. All you've done for me."

She puts a hand on his shoulder. "I've had a soft spot in my heart for quarterbacks for a long time," she says gently.

Dirk puts an arm around Chelsea's back and she puts an arm around Palmer, and the three of them stand arm in arm in front of the fireplace as snow continues to come down outside.

Close to two hours later, Palmer quietly enters Ty's hospital room and finds Vanessa and Ty asleep—Ty on the bed, Vanessa in a chair. For a couple of minutes, Palmer stands still and listens to Ty's labored breathing. Turning over in her chair, Vanessa opens her eyes. "You're not taking him out of the hospital again," she whispers to Palmer.

"I promise," says Palmer. "That's not why I came."

Ty wakes up and Palmer steps close to him. "I had to see you," says Palmer. "One more time before the game."

Vanessa brings Ty some water and he takes a couple of sips. "Wish I could be there," Ty says.

"I'll give you boys a minute," says Vanessa.

Palmer nods and she quietly leaves the room.

"I been meaning to ask," Ty says to Palmer. "Don and Strick?"

Palmer shrugs. "I drove to their house. A god-awful color. Parked up the street. Sat and watched awhile." He exhales as he remembers how sad he felt when he saw them at their home. "They a lot like me, Ty. Living on the edge of poor white trash, like I've done most of my life. They're just meaner than me, is all. So, before too long, I stopped watching and just drove away."

"They'll pay their due sooner or later."

Palmer lays a hand on Ty's shoulder. "You don't deserve this, man. It's not fair."

Ty coughs.

"You the best person I ever met," continues Palmer.

Ty sits up a little and gathers his strength for a moment. "I always wanted to be my Pops," he says. "A natural athlete. But my gene pool had other ideas." Coughing again, he sips from his cup.

"I adjusted," continues Ty. "All A's. Class president. Model citizen. All to make up for being the slowest black quarterback to ever play the game."

Palmer laughs lightly. "I wouldn't say the slowest."

"You're right. Second slowest."

They both chuckle. "I tried to be what my folks wanted," says Ty as he closes his eyes. "But ... I don't know ... Nothing I've done seems to matter. Cancer stripped it all away."

Tears drip down his face and Palmer's too.

"It matters to me," Palmer says. "What you've done. For me."

Palmer hugs Ty close as his strength wanes. "All love, bro," whispers Palmer. "All respect."

Ty licks his lips as Vanessa returns. Palmer backs away from Ty and hugs Vanessa, who accepts it with a tearful smile.

"You gotta win tomorrow," she says.

"I know."

Stepping away from her, Palmer hurries out, down the hall and out the door to his truck. His phone rings as he climbs in. He checks the number and quickly answers.

"Sorry it's taken so long to reach you," says Molly. "Things have been crazy here."

"Your pa all right?"

"Busted nose, stitches in his chin, but nothing too serious. We hoped to drive home tonight, but we're snowed in. Will try again early tomorrow."

"You listen to my messages?"

"Yeah. I finally saw the news too. It's awful."

"Coach is resigning tomorrow."

"She can't do that!"

"You the only one who can stop it." Silence comes to the phone.

"I can't do it," Molly finally says. "Stand in front of a bunch of cameras?

Everybody watching me?"

"I know. And Coach is fine if you don't."

"They won't take your word for what happened? Coach Paul's? Ty's?"

"Nope. You the only one who matters." Palmer tries hard not to press, but a hint of urgency has crept into his voice, and he knows she can hear it.

"I feel so bad for Coach," she laments.

"She wants what's best for you."

Molly's voice rises. "I want to help. You know I do! But Don and Strick will lie! Like they did when they said I had a baby! No telling what they'll say this time! And it's national news now! What about my folks? How will they feel if Don and Strick say something awful?"

"Nobody blames you," says Palmer.

"Please tell Coach I'm sorry."

"Like I said, she's dealing with it. Tell your pa I'm glad he's all right."

They both hang up and Palmer, his last hope gone, slumps against the seat.

CHAPTER THIRTY

S till dressed in her clothes from the previous day, Chelsea wakes up Saturday morning on Dirk's sofa, her body warm and snuggly inside a blanket. She rises slowly and rubs her eyes as sunlight slips into the room. She slides on her shoes and smooths out her hair as Dirk walks in, already dressed. "Coffee?" he asks.

"I'd kill for it."

Dirk disappears into the kitchen as she pulls the blanket around her shoulders and walks to the front window. A couple seconds later, Palmer appears from a back room, also dressed. "Looks like a couple inches of snow," says Chelsea, staring at the ground outside.

Dirk brings a loaded tray from the kitchen. Hands coffee, a bottle of water, and a store-bought muffin to Chelsea. Tosses a muffin and water bottle to Palmer. Sits down on the hearth.

"Molly called me last night," says Palmer, biting the muffin.

Chelsea's heart jumps for a second, but she catches herself and relaxes again. "That ship has sailed," she says quietly but firmly.

"She's trying to get home," continues Palmer. "But the roads are bad."

"Her dad all right?" asks Chelsea, facing Palmer now.

Palmer nods. "She wants to help you, Coach. But she's too scared."

Chelsea nibbles at her muffin. "I understand, Palmer. Really. No need for her to do anything." She drops the blanket onto the sofa. "But I do need to roll."

"Us too," says Dirk.

"Get Palmer back here by eleven," she orders Dirk.

"If the roads are good, we'll be back in plenty of time."

Dirk yanks a tan scarf off a wall peg and wraps it around Chelsea's neck.

"I'll need that returned later," he warns.

She smiles. "I'll guard it with my life."

He grins as she quickly gathers her purse.

"Wonder if the press is still at your house," says Palmer.

"Maybe the snow scared them off."

Pulling the scarf tight around her neck, she gives Dirk a quick hug and rushes out the door.

🏈

A few minutes later, Dirk and Palmer exit the same door and climb into Dirk's truck. Snow blankets the road, and the truck slides a little as they wheel out and speed around a curve. "Whoa," says Dirk, regaining control of his vehicle.

"This truck ain't—isn't built for icy roads," says Palmer.

"Don't criticize a man's truck, kid. Best way I know to get your butt kicked."

"Least the sun's out." Palmer points to the blue sky. "Snow should melt pretty fast."

Palmer checks the weather on his phone. "Looks like the worst of the snow stayed west of us," he says. "Eight inches in north Alabama."

"Any chance Molly will change her mind and tell what happened?" asks Dirk.

"Probably too late, even if she does." Palmer hits the button to roll down his window and sticks a hand into the cold.

"Put the window up!" yells Dirk. "It's freezing out there."

Palmer hits the button again and the window closes. They ride in silence for a few miles. Palmer thinks about the visit he'll be making in an hour or so. "I wish Dad had lived long enough for me to know him," he finally says, his tone wistful as he tries to remember his father.

"He had huge hands," laughs Dirk. "Could pretty much palm you, like a basketball, when you were a baby."

Palmer stares out at the snow. "Before the war? Was he a good man?"

"The best. A positive guy. He laughed easy. Could fix anything electrical or mechanical. Was a big tipper too. Especially for someone with barely any money."

Palmer smiles, his spirits lifting a little. "I remember finding some books under his bed after his death."

"He read a lot. Mysteries. Biographies."

Palmer hesitates, afraid to ask the question he's always wanted to ask but never had the courage to pose. "How did I turn out so dumb?" he whispers.

Dirk glances at him. "You're not dumb, Palmer."

"Mr. Towe would argue with you on that."

"You're not dumb, Palmer."

Palmer drops his eyes. "Miswired then."

Dirk glances at him again. "Yeah, well, we're all miswired one way or another."

Palmer, weighing that thought for a moment, recognizes some truth in it. "Least I can play music," he says, a little more optimistic.

"You got that right. And don't ever forget this: The ladies love musicians."

Palmer smiles, hits the down button on the window again, and holds his hand out as Dirk again yells at him.

Snow blankets the parking lot of a small, one-story motel backed up against a low mountain ridge. A sign by the road out front reads: "Hillgrove Motel." Red and Green Christmas wreaths decorate the front windows.

At the back of the motel, in a small area shoveled clear of snow, Molly leans against a wall and pulls a long drag off a cigarette. A heavy quilted coat, a blue wool cap, and scuffed brown boots protect her against the cold, and a nearby dumpster blocks her from the wind. The back door opens and out strolls an older, African American woman wearing tan slacks and a shirt with a Hillgrove Motel nametag. An unlit cigarette hangs in her fingers.

Molly nods and the woman crunches over the frozen snow to her. Molly peeps at the woman's nametag. "How you doin' today, Mavis?" Molly asks.

"I like snow," answers Mavis, her voice raspy.

"You need a coat on."

"Cold don't bother me."

Molly lights Mavis' cigarette off hers and they lean together on the wall and smoke.

"You in 121?" Mavis asks.

"Me and my folks."

"You up pretty early."

Molly nods. "I like mornings. And I got a lot going on."

"Stuff happens."

Molly flips ashes into the snow. "I work at a motel over in Georgia."

"It ain't the best career path a girl could choose."

A sparrow lands on the edge of the dumpster and peeps at them.

"Choices are hard," says Molly. "Especially when bad things can happen either way you go."

"You young," offers Mavis. "You'll make a million choices before you my age."

Molly considers the statement while taking another drag of her cigarette. "How do you know when you've made the right one?" she asks.

Mavis grunts and studies Molly's face as if staring at the *Mona Lisa*. "I reckon I'm the last person you ought to ask that question to."

Molly thinks of Chelsea. "I barely slept last night," she says.

"That's not a good sign."

Molly snuffs her cigarette out against the wall. "There's this friend," she says. "She's in some trouble and I could help her get out of it. But it will be hard on me if I do."

Mavis exhales a puff of smoke. "You want my advice?" she asks.

"Yeah. Why not?"

Mavis stares at the glowing end of her cigarette. "Choose what lets you sleep peaceful at night. Whatever that is."

Molly weighs the counsel. Wishes she hadn't put out her cigarette.

Mavis drops her cigarette into the snow and steps on it. "Check-out is at eleven," she says.

Molly nods and Mavis pats her on the arm. The bird on the dumpster flits away. Mavis turns to head back inside but suddenly stops and faces Molly again. "Stop smoking, child," she advises. "I hear it'll kill ya."

A bright sun lights the front entrance of the football stadium. The word KNIGHTS, in white, fifteen-foot-high letters, looms over the main gate. A blanket of snow covers the ground. Situated about fifty feet in front of the entrance, Sandra Brinner carefully pushes her hair out of her eyes, adjusts the jaunty red beret she's wearing, and smiles at the camera trained on her. Her producer softly begins his countdown. "Three, two, one."

"This is Sandra Brinner from ESPN," she begins, a wide smile on her face. "Coming to you again from Rabon High School in North Georgia. At noon today, Coach Chelsea Deal, accused of covering up a sexual assault, will make a statement to the media. I don't know exactly what she'll say, but sources tell me she might re-sign, thereby ending her quest to become the first female coach to lead a high school football team to a championship game."

Wind plays with Brinner's hair as she continues. "While we wait on Coach Deal's statement, we've also learned that Rabon High's legal representatives have interviewed at least two other witnesses to the event surrounding the alleged assault, and they've stated that the victim instructed Coach Deal to keep the whole mat-ter quiet."

Brinner strolls slowly toward the main gate. "We've not yet heard the victim's side of the story, but unless she comes forward soon, Coach Deal will remain sus-pended from tonight's game and perhaps never again walk the sideline of a football stadium like this majestic one here in Rabon." She stops in front of the gate, her red beret brilliant in the sun.

Driving in silence, Dirk pilots his truck past a green sign pointing to Bartow, North Carolina. A mile farther, he turns left, sees a sign for Sweetwater Cemetery, and turns right. A couple minutes later, he pulls through a stone gate and follows the road about a hundred yards before reaching a dead end by a row of gravesites. There, he parks and looks at Palmer.

Palmer sighs as he gazes at the snowy ground, the headstones poking out like gray teeth. He never knows how to feel when he visits his dad's grave and today, he's more mixed up than ever.

"Go on now," Dirk finally says.

"You not coming?" asks Palmer.

"You need some time by yourself first."

"I'd like you with me."

"You're old enough now to go it alone."

Palmer drops his eyes. "I don't know what's worse," he says. "Being too young to fend for myself or being old enough to have to deal with things on my own."

Dirk grunts. "It *is* a conundrum. Now move along. I'll join you in a few minutes."

Unable to put it off any longer, Palmer slowly climbs out and walks across the snowy graveyard, counting the rows as he goes. At row seventeen, he turns right and walks three more rows to his dad's plot. Stopping there, he kneels and fingers the lettering on the headstone. "Sergeant Daryl Norman. Father. Husband. Patriot."

Stranger—that's what he is to me, thinks Palmer. *A larger-than-life figure but only as a vague memory, images here and there, a few pictures, a handful of short video clips.* Enough to make him want more but not enough to make him feel close to Daryl Norman.

Palmer wipes his eyes. Snow crunches behind him. He turns and sees Lacy walking toward him.

"Hey, Palmer," she says.

Instantly upset, he stands quickly. "You skip out of rehab again?" he challenges her.

"Dirk signed me out. I got two hours."

"So, it was a conspiracy." He clenches his fists and pivots to leave.

"You need to know what really happened!" Lacy shouts.

Palmer stops, angry now. "We've been over this! I was there, remember? Dad gave you the gun!"

"It's not that simple."

He faces her, his body rigid, ready to pounce. "Okay, Mama!" he shouts. "Make your case!"

Lacy steps closer but Palmer backs up, so she stops and speaks, her voice sad. "You know the war changed your daddy. PTSD. Whatever you call it. Anger, nightmares. That night, like you saw. I talked him down and he handed me the gun. But after you walked away"—she looks Palmer square in the eyes—"your daddy… he rushed me. Grabbed for the gun. We wrestled for it. The gun went off. It was an accident. You know the rest." She waits, her eyes on Palmer.

"I'm supposed to just believe you?" asks Palmer, not blinking. "Trust an addict?"

"I was pregnant, Palmer," she pleads. "You need to understand. I had a miscarriage three weeks later. Fell into a black hole. Took medication for pain, depression. Got hooked. One thing led to another."

Palmer shoves his hands into his pockets, his mind racing. Lacy has failed him so many times—broken his heart, left him alone ... "Why tell me all this now?" he challenges her again. "Why not years ago?"

"I didn't know you saw what you did. So, I didn't talk about it. Figured details didn't matter. After a while, I was so messed up, I just left it alone."

He studies her face, looking for deception in her eyes—deception like he's seen in all the other lies she's told him.

"Even if you telling the truth now," he says, resignation in his voice, "it's too late for me and you."

Lacy steps slowly to him and hands over an envelope.

"What's this?" he asks.

"Just open it."

He opens it with trembling hands and pulls out a picture of an ultrasound.

"Your little sister," whispers Lacy. "She'd be almost nine now. I named her Laura, after my mama."

Palmer stares at the picture for several seconds. Finally hands it back.

"One last chance, Palmer," says Lacy. "That's all I'm asking."

"It's too late," he says.

She puts the picture back in the envelope.

"I need to go," he says, desperate to escape, desperate for some time to think.

"Come see me soon?"

"I don't know." He shakes his head, turns, and walks away.

Palmer rides back to Rabon in almost total silence, too lost in thought to talk. Dirk tries to pull him into conversation a couple of times, but he waves him off and Dirk finally gives up. Snow continues to melt as they reach Georgia again and, by the time they pull up to the middle school football field about half a mile from Rabon High, the roads have pretty much cleared. Palmer checks the time as they park. Ten minutes till eleven. "This shouldn't take long," he tells Dirk.

"I'll wait right here."

Palmer's phone buzzes with a text and he checks it. His math teacher. Palmer holds his breath as he reads the text. "By the skin of your teeth. C-." Palmer grins for the first time all day.

"Why the smile?" asks Dirk.

"A Christmas miracle." Palmer hops out and hustles through the gate.

The team is gathered in the middle of the field and Palmer rushes over and squeezes in at the edge of the circle. Roberts and Eva stand in the middle, Swoops and Johnson beside them.

Russell walks up beside Palmer.

"How's Ty today?" Palmer asks quietly.

Russell drops his eyes and shakes his head.

A murmur rumbles through the group as Chelsea, dressed as usual in khakis, a Knights' jacket, and a whistle around her neck, moves toward them from the back gate. Palmer's phone buzzes and he checks it. Molly! He quickly steps away a couple paces and answers. "Hey, I just have a minute."

"I'll do it," she says. "I'll make a statement."

"I don't understand."

"I'm choosing what lets me sleep peaceful at night."

"What?"

"Don't ask questions."

Palmer's heart races. "Okay. I'm with Coach now. I'll tell her."

"There's just one thing. We're snowed in up here. Close to two hours away."

The players part as Chelsea reaches them and strides to the center of the group.

"I'll come after you!" Palmer hangs up and pushes through the team to Chelsea. "You can't do it, Coach!" he orders as he reaches her.

"It's all right, Palmer."

"No, listen to me," he commands. "Molly just called. She wants to come forward, clear everything up!"

"It's too late," says Chelsea.

Swoops steps towards Chelsea. "No, it's not!" he says.

"There's a minute left on the clock, Coach!" adds Johnson.

Chelsea looks at Palmer, Swoops, and Johnson.

"The team needs you," says Eva.

Chelsea fingers her whistle, glances to the sky, lays the whistle against her jacket, and faces the team. Palmer holds his breath.

"You sure about this?" Chelsea asks the team.

The team yells its approval. "We need you, Coach!"

She faces Palmer again. "I need to talk to Molly," she says.

Palmer quickly calls Molly back. "Hey, Coach wants to talk to you." He hands the phone to Chelsea.

"Are you sure, Molly?" Chelsea asks. "You don't have to do anything."

"Girl power, Coach. We gotta stick together."

"I'm so grateful, Molly," Chelsea says. "Thank you."

Chelsea hands the phone back to Palmer. "Text me your location," he tells Molly. "I'll find a way to reach you."

He hangs up and turns to Chelsea. "I have to go after Molly," he says. "Maybe two hours from here."

Chelsea faces Roberts and Eva. "We have a press conference in half an hour," Roberts reminds her.

"We'll push it back," declares Eva. "Or cancel it altogether. We'll put Molly on record and end Chelsea's suspension before game time. That's the plan."

"The media will raise hell," says Roberts.

"Frankly, George, I don't give a damn!" barks Eva.

Everybody laughs as relief floods through the team. Palmer raises a hand. "Molly is snowed in," he says. "And Dirk's truck" … He starts to say "don't" but stops and starts again. "Dirk's truck doesn't handle snow too well."

"We'll drive Holt's Hummer," asserts Eva.

"You think he'll let us?" asks Roberts.

"If he says 'no,' I'll cut off one of his mammoth ears and feed it to him for breakfast."

"She was in the Navy!" yells Roberts. The team whoops and hollers. "She was in the Navy!"

Not quite two hours later, a "Welcome to Alabama" sign appears on the side of the road and the snow seems to immediately grow deeper. At least six inches cover the asphalt, crunching under the Hummer's thick tires. Roberts rides in the passenger seat beside Holt, with Eva and Chelsea behind them and Palmer and the attorney Pierce in the third row. Palmer stays quiet as they drive, his eyes on the almost-empty road. They pass a rusted old sign with a big arrow pointing left: "Hillgrove Motel. Five miles."

"I appreciate you doing this, Les," says Roberts, breaking the silence as Holt points the Hummer toward the motel.

"I expect full reimbursement for my gas. Eighty-four miles so far. And I'll calculate a fair hourly rate for my time."

Roberts turns to Pierce. "Just confirming. If we get Ms. Cole's statement on video, Coach is good to go?"

"If Ms. Cole affirms in written or video form that she instructed Coach Deal not to report the incident in question, we will immediately lift the suspension on Coach Deal and declare the matter closed."

"Is that a 'yes'?" Palmer says, surprising himself at his sarcastic comment. But he quickly decides he likes it.

Everyone chuckles except Pierce.

Standing again in front of the football stadium with her camera poised to film, Sandra Brinner checks her phone: 1:30. She adjusts her hat, licks her teeth, flips her frown upside down, and faces the camera. "I'm here once again at the Rabon High football complex," she states. "And the curious case of Coach Chelsea Deal has taken another unexpected turn. I'm told she met with the football team this morning, intending to resign. But Palmer Norman, one of the participants in the incident we're investigating, received a call from the victim of the assault. And, our source reports, the victim says she's now ready to speak to the public. Stay tuned to ESPN for the next twist in the fascinating story of a woman coach seeking a last-minute redemption."

Brinner waits until the camera lights turn off, quickly hands her microphone to her producer, and huffs away.

A neon sign for the Hillgrove Motel blinks beside the road and Palmer leans forward as Holt pulls his Hummer into the snow-covered parking lot. Molly's car sits near the front of the motel and Holt parks the Hummer beside it. Eager to see Molly, Palmer hops out first and everyone else quickly follows. A second later, the motel's front door pops open and Molly hurries to them. "They said we can do it in the lobby!" she shouts. "There's a Christmas tree and everything!"

His briefcase in hand, Pierce steps immediately in Molly's direction and positions himself between her and the rest of the group. "Speak only to me, Ms. Cole," he instructs. "We'll permit no outside influence here."

Molly glances at Palmer and he shrugs.

"All right," she says. "This way."

She leads Pierce into the motel and the rest follow, all of them quiet. Once inside, Palmer quickly glances around. A Christmas tree decorated with red lights, red bows, and red bells fills one corner of the lobby. The registration desk stands in the middle and a sitting area with a lit gas fireplace fills the corner to the right.

Molly leads them to the sitting area. A sofa fronted by a coffee table, plus four chairs and an old but functioning grandfather clock furnish the space.

"Let's move this along," says Eva, looking at the clock. "Time is of the essence."

When Mr. and Mrs. Cole appear from the hall past the registration desk, Molly points them to two of the chairs while she quickly takes a seat on the sofa. Clearing his throat, Pierce sits down on a chair across from her, the table in front of him. Everyone else stands behind him. Pierce opens his briefcase, pulls out a yellow legal pad, and places it in his lap. Everyone falls still. Palmer inhales deeply, looks at Molly, and smiles.

"Ms. Cole," starts Pierce, his voice laced with serious intent as he closes his briefcase and places it on the floor, "I have a list of questions here." He holds up the notepad. "I'll ask you these questions. If a simple 'yes' or 'no' suffices to answer the question, please just say 'yes' or 'no.' I'll record my questions and your responses on my phone. I'm also allowing these others"—he indicates everyone behind him—"to videotape this questioning. I'll provide the video to any official investigative body that might need to probe this situation further. Are you comfortable with this set-up?"

"For God's sake, man," grumbles Rob, "get with on with it already."

Molly looks at Palmer and he offers her a thumbs-up. Pierce lifts his phone to face Molly and hits "record." "Is your name Ms. Molly Cole?" Pierce asks.

"Yes." Molly speaks clearly, her chin firm.

"Were you the victim of a sexual assault in the parking lot of the Rabon High football stadium on the night of November 11 of this year?"

"Yes." Molly folds her hands in her lap but doesn't look away from Pierce. Palmer shoves his hands in his pockets, his nerves jangling.

"Why haven't you told your story to anyone before today?"

Molly stares at her hands and her voice quivers as she speaks. "I've been afraid.

The publicity. What people might say."

"Why did you decide to make a statement today?"

Molly glances at Palmer again but he's too nervous to breathe, much less smile.

"I can barely sleep," says Molly. "My conscience is chewing at me. People need to know. As they say, the truth will set you free."

Pierce, checks his notepad, then refocuses on Molly. "Did Coach Chelsea Deal and others assist you in escaping the sexual assault of November 11?"

"Yes." Her voice is firm again.

"Did Coach Deal ask you what you wanted to do in terms of reporting or not reporting this assault?"

"Yes. She asked me twice."

"Did you tell her not to report the assault?"

Molly hesitates, stares at her hands. A door behind the registration desk opens and Mavis slides through. Palmer and everyone else freeze in place. Mavis stops and nods toward Molly.

"Did you tell Coach Deal not to report the assault?" Pierce repeats the question.

Molly faces Palmer again. He knows she needs him, and this time he responds. He tilts his head in a slow nod and a tiny smile appears on his face.

Molly turns to Pierce a final time. "Yes," she says, her voice stronger, decisive now. "I told Coach Deal twice. I didn't want anyone else to know."

"Did Coach Deal pressure you in any way to say 'no' that night?"

"No, she did not pressure me in any way."

"Has she pressured you in any way to say what you've said today?"

"No, she has not."

Pierce leans back and turns off his phone.

"Hot diggity!" yells Rob.

The room erupts with relief and laughter, everyone shouting and hugging. Mr. and Mrs. Cole rush Molly and embrace her as Palmer hugs Chelsea. Eva slaps a high-five with Mr. Roberts. From Palmer's left, Holt approaches Chelsea, his hand out to shake. Palmer steps back to watch and Chelsea pushes Holt's hand away, but then opens her arms and embraces him. Pivoting, Palmer rushes to Molly, lifts her off her feet, and twirls her around and around in celebration.

CHAPTER THIRTY-ONE

Covered scalp to shoes in winter clothes, football fans stuff every seat in Atlanta Stadium. Bands play. Flags fly. Cheerleaders jump and spin.

Sandra Brinner stands in the north end zone, her camera ready, dressed nattily as usual but without a hat this time. Her ever-present smile plastered on, she raises her microphone and speaks. "Good evening. I'm Sandra Brinner with ESPN, and I'm in Atlanta Stadium tonight for a battle for the Georgia State High School Championship between the Rabon Knights and the Conway Tigers. But, as most of us know, this game is about a lot more than football. On one sideline, we have Chelsea Deal, the female coach recently exonerated from a charge of covering-up the sexual assault of a young woman after a football game at Rabon High."

Brinner brushes her hair back with a manicured finger and continues. "On the other sideline, we have Coach Buck Jones, now an analyst with Conway High, and the man who accused Coach Deal of the assault cover-up. Not only do we have the battle-royale between the Knights and the Tigers but also the more personal clash between Coach Chelsea Deal and Buck Jones."

Brinner lowers her microphone and the camera lights blink off as the Knights, clad in purple, rush onto the field from their locker room. Knights' fans erupt and cheers reverberate to the heavens as the team dodges around Brinner and hurry past.

From the opposite end zone, the Conway Tigers appear, dressed in white uniforms with red letters. Buck Jones, in civilian clothes except for a Conway cap pulled low, walks briskly behind the team. Some Knights' fans spot him and rain boos down on him.

Brinner eyes Jones and starts to lead her crew toward him, but Les Holt, wearing a purple tie with his gray suit and white shirt, hustles up and stops her before she reaches Jones. "Hey," says Les. "I left you a message earlier. I've known Buck Jones for years but have supported Chelsea Deal since the day she arrived in Rabon."

Brinner points to her crew and the camera lights blink back on. Quickly arranging Holt directly between the goal posts as the team captains meet at midfield for the coin toss, she nods to her producer, and he counts down: "Three, two, one."

Brinner turns on her high-beam smile and eyes the camera. "I'm here now with Mr. Les Holt," she says, as if introducing a rock star. "A key booster for the Rabon Knights and an early advocate for Coach Chelsea Deal. Mr. Holt, what was it about Ms. Deal that convinced you she was up to the task of leading the Knights?"

She pushes her microphone into his face and Holt smiles. "Well, Coach Deal impressed me from the get-go. She's got *it*, however you define it. We're so grateful she's with us and so proud of Rabon High for standing at the front of the line to support women …"

No more than five minutes later, the Knights gather on the sideline around Chelsea as kickoff time nears. The crowd noise blocks out almost everything else, but the players hang onto every word Chelsea says. "Listen up, gentlemen!" she shouts. "It's been a wild week! But this is the last step! I want you to forget everything that's happened in the last few days and focus on the now! Let's make these next three hours a time we'll talk about the rest of our lives!"

The team cheers, breaks the circle, and lines up for the kickoff. Palmer stands near the goal line, now a returner on the kickoff team. Conway kicks off and the ball floats to Palmer. He grabs it and sprints up field, makes a cut on the twenty-five-yard line to miss a tackler, sees an opening, and darts through it, outrunning the defense. He reaches the forty, the fifty, spins away from a tackle, and takes a vicious hit to his helmet as he turns. He instantly blacks out and the ball drops as he falls to the turf. The trailing referee reaches for his penalty flag but pulls back his hand as a Conway player scoops up the ball and runs it in for a touchdown.

Chelsea and her coaches explode, yelling at the referee. "That's a personal foul!" screams Chelsea.

Boos from Knights' fans fill the stadium.

"A blatant, direct, deliberate hit to the head!" Chelsea shouts again. "A direct hit to the head!"

A trainer runs to Palmer as he stands, wobbles, falls, stands again. Chelsea, still yelling at the referee, rushes out to Palmer with the trainer and helps him up. The trainer pulls off Palmer's helmet and flashes a light into his eyes. "I'm all right," pants Palmer.

"You sure?" asks Chelsea. Palmer nods.

"Let's move him to the sideline," says the trainer. "I'll check him out better there." They lead him off and the trainer lays Palmer on the bench, flashes the light into his eyes again, holds up three fingers.

On the field, the referee blows his whistle for play to start again. Chelsea pats Palmer on the shoulder pads, then turns her focus back to the game. "Kick-off return team," she yells, stepping away from Palmer. "Swoops, you're in for Palmer!"

About an hour and a half later, Russell and Vanessa sit by Ty in the hospital, numerous wires hooking him to monitors. Tanya is also there, quiet in the corner. A sad pall hangs over the room, not only because of Ty's frailty but also the football game. A TV screen on the wall opposite the bed shows the halftime score at Atlanta Stadium: Conway Tigers: 22. Rabon Knights: 3.

Ty shakes his head at the TV. "This is so bad," he says, his voice barely a whisper.

"Hopeless," says Russell. "Want me to turn it off?"

"You turn it off, I'll take a crutch to your face."

Standing in the middle of the locker room with half an orange in her hand, Chelsea studies the team. Swoops and Johnson sit side by side with the rest of the offense on benches nearest the exit door. Coach Paul stands in front of them, a white board in one hand, a black marker in the other. He's sketching, pointing, coaching the offense for all he's worth.

On the other side of the room, Dub walks from one defensive player to another, bends to each one, whispers in his ear, pats him on the back, hugs him around the neck.

The players suck down fluids and listen to the coaches, but the energy level in the room hangs low. The trainer talks quietly to Palmer in a corner and Chelsea eases over to them and listens. "One more time," says the trainer. "I need to ask.

Does your head hurt?"

"No," says Palmer.

"Do you feel dizzy? Anything unusual?"

"I told you an hour ago, I feel fine."

The trainer turns to Chelsea. "I've run the protocols," he says. "Don't see any concussion symptoms."

"Should we send him to an emergency room?' she asks. "Let a doctor check him out?"

The trainer shrugs. "You can," he says. "But I don't believe that's necessary."

"Good." Chelsea turns back to the team and tries to figure out something to say or do to inspire her players. A thought occurs to her, but she pushes it back. Not here, not now.

Sighing, she moves back to the middle of the room, her orange still in her hand. Once she blows her whistle, all eyes turn to her. "Listen up, gentlemen," she offers softly. "It's almost time to head out for the second half."

She scans the room. "In that first half, we laid a big fat egg," she says calmly, taking a bite from the orange. "So now we have two options. One, we can give up and take the rest of our beating like a whiny dog."

"What's the second option, Coach?" asks Johnson.

Chelsea stares at the floor as a memory suddenly floods through her. No. Not here. Not now. The memory pushes again, this time with emotions along with it, and she fights unsuccessfully to shove them down. They stand steady, determined to be seen, heard, and felt for the first time in years. Chelsea breathes slowly, struggling to keep her composure. Finally, she raises her head and speaks, almost in a whisper.

"I had a twin brother, gentlemen," she starts. "Named Mitchell. He wore number 2 because I was the oldest, by seven minutes. I wore number 1. Mitchell loved football. Played quarterback."

Her eyes water as she relives a football game played fourteen years earlier. "We had thirteen seconds left in the last game of our senior year. Our Rockets against our archrivals, the Piedmont Pirates. Score stood at 17-16 in favor of the Pirates. I lined up to kick a 27-yard field goal to win the game. Mitchell, my holder, always winked at me right before the snap."

Chelsea wipes her eyes and continues. "Mitchell turned to me, winked, and faced the line again. Caught the snap from center and set the ball down for my kick. The defense rushed. I kicked the ball, but it was low, and the defense blocked it."

The team sits entranced, no one moving.

"Everybody scrambled for the ball," Chelsea continues quietly. "Me and Mitchell in the middle of the pile. The ball bounced toward us. Mitchell reached for it as a defender hit him, helmet to helmet. I can still hear it, to this day, like a baseball bat cracking a ball. I'll hear that sound the rest of my life."

Unable to continue, she stops as tears flow. Nobody moves or breathes. Chelsea slowly composes herself and finds the strength to finish the story. "Mitchell fell," she whispers. "Face down, the ball in his arms. He wasn't moving. I knelt beside him. My face next to his. He tried to breathe but couldn't. I begged him, 'Mitchell, get up. Come on, get up.'"

She wipes away her eyes, her voice even lower. "Mitchell never got up, gentlemen. He died on that field, me beside him, his teammate, his sister."

She stares at the floor. The team remains still, silent.

"I returned to coaching this year," she says. "Because being on the field—under the lights, with the band playing, the smell of the grass, the roar of the crowd—it all made me feel close to my brother again, almost like I'd never lost him."

She looks up at the team, her teary eyes searching theirs. "But I've discovered something these past few weeks," she says, her voice rising as she hurries to finish. "Yes, I love coaching. But not just because of Mitchell. I love coaching because of you, the sacrifices you make, the love you share, the support you've given me, the support you give each other. That's why I do it." She stops and wipes her eyes, her head down again, the orange in her hand.

Swoops and Johnson quietly stand and raise their helmets toward the ceiling. The rest of the team quickly joins them, each player dead silent with helmets over their heads.

"Here's the second option," says Chelsea, gathering herself with renewed purpose. "Ask yourself why you play this game. Because you like beating on the guy across the line from you? Because it helps you get a girl? Because it makes your mama and daddy proud? I want you to play this second half for that, whatever it is. Play this next half for that reason. Go play for that!" She shouts the last words and the team roars and follows her out of the locker room, their helmets raised, their faces set.

Chelsea pulls Palmer aside as the team hustles out toward the field. "You're sure you're all right?" she asks.

"I'm good, Coach. You bet."

"You're starting this half. Have one series to show me what you can do. I've already told Johnson."

Palmer's eyes widen as his heart notches higher.

"Just play ball," encourages Chelsea as they reach the field. "It's all good. No matter what happens."

Too stunned to speak, Palmer runs onto the field, Chelsea beside him. At about the forty-yard line, he reaches the benches and stops as Swoops tosses him a ball. He catches it and throws it back, loosening his arm. When the Knights' crowd starts booing, he glances behind him and sees Buck Jones at the fifty-yard line, just ten yards away, studying him and Chelsea.

Palmer turns to Chelsa. "What's he staring at?" he asks.

"Ignore him," says Chelsea.

"Running your twelve plays, Chelsea?!" Buck yells.

"Selling your soul, Buck?!" snarls Chelsea.

"You took my job!" shouts Buck.

"You betrayed your players! Lied about me!"

Buck rushes toward her, his eyes blazing, jaw set. Chelsea stalks to him too, equally furious. They're chin to chin now.

"If you weren't a woman..." Buck bellows.

If you WERE a man..." Chelsea growls.

Coach Paul sprints up and pushes himself between them. "Both of you, back off!" he shouts.

They hesitate and Paul puts a hand on each one, holding them back. "Truth is," he shouts as he pushes them away, "I'd pay good money to see it!"

Chelsea and Jones back up and Palmer steps towards Chelsea. "What happened to 'ignore him'?" he asks.

Chelsea shakes her head and Palmer laughs as he shoves on his helmet and sets his mind on the game.

Ten minutes later, the Knights' kickoff drops into a Tiger hands, and the return guy sprints up field, breaks past the first wave of tacklers, then sprints past the fifty-yard line. Desperately chasing him, Johnson leaps at the last second and knocks him sideways. The ball pops loose and Johnson falls on it.

The Knights' crowd roars as Chelsea pulls Palmer close. "Keep it simple," she instructs. "Run play number 7. Drop it off to the back in the flat."

"I can run the whole Playbook, Coach," Palmer says, his confidence high for the first time ever on a football field. "I told you that."

"Run the play I call, Palmer."

"You said I had a series," argues Palmer.

Chelsea blinks in surprise. "You ready to take that chance?" she asks.

"I'm a better bet than I was, Coach."

Chelsea arches an eyebrow. "All right. It's your opportunity. Make the best of it."

Palmer smiles and leads the offense into the huddle. "Okay, gentlemen," he says.

"You're not Coach Deal," says Swoops.

"Yeah, my bad," says Palmer. "Okay, idiots. We're running Gun Bunch, Weak ' 324, Z post, 1 go."

"That's not one of the twelve," says Swoops.

Palmer stares at Swoops. "I hope Conway is as surprised as you are."

The huddle breaks and Palmer steps to the line, closes his eyes, and sees a quote from Malcom Forbes from page 99 of the Playbook: "Victory is sweetest when you've known defeat." He hums and sees the play. Opens his eyes. The center snaps the ball.

Palmer drops back. Receivers run their routes. The flanker sprints straight down field, then angles toward the middle of the gridiron. Palmer uncorks his throw, fifty yards in the air. The flanker catches the ball in stride and sprints in for a touchdown.

On the Conway sideline, Buck Jones huddles with the Tigers' head coach, a stocky man with a beard, broad face, and black glasses. "You said the Norman kid only knew twelve plays!" screams the Tigers' coach.

"So maybe thirteen," says Buck.

"You think that's it? That plus the twelve?"

"Probably. The kid's brain is oatmeal."

"You think we're good?" the coach asks hopefully.

"If he's got more than that, you're in for a hell of a fight."

Out on the field, the Knights' defense faces the Tigers' offense. Dub yells the defensive formation and his players line up. The Tiger quarterback receives the snap and hands off to a running back. A Knights' lineman smacks the back hard and the ball squirts from his hand. The Knights recover on the Tigers' thirty-seven-yard line. Knights' fans roar again as the momentum shifts.

On the sidelines, Palmer glances into the stands and sees Molly jumping up and down beside Dirk. Chelsea grabs him by the shoulder pads. "Pay attention to the game, Palmer!" she shouts.

He focuses again. "One of the twelve?" he asks.

"I'm still not sure you're a master of the Playbook," she responds. "But let's test it. I like Gun, 2 right, Outside Stick, RPO. 1 go."

Palmer closes his eyes. "To make a comeback, you have to have a setback," says Mr. T on Playbook page 12." Palmer hums and the play appears.

"Open your eyes, Palmer!" yells Chelsea. "And stop that humming! You need to concentrate on football, not music!"

Palmer grins, runs onto the field, huddles up with the offense, and calls the play. The offense sets up, the Tigers across the line. The center snaps the ball. Palmer fakes a handoff to a running back and rolls right, fakes a reverse to Swoops, dodges a linebacker, and breaks into the open field. A safety desperately tries to cut him off but Palmer hits another gear and outruns the safety down the sideline for another touchdown.

Back in the hospital, Russell jumps out of his chair, high-fives Vanessa and Tanya, then bends to Ty, who's awake but barely. "We're back in the game, Ty!" says Russell. "Palmer has brought us back!"

Dr. Ramirez suddenly enters, a folder in hand. Russell and Vanessa step quickly to him. He opens the folder and points to an image from a scan.

Vanessa grabs Russell's hand and they both start crying. Tanya quickly joins them, and they stand in a circle with tears on their cheeks as Ty lies in bed, his eyes closed.

His face red all the way to his ears, the Tigers' coach screams at Jones on the sideline. "What was that, Buck?"

Buck shrugs. "That was a player making a play."

"Get out of my face! You're useless!"

"I told you he was talented."

"You told me his brain was oatmeal!"

Jones pivots and walks away as the coach gathers his defense. "He's running more than the twelve plays!" shouts the coach. "But if we stop him now, we still win!"

The game settles into a defensive struggle. Neither offense can move the ball much. The third quarter ends and the fourth begins. The teams exchange punts. Palmer throws a long pass three minutes into the fourth quarter, but it bounces off Snoops' fingers and the Knights have to punt again.

The Tigers score a touchdown on a long run by their quarterback but a holding penalty on the offense brings the play back and the Tigers miss a field goal.

Time ticks away. Eight minutes left, then five, then two, and the players breathe harder as the tension mounts. The offensive coaches on both sidelines scheme away, black markers busy on whiteboards as they search for ways to score but come up empty.

On the sidelines near Chelsea, Palmer feels the stress like everyone else. His breathing grows quicker, and his hands sweat, even in the cold of the night. He checks the scoreboard: Knights: 17. Tigers: 22. One minute and twenty seconds left in the game.

The Tigers possess the ball. After their quarterback throws a slant pass for a six-yard second-down gain, it's now third down with four yards to go at the 50-yard line. One minute and six seconds left. Chelsea calls a time-out and waves the whole team together. The defense fights to catch its breath as the players surround her. Chelsea turns to Dub. "We have to stop them here! What's the call?"

"They'll throw it," says Dub. "It's what they do best. We're going to do an all-out blitz. Knock that quarterback to the dark side of the moon."

The referee blows the whistle to resume play and the defense jogs back onto the field. The Tigers quarterback calls the signal and takes the snap. He rolls to the right with seven Knights rushing him. The quarterback dodges left, then right, and defenders reach for him but come up empty. The quarterback tosses the ball down-field. The receiver stretches for it... but his arms come up a couple of inches short. The ball bounces off his hands and the Knights intercept. Tiger fans moan, cuss, throw hats onto the bleachers. Fifty-four seconds left.

The Knights' offense gathers around Chelsea. "We're going to confuse the defense," she says calmly. "Will run two of our twelve plays back-to-back. That'll make them expect another of the twelve on the third play. That's when we drop the hammer." She faces Palmer. "You good with that?"

Palmer stares at the ground, his emotions churning. He feels the tension, but it suddenly seems like a good thing. Necessary even, like an electric current pulsing through a wire, dangerous but required to provide energy at the terminal.

Palmer looks straight at Chelsea. "I got you, Coach."

"Don't be cocky," she warns.

Eager now, Palmer leads the offense onto the field and runs the first play. A pitch to a running back gains four yards. The clock runs as Palmer checks the sidelines. Thirty seconds left. Chelsea signals in the play and Palmer runs it as instructed, a sprint-out sweep for another four-yard advance.

The clock ticks. Eleven seconds left and Chelsea calls her last time out.

On the Tigers sideline, the head coach waves Jones over. "What's her move, Buck?"

"I thought I was useless," chides Buck.

"I got no time for that!" barks the coach. "What's she gonna do?"

"I think she's setting you up."

"I don't know. I think she's emptied her bag of tricks. She's run two of the twelve in a row."

"She's a cat and you're the mouse."

"You *are* useless."

"She's a competitor, man. It burns my bacon to say it, but you have to tip your cap to her."

The Tigers' coach steps to the huddle with his defense. "They only got time for one, maybe two passes!" he reminds them. "Expect them to be from the six pass plays we've prepared for!"

Thirty seconds later, the two teams face off again on the line of scrimmage. The players brace for contact, each one tired, sweating, but poised to fight. The fans on both sides of the stadium roar their support.

Palmer studies the defense as Swoops shifts from the left of the formation to the right. Palmer calls the cadence, rolls out, and whips the ball downfield. The defender tackles Swoops before the ball arrives, an obvious pass interference penalty. The pass falls incomplete, but the referee keeps his flag in his pocket. Knights' fans boo again. Chelsea holds Coach Paul back as he screams at the referee.

Palmer yells at the official too but Swoops yanks him away and they hustle toward the huddle. "Focus, Palmer!" Swoops commands. "It's the last play!"

Palmer checks the clock and tries to calm down. Three seconds left. Chelsea yells a play from the sideline, but Palmer shakes his head "no" and darts into the huddle. Chelsea keeps shouting but Palmer ignores her and faces his offense. The players stare at him, waiting for the play call, depending on him to lead. The looks scare him a little but excite him too, make him feel needed, trusted.

A strange peace suddenly flows through him, and everything slows down. The roar of the crowd fades. The lights burn but they're far away. He hears his heart beating in his chest, but it sounds smooth, even soothing and he knows exactly what play to call.

"We're running Ecclesiastes 4:12," he calmly instructs his teammates.

"What?" asks Swoops.

Palmer smiles, surprising himself with the confidence he feels. "Sorry," he says to the offense. "Gun, Empty Trips, Right 868, X Fade, 2 go."

"Coach didn't call that play!" argues Swoops.

Palmer pats him on the helmet. "It's Ty's favorite, Swoops. Ride or die with Ty. That's what we're running."

Swoops stares at him like he's smoking mushrooms. "You sure?"

Palmer nods and Swoops shrugs. "You da man, Palmer. Let's do this."

Palmer eyes the rest of the offense. "For Ty," he says.

The offense claps its hands in unison, breaks the huddle, and lines up across from the Tigers.

Standing behind the center, Palmer briefly closes his eyes and the quote appears in his head: "Though a man might prevail against one who is alone, two will withstand him. A threefold cord is not easily broken." Palmer hums and sees the play, opens his eyes, takes the snap, and drops back.

The receivers speed downfield. Palmer darts right as the defense rushes him with an all-out blitz. He dodges one defender, ducks another, reverses field and almost falls but pulls himself straight again and reaches the line of scrimmage. Staring downfield, he sees no one open and almost runs but suddenly spots Swoops breaking free from his defender. The world slows. Quiet falls. Swoops runs. Palmer feels at peace. He draws back his arm and zips the ball through the night sky. It floats over the defense like a silent, oblong missile and Swoops reaches for it...

CHAPTER THIRTY-TWO

TEN YEARS LATER

A new, bigger sign flashes outside the stadium: "Rabon High School Knights." Cars and trucks line the streets in every direction. Inside the stadium, people stand and wave banners. A camera crew in a helicopter videos the scene. Lasers flash in all colors. Music rocks the night. The lights go out except for the lasers. A strobe effect bathes the stadium.

A spotlight suddenly flashes on the north end zone and lights up a spot where Chelsea stands with a microphone. She's dressed in khakis and a Knights' white jacket with a purple tee-shirt under it. "Good evening, ladies and gentlemen!" she calls out through the microphone.

The crowd erupts in a thunderous roar. Chelsea basks in the sound for several seconds before continuing. "I'm so thrilled tonight to celebrate with you the tenth anniversary of our Rabon Knights state championship football team!" she shouts.

The crowd cheers even louder as the spotlight shifts to the south end zone, where Johnson, Swoops, and the rest of the team, except for Ty and Palmer, are lined up.

The spotlight switches back to Chelsea. "Now, please turn your attention to the center of the field!" she instructs the crowd.

The spotlight suddenly focuses on a stage where Dirk and three other band members lift their instruments and wave to the crowd. The crowd again goes berserk.

The stadium falls fully dark.

"To make this night even more fantastic, we have with us our most famous player from that team," announces Chelsea, still in the dark. "The player who led us to a championship as a sophomore and again as a senior!"

The spotlight jumps around, one spot to another, as if searching for someone. Chelsea's voice booms a final time. "Let's hear it for the four-time Platinum Award winner and Top Country Music Performer two of the past five years, Mr. Palmer Norman!"

The crowd loses its mind as the spotlight finds Palmer and he hustles onto the stage with a guitar in his hands. Waving to the crowd, he straps the guitar over his shoulder, steps to a microphone, and clears his throat. The place falls dead quiet.

"Ten years ago, I came to Rabon High," Palmer begins in a conversational tone. "I lived with my Uncle Dirk." He points to Dirk and the spotlight focuses on him.

Dirk wears a purple tee-shirt with the words "I Taught Him to Play the Guitar" printed in white.

Palmer continues, louder now. "This town gave me a chance to play football. Thank you, Coach Chelsea!"

The spotlight lands on Chelsea again. She unbuttons her jacket. Her tee- shirt reads: "He Made Me What I Am Today: A Football Coach." The fans cheer again.

"I met my best friend here," continues Palmer. The spotlight shifts to Ty in the stands at the fifty-yard line. His tee-shirt says: "I Manage His Finances. And That's a Lot of Finances!"

Sitting beside Ty is Coach Dub. His tee shirt says: "I Wish I Managed His Finances."

Behind Dub sits Gerty from the gas station. Her tee shirt says, "I Let Him Sleep Behind My Dumpster."

Beside Gerty is the smiling hostess from the Busted Spoke. Her tee-shirt reads, "I Told Him Not to Give Up."

The spotlight moves back to Palmer and his voice softens and the stadium hushes. "I reconnected with my mama here," he almost whispers. "She passed a year ago, but I was with her when it happened."

He adjusts his guitar strap, wipes his eyes, and pauses. The crowd waits. After a few seconds, a smile crawls onto Palmer's face and he shouts into the microphone. "I met the love of my life here, my wife Molly, who's the mother of my son, Ty!"

The spotlight flashes on Molly. Her tee-shirt says, "Sometimes He's an Idiot. But I Still Love Him."

She holds Ty up so everyone can see him. His tee-shirt says, "I Let Him Be My Daddy." The crowd roars.

The spotlight lands on Palmer again and, as he pauses one last time to gather himself, the crowd goes quiet in anticipation. "Thank you, Rabon," he whispers, head down as if in prayer. "For taking me in. For becoming my family. For forgiving me when I screwed up. For lifting me up when I fell down. For teaching me to be a man."

Palmer looks up at the crowd again and smiles. "Are you ready?!" he shouts.

The crowd in one corner of the stadium begins to chant. "Palmer! Palmer! Palmer!" The chant spreads until the whole stadium reverberates with the sound: "Palmer! Palmer! Palmer!"

He raises a hand into the night sky. "Are you ready?!"

The chant continues. Palmer starts jumping up and down and the crowd joins him. "Let's rock some music!" he roars.

The band hits it and the crowd goes crazy as Palmer leaps to the microphone and begins to sing.

ABOUT THE AUTHOR

G ary E. Parker is the best-selling author of 23 published books (19 novels/novellas), including numerous genre best-sellers and fiction award-winners. A Christy Award finalist for Highland Hopes, Parker has become a leading source for sweeping sagas of family and faith.

A BA graduate of Furman University and the holder of a PhD from Baylor University, he has written six screenplays, including an adaptation of *The Playbook*.

A frequent and much sought-after speaker before national and local conventions and conferences, he currently lives in the Atlanta suburbs.